MW00756053

TALES FROM
THE NIGHTSIDE

Novels of the Nightside

SOMETHING FROM THE
NIGHTSIDE
AGENTS OF LIGHT AND
DARKNESS
NIGHTINGALE'S LAMENT
HEX AND THE CITY
PATHS NOT TAKEN
SHARPER THAN A SERPENT'S
TOOTH

HELL TO PAY
THE UNNATURAL INQUIRER
JUST ANOTHER JUDGEMENT
DAY
THE GOOD, THE BAD, AND
THE UNCANNY
A HARD DAY'S KNIGHT
THE BRIDE WORE BLACK
LEATHER

Ghost Finders Novels

GHOST OF A CHANCE
GHOST OF A SMILE
GHOST OF A DREAM

SPIRITS FROM BEYOND
VOICES FROM BEYOND

Secret Histories Novels

THE MAN WITH THE
GOLDEN TORC
DAEMONS ARE FOREVER
THE SPY WHO HAUNTED ME
FROM HELL WITH LOVE

FOR HEAVEN'S EYES ONLY
LIVE AND LET DROOD
CASINO INFERNALE
PROPERTY OF A LADY FAIRE

Deathstalker Novels

DEATHSTALKER
DEATHSTALKER REBELLION
DEATHSTALKER WAR
DEATHSTALKER HONOR

DEATHSTALKER DESTINY
DEATHSTALKER LEGACY
DEATHSTALKER RETURN
DEATHSTALKER CODA

Hawk and Fisher Novels
SWORDS OF HAVEN
GUARDS OF HAVEN

Also by Simon R. Green

BLUE MOON RISING
BEYOND THE BLUE MOON

ONCE IN A BLUE MOON
DRINKING MIDNIGHT WINE

Omnibus
A WALK ON THE NIGHTSIDE

Anthology
TALES FROM THE NIGHTSIDE

TALES FROM THE NIGHTSIDE

Including "The Big Game,"
a never-before-published Nightside novella, and nine
other Nightside favorites now in one volume

SIMON R. GREEN

ACE BOOKS, NEW YORK

THE BERKLEY PUBLISHING GROUP
Published by the Penguin Group
Penguin Group (USA) LLC
375 Hudson Street, New York, New York 10014

USA • Canada • UK • Ireland • Australia • New Zealand • India • South Africa • China

penguin.com

A Penguin Random House Company

Copyright © 2015 by Simon R. Green.
"The Nightside, Needless to Say" copyright © 2004 by Simon R. Green.
"Razor Eddie's Big Night Out" copyright © 2006 by Simon R. Green.
"Lucy, at Christmastime" copyright © 2008 by Simon R. Green.
"Appetite for Murder" copyright © 2008 by Simon R. Green.
"The Difference a Day Makes" copyright © 2009 by Simon R. Green.
"Some of These Cons Go Way Back" copyright © 2009 by Simon R. Green.
"The Spirit of the Thing" copyright © 2011 by Simon R. Green.
"Hungry Heart" copyright © 2011 by Simon R. Green.
"How Do You Feel?" copyright © 2012 by Simon R. Green.
Penguin supports copyright. Copyright fuels creativity, encourages diverse voices,
promotes free speech, and creates a vibrant culture. Thank you for buying an authorized
edition of this book and for complying with copyright laws by not reproducing, scanning,
or distributing any part of it in any form without permission. You are supporting writers
and allowing Penguin to continue to publish books for every reader.

Ace Books are published by The Berkley Publishing Group.
ACE and the "A" design are trademarks of Penguin Group (USA) LLC.

Library of Congress Cataloging-in-Publication Data

Green, Simon R., 1955–
[Short stories. Selections]
Tales from the nightside / Simon R. Green.
pages ; cm.
ISBN 978-0-425-27075-2 (hardcover)
I. Title.
PR6107.R44A6 2015
823'.92—dc23
2014035729

FIRST EDITION: January 2015

PRINTED IN THE UNITED STATES OF AMERICA

10 9 8 7 6 5 4 3 2 1

Cover illustration © Jonathan Barkat.
Cover design by Judith Lagerman.

"The Nightside, Needless to Say" was previously published in the
anthology *Powers of Detection*.
"Razor Eddie's Big Night Out" was previously published in the magazine *Cemetery Dance* 55.
"Lucy, at Christmastime" was previously published in the anthology *Wolfsbane and Mistletoe*.
"Appetite for Murder" was previously published in the anthology *Unusual Suspects*.
"The Difference a Day Makes" was previously published in the anthology *Mean Streets*.
"Some of These Cons Go Way Back" was previously published in the magazine *Cemetery Dance* 60.
"The Spirit of the Thing" was previously published in the anthology *Those Who Fight Monsters*.
"Hungry Heart" was previously published in the anthology *Down These Strange Streets*.
"How Do You Feel?" was previously published in the anthology *Hex Appeal*.

This is a work of fiction. Names, characters, places, and incidents either are the product
of the author's imagination or are used fictitiously, and any resemblance to actual persons,
living or dead, business establishments, events, or locales is entirely coincidental.

CONTENTS

Introduction   **vii**

The Nightside, Needless to Say   **1**

Razor Eddie's Big Night Out   **17**

Lucy, at Christmastime   **39**

Appetite for Murder   **45**

The Difference a Day Makes   **63**

Some of These Cons Go Way Back   **129**

The Spirit of the Thing   **141**

Hungry Heart   **155**

How Do You Feel?   **179**

The Big Game   **211**

INTRODUCTION

Welcome to the Nightside.

The secret, hidden heart of London, where the long night never ends, the sun never shines, and dawn never comes. Where it's always three o'clock in the morning, the hour that tries men's souls. The Nightside, where hot neon burns bright and gaudy as Hell's candy, where gods and monsters walk hand in hand, and angels from Above and Below go fist-fighting through alleyways. Where you can find anything, anything at all, if it doesn't find you first. Where all your dreams can come true, especially the really bad ones.

I've never made any secret of the fact that the Nightside is based largely on London's Soho area. Or, to be exact, old Soho, as it used to be, before it was cleaned up and gentrified, made safe and boring. I was there for the last days of old Soho, when the bad old days were mostly gone, but there was still enough sin to go around if you knew where to look. Pubs and bars and night-clubs, and the very private Members Only establishments, where you could still find all the things that people aren't supposed to want but still do. I talked to a lot of people who were only too happy to reminisce about how things used to be. Telling tales of lust and glory, when show business and gangsters and all the twilight people got together, to play the kind of games that might not have any rules but certainly had a price. Of the days when love was for sale, or at least for rent, when everything that was bad for you was openly for sale, and there was always some minor celebrity hanging around a street-corner, doing something unwise.

The legend of old Soho eventually produced the modern legend of the Nightside. A nice place to visit, but you wouldn't want to die there. Where tarnished heroes and charming villains, broken men and hard-hearted women, found their way home, at last.

The Nightside. Neon noir. Don't say you weren't warned.

THE NIGHTSIDE, NEEDLESS TO SAY

The Nightside is the secret, sick, magical heart of London. A city within a city, where the night never ends and it's always three o'clock in the morning. Hot neon reflects from rain-slick streets, and dreams go walking in borrowed flesh. You can find pretty much anything in the Nightside, except happy endings. Gods and monsters run confidence tricks, and all desires can be satisfied, if you're willing to pay the price. Which might be money and might be service, but nearly always ends up meaning your soul. The Nightside, where the sun never shows its face because if it did, someone would probably try to steal it. When you've nowhere else to go, the Nightside will take you in. Trust no-one, including yourself, and you might get out alive again.

Some of us work there, for our sins. Or absolution, or atonement. It's that kind of place.

Larry! Larry! What's wrong?
The sharp, whispered voice pulled me up out of a bad

dream; something about running in the rain, running from something awful. I sat up in bed, looked around, and didn't know where I was. It wasn't my bedroom. Harsh neon light flickered red and green through the slats of the closed shutters, intermittently revealing a dark dusty room with cheap and nasty furniture. There was nobody else there, but the words still rang in my ears. I sat on the edge of the bed, trying to remember my dream, but it was already fading. I was fully dressed, and there were no bedsheets. I still had my shoes on. I had no idea what day it was.

I got up and turned on the bedside light. The room wasn't improved by being seen clearly, but at least I knew where I was. An old safe house, in one of the seedier areas of the Nightside. A refuge I hadn't had to use in years. I still kept up the rent; because you never know when you're going to need a bolt-hole in a hurry. I turned out my pockets. Everything where it should be, and nothing new to explain what I was doing here. I shook my head slowly, then left the room, heading for the adjoining bathroom. Explanations could wait, until I'd taken care of something that couldn't.

The bathroom's bright fluorescent light was harsh and unforgiving as I studied my face in the medicine cabinet mirror. Pale and washed-out, under straw-blond hair, good bone structure, and a mouth and eyes that never gave anything away. My hair was a mess, but I didn't need a shave. I shrugged, dropped my trousers and shorts, and sat down on the porcelain throne. There was a vague uneasy feeling in my bowels and then a sudden lurch as something within made a bid for freedom. I tapped my foot impatiently, listening to a series of splashes. Something bad must have happened, even if I couldn't remember it. I needed to get out of here and start asking pointed questions of certain people. Someone would know. Someone always knows.

The splashes finally stopped, but something didn't feel

right. I got up, turned around, and looked down into the bowl. It was full of maggots. Curling and twisting and squirming. I made a horrified sound and stumbled backward. My legs tangled in my lowered trousers, and I fell full length on the floor. My head hit the wall hard. It didn't hurt. I scrambled to my feet, pulled up my shorts and trousers, and backed out of the bathroom, still staring at the toilet.

It was the things that weren't happening that scared me most. I should have been hyperventilating. My heart should have been hammering in my chest. My face should have been covered in a cold sweat. But when I checked my wrist, then my throat, there wasn't any pulse. And I wasn't breathing hard because I wasn't breathing at all. I couldn't remember taking a single breath since I woke up. I touched my face with my fingertips, and they both felt cold.

I was dead.

Someone had killed me. I knew that, though I didn't know how. The maggots suggested I'd been dead for some time. So, who killed me, and why hadn't I noticed it till now?

My name's Larry Oblivion, and with a name like that I pretty much had to be a private investigator. Mostly I do corporate work: industrial espionage, checking out backgrounds, helping significant people defect from one organization to another. Big business has always been where the real money is. I don't do divorce cases, or solve mysteries, and I've never even owned a trench-coat. I wear Gucci, I make more money than most people ever dream of, and I pack a wand. Don't snigger. I took the wand in payment for a case involving the Unseelie Court, and I've never regretted it. Two feet long, and carved from the spine of a species that never existed in the waking world, the wand could stop time, for everyone except me. More than enough to give me an edge, or a running start. You take all the advantages you can get when you operate in the Nightside. No-one else knew I had the wand.

Unless . . . someone had found out and killed me to try and get their hands on it.

I found the coffeemaker and fixed myself my usual pick-me-up. Black coffee, steaming hot, and strong enough to jump-start a mummy from its sleep. But when it was ready, I didn't want it. Apparently the walking dead don't drink coffee. Damn. I was going to miss that.

Larry! Larry!

I spun round, the words loud in my ear, but still there was no-one else in the room. Just a voice, calling my name. For a moment I almost remembered something horrid, then it was gone before I could hold on to it. I scowled, pacing up and down the room to help me think. I was dead, I'd been murdered. So, start with the usual suspects. Who had reason to want me dead? Serious reasons; I had my share of enemies, but that was just the price of doing business. No-one murders anyone over business.

No; start with my ex-wife, Donna Tramen. She had reasons to hate me. I fell in love with a client, Margaret Boniface, and left my wife for her. The affair didn't work out, but Maggie and I remained friends. In fact, we worked so well together I made her a partner in my business. My wife hadn't talked to me since I moved out, except through her lawyer, but if she was going to kill me, she would have done it long ago. And the amount of money the divorce judge awarded her gave her a lot of good reasons for wanting me alive. As long as the cheques kept coming.

Next up: angry or disappointed clients, where the case hadn't worked out to everyone's satisfaction. There were any number of organizations in and out of the Nightside that I'd stolen secrets or personnel from. But none of them would take such things personally. Today's target might be tomorrow's client, so everyone stayed polite. I never got involved in the kinds of cases where passions were likely to be raised. No-one's ever made movies about the kind of work I do.

I kept feeling I already knew the answer, but it remained stubbornly out of reach. Perhaps because . . . I didn't want to remember. I shuddered suddenly, and it wasn't from the cold. I picked up the phone beside the bed, and called my partner. Maggie picked up on the second ring, as though she'd been waiting for a call.

"Maggie, this is Larry. Listen, you're not going to believe what's happened . . ."

"Larry, you've been missing for three days! Where are you?"

Three days . . . A trail could get real cold in three days . . .

"I'm at the old safe house on Blaiston Street. I think you'd better come and get me."

"What the hell are you doing there? I didn't know we still had that place on the books."

"Just come and get me. I'm in trouble."

Her voice changed immediately. "What kind of trouble, Larry?"

"Let's just say . . . I think I'm going to need some of your old expertise, Mama Bones."

"Don't use that name on an open line! It's been a long time since I was a mover and shaker on the voodoo scene, and hopefully most people have forgotten Margaret Boniface was ever involved. I'm clean now. One day at a time, sweet Jesus."

"You know I wouldn't ask if it wasn't important. I need what you used to know. Get here as fast as you can. And, Maggie, don't tell anyone where you're going. We can't trust anyone but each other."

She laughed briefly. "Business as usual, in the Nightside."

• • •

I did a lot more pacing and thinking in the half hour it took Maggie to reach Blaiston Street, but I was no wiser at the end of it. My memories stopped abruptly three days ago, with no warning of what was to come. I kept watch on and off through the slats of the window shutters, and was finally rewarded with the sight of Maggie pulling up to the curb in her cherry-red Jaguar. Protective spells sparked briefly around the car as she got out and looked up at my window. Tall and slender, an ice-cool blonde with a buzz cut and a heavy scarlet mouth. She dressed like a diva and walked like a princess, and carried a silver-plated magnum derringer in her purse, next to her aboriginal pointing bone. She had a sharp, incisive mind, and given a few more years' experience and the right contacts, she'd be ten times the operative I was. I never told her that, of course. I didn't want her getting overconfident.

She rapped out our special knock on the door, the one that said yes she had checked, and no, no-one had followed her. I let her in, and she checked the room out professionally before turning to kiss my cheek. And then she stopped, and looked at me.

"Larry . . . you look half-dead."

I smiled briefly. "You don't know the *half* of it."

I gave her the bad news, and she took it as well as could be expected. She insisted on checking my lack of a pulse or heartbeat for herself, then stepped back from me and hugged herself tightly. I don't think she liked the way my cold flesh felt. I tried to make light of what had happened, complaining that my life must have been really dull if neither Heaven nor Hell were interested in claiming me, but neither of us was fooled. In the end, we sat side by side on the bed, and discussed what we should do next in calm, professional voices.

"You've no memory at all of being killed?" Maggie said finally.

"No. I'm dead, but not yet departed. Murdered, but still walking around. Which puts me very much in your old territory, oh mistress of the mystic arts."

"Oh please! So I used to know a little voodoo . . . Practically everyone in my family does. Where we come from, it's no big thing. And I was never involved in anything like this . . ."

"Can you help me, or not?"

She scowled. "All right. Let me run a few diagnostics on you."

"Are we going to have to send out for a chicken?"

"Be quiet, heathen."

She ran through a series of chants in Old French, lit up some incense, then took off all her clothes and danced around the room for a while. I'd probably have enjoyed it if I hadn't been dead. The room grew darker, and there was a sense of unseen eyes watching. Shadows moved slowly across the walls, deep disturbing shapes, though there was nothing in the room to cast them. And then Maggie stopped dancing, and stood facing me, breathing hard, sweat running down her bare body.

"Did you feel anything then?" she said.

"No. Was I supposed to?"

Maggie shrugged briefly and put her clothes back on in a businesslike way. The shadows and the sense of being watched were gone.

"You've been dead for three days," said Maggie. "Someone killed you, then held your spirit in your dead body. There's a rider spell attached, to give you the appearance of normality, but inside you're already rotting. Hence the maggots."

"Can you undo the spell?" I said.

"Larry, you're *dead*. The dead can be made to walk, but no

one can bring them all the way back, not even in the Nightside. Whatever we decide to do, your story's over, Larry."

I thought about that for a while. I always thought I would have achieved more, before the end. All the things I meant to do, and kept putting off, because I was young and imagined I had all the time in the world. Larry Oblivion, who always dreamed of something better, but never had the guts to go after it. One ex-wife, one ex-lover, no kids, no legacy. No point and no purpose.

"When all else fails," I said finally, "there's always revenge. I need to find out who killed me and why, while I still can. While there's still enough of me left to savor it."

"Any ideas who it might have been?" said Maggie. "Anyone new you might have upset recently?"

I thought hard. "Prometheus Inc. weren't at all happy over my handling of their poltergeist saboteur. Count Entropy didn't like what I found out about his son, even though he paid me to dig it up. Big Max always said he'd put me in the ground someday . . ."

"Max," Maggie said immediately. "Has to be Max. You've been rivals for years, hurt his business and made him look a fool, more than once. He must have decided to put an end to the competition."

"Why would he want to keep me around after killing me?"

"To gloat! He hated your guts, Larry; it has to be him!"

I thought about it. I'd rubbed Max's nose in it before, and all he ever did was talk. Maybe . . . he'd got tired of talking.

"All right," I said. "Let's go see the big man and ask him a few pointed questions."

"He's got a lot of protection," said Maggie. "Not at all an easy man to get to see."

"Do I look like I care? Are you in or not?"

"Of course I'm in! I'm just pointing out that Big Max is known for surrounding himself with heavy-duty firepower."

I smiled. "Baby, I'm dead. How are they going to stop me?"

We went out into the streets, and walked through the Nightside. The rain had stopped, and the air was sharp with new possibilities. Hot neon blazed on every side, advertising the kinds of love that might not have names, but certainly have prices. Heavy bass lines surged out of open club doors, reverberating in the ground and in my bones. All kinds of people swept past us, intent on their own business. Only some of them were human. Traffic roared constantly up and down the road, and everyone was careful to give it plenty of room. Not everything that looked like a car was a car, and some of them were hungry. In the Nightside, taxis can run on deconsecrated altar wine, and motorcycle messengers snort powdered virgin's blood for that extra kick.

Max's place wasn't far. He holed up in an upmarket cocktail bar called the Spider's Web. Word is he used to work there once. And that he had his old boss killed when he took it over, then had the man stuffed and mounted and put on display. Max never left the place any more, and held court there from behind more layers of protection than some presidents can boast. The big man had a lot of enemies, and he gloried in it.

Along the way I kept getting quick flashes of déjà vu. Brief glimpses of my dream of running through the rain. Except I was pretty sure by now that it wasn't a dream but a memory. I could feel the desperation as I ran, pursued by something without a face.

The only entrance to the Spider's Web was covered by two large gentlemen with shoulder holsters, and several layers of defensive magics. I knew about the magics because a client had once hired me to find out exactly what Max was using. Come to think of it, no-one had seen that client for some time. I murmured to Maggie to hang on to my arm, then drew my wand and activated it. It shone with a brilliant light, too bright to look at, and all around us the world seemed to slow down, and become flat and unreal. The roar of the traffic shut off, and the neon stopped flickering. Maggie and I were outside Time. We walked between the two bodyguards, and they didn't even see us. I could feel the defensive magics straining, reaching out, unable to touch us.

We walked on through the club, threading our way through the frozen crowds. Deeper and deeper, into the lair of the beast. There were things going on that sickened even me, but I didn't have the time to stop and do anything. I only had one shot at this. Maggie held my arm tightly. It would probably have hurt if I'd still been alive.

"Well," she said, trying for a light tone and not even coming close. "A genuine wand of the Faerie. That explains a lot of things."

"It always helps to have an unsuspected edge."

"You could have told me. I am your partner."

"You can never tell who's listening, in the Nightside." I probably would have told her, if she hadn't ended our affair. "But I think I'm past the point of needing secrets any more."

We found the big man sitting behind a desk in a surprisingly modest inner office. He was playing solitaire with tarot cards, and cheating. Thick mats of ivy crawled across the walls, and the floor was covered with cabalistic symbols. I closed the door behind us so we wouldn't be interrupted, and shut down the wand. Max looked up sharply as we appeared suddenly in front of him. His right hand reached for something, but Maggie already had her silver magnum derringer out and covering him. Max shrugged, sat back in his chair, and studied us curiously.

Max Maxwell, so big they named him twice. A giant of a man, huge and lowering even behind his oversized mahogany desk. Eight feet tall and impressively broad across the shoulders, with a harsh and craggy face, he looked like he was carved out of stone. A gargoyle in a Savile Row suit. Max traded in secrets, and stayed in business because he knew something about everyone. Or at least, everyone who mattered. Even if he hadn't killed me, there was a damned good chance he knew who had.

"Larry Oblivion," he said, in a voice like grinding stone. "My dearest rival and most despised competitor. To what do I owe the displeasure of this unexpected visit?"

"Like you don't already know," said Maggie, her derringer aimed directly between his eyes.

Max ignored her, his gaze fixed on me. "Provide me with one good reason why I shouldn't have both of you killed for this impertinence?"

"How about, you already killed me? Or haven't you noticed that I only breathe when I talk?"

Max studied me thoughtfully. "Yes. You are dead. You have no aura. I wish I could claim the credit, but alas, it seems someone else has beaten me to it. And besides, if I wanted you dead, you'd be dead and gone, not hanging around to trouble me."

"He's right," I said to Maggie. "Max is famous for never leaving loose ends."

"You want me to kill him anyway?" said Maggie.

"No," I said. "Tell me, Max. If you didn't kill me, who did?"

"I haven't the faintest idea," said Max, smiling slowly, revealing grey teeth behind the grey lips. "Which means it isn't any of your usual enemies. And if I don't know, no-one does."

I felt suddenly tired. Max had been my best bet, my last hope. He could have been lying, but I didn't think so. Not when he knew the truth could hurt me more. My body was decaying, I had no more leads, and I didn't have the time left to go anywhere else. So Maggie and I walked out the way we came in. Maggie would have killed Max, if I'd asked, but I didn't see the point. Feuds and vendettas are for the living; when you're dead you just can't be bothered with the small shit.

Maggie took me back to her place. I needed time out, to sit and think. I was close to despair. I didn't have enough time left to investigate all the enemies I'd made in my personal and professional life. A disturbing and depressing thought, for someone facing eternity. So many enemies, and so few friends . . . I sat on Maggie's couch, and looked fondly at her as she made us some coffee. We'd been so good together, for a while. Why didn't it work out? If I knew the answer to that, we'd still be together. She came in from the kitchen, carrying two steaming mugs. I took one, and held it awkwardly. I wanted to drink the coffee to please her, but I couldn't. She looked at me, puzzled.

"Larry? What's the matter?"

And just like that, I knew. Because I finally recognized the voice I'd been hearing ever since I woke up dead.

I was at Maggie's place, drinking coffee. It tasted funny. Larry? she said. Larry? What's wrong? I felt something burning in my throat, and knew she'd poisoned me. I stopped time with my wand, and ran. It was raining. I didn't dare go home. She'd find me. I didn't know where to go for help, so I went to ground, in my old safe house at Blaiston Street. And I died there, still wondering why my partner and ex-lover had killed me.

"It was you," I said, and something in my voice made her flinch. "You poisoned me. Why?"

"The how is more interesting," Maggie said calmly. She sat down opposite me, entirely composed. "An old voodoo drug in your coffee, to kill you and set you up for the zombie spell. But of course I didn't know about the wand. It interacted with my magic, buying you more time. The wand's magic is probably what's holding you together now."

"Talk to me, Maggie. We were lovers. Friends. Partners."

"That last one is the only one that matters." She blew on her coffee, and sipped it cautiously. "I wanted our business. All of it. I was tired of being the junior partner, especially when I did most of the work. But you had the name, and the reputation, and the contacts. I didn't see why I should have to go on sharing my money with you. I was the brains in our partnership, and you were only the muscle. You can always hire muscle. And . . . I was bored with you. Our affair was fun, and it got me the partnership I wanted; but, Larry darling, while you might have been adequate in bed, you were just so damned dull out of it.

"I couldn't split up the business. I needed the cachet your name brings. And I couldn't simply have you killed, because under the terms of your will, your ex would inherit your half of the business. And I really didn't see why I should have to go to all the trouble and expense of buying her out.

"So I got out my old books and put together a neat little package of poisons and voodoo magics. As a zombie under my control, you would have made and signed a new will, leaving everything to me. Then I'd dispose of your body. But clearly I didn't put enough sugar in your coffee. Or maybe you saw something in my face, at the last. Either way, that damned secret wand of yours let you escape. To a safe house I didn't even know we had any more. You have no idea how surprised I was when you rang me three days later.

"Why didn't you remember? The poison, the spells, the trauma? Or maybe you just didn't want to believe your old sweetie could have a mind of her own and the guts to go after what she wanted."

"So why point me at Max?" I said numbly.

"To use up what time you've got left. And there was always the chance you'd take each other out and leave the field even more open for me."

"How could you do this? I loved you, Maggie!"

"That's sweet, Larry. But a girl's got to live."

She put aside her coffee, stood up, and looked down at me. Frowning slightly, as though considering a necessary but distasteful task. "But it's not too late to put things right. I made you what you are, and I can unmake you." She pulled a silver dagger out of her sleeve. The leaf-shaped blade was covered with runes and sigils. "Just lie back and accept it, Larry. You don't want to go on as you are, do you? I'll cut the consciousness right out of you, then you won't care any more. You'll sign the necessary papers like a good little zombie, and I'll put your body to rest. It's been fun, Larry. Don't spoil it."

She came at me with the dagger while she was still talking, expecting to catch me off guard. I activated my wand, and time crashed to a halt. She hung over me, suspended in mid-air. I studied her for a moment; and then it was the easiest thing in the world to take the dagger away from her and slide it slowly into her heart. I let time start up again. She fell forward into my arms, and I held her while she died, because I had loved her once.

I didn't want to kill her, even after everything she'd done and planned to do. But when a man's partner kills him, he's supposed to do something about it.

❦

So here I am. Dead, but not departed. My body seems to have stabilized. No more maggots. Presumably the wand interacting with the voodoo magics. I never really understood that stuff. I don't know how much longer I've got, but then, who does? Maybe I'll have new business cards made up. Larry Oblivion, deceased detective. The postmortem private eye. I still have my work. And I need to do some good, to balance out all the bad I did while I was alive. The hereafter's a lot closer than it used to be.

Even when you're dead, there's no rest for the wicked.

RAZOR EDDIE'S
BIG NIGHT OUT

London has a secret. Deep in the heart of that ancient city, there is a place where gods and monsters walk openly, often hand in hand, and all the forbidden knowledge and unnatural pleasures of the world are up for sale if you can afford the price. Which might be your soul, or someone else's. Far older than the city that surrounds and conceals it, and far more dangerous, the Nightside waits for all of us. Here the sun has never shone and never will, and it's always three o'clock in the morning; the hour of the wolf, when most babies are born and most people die. The Nightside is a terrible, vicious place, but it doesn't bother me. I come from somewhere much worse.

I walked unhurriedly through streets lit by hot neon, past the propped-open doors of clubs where the music never stops, and you can dance till your feet bleed, and the Devil's music is always in season. Shops and establishments offered ecstasy and damnation, lost treasures and your heart's desire, all at knock-down prices and only a little shop-soiled. In the Nightside, you can talk with spirits or lie down with demons, and no-one will give a damn as long as your credit holds out.

None of it tempted me.

Men and women, and things that were both and neither, hurried past me as I made my way through the crowded streets. They were all careful to give me plenty of room. People tend not to bother priests in the Nightside. You can never be sure what kind of backup they might have. I smiled and nodded pleasantly to everyone I passed because nothing upsets the lost souls of the Nightside more than a confident smile. And, finally, I came to Uptown, which passes for the fashionable end of the Nightside. Here the swells and celebrities and Major Players gather to enjoy the very best clubs and restaurants and meeting-places. I passed them all by. The man I was looking for wouldn't be seen dead in such establishments. Unless he was there to kill someone. Behind the expensive and brightly lit watering holes is a darker place called Rats' Alley. A cold and miserable square of stained stone walls and grimy cobble-stones, where the homeless and the down-and-outs gather, to beg food from the backdoors and service entrances of the Uptown restaurants. Sometimes they sleep there, in cardboard boxes or improvised lean-tos, or wrapped in whatever blankets or heavy coats they can beg, borrow, or steal. The wheel turns for everyone, and nowhere more so than in the Nightside.

Rats' Alley was a mess, with dirt and grime and slime everywhere. Ragged forms huddled together, people who had lost everything, or at least, everything that mattered. Sister Morphine, in her ragged robes, arguing resignedly with one of the Little Sisters of the Immaculate Chain-saw. Herne the Hunter, once a god in his own right and spirit of the wild woods, but now much diminished, snarling miserably from under soggy cardboard. A single Grey alien, left behind by his abducting fellows, with a sign saying WILL

PROBE FOR FOOD. I stopped abruptly as a hunger-thin and ghostly pale woman lurched out of the shadows to block my way, clutching her filthy rags about her.

"This is no place for tourists. Leave now, while you still can."

"Hello, Jacqueline," I said gently. "It's all right. I'm not here for you. I'm looking for Eddie."

Her bony hands clenched into fists. "You know me?"

"Yes. You're Jacqueline Hyde."

"Wrong! I'm Jacqueline; he's Hyde. And we don't like snoopers!"

She changed in a moment, her bones cracking loudly as they lengthened, her scrawny body bulking out with new muscle. The shoulders broadened, the face coarsened, and just like that, the man called Hyde was blocking my way, a great hulking brute scowling at me from under a lowering brow. His large, hairy hands twitched eagerly, ready to maim or murder. The homeless and down-and-outs only watched listlessly, from a safe distance. None of them would help.

"Leave him alone."

It was a quiet, almost ghostly voice, but it stopped Hyde in his tracks. He glanced back over his shoulder. He knew the voice, and he was afraid. His clenched hands beat on the air in frustration, then he lurched back into the concealing shadows, his face and form already shrinking, changing back. At the back of the square, a length of plastic sheeting had been formed into a lean-to, from which Razor Eddie studied me thoughtfully with his cold, cold eyes. He emerged unhurriedly, pulling his ancient coat about him, and came forward to join me.

"A sad tale," he said. "Jacqueline is in love with Hyde, and he with her, but they can never meet."

"The Nightside is full of sad tales," I said. "That's why I'm here, Eddie."

He nodded. No-one ever came to see Razor Eddie unless they wanted something from him, and mostly he liked it that way. Razor Eddie, the Punk God of the Straight Razor, was a tall, thin presence in an oversized grey raincoat held together by accumulated filth and grease. His face was sallow and unshaven, with deep hollows and fever-bright eyes. Flies hung around him, and he smelled really bad.

A wild child, and already an experienced killer by the age of fourteen, Eddie was a street kid who'd run with any gang that promised him kicks or killing. But he finally went too far, even for them, and so he ran to the Street of the Gods for shelter. The one place even his many enemies might not dare follow. The Street of the Gods is where all the Powers and Forces and Beings too powerful for the Nightside are segregated. You can find any kind of church or temple there, any kind of faith or racket, and pretty much any kind of god or devil you can think of. Big or small, famous or forgotten by the outside world, you can find whatever you're looking for on the Street of the Gods.

A place where prayers are heard and answered whether you want it or not.

Eddie had an epiphany on the Street of the Gods, and it changed him forever. He came back into the Nightside with a new and terrible power in him, determined to do penance for his old, evil ways. But since all he knew was killing, he turned his rage upon the Bad Guys, the important people no-one else could touch. He killed them in horrible, disturbing ways, and his reputation grew. He lived on hand-outs and slept in shop doorways, a god of back streets and shadows, whose name was known and feared in all the highest and lowest places of the Nightside. And that was Razor Eddie—an extremely upsetting force for the Good. (And no, the Good didn't get a say in the matter.)

Eddie and I are friends, I suppose. It's hard to tell, with people like us.

Mad Old Alice passed by, muttering querulously to herself, still searching for the giant white rabbit she says led her into the Nightside, then abandoned her. Still, that's Pookahs for you. Eddie led me a little away from watching eyes and ears, so we could talk privately.

"What do you want?" he said, blunt as always.

"Bad things are happening on the Street of the Gods," I said.

"Good. Let them all fall. Gods always were more trouble than they're worth."

I had to smile. "How can you not approve of gods when you are one?"

He sniffed. "I never asked to be worshipped. Feared, yes."

"That's how most religions start. Eddie, the Street is in danger, and so am I."

He studied me with his bright, unblinking gaze, but I didn't flinch or back away, and after a while, he sighed heavily.

"I never wanted to go back there. But I owe you. Let's go."

We left the gloom of Rats' Alley for the sleazy neon and endless roar of the Nightside streets. Everyone gave Razor Eddie plenty of room. Some even turned and ran when they saw him coming. We headed for the nearest Underground tube station. The Street of the Gods isn't actually in the Nightside, as such, for security reasons, but there are trains that will take you there. You can get to pretty much anywhere from the Nightside, including places that don't officially exist any more.

It should have taken the best part of half an hour to reach the nearest station, but Eddie led me suddenly down a narrow alleyway that hadn't been there a moment before, and when we came out the other end, we were right at the station entrance. Eddie didn't make a big deal out of it, but then he never does. The one time I asked him about it, he smiled his disturbing smile, and said, *I can move in mysterious ways, too, when I feel like it.*

We went down into the station. The crowds were even thicker here, with eager eyes and impatient mouths, bad intentions heavy on the air. The white-tiled walls were covered in the usual graffiti, in a variety of languages, some of which hadn't been spoken in centuries. Deeply gouged claw-marks and recent blood and hair crusted high up on the walls. A busker with Multiple Personality Disorder sang close harmony with himself, while a small, winged monkey plaintively held out a plastic cup for spare change. I dropped in a few coins. It never hurts to have some spare karma in the bank.

The platform was packed with all sorts of interesting types, but then, the Nightside has interesting like a dog has fleas. A small group of furry animals walked on two legs with bowed heads, following a bear in priestly robes, holding up a cross with the image of a small green frog nailed to it. A princess chatted amiably with her unicorn. A fifteenth-century Crusader in full plate armour scowled disapprovingly about him. A red cross was painted on his breast-plate, in what looked like fresh blood.

The train pulled in. A long, shining silver bullet with no windows anywhere. You have to pass through strange, dangerous places getting to and from the Nightside, and you really don't want to see them. Eddie and I sat alone in our carriage. No-one felt like joining us. I didn't blame them. Eddie's smell got really bad in confined spaces, and the leather seats were already beginning to sweat.

And so we came at last to the Street of the Gods. Where everything that has ever been worshipped, or ever will be, makes its home. No-one knows for sure how long the Street is. Some say it expands and contracts to fit in all the sanctity and abominations available. I warned Eddie the place had changed a lot since he was last here, but even so, I think he was shocked. These days the Street of the Gods is determinedly modern, very now, and in your face. Church fronts blazed with gaudy neon, promising delights and damnations, while barkers worked the crowds, tempting and cajoling the passers-by.

Beings and Powers walked openly on the Street, showing off their peacock glory, out and about to See and be Seen. Animal-headed gods from antiquity, elemental spirits, awful creatures from higher and lower dimensions, and energy forms so abstract you sensed as much as saw them. In the old days, they would have stopped to chat pleasantly together, share the latest news and catch up on the gossip. It was a big Street, and there was room for everyone. But not now. There was a distinct tension on the air, and the gods walked like gun-slingers, wary for insult or attack. Their followers banded together like street gangs, shouting slogans and dogmas at each other.

And here and there, burned and bombed-out churches left gaps in the Street like pulled teeth. What had once been unthinkable was now a sign of the times, of gods no longer able to protect themselves.

We passed by the Egyptian cat goddess Bast, now reduced to singing "Memory" out on the Street, for the tourists.

"This isn't the way to your church," said Eddie, after a while.

"I don't have a church any more," I said steadily. "As the one and only representative of my religion, I have been evicted from my church, so it could be handed over to some more successful god. I have a street stall now."

Eddie stopped and looked at me, so I stopped, too, and met his angry gaze calmly. He started to say something, but we were interrupted by an approaching zealot, calling out

Eddie's name like an insult. He was a Kali worshipper, in black leather bondage trousers under an open robe, pulled back to show off the ritual scars on his shaven chest. A thugee strangling cord hung ostentatiously from his fist. He was big and muscular but very young. Anyone else would have had more sense. No doubt Someone else put him up to it, to see if Razor Eddie still had it.

The zealot shoved his face right into Eddie's. I decided to retreat several steps, so I wouldn't get any of the blood on me.

"Have You Been Saved?" the zealot barked.

"I saved myself," said Razor Eddie. "But who will save you from me?"

"I serve Kali, mistress of death!"

"Met her once. We didn't get on. She said I was too extreme."

An old-fashioned pearl-handled straight razor appeared in his hand, out of nowhere. The steel blade shone supernaturally bright. The zealot brought up his strangling cord, and Razor Eddie fell upon him. He moved supernaturally quickly, his razor rising and falling, and the zealot cried out in terror as his clothes fell away in tatters, sliced clean through. In a moment, he was entirely naked, his strangling cord in pieces on the ground. Eddie stood with his razor pressed lightly against the zealot's throat, and he wasn't even breathing hard.

"I've been away too long," said the Punk God of the Straight Razor, in his soft, ghostly voice. "I think I need to set an example. So I'm going to flay every inch of skin from your body. Nothing personal, you understand."

The young zealot cried out miserably, but no-one came forward to help him.

"No," I said. Eddie looked at me. One doesn't say *No* to the Punk God of the Straight Razor, even if he is an old friend. "Please," I said.

Eddie sighed and shrugged. "You always were too soft for your own good."

His razor flashed once, briefly, and the zealot cried out in agony as he was instantly and expertly circumcised.

"You can go now," said Razor Eddie, and the zealot ran, howling all the way down the Street. And everyone who'd been watching went about their business again.

"Well," I said, trying to keep it light. "At least he's not a complete prick any more."

"It's all in the wrist action," said Eddie.

We continued down the Street of the Gods, Razor Eddie studying everything and everyone with his hot, intense gaze. Some of the names on the churches were clearly familiar to him even though their exteriors had changed greatly. The Speaking Stone, Soror Marium, The Carrion In Tears, and a whole bunch of the Transient Beings, honoured mostly in the hope they'd stay away. The Transient Beings aren't actually gods, but it doesn't stop them behaving as though they are.

"I don't see the problem," Eddie said finally. "The Street of the Gods may have undergone a make-over, but it all still seems very much business as usual. A business where souls are currency, and the suckers still get fleeced."

"Not everyone is doing well," I said. "A lot of the lesser gods are suffering."

He looked sideways at me. "Do the gods who can't hack it any more still suffer the same fate?"

"Oh yes," I said. "Faith and worshippers bestow power, and without that, the gods are as vulnerable as anyone else. Take away a god's congregation, and they wither up and fade away. Some keep going by merging with other, more successful gods and pantheons, and some choose to become mortal rather than disappear entirely. There's always a chance of a comeback. This is a place of miracles, after all."

"The Street . . . feels different," said Eddie. He might have been listening to me, or he might not. "There's no . . . community any more. Tell me what's been happening here.

What's so important that you would leave the Street to look for me?"

"There are moves afoot," I said carefully, "to modernise, organise, and regulate all the various gods and religions that make up the Street. Those with the most worshippers, the most powerful and adored, are to be given dominion over all the best locations. The rest will be ranked, according to power and status, and positioned accordingly on the Street. The lowest will actually have to pay the highest, in order to be allowed to stay on the Street. Those at the very bottom, like Bast, are being forced out. It seems we lesser religions lower the tone and might scare off the paying customers. At the end of the day, it's all about the Big Boys wanting more power and more money and less competition. It seems doctrines and articles of faith aren't enough any more. The Big Boys want job security."

"That sounds more like Nightside thinking than Street of the Gods," said Eddie. "Who brought it here?"

"Who do you think?" I said. "Who's behind all the bad news in our lives?"

"How unkind," murmured a calm, cultured voice behind us. "After all, I was invited."

We both looked round. Walker was standing right behind us even though neither of us had heard him approach. A smart city gent in a smart city suit, complete with old-school tie and a bowler hat, Walker was the public face of the Authorities: those shadowy background figures who run the Nightside, inasmuch as anybody does. Walker's word is law, and he can call on all kinds of nasty people to back him up. Few people argue with him. They say he once made a dead man sit up on his mortuary slab and answer questions. Walker smiled easily at Eddie, ignoring me.

"It had to happen eventually, Eddie. The Street of the Gods was getting terribly old-fashioned. It was time to spruce the place up, clear out the dead wood, bring a little order and efficiency to things. Just because you're immortal doesn't mean you're guaranteed a job for life. Think of what's happening here as survival of the fittest, divine evolution in action."

"I've always been on the side of the underdog," said Eddie. "And the undergod. There's room enough here for everyone, Walker."

"Yes, there is," said Walker. "But the Big Boys have decided they don't want to share any more."

Eddie smiled slowly. "I wonder who put that idea into their heads. And I wonder how much they've had to promise the Authorities in return for your help, Walker. Who's working with you on this? You couldn't hope to pull this off without really heavy-duty backup."

"True," said Walker. "But even gods can be smacked down and made to behave if you have powerful enough attack dogs. Let me present the Holy Trio."

A man and a woman appeared suddenly out of nowhere on either side of Walker. Tall, cadaverous, and dressed in long black priestly robes, I could feel magic crackling threateningly on the air around them. Their eyes were cold, and their smiles colder still.

"Don't you need three for a Trio?" said Eddie, entirely unmoved.

"The Holy Trio consists of a man, a woman, and a disembodied spirit," Walker said calmly. "All of them Jesuit demonologists. They specialise in the flip side of tantric magic, channelling the accumulated tensions of a lifetime's celibacy to power their magics. They have energy to burn and a really spiteful attitude towards the world in general. It helps that they strongly disapprove of worshipping any god except their own. Perfect enforcers for whipping the gods into shape. I have dozens of units like this, working the whole length of the Street."

"Spiritual storm-troopers," said Eddie. "What next, the Inquisition?"

Walker sighed. "I knew you were going to be difficult," he murmured. "Jonathon, Martha, Francis, if you wouldn't mind . . ."

The two visible members of the Holy Trio stepped forward, their cold smiles widening, and I could feel a power building around them, like a coming storm. I could feel a third presence, too, even if I couldn't see it. A bitter wind blew out of nowhere, and all around us the shadows were very dark. On the Street, men and gods ran for cover. Lightning bolts slammed down around us, blasting holes in the road. Eddie didn't move an inch. The man and woman in black raised their hands, and dark energies manifested. My feet were suddenly very cold, and I looked down to find a vast black pool forming under me, and under Eddie. Already, we had sunk a few inches into it. Eddie laughed softly.

"Is that it? Open up a bottomless hole, drop us into it, then disappear the hole? I'm disappointed in you, Walker. You used to have style; this is just a cheap party trick. I prefer something a little more . . . humorous."

He moved suddenly, in a direction I couldn't comprehend, and abruptly we were all somewhere else, leaving the black pool behind. Eddie had moved in his mysterious way again, and we were all standing before a completely different church. Tall white pillars of the purest marble fronted the Church of the Glorious Marilyn. A huge statue of the modern goddess towered over us, holding down her iconic flapping white dress. Raw sexuality poured out of the church, beating on the air like heavy breathing. Walker and I had the sense to step back immediately, moving out of range, but Jonathon and Martha were rooted to the spot by unfamiliar feelings and emotions surging through them. Eddie's razor flashed, and all their clothes fell away. Naked, and overwhelmed by sudden lust and a lifetime's frustrated needs, Jonathon and Martha fell upon each other, and did it right there in the Street. There was a horrified howl from the unseen presence, fading rapidly away to nothing as the living pair's ecstasy exorcised the unquiet spirit.

Eddie smiled briefly at Walker. "Holy Trio, eh? I liked them. They were fun. What else have you got?"

"You're going to be trouble, aren't you?" said Walker.

"Always," said Razor Eddie.

Walker sighed again, tipped his bowler hat to Eddie and to me with his usual impeccable manners, and turned away and strode unhurriedly off down the Street of the Gods. He'd be back, once he'd thought of something sufficiently distressing to do to us. Eddie looked at me thoughtfully.

"What happened to your old church? You were the last follower of Dagon. Is he to be forgotten now?"

"Oh no," I said. "Nothing's ever wasted under the new regime. That wouldn't be efficient. They've installed a new, modernised Dagon in my old church—a Dagon for the twenty-first century."

"A new Dagon?"

I shrugged. "Some semi-divine wannabe, looking for his big break. A lot of the more recalcitrant weaker gods are being ousted and replaced."

"A new Dagon, in the church where I was . . . reborn." Eddie shook his head slowly. "No. I won't have that. Take me there."

"Are you going to make trouble?"

"Yes."

"Then let's go. But I have to warn you, Eddie; the church won't look at all like you remember. It's been remade, in the image of its new deity, along with all new dogmas and doctrines."

"How can he be Dagon if everything that used to represent Dagon has been changed?"

"The name is everything, these days," I said. "The name and the brand and the logo are all anyone cares about."

Eddie could have transported us both to my old church in a moment if he'd wanted, but I think he needed to walk, to give him time to think and consider and remember. I remembered him, as he was then. Fourteen years old and on the lam, having outraged absolutely everybody. He'd kill anyone back then, striking out blindly at a world that had always hurt him and done him wrong. He was out-of-control, and everyone knew it. The word went out, and Eddie ran, and once on the Street of the Gods, dazzled and overwhelmed by forces even more dangerous than he, he somehow found his way to the old, small church of Dagon, a fish god once worshipped by the Pharisees. Forgotten by pretty much everyone except the one man who still maintained his church.

Eddie came in like a wild dog seeking shelter from the storm, and he let me feed and look after him, perhaps because he could tell I was never going to be any threat to him. He didn't care about the god of my church, but my stubborn persistence fascinated him. He stayed with me, and somehow . . . we connected. Perhaps because we both had nobody else. I gave him sanctuary, and we talked for many hours. I asked him what he believed in.

"I don't know," he said. "I never came across anything or anyone worth believing in."

"Then why not try believing in yourself," I said. "That you can be more than you are, better than you are. That's a start, at least."

"What if I'm not . . . worth believing in?" he said.

"Everyone can change," I said. "You wouldn't believe how much I've changed, down the years."

Sometime later, another lost soul came bursting into my

church, desperate and bedraggled, begging for sanctuary and protection. He was a flower child from the 1960s who'd been attending the Summer of Love festival when he fell through a Timeslip and ended up on the Street of the Gods. Half out of his mind with fear and culture shock, he'd made the mistake of appealing to the wrong god for help, and now he had a killer on his trail.

Another figure came striding into my church, a broad and stocky man in old-fashioned armour, carrying a short-sword. He had come for the flower child, and his scarred face was ugly with rage and contempt. Mithras was an old soldier's god. He had fallen far from what he once was, but he still had his pride and the convictions of his old beliefs. The flower child was everything he detested. The very idea that a man could turn his back on war and embrace peace was anathema to Mithras. It offended everything he was.

He advanced on the young man, murder in his eyes. I stepped forward and stood between the soldier and his victim.

"Not in my church," I said.

"This isn't a church," said Mithras. "How can it be a church when its god is no more? You're just a man. Get out of my way."

"I still follow the way of Dagon," I said. "I have given this man sanctuary."

"Get out of the way, or I'll kill you, too."

I don't know what made me so stubborn. Perhaps all those hours of talking with Eddie had reminded me of what I used to be. But I wouldn't move. Mithras drew back his sword to run me through. And Eddie, wild child, cut-throat, and killer, who had never had a friend before, threw himself forward. Mithras turned at the unexpected attack, and Eddie opened up the god's throat with his straight razor. Mithras staggered backwards, choking on his own blood, then fell to his knees, more mortal than he had realised. He tried to lift his sword, but it fell from his hand.

Eddie stepped forward and finished the job, and Mithras fell dead at his feet.

And Razor Eddie cried out in shock and astonishment, as all of Mithras's remaining power flooded out of the dead god and into him. All in a moment the street kid was gone, and a new god was created. Razor Eddie, Punk God of the Straight Razor.

I found a way to send the flower child back to where and when he belonged, and Eddie stayed with me for some time. We learned much from each other. It was fascinating to watch a new person being born, right before my eyes. He asked me once exactly what it was I believed in since Dagon no longer existed as a god. I thought for a long while before I answered.

"I've been here a long time," I said finally. "But I think what I truly believe in is people. They can always surprise you. They have such potential . . . They can change and grow and become so much more than they or anyone else would ever have thought possible. Unlike gods. And at the end of the day, I believe that people should be kind to each other. Because there's more than enough evil in the world already."

"I've seen many strange things in the Nightside," said Eddie. "Monsters and men, and men who were monsters. Wonders and terrors and odd things passing through; but none of them impressed me as much as the bravery of your stand against Mithras. I don't want to be . . . like I was. Before. I want to be like you."

He left, not long after that, to begin his long penance in the Nightside for all the evils he'd done. When he first mentioned his intention, I thought he meant good deeds and charity. I should have known better.

The more bad people he killed, the more everyone believed in this new appalling god, and so his power grew. The whole of the Nightside was his church and the killings his doctrine.

Never worshipped, ever feared. Doing penance in his own way. Poor Eddie. I did offer to absolve him, but he would not accept my forgiveness. He did not forgive himself, for who and what he used to be and all the terrible things he'd done.

I don't think he realises how close he still is to what he was, and that a man who murders in the name of the Good is still a murderer. Certainly I'll never tell him.

We came at last to the church of the Twenty-First-Century Dagon. I hardly recognised the old place, but then I had been away for a while, and they'd tarted up the old girl something fierce. More sleazy neon and blatant come-ons than a Nightside brothel. Eddie stared down a doorman who had the nerve to demand an entrance fee, and we went inside. It looked like some ghastly Hollywood theme restaurant. The walls had been painted the colours of the sea, the pews had been artfully draped with plastic seaweed, and the air stank of artificial brine. The new Dagon came striding forward to meet us. He was big and green and scaly, and looked like a cross between the Creature from the Black Lagoon and one of those plastic He-Man steroid-abuse toys. He glared at us and opened his fanged mouth to speak, and Razor Eddie cut his head off. The few worshippers in the church ran out, screaming. The scaly body was still standing, so Eddie pushed it over and kicked the head away like a football. He smiled briefly at me.

"Fancy some sushi later?"

There was the sound of unhurried footsteps behind us, so we looked round. I was half expecting to see Walker back again, with major reinforcements, but it was only the goddess from the church next door, come to see what was up. She'd faced the same choice I had, but had chosen to be reinvented rather than evicted and replaced. I nodded politely. I make no judgements.

"Greetings, patron of witches. It's been a while. Eddie, you remember Hecate, the goddess next door."

"Not like this I don't," said Eddie.

He had a point. Hecate, that ancient inspiration for all witches, had been made over into the ultimate Goth diva. Pale, colourless skin, night-dark hair, jet-black leathers, and so many face and body piercings she had to be a danger during thunder-storms. It didn't suit the mystical and mysterious goddess I remembered, but this was a new Hecate, for a New Age. Half a dozen acolytes clustered around her, cute little gothettes in black basques, torn stockings, and sinister face make-up. They all carried switch-blades and looked like they'd be glad of a chance to use them.

"I know," said Hecate. "It's not a look I would have chosen, either. But needs must when the Authorities drive, and I have always done my best to reflect the times I move in. After all, seduction spells and murder magic are never out of fashion."

"You've given in," said Eddie. "Given up. I thought better of you than that, Hecate."

The acolytes stirred menacingly at such open disrespect, but Hecate hushed them with a glance. "I knew you'd be back, Eddie. Blood and death call to you like a lover, and there has been so much of both here on the Street, of late. But you should consider that some of us are reasonably happy with the way things are. I'm still running the same old racket I always was; give me blood and suffering and regular live sacrifices, and I'll answer your prayers. I'm really a very easy goddess to get along with."

"You look . . . silly," said Eddie.

She shrugged, not offended. "Like you know anything about fashion. It's only a new face for a very old game."

"I don't like it," said Eddie. "I don't like any of this. Faith should mean something. Gods . . . should stand for something, not chop and change with every breeze that blows. Gods should be worshipped for the truths they represent, not what party favours they might dispense."

"You always were a romantic, Eddie," said Hecate. "In your own disturbing way. But the times they are a-changing, and not even you can hold back this tide."

Razor Eddie smiled slowly. "Want to bet?"

Hecate didn't even try to meet his gaze. She turned to leave, and her acolytes hissed with rage at seeing their goddess so slighted. They surged forward as one, their switchblades gleaming brightly in the undersea lighting. Eddie was kind and killed them quickly. Their young bodies lay sprawled across the floor of what had once been my church like so many bloody, broken toys. I looked on them sadly, and Hecate came back to join me.

"Ah well," she said. "I suppose I'll have to find some more fools. It's not like there's a shortage . . ."

"You're a hard woman, Hecate," I said.

She smiled. "I told you I hadn't changed."

"You should leave now," said Razor Eddie. "This church is corrupted. Beyond saving. I'm bringing it down."

There was something in his voice. I grabbed Hecate's hand, and we ran from the church. Behind us, I could feel Razor Eddie's power growing as his implacable presence filled the whole church. He wasn't just a street person in a filthy overcoat any more, or even an extremely disturbing agent for the Good; he was the Punk God of the Straight Razor, and he was terrible in his rage. The whole building shook as though in the grip of some great beast, then collapsed in upon itself. A massive cloud of smoke billowed out the front door as the walls fell in, and the ceiling crashed through. Within moments, there was nothing left but a pile of rubble, and standing before it like some shopsoiled avenging angel, Razor Eddie.

He strode past Hecate and me, not even looking in our direction, and headed down the Street. I hurried after him and watched aghast as, one by one, he brought down all the churches of the new and reinvented gods. His power roared and crackled on the air around him like a living thing, awful and potent, and none of the new gods and goddesses could stand against him. Wherever he looked, buildings exploded or caught on fire, and all the gods who could not, dared not, face him ran screaming and sobbing down the Street of the Gods. Because they believed in the Punk God of the Straight Razor.

In the end, Eddie tired, and even his rage ran dry. He stood alone, surrounded by smoke and fire and destruction, and the cries of those who'd seen their gods thrown down. Eddie looked upon his work, and knew it to be Good. He flicked a few drops of blood from the blade of his straight razor, and it vanished from his hand. I came forward to join him.

"Oh, Eddie," I said. "Still over-reacting."

"It's what I do best. Isn't that why you brought me here?"

I had no answer to that.

Walker came strolling down the Street and stopped a respectful distance away. "You know the Authorities will send me after you for this, Eddie."

"Let them come," said Razor Eddie, in his soft, ghostly voice. "Let them all come."

"You haven't really stopped anything here."

"I haven't really started yet."

Walker looked at me. "All this because we put you out of a church no-one came to anyway?"

"It was my church," I said. "Beware the man with nothing left to lose."

Walker nodded. "Or the god."

"Take me home," Razor Eddie said to me. "I think I've done all the Good I can stand, for one day."

•   •   •

Eddie and I made our way back to the Nightside, where everyone gave him even more room than usual. Word of his latest exploits was already making the rounds, growing wildly in the telling, as always. And thus his power grew. We went back to Rats' Alley, to the homeless and the cardboard boxes. Razor Eddie could have lived well, with every luxury. No-one would have dared deny him anything. But Eddie had very old-fashioned ideas about doing penance. I could understand that. We shook hands, a little awkwardly. We've never found it very easy, being friends, being what we are.

"Good-bye, Eddie," I said.

He nodded. "Good-bye, Dagon."

LUCY, AT CHRISTMASTIME

You never forget your first; and mine was Lucy.

It was Christmas Eve in the Nightside, and I was drinking wormwood brandy in Strangefellows, the oldest bar in the world. The place was crowded, the air was thick with good cheer, the ceiling trailed long streamers of the cheapest paper decorations money could buy; and as midnight approached, the revellers grew so festive they could barely stand up. Even so, everyone was careful to give me plenty of room as I sat on my stool at the bar, nursing my drink. I'm Leo Morn, and that's a name you can scare people with. Of course, my Lucy was never scared of me, even though everyone told her I was a bad boy, and would come to a bad end. Lucy sat on the stool beside me at the bar, smiling and listening while I talked. She didn't have a drink. She never does.

The music system was playing "Jingle Bells" by the Sex Pistols, a sure sign the bar's owner was feeling nostalgic. Farther down the long (and only occasionally polished) wooden bar, sat Tommy Oblivion, the existential private eye. He was currently doing his best to convince a pressing creditor that his bill might or might not be valid in this particular reality. Not that far away, Ms. Fate, the Nightside's very own leather-costumed transvestite superheroine, was dancing on a tabletop with demon girl reporter Bettie Divine. Bettie's cute little curved horns peeped out from between the bangs of her long dark hair.

The Prince of Darkness was sulking into his drink over the cancellation of his TV reality show; the Mistress of the Dark was trying to tempt Saint Nicholas with a sprig of plastic mistletoe; and a reindeer with a very red nose was lying slumped and extremely drunk in a corner, muttering something about unionization. Brightly glowing wee-winged fairies swept round and round the huge Christmas tree, darting in and out of the heavy branches at fantastic speed in some endless game of tag. Every now and again one of the fairies would detonate like a flashbulb, from sheer overpowering joie de vivre, before re-forming and rejoining the chase.

Just another Christmas Eve, in the oldest bar in the world. Where dreams can come true, if you're not careful. Especially at the one time of the year when gods and monsters, good men and bad, can come together in the grand old tradition of eating and drinking yourself stupid, and making a fool of yourself over past loves.

Alex the bartender noticed my glass was empty, and filled it up again without having to be asked. Since he knows me really well, he usually has the good sense to insist I pay in advance for every drink; but even nasty mean-spirited Alex Morrisey knows better than to disturb me on Christmas Eve. I saluted Lucy with my new drink, and she smiled prettily back. My lovely Lucy. Short and sweet, pleasantly curved, tight blonde curls over a heart-shaped face, bright flashing eyes and a smile to break your heart. Wearing the same long white dress she'd been wearing just before she left me forever. Lucy was . . . sharp as a tack, sweet as forbidden fruit, and honest as the day is long. What she ever saw in me, I'll never know. She was sixteen, going on seventeen. Of course, I'm a lot older than her now.

I only ever see her here, on Christmas Eve. I don't have to come here, tell myself every year that I won't; but I always do. Because no matter how much it hurts, I have to see her. *Silly boy,* she always says. *I forgave you long ago.* And I always nod, and say, *I don't forgive me. And I never will.*

Were we in love, really? We were very young. And every-thing seems so sharp and intense, when you're a teenager. Emotions surge through you like tidal waves, and a sudden smile from a girl can explode in your heart like a firecracker. Immersed in the moment, transfixed in each other's eyes like rabbits caught in the glare of approaching head-lights . . . Yes; she was my first love, and I have never forgot-ten the time we had together.

All the things we were going to do, all the people we could have been . . . thrown away, in a moment of madness.

I reminded Lucy of how we first met; standing in a rail-way station late at night, waiting for a train that seemed like it would never come. I looked at her, she looked at me, we both smiled; and next thing I knew we were chatting away as though we'd known each other all our lives. After that, we were never apart. Laughing and teasing, arguing and making up, walking hand in hand and arm in arm because we couldn't bear not to be touching each other. Running through the thick woods under Darkacre; drinking and singing in a late-night lockup, even though we were still underage, because the owner was an old romantic who believed in young love; and later, slow dancing together on the cobbled street of a back alley, to the sound of sentimen-tal music drifting out of a half-open window up above.

You never forget your first love, your first great passion.

I was jolted out of my mood, as Harry Fabulous lurched out of the crowd to greet me with his best salesman's smile. He should have known better, but Harry would try and sell a silencer to the man who was about to shoot him. Always affable and professionally charming, Harry was a con man, a fixer, a specialist in the kind of deal that leaves you counting your fingers afterwards. Always ready to sell you something that was bad for you, or someone else. A hard man to dislike, but worth the effort. He went to sit on the stool next to me, and then froze as I fixed him with my stare. I smiled at him, showing my teeth, and he went pale. He eased back from the stool, holding his empty hands out before him to show how sorry and harmless he was. I let him go. My time with Lucy was too precious to interrupt with the likes of Harry Fabulous.

I remembered running through the woods, chasing Lucy in and out of the tall dark trees as she ran giggling before me, teasing and taunting me, always just out of reach, but careful never to get so far ahead I might think she didn't want to be caught. It was late at night, but the woods were lit up with the shimmering blue-white glare of a full moon. The whole world seemed to come alive around me as I ran, rich with scents and sounds I'd never noticed before. I felt strong and fast and indomitable, like I could run and run forever.

Lucy ran ahead of me, in her long white dress, like a ghost fleeting through the trees.

The moonlight filled my mind, and boiled through my body. My senses were so sharp now they were almost painful. I'd never felt so alive, so happy. The change swept over me like a red rolling tide. Bones creaked and cracked as they lengthened, and I didn't care. Fur burst out of me, covered me, made me whole. My mouth stretched out into a long muzzle, so I could howl my thanks to the full moon that gave me birth. I hardly even noticed as I fell forward and continued to run on four feet. I was a wolf, under the glorious moon, doing what I was born to do. The ancient imperative of the hunt was upon me. I forgot about Leo Morn, forgot about Lucy. I ran howling through the trees, maddened by the moon and the exhilaration of my very first change. The real me had finally burst out of its human cocoon, its human trap; released to run and hunt as I was meant to.

I ran and ran, driven on by the marvellous strength and speed of my new four legs, lord of all I surveyed; as though the whole world and everything in it was nothing more to me than prey.

I shot back and forth, questing between the trees, crested a ridge, and threw myself down onto the prey cringing below. I slammed it to the ground, and tore out its throat with one easy snap of my jaws. The blood was hot and wet and wonderful in my mouth. The prey kicked and struggled as I tore it apart, but not for long. I feasted on the hot and steaming meat, savouring the way it tore easily between my fine new teeth. I ate till I was full, and then raised a leg and urinated over what was left, so no other beast would dare to touch my kill. I licked my blood-flecked muzzle clean, and felt as if I'd come home at last.

When I came to myself again, Lucy was gone.

And now, all these years later, it was Christmas Eve in Strangefellows; and the crowd was singing a carol, or something like it. The night was almost over. I didn't tell Lucy what I'd been thinking about, but I think she knew. She only ever looks sad when I do. But it's all I can think about, on this night of all nights; the night that separated us, forever. Christmas Eve, when the world seems full of promise; the night I told Lucy I loved her, and that I'd love her forever, forever and a day. I told her there was nothing else in the world I wanted as much as her, and I meant it, then. It was the wolf within that made me a liar. That's why I come here every Christmas Eve, to the oldest bar in the world . . . where sometimes stories can still end in lovers' meeting.

I don't have to show up, but I do, because I promised her I'd love her forever and a day.

The clock struck midnight, the revellers cheered the coming of Christmas Day, and Lucy softly and silently faded away. Gone again, for another year.

When the change first takes you, it's only too easy to mistake one passion for another.

You never forget your first victim.

APPETITE FOR MURDER

I never wanted to be a Detective. But the call went out, and no-one else stood up, so I sold my soul to the company store, for a badge and a gun and a shift that never ends.

The Nightside is London's very own dirty little secret: a hidden realm of gods and monsters, magic and murder, and more sin and temptation than you can shake a wallet at. People come to the Nightside from all over the world, to indulge the pleasures and appetites that might not have a name but certainly have a price. It's always night in the Nightside, always three o'clock on the morning, the hour that tries men's souls and finds them wanting. The sun has never shone here, probably because it knows it isn't welcome. This is a place to do things that can only be done in the shadows, in the dark.

I'm Sam Warren. I was the first, and for a long time the only, Detective in the Nightside. I worked for the Authorities, those grey and faceless figures who run the Nightside, inasmuch as anyone does, or can. Even in a place where there is no crime, because everything is permitted, where sin and suffering, death and damnation are just business as usual . . . there are still those who go too far and have to be taken down hard. And for that, you need a Detective.

We don't get many serial killers in the Nightside. Mostly because amateurs don't tend to last long amongst so much professional competition. But I was made Detective, more years ago than I care to remember, to hunt down the very first of these human monsters. His name was Shock-Headed Peter. He killed 347 men, women, and children before I caught him. Though that's just an official estimate; we never found any of his victims' bodies. Just their clothes. Wouldn't surprise me if the real total was closer to a thousand. I caught him and put him away; but the things I saw, and the things I had to do, changed me forever.

Made me the Nightside's Detective, for all my sins, mea culpa.

I'd just finished eating when the call came in. From the H P Lovecraft Memorial Library, home to more forbidden tomes under one roof than anywhere else. Browse at your own risk. It appeared the Nightside's latest serial killer had struck again. Only this time he'd been interrupted, and the body was still warm, the blood still wet.

I strode through the Library accompanied by a Mr. Pettigrew, a tall, storklike personage with wild eyes and a shock of white hair. He gabbled continuously as we made our way through the tall stacks, wringing his bony hands against his sunken chest. Mr. Pettigrew was Chief Librarian, and almost overcome with shame that such a vulgar thing should have happened in his Library.

"It's all such a mess!" he wailed. "And right in the middle of the Anthropology Section. We've only just finished refurbishing!"

"What can you tell me about the victim?" I said patiently.

"Oh, he's dead. Yes. Very dead, in fact. Horribly mutilated, Detective! I don't know how we're going to get the blood out of the carpets."

"Did you happen to notice if there were any . . . pieces missing, from the body?"

"Pieces? Oh dear," said Mr. Pettigrew. "I can feel one of my heads coming on. I think I'm going to have to go and have a little lie down."

He took me as far as the Anthropology Section, then disappeared at speed. It hadn't been twenty minutes since I got the call, but still someone had beaten me to the body. Crouching beside the bloody mess on the floor was the Nightside's very own superheroine, Ms. Fate. She wore a highly polished black-leather outfit, complete with full face mask and cape; but somehow on her it never looked like a costume or some fetish thing. It looked like a uniform. Like work clothes. She even had a utility belt around her narrow waist, all golden clasps and bulging little pouches. I thought the high heels on the boots were a bit much, though. I came up on her from behind, making no noise at all, but she still knew I was there.

"Hello, Detective Warren," she said, in her low, smoky voice, not even glancing round. "You got here fast."

"Happened to be in the neighbourhood," I said. "What have you found?"

"All kinds of interesting things. Come and have a look."

Anyone else I would have sent packing, but not her. We'd worked a bunch of cases together, and she knew her stuff. We don't get too many superheroes or vigilantes in the Nightside, mostly because they get killed off so damn quickly. Ms. Fate, that dark avenger of the night, was different. Very focused, very skilled, very professional. Would have made a good Detective. She made room for me to crouch down beside her. My knees made loud cracking noises in the Library hush.

"You're looking good, Detective," Ms. Fate said easily. "Have you started dyeing your hair?"

"Far too much grey," I said. "I was starting to look my age, and I couldn't have that."

"I've questioned the staff," said Ms. Fate. "Knew you wouldn't mind. No-one saw anything, but then no-one ever does, in the Nightside. Only one way into this Section, and only one way out, and he would have had blood all over him, but . . ."

"Any camera surveillance?"

"The kind of people who come here, to read the kind of books they keep here, really don't want to be identified. So, no surveillance of any kind, scientific or mystical. There's major security in place to keep any of the books from going walkabout, but that's it."

"If our killer was interrupted, he may have left some clues behind," I said. "This is his sixth victim. Maybe he got sloppy."

Ms. Fate nodded slowly, her expression unreadable behind her dark mask. Her eyes were very blue, very bright. "This has got to stop, Detective. Five previous victims, all horribly mutilated, all with missing organs. Different organs each time. Interestingly enough, the first victim was killed with a blade, but all the others were torn apart, through brute strength. Why change his MO after the first killing? Most serial killers cling to a pattern, a ritual, that means something significant to them."

"Maybe he decided a blade wasn't personal enough," I said. "Maybe he felt the need to get his hands dirty."

We both looked at the body in silence for a while. This one was different. The victim had been a werewolf and had been caught in midchange as he died. His face had elongated into a muzzle, his hands had claws, and patches of silver-grey fur showed clearly on his exposed skin. His clothes were ripped and torn and soaked with blood. He'd been gutted, torn raggedly open from chin to crotch, leaving a great crimson wound.

There was blood all around him, and more spattered across the spines of books on the shelves.

"It's never easy to kill a werewolf," Ms. Fate said finally. "But given the state of the wound's edges, he wasn't cut open. That rules out a silver dagger."

"No sign of a silver bullet either," I observed.

"Then we can probably rule out the Lone Ranger." She rubbed her bare chin thoughtfully. "You know, the extent of these injuries reminds me a lot of cattle mutilations."

I looked at her. "Are we talking little grey aliens?"

She smiled briefly, her scarlet lips standing out against the pale skin under the black mask. "Maybe I should check to see if he's been probed?"

"I think that was the least of his worries," I said. "This must have been a really bad way to die. Our victim had his organs ripped out while he was still alive."

Ms. Fate busied herself taking samples from the body and the crime scene, dropping them into sealable plastic bags and tucking them away in her belt pouches.

"Don't smile," she said, not looking round. "Forensic science catches more killers than deductive thought."

"I never said a word," I said innocently.

"You didn't have to. You only have to look at my utility belt, and your mouth starts twitching. I'll have you know the things I store in my belt have saved my life on more than one occasion. Shuriken, smoke bombs, nausea-gas capsules, stun grenades . . . A girl has to be prepared for everything." She stood up and looked down at the body. "It's such a mess I can't even tell which organs were taken; can you?"

"The heart, certainly," I said, standing up. "Anything else, we'll have to wait for the autopsy."

"I've already been through the clothing," said Ms. Fate. "If there was any ID, the killer took it with him. But I did find a press pass, tucked away in his shoe. Said he worked for the

Night Times. But no name on the pass, which is odd. Could be an investigative reporter, I suppose, working undercover."

"I'll check with the editor," I said.

"But what was he doing here? Research?"

We both looked around, and Ms. Fate was the first to find a book lying on the floor, just outside the blood pool. She opened the book and flicked through it quickly.

"Anything interesting?" I said.

"Hard to tell. Some doctoral dissertation, on the cannibal practices of certain South American tribes."

I gestured for the book, and she handed it over. I skimmed quickly through the opening chapter. "Seems to be about the old cannibal myth that you are what you eat. You know—eat a brave man's heart to become brave, a runner's leg muscles to become fast . . ."

We both looked at the torn open body on the floor, with its missing organs.

"Could that be our murderer's motivation?" said Ms. Fate. "He's taking the organs so he can eat them later, and maybe . . . what? Gain new abilities? Run me through the details of the five previous victims, Detective."

"First was a minor Greek godling," I said. "Supposedly descended from Hercules, at many removes. Very strong. Died of a single knife wound to the heart. Chest and arm muscles were taken."

"Just the one blow, to the heart," said Ms. Fate. "You'd have to get in close for that. Which suggests the victim either knew his killer or had reason to trust him."

"If the killer has acquired a godling's strength, he wouldn't need a knife any more," I said.

"There's more to it than that." She looked like she might be frowning, behind her mask. "This whole hands-on thing shouts . . . passion. That the killer enjoyed it, or took some satisfaction from it."

"Second victim was a farseer," I said. "What they call a

remote viewer these days. Her head was smashed in, and her eyes taken. After that, an immortal who lost his testicles, a teleporter for a messenger service who had his brain ripped right out of his skull, and, finally, a minor radio-chat-show host, who lost his tongue and vocal cords."

"Why that last one?" said Ms. Fate. "What did the killer hope to gain? The gift of the gab?"

"You'll have to ask him," I said. "Presumably the killer believed that eating the werewolf's missing organs would give him shape-changing abilities, or at least regeneration."

"He's trying to eat himself into a more powerful person . . . Hell, just the godling's strength and the werewolf's abilities will make him really hard to take down. Have you come up with any leads yet, from the previous victims?"

"No," I said. "Nothing."

"Then I suppose we'd better run through the usual suspects, if only to cross them off. How about Mr. Stab, the legendary uncaught immortal serial killer of Old London Town?"

"No," I said. "He always uses a knife, or a scalpel. Always has, ever since 1888."

"All right; how about Arnold Drood, the Bloody Man?"

"His own family tracked him down and killed him, just last year."

"Good. Shock-Headed Peter?"

"Still in prison, where I put him," I said. "And there he'll stay, till the day he dies."

Ms. Fate sniffed. "Don't know why they didn't just execute him."

"Oh, they tried," I said. "Several times, in fact. But it didn't take."

"Wait a minute," said Ms. Fate. She knelt again suddenly, and leaned right over to study the dead man's elongated muzzle. "Take a look at this, Detective. The nose and mouth tissues are eaten away. Right back to the bone in places. I wonder . . ." She produced a chemical kit from her belt and ran some quick tests. "I thought so. Silver. Definite traces of silver dust, in the nose, mouth, and throat. Now that was clever . . . Throw a handful of silver dust into the werewolf's face, he breathes it in, unsuspecting, and his tissues would immediately react to the silver. It had to have been horribly painful, certainly enough to distract the victim and interrupt his shape change . . . while leaving him vulnerable to the killer's exceptional strength."

"Well spotted," I said. "I must be getting old. Was a time I wouldn't have missed something like that."

"You're not that old," Ms. Fate said lightly.

"Old enough that they want to retire me," I said.

"You? You'll never retire! You live for this job."

"Yes," I said. "I've done it so long it's all I've got now. But I am getting old. Slow. Still better than any of these upstart latecomers, like John Taylor and Tommy Oblivion."

"You look fine to me," Ms. Fate said firmly. "In pretty good shape, too, for a man of your age. How do you manage it?"

I smiled. "We all have our secrets."

"Of course. This is the Nightside, after all."

"I could have worked out your secret identity," I said. "If I'd wanted to."

"Perhaps. Though it might have surprised you. Why didn't you?"

"I don't know. Professional courtesy? Or maybe I just liked the idea of knowing there was someone else around who wanted to catch murderers as much as I did."

"You can depend on me," said Ms. Fate.

Our next port of call was the Nightside's one and only autopsy room. We do have a CSI, but it only has four people in it. And only one Coroner, Dr. West. Short, stocky fellow with a smiling face and flat straw-yellow hair. I wouldn't leave him alone with the body of anyone I cared about, but he's good enough at his job.

By the time Ms. Fate and I got there, Dr. West already had the werewolf's body laid out on his slab. He was washing the naked body with great thoroughness and crooning a song to it as we entered. He looked round unhurriedly and waggled the fingers of one podgy hand at us.

"Come in, come in! So nice to have visitors. So nice! Of course, I'm never alone down here, but I do miss good conversation. Take a look at this."

He put down his wet sponge, picked up a long surgical instrument, and started poking around inside the body's massive wound. Ms. Fate and I moved closer, while still maintaining a respectful distance. Dr. West tended to get over-excited with a scalpel in his hand, and we didn't want to get spattered.

Dr. West thrust both his hands into the cavity and started rooting around with quite unnecessary enthusiasm. "The heart is missing," he said cheerfully. "Also, the liver. Yes. Yes . . . Not cut out, torn out . . . Made a real mess of this poor fellow's insides, hard to be sure of anything else . . . Not sure what to put down as actual cause of death: blood loss, trauma, shock . . . Heart attack? Yes. That covers it. So, another victim for our current serial killer. Number six . . . how very industrious. Oh yes. Haven't even got a name for your chart, have we, boy? Just another John Doe . . . But not to worry; I've got a nice little locker waiting for you, nice and cosy, next to your fellow victims."

"You have got to stop talking to the corpses like that," I said sternly. "One of these days someone will catch you at it."

Dr. West stuck out his tongue at me. "Let them. See if I care. See if they can get anyone else to do this job."

"How long have you been Coroner, Dr. West?" said Ms. Fate, tactfully changing the subject.

"Oh, years and years, my dear. I was made Coroner the same year Samuel here was made Detective. Oh yes, we go way back, Samuel and I. All because of that nasty Shock-Headed Peter . . . The Authorities decided that such a successful serial killer was bad for business, and therefore Something Must Be Done. It's all about popular perception, you see . . . There are many things in the Nightside far more dangerous than any human killer could ever hope to be, but the Authorities, bless their grey little hearts, wanted visitors to feel safe, so . . ."

He stopped and looked at me sourly. "You'd never believe he and I were the same age, would you? How do you do it, Samuel?"

"Healthy eating," I said. "And lots of vitamins."

"Why haven't you called in Walker?" Ms. Fate said suddenly. "He speaks for the Authorities, with a Voice everyone has to obey; and I've heard it said he once made a corpse sit up on a slab and answer his questions."

"Oh he did, he did," said Dr. West, pulling his hands out of the body with a nasty sucking sound. "I was there at the time, and very edifying it was, too. But unfortunately, all six of our victims had their tongues torn out. After our killer had taken the bits and pieces he wanted. Which suggests our killer had reason to be afraid of Walker."

"Hell," I said. "Everyone's got good reason to be afraid of Walker."

Dr. West shrugged, threw aside his scalpel and slipped off his latex gloves with a deliberate flourish, as though to make clear he'd done all that could reasonably be expected of him.

Ms. Fate stared into the open wound again. "Our killer really does like his work, doesn't he?"

"He's got an appetite for it," I said solemnly.

"Oh please," said Ms. Fate.

I moved in beside her, staring down into the cavity. "Took the heart out first, then the liver. Our killer must believe they hold the secret of the werewolf's abilities. If he is a shape-changer now, he'll be that much harder to take down."

Ms. Fate looked at me thoughtfully, then turned to Dr. West. "Do you still have all the victims' clothes and belongings?"

"Of course, my dear, of course! Individually bagged and tagged. Help yourself."

She opened every bag, and checked every piece of torn and blood-soaked clothing. It's always good to see a real professional at work. Eventually, she ran out of things to check and test, and turned back to me.

"Six victims. Different ages, sexes, occupations. Nothing at all to connect them. Unless you know something, Detective."

"There's nothing in the files," I said.

"So how were the victims chosen? Why these six people?"

"Maybe the people don't matter," I said. "Just their abilities."

"Run me through them again," she said. "Names and abilities, in order, from the beginning."

"First victim was the godling, Demetrius Heracles," I said patiently. "Then the farseer, Barbara Moore. The immortal, Count Magnus, though I doubt very much that was his real name. The teleporter, Cainy du Brec. The chat-show host, Adrian Woss, and finally the werewolf, Christopher Russell."

"This whole business reminds me unpleasantly of Shock-Headed Peter," Ms. Fate said slowly. "Not the MO, but the sheer ruthlessness of the murders. Are you sure he hasn't escaped?"

"Positive," I said. "No-one escapes from Shadow Deep."

She shook her masked head, her heavy cloak rustling loudly. "I'd still feel happier if we checked. Can you get us in?"

"Of course," I said. "I'm the Detective."

•   •   •

So we went down into Shadow Deep, all the way down to the darkest place in the Nightside, sunk far below in the cold bedrock. Constructed . . . no-one knows how long ago, to hold the most vicious, evil, and dangerous criminals ever stupid enough to prey on the Nightside. The ones we can't, for one reason or another, just execute and be done with. The only way down is by the official transport circle, maintained and operated by three witches from a small room over a really rough bar called the Jolly Cripple. If the people who drank in the bar knew what went on in the room above their heads . . . they'd probably drink a hell of a lot more.

"Why here?" said Ms. Fate, as we ascended the gloomy back stairs. "Secrecy?"

"Partly, I suppose," I said. "More likely because it's cheap."

The three witches were the traditional bent-over hags in tattered cloaks, all clawed hands and hooked noses. The great circle on the floor had been marked in chalk mixed with sulphur and semen. You don't want to know how I found out. Ms. Fate glowered at the three witches.

"You can stop that cackling right now. You don't have to put on an act; we're not tourists."

"Well, pardon us for taking pride in our work," said one of the witches, straightening up immediately. "We are professionals, after all. And image is everything, these days. You don't think these warts just happened, do you?"

I gave her my best hard look, and she got the transport operation under way. The three witches did the business with a minimum of chanting and incense, and down Ms. Fate and I went, to Shadow Deep.

It was dark when we arrived. Completely dark, with not a ghost of a light anywhere. I only knew Ms. Fate was there with me because I could hear her breathing at my side. Footsteps approached, slow and heavy, until finally a pair of night-vision goggles were thrust into my hand. I nearly jumped out of my skin, and from the muffled squeak beside me, so did Ms. Fate. I slipped the goggles on, and Shadow Deep appeared around me, all dull green images and fuzzy shadows.

It's always dark in Shadow Deep.

We were standing in an ancient circular stone chamber, with a low roof, curving walls, and just the one exit, leading on to a stone tunnel. Standing before us was one of the prison staff, a rough clay golem with simple preprogrammed routines. It had no eyes on its smooth face, because it didn't need to see. It turned abruptly and started off down the tunnel, and Ms. Fate and I hurried after it. The tunnel branched almost immediately, and branched again, and as we moved from tunnel to identical tunnel, I soon lost all track of where I was.

We came at last to the Governor's office, and the golem raised an oversized hand and knocked once on the door. A cheery voice called out for us to enter, and the door swung open before us. A blinding light spilled out, and Ms. Fate and I clawed off our goggles as we stumbled into the office. The door shut itself behind us.

I looked around the Governor's office with watering eyes. It wasn't particularly big, but it had all the comforts. The Governor came out from behind his desk to greet us, a big blocky man with a big friendly smile that didn't touch his eyes at all. He seemed happy to see us, but then, he was probably happy to see anyone. Shadow Deep doesn't get many visitors.

"Welcome, welcome!" he said, taking our goggles and shaking my hand and Ms. Fate's with great gusto. "The great Detective and the famous vigilante; such an honour! Do sit down, make yourselves at home. That's right! Make yourselves comfortable! Can I offer you a drink, cigars . . . ?"

"No," I said.

"Ah, Detective," said the Governor, sitting down again behind his desk. "It's always business with you, isn't it?"

"Ms. Fate is concerned that one of your inmates might have escaped," I said.

"What? Oh no; no, quite impossible!" The Governor turned his full attention and what he likes to think of as his charming smile on Ms. Fate. "No-one ever escapes from here. Never, never. It's always dark in Shadow Deep, you see. Light doesn't work here, outside my office. Not any kind of light, scientific or magical. Not even a match . . . Even if a prisoner could get out of his cell, which he can't, there's no way he could find his way through the maze of tunnels to the transfer site. Even a teleporter can't get out of here because there's no way of knowing how far down we are!"

"Tell her how it works," I said. "Tell her what happens to the scum I bring here."

The Governor blinked rapidly and tried another ingratiating smile. "Yes, well, the prisoner is put into his cell by one of the golems, and the door is then nailed shut. And sealed forever with preprepared, very powerful magics. Once in, a prisoner never leaves his cell. The golems pass food and water through a slot in the door. And that's it."

"What about . . . ?" said Ms. Fate.

"There's a grille in the floor."

"Oh, ick."

"Quite," said the Governor. "You must understand, our prisoners are not here to reform or repent. Only the very worst individuals ever end up here, and they stay here till they die. However long that takes. No reprieves, and no time off for good behaviour."

"How did you get this job?" said Ms. Fate.

"I think I must have done something really bad in a previous existence," the Governor said grandly. "Cosmic payback can be such a bitch."

"You got this job because you got caught," I said.

The Governor scowled. "Yes, well . . . It's not that I did anything really bad . . ."

"Ms. Fate," I said, "allow me to introduce to you Charles Peace, villain from a long line of villains. Burglar, thief, and snapper-up of anything valuable not actually nailed down. Safes opened while you wait."

"That was my downfall," the Governor admitted. "I opened Walker's safe, you see; just for the challenge of it. And I saw something I really shouldn't have seen. Something no-one was ever supposed to see. I ran, of course, but the Detective tracked me down and brought me back, and Walker gave me a choice. On-the-spot execution, or serve here as Governor until what I know becomes obsolete and doesn't matter any more. That was seventeen years ago, and there isn't a day goes by where I don't wonder whether I made the right decision."

"Seventeen years?" said Ms. Fate. She always did have a soft spot for a hard-luck story.

"Seventeen years, four months, and three days," said the Governor. "Not that I obsess about it, you understand."

"Is Shock-Headed Peter still here?" I said bluntly. "There's no chance he could have got out?"

"Of course not! I did the rounds only an hour ago, and his cell is still sealed. Come on, Detective; if Shock-Headed Peter was on the loose in the Nightside again, we'd all know about it."

"Who else have you got down here?" said Ms. Fate. "Anyone . . . famous?"

"Oh, quite a few; certainly some names you'd recognise. Let's see; we have the Murder Masques, Sweet Annie Abattoir, Max Maxwell the Voodoo Apostate, Maggie Malign . . . But they're all quite secure, too, I can assure you."

"I just needed to be sure this place is as secure as it's supposed to be," said Ms. Fate. "You'd better prepare a new cell, Governor; because I've brought you a new prisoner."

And she looked at me.

I rose to my feet, and so did she. We stood looking at each other for a long moment.

"I'm sorry, Sam," she said. "But it's you. You're the murderer."

"Have you gone mad?" I said.

"You gave yourself away, Sam," she said, meeting my gaze squarely with her own. "That's why I had you bring me here to Shadow Deep, where you belong. Where even you can't get away."

"What makes you think it was me?" I said.

"You knew things you shouldn't have known. Things only the killer could have known. First, at the Library. That anthropology text was a dry, stuffy, and very academic text. Very difficult for a layman to read and understand. But you just skimmed through it, then neatly summed up the whole concept. The only way you could have done that was if you'd known it in advance. That raised my suspicions, but I didn't say anything. I wanted to be wrong about you.

"But you did it again, at the autopsy. First, you knew that the heart had been removed *before* the liver. Dr. West hadn't worked that out yet, because the body's insides were such a mess. Second, when I asked you to name the victims in order, you named them all, including the werewolf. Who hasn't been identified yet. Dr. West still had him down as a John Doe.

"So, it had to be you. Why, Sam? Why?"

"Because they were going to make me retire," I said. It was actually a relief, to be able to tell it to someone. "Take away my job, my reason for living, just because I'm not as young as I used to be. All my experience, all my years of service, all the things I've done for them, and the Authorities were going to give me a gold watch and throw me on the scrap heap. Now, when things are worse than they've ever been. When I'm needed more than ever. It wasn't fair. It wasn't right.

"So I decided I would just take what I needed, to make myself the greatest Detective that ever was. With my new abilities, I would be unstoppable. I would go private, like John Taylor and Larry Oblivion, and show those wet-behind-the-ears newcomers how it's done . . . I would become rich and famous, and if I looked a little younger, well . . . this is the Nightside, after all.

"Shed no tears for my victims. They were all criminals, though I could never prove it. That's why there was no paper-work on them. But I knew. Trust me; they all deserved to die. They were all scum.

"I'd actually finished, you know. The werewolf would have been my last victim. I had all I needed. I teleported in and out of the Library, which is why no-one saw me come and go. But then . . . you had to turn up, the second-best Detective in the Nightside, and spoil everything. I never should have agreed to train you . . . but I saw in you a passion for justice that matched my own. You could have been my partner, my successor. The things we could have done . . . But now I'm going to have to kill you, and the Governor. I can't let you tell. Can't let you stop me, not after everything I've done. The Nightside needs me.

"You'll just be two more victims of the unknown serial killer."

I surged forward with a werewolf's supernatural speed and grabbed the front of Ms. Fate's black-leather costume with a godling's strength. I closed my hand on her chest and ripped her left breast away. And then I stopped, dumb-struck. The breast was in my hand, but under the torn-open leather there was no wound, no spouting blood. Only a very flat, very masculine chest. Ms. Fate smiled coldly.

"And that's why you'd never have guessed my secret identity, Sam. Who would ever have suspected that a man would dress up as a superheroine to fight crime? But then, this is the Nightside, and like you said; we all have our secrets."

And while I stood there, listening with an open mouth, she palmed a nausea-gas capsule from her belt and threw it in my face. I hit the stone floor on my hands and knees, vomiting so hard I couldn't concentrate enough to use any of my abilities. The Governor called for two of his golems, and they came and dragged me away. They threw me into a cell, then nailed the door shut and sealed it forever.

No need for a trial. Ms. Fate would have a word with Walker, and that would be that. That's how I always did it.

So here I am, in Shadow Deep, in the dark that never ends. Guess whose cell they put me next to. Just guess.

One of these days they'll open this cell and find nothing here but my clothes.

THE DIFFERENCE
A DAY MAKES

ONE

It was three o'clock in the morning, in the oldest bar in the world, and I was killing time drinking with a dead man. Dead Boy is an old friend, though he's only seventeen. He's been seventeen for some thirty years now, ever since he was mugged and murdered for the spare change in his pockets. He made a deal to come back from the dead and take his revenge on his killers; but he should have read the small print. He's been trapped inside his dead body ever since, searching for a way out. He's surprisingly good company, for a man with so many strikes against him.

I'm John Taylor, private investigator. I don't do divorce work, I don't chase after the Maltese Falcon, and I am most definitely not on the side of the angels. Either variety. I do, however, wear a white trench coat, get in over my head more often than not, and get personally involved with my female clients far more often than is good for me. I have a gift, for finding things and people.

I'd just finished a case that hadn't ended well. A man hired me because his imaginary friend had gone missing, and he wanted me to find out why. Apparently this man's imaginary friend had been his constant companion since childhood, and had never gone off on his own before. The client got quite tearful about it, so I gave him my best professional look, and my most reassuring smile, and promised him I would waste no time in tracking down his imaginary friend. As cases go, it wasn't that difficult. I found the imaginary bastard in the first place I looked. He was having an affair with the client's wife. I put the three of them together in the same hotel room, and left them to it, knowing there was no point in even sending in my bill.

It was all the client's fault, really. Far too imaginative, except when it came to his wife.

And there I was, consoling myself with a large glass of wormwood brandy, while Dead Boy made heavy going of something that heaved back and forth, and looked like it was trying to eat its way through the glass. Being very thoroughly dead, though not in the least departed, Dead Boy doesn't need to eat or drink, but he likes to pretend. It makes him feel more real. And since his taste-buds are quite definitely damaged, it takes more than the usual hard stuff to hit his spot. Dead Boy knows this appalling old Obeah woman who whips up pills and potions especially for him, potent enough to make a corpse dance and a ghoul show you her underwear. God alone knows what it would do to the living; certainly I've never been tempted to find out. For the moment, Dead Boy was drinking a graveyard punch, made with ingredients from real graveyards. I just hoped it was no-one I knew.

For once, Dead Boy was in a better financial state than me, so he was paying for the drinks. He'd just started a new job, as doorman for Club Dead, the special club for zombies, vampires, mummies, and all the other forms of the mortally challenged. (Club motto: *We Belong Dead.*) I didn't see the job lasting. Dead Boy has all the social graces of a lemming in heat or a sewer rat with bleeding haemorrhoids. But, since he was in the money, I was ordering the best of everything, in a big glass.

The oldest bar in the world is called Strangefellows, these days. You get all sorts in here, the living and the dead and those who haven't made their minds up yet, along with gods and monsters, aliens and shapeshifters, and a whole bunch of things that shouldn't exist but unfortunately do. Something from a Black Lagoon was sitting slumped in one corner, big and green and mossy and stinking of brine, drinking whiskey sours one after the other and mourning over *the one that got away.* The Tribe of the Gay Barbarians, tall muscular fellows resplendent in fringed leather chaps, nipple piercings, and tall ostrich feather headdresses, were challenging all comers to a game of Twister. A dancing bear was giving it his best John Travolta moves. He looked pretty silly in the white jacket, but given his size no-one felt like telling him. And a group of rather disreputable-looking dwarves were selling tickets to see The Incredible Sleeping Woman. (I'd seen her. Forty years of catatonia had not been kind, which was why the dwarves were no longer allowed to bill her as The Incredible Sleeping Beauty.)

One of Frankenstein's female creations was singing a torch song, the transvestite superheroine Ms. Fate was reading a gossip tabloid with great concentration, to see if he was in it that week, and Harry Fabulous was doing his rounds, selling chemical adventures, knockoff Hyde formula, and short-time psychoses, for really quite reasonable prices.

Just another night, at Strangefellows.

But while the oldest bar in the world has few rules and even fewer standards, we do draw the line at weeping women.

So when the tall slender brunette in the expensive outfit came stumbling into the bar, crying her eyes out, everyone fell quiet and turned to look. Weeping women always mean trouble, for someone. She lurched to a halt in the middle of the room and looked about her, and I quickly realised that she was crying hot angry tears of rage and frustration, rather than sorrow. The tears ran jerkily down her cheeks, the sheer force of them shaking her whole body. Something about her gave me the feeling she wasn't a woman who often gave in to tears. She sniffed them back with an effort, and glared about her as defiantly as her puffy eyes and streaked makeup would allow. And then she looked in my direction, and my heart sank as she fixed her attention on me. She pushed her way quickly through the packed tables, and marched right up to me. The bar's normal bedlam resumed, as everyone celebrated someone else getting hit by the bullet. I sighed inwardly, and turned unhurriedly on my bar stool to nod politely to the woman as she crashed to a halt before me and fixed me with dark, haunted eyes.

She was good-looking enough, in an undemanding way, her long lean body positively burning with thwarted nervous energy. Her clothes were expensive, though somewhat dishevelled. She was clutching a white leather shoulder bag as though she would never let it go, and her whole stance screamed stress and tension. Her mouth was compressed into a thin dark red line, and she held herself very stiffly, as though she might fall apart if her control lapsed for just one moment. And yet, behind the clear anger in her eyes, I could see an awful, unfocused fear.

"Hi," I said, as kindly as I could. "I'm John Taylor."

"Yes," she said jerkily, the words coming out clipped, in sudden bursts. "I know. You were described to me. The man in the white trench coat. The knight in cold armour. He said you'd help me. Sorry. I'm not making myself clear . . . I've had something of a shock. My name is Liza Barclay. I'm lost. I don't know what I'm doing here. I've lost all memory of the last twenty-four hours of my life. I want you to find them for me."

I sighed again, still inwardly, and handed her my glass. "Take a sip of brandy," I said, doing my best to sound kind and helpful and not at all threatening.

She grabbed the brandy glass with both hands, took a good gulp, and immediately pulled a face and thrust the glass back into my hand.

"God, that's awful. You drink that for fun? You're tougher than you look. But then, you'd have to be. Sorry. I'm rambling."

"It's all right," I said. "Take your time, get your breath back. Then tell me how you got here. This isn't an easy place to get to."

"I don't know!" she said immediately. "I've lost a day. A whole day!"

I slipped off my bar stool and offered her a seat, but she shook her head quickly. So I just leaned back against the long wooden bar and studied her openly as she looked around Strangefellows, making it very clear with her face and body language that not only had she never seen anything like it, but that she was quite definitely slumming just by being there. I was impressed. The oldest bar in the world isn't for just anyone. Most people take one look and run away screaming, and we like it that way. Strangefellows is a place of old magic and all the very latest sins and indulgences. This is not the kind of bar where everyone knows your name; it's the kind of bar where you can wake up robbed and rolled in someone else's body.

Liza Barclay deliberately turned her back on the disturbing sights and the appalling patrons, and fixed her full attention on me. I did my best to look tall, dark, and handsome, but I couldn't have been that successful because after only a moment she nodded briskly, as though I'd passed some necessary test, but only just. She switched her gaze to Dead Boy, who smiled vaguely and toasted her with his glass. The graveyard punch made a valiant attempt to escape, and he had to push the stuff back in with his fingers.

Dead Boy was tall and adolescent thin, wrapped in a long purple greatcoat spotted with various food and drink stains, and topped with a fresh black rose on his lapel. Scuffed black leather trousers over muddy calfskin boots completed the ensemble. He let his coat hang open, to reveal a bare torso covered with old injuries, bullet holes, and one long Y-shaped autopsy scar. Dead Boy might be deceased, but he still took damage, even if he couldn't feel it. He was mostly held together with stitches and staples and superglue, along with a certain amount of black duct tape lashed around his middle. His skin was a pale grey, and dusty-looking.

He had the face of a debauched and very weary Pre-Raphaelite poet, with dark fever-bright eyes, a sulky mouth with no colour in it, and long dark curly hair crammed under a large floppy hat. He didn't smile at Liza Barclay. He didn't care. Her tears hadn't touched him at all.

Liza shuddered, but didn't look away. She was impressing me more and more. Most people can't stand being around the dead, and that goes double for Dead Boy. Liza glanced around the bar again, at its various strange and unnatural patrons, and rather than being scared or appalled, she just sniffed loudly and turned her back on them again. They were no help to her, or her problem, so they didn't matter. Liza Barclay, it seemed, was a very single-minded lady.

"How can you stand being in a place like this?" she said to me, quite seriously.

"What, Strangefellows?" I said. "There are worse places

to drink in. The ambience isn't up to much, I'll grant you, but . . ."

"I don't mean just here! I mean . . . everywhere! This whole area!" A tinge of hysteria had entered her voice. Liza heard it, and clamped down hard on it. She hugged herself suddenly, as though a cold wind had blown over her grave. "I've been walking back and forth in the streets for ages. This *terrible* place. I've seen things . . . awful things. Creatures, walking right out in the open, with normal people, and none of them batted an eye! Where am I? Am I dead? Is this Hell?"

"No," I said. "Though on a good day you can see Hell from here. As far as I can tell, you are a perfectly normal woman who has had the misfortune to somehow find her way into the Nightside."

"The Nightside." She grabbed on to the word, considered it, and then looked to me for more information. And it wasn't a request; it was a demand. I was liking her more and more.

"The Nightside," I said, "the dark secret hidden in the heart of London. The longest night in the world, where the sun has never shone and never will. Where it's always three o'clock in the morning, the hour that tries men's souls. This is where all the secret people come, in search of forbidden knowledge and all the pleasures people aren't supposed to want, but still do. You can pursue any dream here, or any nightmare. Sell your soul or someone else's. Run wild in the streets and satisfy any fantasy you ever had. As long as your credit holds out. This is the Nightside, Liza Barclay, and it is not a place for normal people like you."

"It's not an easy place to find your way into," said Dead Boy. "How did you get here?"

"I don't know! I can't remember!" Her shoulders slumped, and her strength seemed to seep out of her. I understood. She was having to take in a lot at one go. And the Nightside does so love to break people . . . I thought for a moment she might start crying again, but her chin lifted, her eyes flashed, and just like that she was back in control again. "I live in London, have done all my life. And I never heard of the Nightside. I just . . . came to, and found myself here. Lost, and alone."

"And now you're among friends," I said.

"More or less," said Dead Boy.

"I am John Taylor," I said, ignoring Dead Boy with the ease of long practice. "And I'm a private eye. Yes, really."

Her mouth twitched in a brief smile. "I suppose I shouldn't be surprised, to find one more mythical creature, among so many."

"And my appalling friend here is Dead Boy. Yes, really."

"Hi," said Dead Boy, leaning forward and offering a pale dead hand for her to shake. "Yes, that is formaldehyde you're smelling, so get used to it. I'm dead, I'm wild and exciting and extraordinarily glamorous, and you're very pleased to meet me."

"Don't put money on it," said Liza. "What's it like, being dead?"

"Cold," said Dead Boy, unexpectedly. "It's getting hard for me to even remember what being warm feels like. Though I think I miss sleep the most. Never being able to just lie down and switch off. No rest, no dreams . . ."

"Don't you get tired?" said Liza, fascinated despite herself.

"I'm always tired," Dead Boy said sadly.

"Cut it out," I said firmly. "You think I don't know you mainline that synthetic adrenaline when no-one's looking?" I shrugged apologetically at Liza. "Sorry, but you mustn't encourage him. He's not really as self-pitying as he likes to make out. He just thinks it makes him more attractive to women."

"Never dismiss the pity factor," Dead Boy said easily. "Suicide girls go crazy for dead flesh."

"That's disgusting," said Liza, very firmly.

He leered at her. "You haven't lived till you've rattled a coffin with someone on graveyard Viagra."

"Changing the subject right now," I said loudly. "Tell me about your memory loss, Liza. What's the last thing you do remember, before waking up here?"

She frowned, concentrating. "The last twenty-four hours are just gone. A whole day. The last thing I'm sure of, I was in London. The real London. Down in Tottenham Court Road Underground station . . . though I can't quite seem to remember why . . . I think I was looking for someone. The next thing I knew, I was here. Running through the streets. Crying as though my heart would break. I don't know why. I'm not the crying kind, usually. I'm just not."

"It's all right," I said. "What happened next?"

"I was attacked! They came out of nowhere . . . Tall spindly men in top hats and old-fashioned clothes, with great smiling faces, and . . . knives for hands."

"Scissormen," I said. "Always looking for someone weaker to prey on. They can home in on guilt and horror like sharks tasting blood in the water."

"I haven't done anything to feel guilty about," said Liza.

"As far as you know," said Dead Boy, reasonably. "Who knows what you might have done, in the missing twenty-four hours? It's amazing how much sin a determined person can cram into twenty-four hours. I speak from experience, you understand."

"Ignore him," I said. "He's just boasting."

"But . . . Scissormen?" said Liza.

"Everything comes to the Nightside," I said. "Especially all the bad things, with nowhere else to go. Still, it's always a shame when childhood characters go bad. How did you get away from them?"

"I didn't," said Liza, her eyes and her voice becoming uncertain again as she remembered. "They were all around me, smiling their awful smiles, opening and closing their . . . scissorhands, chanting something in German in shrill mocking voices. They cut at me, always drawing back at the very last moment, and laughing as I jumped this way and that to avoid them. Scuttling round and round me, always pressing closer, smiling and smiling . . . And nobody did anything! Most people didn't even stop to watch! I was screaming by then, but no-one helped. Until this . . . strange man appeared out of nowhere, and the Scissormen stopped, just like that. They huddled together, facing him like a pack of dogs at bay. He said his name, and the Scissormen just turned and ran. I couldn't believe it."

"What was his name?" I said.

"Eddie. He was very sweet, though he looked like some kind of vagrant. And from the smell of him, he'd been sleeping rough for some time. I tried to give him some money, but he wasn't interested. He listened to my story, though I don't know how much sense I made, and then he brought me here. Told me to look for you. John Taylor. That you'd be able to help me. Do you know this man?"

"Oh, sure," said Dead Boy. "Everyone here knows Razor Eddie. Punk God of the Straight Razor. No wonder the Scissormen cut and ran. Most people do."

Liza looked at me, and I nodded. "Eddie's a good man, in his own disturbing way. And he's right; I can help you. I have a gift for finding things."

"Even missing memories?" Liza managed a real, hopeful smile for the first time.

"Anything," I said. "But I have to ask . . . are you sure you want to remember? A lot of the time, people forget things for a reason."

She looked at me steadily. "Of course I want to remember. I think I need to. I think . . . something bad happened."

"In the Nightside? I can practically guarantee it," said Dead Boy.

"You're really not helping," I said. "Liza, you're sure you've never even heard of the Nightside before? It's not unheard of for innocents to wander in by accident, but usually you have to want it pretty bad."

"I never knew places like this existed," Liza said stubbornly. "I never knew monsters were real."

"The world is a much bigger place than most people realise," I said. "Magic still exists, though it's grown strange and crafty and maybe just a bit senile."

"Magic?" she said, raising one perfectly plucked eyebrow.

"Magic, and other things. Time isn't as firmly nailed down in the Nightside as it might be. We get all sorts turning up here, from the Past and any number of alternate Futures. Not to mention all kinds of rogues, adventurers, and complete and utter scumbags from other worlds and dimensions, all looking for a little excitement, or a nice bit of sin that isn't too shop-soiled." I stopped, and considered her thoughtfully. "You really don't care about any of this, do you? It doesn't interest or attract you in the least."

"No," said Liza. "I don't belong in a madhouse like this. I have no business being here."

"I could just take you home," I said. "Back to the safe and sane London you've always known."

"No," she said immediately. "There's a whole day of my life missing. It's mine, and I want it back."

"But what if you've done something really bad?" said Dead Boy. "Most people come to the Nightside to do something really bad."

"It's always better to know," Liza said firmly.

"No," I said. "Not always. And especially not here. But if that's what you want, then that's what you get. The client is always right. Now, the odds are you came here looking for something. Or someone. So let's take a look in that shoulder bag of yours. The way you've been clinging to it since you got here, it must hold something important."

She looked down at the bag as though she'd honestly forgotten it was there. And when I reached out a hand to take it, she actually shrank back for a moment. But once again her stern self-control reasserted itself, and she made herself hand over the bag. But there was a subtle new tension in her that hadn't been there before.

I hefted the bag. It wasn't that large, and it didn't feel like there was that much in it. Nothing obviously special about it. Expensive, yes; white leather Gucci without a mark on it. I opened the bag, and spilled the contents out onto the wooden bar top. All three of us leaned in for a closer look. But it was just the usual feminine clutter, with nothing out of the ordinary. Apart from a single colour photograph, torn jaggedly in two. I fitted the pieces together as best I could, and we all studied the image in silence for a while. The photo showed a somewhat younger Liza Barclay in a stylish white wedding dress, hugging a handsome young man in a formal suit. They were both laughing at the camera, clearly caught a little off guard. They looked very happy. As though they belonged together, and always would. Someone had torn the photo fiercely in two, right down the middle, as though trying to separate the happy couple.

"That's Frank," said Liza, frowning so hard her brow must have ached. "My husband, Frank. That's our wedding day, just over seven years now. I was never so happy in my life, the day we got married. Poor Frank, he must be worried sick by now, wondering where I am. But . . . this is my favourite photo ever. I must have worn out half a dozen copies, carrying it around in my bag and showing it to people. Who could have torn it like this?"

"Maybe you tore it," said Dead Boy. "Been having problems recently, have you?"

"No! No . . ." But even as she objected, I could practically see the beginnings of memories resurfacing in her. She concentrated on the two pieces of the photo, speaking only to them. "We were always so much in love. He meant everything to me. Everything. But . . . I followed him. All the way across London, on the Underground. He never saw me. He'd been so . . . preoccupied, the last few months. I could tell something was wrong. I was worried about him. He'd been keeping things from me, and that wasn't like him. There were letters and e-mails I wasn't allowed to read, phone calls he wouldn't talk about. He'd never done that before. I thought he might be in some kind of trouble. Something to do with his business. I wanted to help. He was my love, my life, my everything. I was so worried . . ."

"Sounds like another woman," Dead Boy said wisely, and was genuinely surprised when I glared at him. "Well, it does."

But Liza was smiling, and shaking her head. "You don't know my Frank. He loves me as much as I love him. He's never even looked at another woman."

"Come on," said Dead Boy. "Every man looks at other women. When he starts pretending he doesn't, that's when you know he's up to something."

"You followed Frank through the Underground," I said to Liza, ignoring Dead Boy. "What happened then?"

"I don't know." Liza reached out to touch the photo, but didn't, quite. "The next thing I remember, I'm here in the Nightside, and there's no sign of Frank anywhere. Could we have been kidnapped, dragged here against our will, and I somehow escaped?"

"Well," I said diplomatically, "it's possible, I suppose."

"But you don't think so."

"It's not the way I'd bet, no. But at least now we know you're not here alone. If you're here, then the odds are Frank is, too. I can find him with my gift, and see if perhaps he holds the answer to your missing memories."

"No!" said Liza. "I don't want my Frank involved in all this . . . madness."

"If he's here, he's involved," said Dead Boy. "If only because the Nightside doesn't take kindly to being ignored."

She shook her head again, still smiling. "You don't know my Frank."

"And you don't know the kind of temptations on offer here," said Dead Boy. "Sex and love and everything in between, sweet as cyanide and sprinkled with a little extra glamour to help it go down easier. Sin is always in season in the Nightside."

"And you followed him here," I said.

She glared at me. "How could he know the way to a place like this?"

"Because he'd been here before," said Dead Boy. "Sorry, but it's the only answer that makes sense."

Liza glared at him, and then looked me right in the eye. "Find him. Find my Frank for me. If only so he can tell us the truth, and throw these lies back in your faces."

"I'll find him," I said. "Anything else . . . is up to you, and him."

I picked up the two pieces of the photo, holding them firmly between thumb and forefinger, and held them up before me. I took a deep breath and concentrated, reaching deep inside myself for my gift, my special gift, that allowed me to find anyone or anything. I concentrated on the photo until I couldn't see anything else, and then slowly, my inner eye opened; my third eye, my private eye . . . from which nothing can hide. With my inner eye all the way open, I could See the world as it really was, every last bit of it. All the things that are hidden from Humanity, because if we could all See the true nature of this world, and the kinds of things we share it with, Humanity would go stark staring mad with horror.

I can only bear to See it for a little while.

I sent my Sight soaring up out of my body, shooting up through the roof of my skull and the roof of Strangefellows, until I was high in the star-speckled sky, looking down on the Nightside spread out below me, turning slowly, like the circles of Hell. Hot neon burned everywhere, like balefires in the night. Sudden bright glares detonated in this place or that; as souls were bartered, great magical workings rewrote the world, or some awful new thing was born to plague Mankind. There were great Voices abroad in the night, and terrible rumblings deep in the earth, as Powers and Dominations went about their unknowable business.

Ghosts howled in the streets, trapped in moments of Time like insects in amber. Demons rode their human hosts, whispering in their ears. And vast and powerful creatures walked the night in majesty, wonderful and terrible beyond human ability to bear.

I dropped down from my high vantage point, sending my Sight flashing through the packed narrow streets, slamming in and out of buildings with the quickness of thought, following a trail only I could See. The photo of Frank Barclay had let me sink my mental hook in his consciousness, if not his soul, and I could See the ghost of him still striding purposefully through the streets. Semi-transparent and fragile as a soap bubble, the mark he'd made in the Nightside was still clear, his imprint on Time itself, still walking the streets that he had walked not so long ago . . . and would do until the last vestiges of it faded away.

Frank Barclay showed no interest in any of the usual pleasure joints or temptations. The open doors of night-clubs where the music never ends, the heavy-lidded glances from dark-eyed ladies of the twilight, had no attraction for him. He never hesitated once, or paused to check directions. He knew where he was going. And from the increasingly intense, almost desperate anticipation in his face, wherever he was going promised something none of the usual temptations could hope to satisfy. I could See him clearly now, and he was smiling. And something in the smile chilled me all the way to my soul.

I pulled back, as I realised where he was going. There are some places you just don't go into with your spirit hanging out. Some parts of the Nightside are hungrier than others. I slowly closed my third eye, my inner eye, until I was safely back inside my own head again. And then I dropped the two pieces of the photo back onto the bar top as though they burned my fingers. I looked at Liza.

"Good news and bad news," I said. "I've found him. I've found husband Frank."

"Then what's the bad news?" said Liza, meeting my gaze unflinchingly.

"He's in the badlands," I said. "Where the really wild things are, and hardly anyone gets out alive. You only go into the badlands in search of the pleasures too sick, too twisted, and too nasty for the rest of the Nightside."

"If that's where he is," Liza said steadily, "then that's where I have to go."

"You can't go there alone," I said. "They'd eat you up and chew on the bones."

"But I have to know!" said Liza, her chin jutting stubbornly. "I have to know what's wrong with him, what could possibly bring him to an awful place like this. And I have to know what, if anything, this has to do with my missing memories. I have to go there."

"Then I guess I'll have to take you," I said.

"I . . . don't have much money on me, at the moment," said Liza. "Is my credit good?"

"Put the plastic away," I said. "No charge, this time. Razor Eddie owes me a favour, for dumping you on me, and that's worth more than you could ever pay."

I leaned over and nudged Dead Boy, who'd lost interest in all this long ago. His eyes snapped back into focus.

"What is it, John? I have some important existential brooding I need to be getting on with."

"I'm taking Liza into the badlands in pursuit of her missing husband, and her missing memories," I said briskly. "Bound to be some trouble. Interested?"

"Oh, sure," said Dead Boy. "You can't get too much excitement, when you're dead. How much are you offering?"

"Tell you what," I said. "You can have half of my fee. But only if we can use your car."

"Done!" said Dead Boy.

"Why do we need his car?" said Liza.

"Because we have to travel all the way across town," I said. "And the rush hour can be murder."

TWO

She'd never seen the sky before. Preoccupied with so much new sin and strangeness right before her, it had never even occurred to her to stop and look up. Now, on the rain-slick pavement outside the oldest bar in the world, Liza Barclay followed my pointing finger and stood very still, held to the spot by awe and enchantment, quite unaware of all the people, and others, hurrying by on every side. In the Nightside, the sky is full of stars, thousands and thousands of them, burning bright and sharp in constellations never seen in the outside world. And the moon . . . ah, the moon is big and bright indeed in the Nightside, unnaturally luminous and a dozen times larger than it should be, hanging over us all like a great mindless eye, like an ancient guardian that has quite forgotten its duty and purpose. Seeing all, judging nothing.

I often think that it isn't a matter of where the Nightside is, so much as when.

Meanwhile, all kinds and manner of Humanity, and many things not in any way human, pushed past with brisk impartial haste, intent on their own personal salvations and damnations. No-one got too close, though. They might not give a damn about Liza, clearly just another starstruck tourist, but everyone in the Nightside knows me. Or knows enough to give me plenty of room. Liza finally tore her gaze away from the overcrowded heavens, and gave her attention to the crowds bustling around us. The street, as always, positively squirmed with life and energy and all manner of hopes, the pavements packed with desperate pilgrims come in search of sin and temptation and the kinds of love that might not have a name but most certainly have a price. Hot neon blazed and burned up and down the street, gaudy as a hooker's smile, signposts to all the most succulent hells. If you can't find it in the Nightside, it doesn't exist.

Liza clung to my arm like a drowning woman, but to her credit she never flinched or looked away. She took it all in, staring grimly about her, refusing to allow the strange sights and tacky glamour to overwhelm her. She pressed a little more closely to me, as a bunch of eight-foot-tall insect things paused to bow their devilish heads before me. Bones glowed through their flesh, filmy wings fluttered uncomfortably on their long chitinous backs, and their iridescent compound eyes didn't blink once. Their absurdly jointed legs lowered them almost to the ground as they abased themselves, speaking in unison with urgent breathy children's voices.

"All hail to thee, sweet prince of a sundered line, and remember us when you choose to come into your kingdom."

"Move on," I said, as kindly as I could.

They waited a while, antennae twitching hopefully, until they realised I wasn't going to say any more, and then they moved on. Liza watched them go, and then looked at me.

"What the hell was that all about? Who . . . what were they?"

"They are all that remains of the Brittle Sisters of the Hive," I said. "They were just being polite."

"So you're . . . someone special here?"

"I might have been, once," I said. "But I abdicated."

"So what are you now?"

"I'm a private investigator," I said. "And a bloody good one."

She favoured me with another of her brief smiles, and then looked out at the traffic, thundering ceaselessly through the Nightside. There was a lot of it to look at. Vehicles of all kinds and natures flashed past, never slowing, never stopping, jockeying endlessly for position and dominance. Some of them carried goods and some of them carried people, and many of them carried things best not thought about at all. Most were just passing through, on their way to somewhere more interesting; mysteries and enigmas, never to be understood.

A horse-drawn diligence from the eighteenth century clattered past, overtaken by a lipstick-red Plymouth Fury with a dead man grinning at the wheel. An articulated rig bore the logo of a local long-pig franchise, while a motorcycle gang of screaming skeletons burning forever in hellfire chased something very like a tank crossed with an armadillo. The Boggart On Stilts, one of the Lesser Atrocities, strode disdainfully down the middle of the road, while smaller vehicles nipped in and out of its tall bone stilts. A great black beauty of a car cruised past, driven by an Oriental in black leathers, and the man in the back in the green face mask and snap-brimmed hat nodded respectfully to me in passing. Liza turned and looked at me speechlessly, demanding an explanation.

"In the Nightside, the traffic comes and goes, but not everything that looks like a car is a car," I explained patiently. "Here, ambulances run on distilled suffering, motorcycle couriers snort powdered virgin's blood for that extra kick, and sometimes the bigger vehicles sneak up behind the smaller ones and eat them. Pretty much everything passes through the Nightside, at one time or another and sometimes simultaneously, and it's always in a hurry. Foot down, everything forward and trust in the Lord, and Devil take the hindmost. That isn't traffic out there; that's evolution in action. Which is why we can't get where we're going by just hopping on the crosstown bus. We are waiting for Dead Boy, and his marvellous car of the future."

"The sky, the traffic, creatures and demons walking openly in the street . . ." Liza shook her head just a bit dazedly. "Where is this place, John?"

"Good question," I said. "Of this world, but not necessarily in it. Half-way between Heaven and Hell, but beholden to neither. A place of infinite jest and appalling possibilities. But don't let it get to you. The Nightside is just a place where people go, in search of all the things they're not supposed to want. Forbidden knowledge, forgotten secrets, and all the nastier kinds of sex. A place where the shadows are comfortably deep, and the sun never rises because some things can only be done in the dark.

"It's the Nightside."

Liza looked at me. "You do like the sound of your own voice, don't you?"

"You asked," I said.

Perhaps fortunately, Dead Boy arrived at that moment in his fabulous futuristic car, and Liza had something else to stare at. Dead Boy's car is always worth a good look. It glided silently to a halt before us, hovering a few feet above the ground. A car from the future, so stylish it didn't even

bother with wheels any more. It originally arrived in the
Nightside through a Timeslip, from some future time line,
and adopted Dead Boy as its driver. Bright gleaming silver,
long and sleek and streamlined to within an inch of its
life, the car hovered arrogantly before us, looking like it ran
on distilled starlight. The long curving windows were polarised so no-one could see in, and the mighty engines didn't
so much as deign to murmur.

・ The driver's door swung open, to reveal Dead Boy loung-
ing languidly behind the steering wheel. He had a half-empty
bottle of vodka in his hand.

"All aboard for the badlands, boys and girls! Feel free to
admire my beautiful ride's elegance and style. This is what
every car would be, if they only had the ambition."

"You're late," I said sternly.

"I'm always late. I'm the late Dead Boy." He sniggered at
his own joke, and took a healthy pull from his vodka bottle.

"I am not getting into that!" Liza said firmly. "It hasn't
got any wheels. It looks like something from a bad seven-
ties sci-fi movie."

"Hush, hush, my beauty!" Dead Boy said soothingly to
his car. "She is an uneducated barbarian, and doesn't mean
it." He appeared to listen for a moment. "All right, yes, she
probably did mean it, but you mustn't take it personally.
She is a mere tourist, and knows nothing of cars. Please let
her in. And please don't activate the ejector seat, no matter
how annoying she gets."

There was a pause, and then the other doors opened, slowly
enough to express a certain reluctance. Liza looked at me.

"Does he often have conversations with his car?"

"Oh, yes," I said. "Only he can hear her, though."

"I see. And does this car really have an ejector seat?"

"Oh, yes. More than powerful enough to blast you into a
whole different dimension."

"I'll be more polite to the car from now on," said Liza.

"I would," I said.

"But I'm still not sitting next to Dead Boy."

So we both got in the back. Liza jumped just a bit as the door shut itself behind us. The seats were bloodred leather, and very comfortable. There was a faint perfume of crushed roses on the slightly pressurised air. There were no seat belts, of course. Their very existence would have been an insult to the car's driving skills. Liza leaned forward and stared openly at the frankly futuristic display screens where the dashboard dials should have been. In fact, there were enough screens and displays and flashing lights to suggest anything up to and including warp speed.

"Can you get warp speed on this thing?" said Liza, proving that great minds think alike.

"Only in emergencies," said Dead Boy. He didn't seem to be kidding.

Liza took in the whiskey, brandy, and gin bottles lined up on top of the monitor screens, all of which showed signs of extensive sampling, and sniffed loudly. Dead Boy took this as a hint, and gestured generously at the bottles, and the open dashboard compartment full of honeyed locusts, spiced potato wedges, and assorted chocolate biscuits.

"Help yourself," he said, around a mouthful of chocolate Hobnob. Liza declined. Dead Boy shrugged, finished his biscuit, knocked back a handful of glowing green pills, finished off the last of the vodka, and slung the bottle through the window, which didn't happen to be open. The bottle passed right through the glass without stopping. They really have thought of everything, in the future.

"Where to, John?" Dead Boy said easily. "My car requires directions. She is powerful and lovely and full of surprises, but she is not actually prescient. Apparently that only came as an optional extra."

"Head for the badlands," I said. "I should be able to provide more specific directions once we get there."

"I love mystery tours," Dead Boy said happily. "Off you go, girl."

The futuristic car moved smoothly out into the vicious traffic, and absolutely everything slammed on the brakes or changed lanes in a hurry, to give us plenty of room. Everybody knew Dead Boy's car, and the awful things it could and would do if it got even slightly annoyed.

"I can't help noticing you're not even touching the steering wheel," Liza said to Dead Boy.

"Oh, I wouldn't dare," he said. "My sweetie's a much better driver than I'll ever be. I don't interfere."

Liza leaned back in her seat, watched the traffic for a while, and then looked thoughtfully at me. "Why are you helping me, John? It's not like I'm even paying you for your services."

"I'm curious," I said honestly. "And . . . I don't like to see an innocent caught up and crushed under the Nightside's wheels. There's enough real evil here, without adding cruel and casual stuff. Good people shouldn't end up here, but if they do, they need to be protected. Just on general principles."

"If this is such a bad place," she said, "what are you doing here?"

"I belong here," I said.

She settled for that, and went back to watching the traffic. I took out the two pieces of her photo, fitted them together, and concentrated on the image of her husband. My gift barely stirred, manifesting just enough to keep a firm hold on Frank's location. Husband Frank. He'd better be worth all this trouble. Liza clearly loved him with all her heart; but women have been known to fall for complete bastards before now. His face in the photo didn't give anything away. The smile seemed genuine enough, but I wasn't so sure about the eyes.

Frank hadn't moved since I first sensed his location, and I got the feeling he hadn't moved in some time. As I concentrated on his image, I began to get a feel for his surroundings, and the first thing I felt was the presence of technology. Advanced, future tech, not from this time and place. Frank seemed to be surrounded by it, fascinated by it . . . and the more I concentrated, the more my images of this future technology were tainted by distinctly organic touches.

Sweating steel and cables that curled like intestines; lubricated pistons rising and falling, and machines that murmured like people disturbed in their sleep. Strange nightmare devices, performing unnatural tasks, with hot blood coursing through their systems.

What had Frank got himself into?

I was beginning to get a really bad feeling about this. Especially when Frank's image in the photo suddenly turned its head to look right at me. His face was drawn, tired, and burning with a strange delirium. His eyes were dark and fever-bright . . . and he never even glanced at his wife, Liza, sitting right next to me. He locked his gaze onto mine, and his faraway voice sounded in my head.

Go away. I don't want you here. Don't try and find me. I don't want to be found.

"Your wife's here," I said silently to the photo. "Liza's here, in the Nightside. Looking for you. She's very worried about you."

I know. Keep her away. For her sake.

And just like that, the photo was only a photo, and his face was just an image from the past. I didn't tell Liza what had just occurred. It didn't matter to me whether Frank wanted to be found or not; I was working for his wife. And she wanted to know what her husband was up to, even if she hadn't actually put it that way. This is why I don't do divorce work. No matter what the client says, they never really want the truth. Still, the unexpected contact with Frank, brief as it was, had given me a more definite fix on his position.

"I've found Frank," I announced, to Liza and Dead Boy. "He's on Rotten Row."

"Ah," said Dead Boy, sucking noisily on his whiskey bottle. "That is not good."

"Why?" Liza said immediately. "What happens on Rotten Row? What do people do there?"

"Pretty much everything you can think of, and a whole lot of things most people have never even contemplated," said Dead Boy. "Rotten Row is for the severely sick and disturbed, even by the Nightside's appalling standards."

Liza turned to me. "What is he talking about?"

"Rotten Row is where people go to have sex with the kind of people, and things, that no sane person would want to have sex with," I said, just a bit reluctantly. "Sex with angels, or demons. With computers or robots, slumming gods or other-dimensional monsters; worms from the earth or some of the nastier versions of the living dead. Rotten Row is where you go when the everyday sins of the flesh just don't do it for you any more. Where men and women and all the many things they can do together just don't satisfy. Sex isn't a sin or a sacrament on Rotten Row; it's an obsession."

Liza looked at me, horrified. "Sex with . . . How is any of that even *possible?*"

"Love finds a way," Dead Boy said vaguely.

Liza shook her head stubbornly, as though she could prove me a liar if she was just firm enough. "No. You must be wrong, John. My Frank would never . . . never lower himself to . . . He just wouldn't! He's always been very . . . normal. He'd never go to a place like that!"

"We all find love where we can," said Dead Boy.

"You're talking about sex, not love!" snapped Liza.

"Sometimes . . . you have to go a little off the beaten path to get what you really need," said Dead Boy philosophically. "There's more to life than just boy meets girl, you know."

And that was when all the car's alarms went off at once. Flashing red lights, followed by a rising siren, and the sound of an awful lot of systems arming themselves. Dead Boy sat bolt upright, tossed his whiskey bottle onto the passenger seat, and studied his various displays with great interest. Dead Boy lived for action and adventure.

"All right, car, turn off the alarms, I see them. Proximity alert, people. We are currently being boxed in by three, no four, vehicles. In front and behind, left and right. Look out the windows, see if you can spot the bastards."

It wasn't difficult; they weren't being exactly furtive about it. Four black London taxicabs were forcing their way through the crowded lanes of traffic to surround us on every side, positioning themselves to cut off all possible exits and escapes. The cabs bore no name or logo on their flanks, just flat black metal, like so many malignant beetles. They all had cyborged drivers, human only down to the waist. The head and torso hung suspended in a complex webbing of cables, tubes, and wires that made them a part of their taxis. The car was just an extension of its tech-augmented driver, so it could manoeuvre as fast as they could think. Human consciousness given inhuman control and reaction times. By the time I'd finished peering out of every window, there were black cabs speeding in perfect formation all around us.

And long machine-gun barrels protruded from each and every one of them, covering us.

"Put your foot down," I said to Dead Boy. "Try and lose them."

"You go, girl, go!" said Dead Boy, and the futuristic car surged forward.

The back of the taxicab in front of us loomed up disturbingly fast, and for a moment I thought we were going to ram it, but the taxi accelerated, too, maintaining its distance. The other cabs swiftly increased their speed, too, suggesting the cyborged drivers and the protruding machine guns weren't the taxis' only special features. These black cabs had been seriously souped up. We were all moving incredibly fast now, hurtling through the Nightside at insane speed, streets and buildings just gaudy blurs of colour. All around us, traffic hurried to get out of our way. Vehicles that didn't, or couldn't, move quickly enough were slammed and shunted aside by the taxis. Cars ran careering off the road, into defenceless storefronts, or smashed into one another, crying out like living things. Screams and shouts of outrage rang briefly behind us, Dopplering away into the distance.

The cabs decided enough was enough, closed in on us from every side, and slammed on their brakes simultaneously. We had to slow down with them or risk a collision, and the futuristic car was clearly cautious enough not to want to risk direct contact until it had to. Just because they looked like cabs, it didn't mean they were. Protective camouflage is a way of life in the Nightside.

Why do you think I work so hard to look like a traditional private eye?

Dead Boy beat on the steering wheel with his pale fists, hooting with the excitement of the chase and shouting helpful advice that the car mostly ignored. Liza peered out of one window after another, her small hands unconsciously clenched into fists. I wasn't that worried, yet. The car could look after itself.

One cab pressed in from the left, trying to pressure us into changing lanes. The cyborged driver wasn't even looking at us. The other cabs gave way a little, to entice us, trying to persuade us away from the badlands exit, some way up ahead. To keep us away from Frank . . . and probably to herd us into a previously chosen killing zone where they'd have all the advantages. The futuristic car swayed back and forth, looking for a way out between the cabs, but they constantly manoeuvred with their more-than-human reflexes to block our way. And then, without warning, all four sets of machine guns opened fire on us. The sound was painfully loud, as bullets raked our car from end to end, and slammed viciously into front and back. Liza cried out, but quickly calmed down again as she realised I wasn't even ducking. The machine-gun fire roared and stuttered, but none of it could touch us. Whatever Dead Boy's car was made of, it wasn't just steel. Bullets ricocheted harmlessly away in flurries of sparks and metallic screeches, but the futuristic car didn't even shudder under the impact. The gunfire continued, as though the taxis thought they could break through our defences through sheer perseverance.

"Time for Puff the Magic Dragon, I think," Dead Boy said cheerfully, entirely unmoved by the massed firepower aimed at him from all sides.

"What?" said Liza. "What did he just say? He's got a bloody dragon in here somewhere?"

"Not as such," I said. "More of a nickname, really. Because it breathes fire and makes problems disappear. Go for it, Dead Boy."

Lights gleamed brightly all across the display screens, and there was the sound of something large and heavy moving into position. To be exact, a large gun muzzle was slowly protruding from the car's radiator grille. Puff the Magic Dragon fired two thousand explosive fléchettes a second, pumping them out at inhuman speed and with appalling vigour. Puff is a gun's gun. The futuristic car opened up on the taxicab in front of us, and the whole back of the cab just exploded, black steel disintegrating under the impact, throwing ragged shrapnel in all directions. The cab surged wildly back and forth, but Puff moved easily to follow it, tearing the cab apart with invisible hands. The cab burst into flames, and was thrown this way and that by a series of explosions, before the endless stream of explosive fléchettes picked the cab up and threw it end over end across several lanes of traffic, leaving a trail of blazing debris and drifting smoke behind it. I caught a brief glimpse of the cyborged driver, trapped behind his wheel in his ruptured webbing, screaming horribly as he burned alive in the wreckage.

I couldn't bring myself to care, much. He would have done worse to us, if he could.

The taxi to our left accelerated wildly, forcing its way in front of us to block our escape, machine guns blazing fiercely from its rear. A brave and determined move, but the driver really shouldn't have taken his eyes off the main threat. The other traffic.

A long dark limousine with dull unreflective black windows moved effortlessly in beside the cab, having sneaked up in the driver's blind spot while he was concentrating on us. I winced, despite myself. I'd seen the limousine in action before. It moved in beside the taxicab, matching speeds perfectly until it was right opposite the driver's window; and then the black window surface erupted into dozens of long grasping arms with clawed hands. Hooked fingers sank deep into the steel side of the cab, holding it firmly in place, while powerful black arms smashed through the window to get at the cyborged driver. The limousines can smell human flesh, and they're always hungry. The cyborged driver screamed shrilly as a dozen hands gripped him fiercely, long barbed fingers sinking deep into flesh and bone, and then they hauled the driver right out of his webbing, tearing the human torso free from its rupturing tubes and cables. They dragged the screaming head and torso out through the shattered window, and into the interior of the limousine. The driver's mouth stretched wide in an endless howl of horror, his eyes almost starting from his head at what he saw waiting for him. He disappeared inside the limousine, there was a brief spurt of blood out the window, and then the black arms snapped back in, the window re-formed itself, and the dark limousine accelerated smoothly away. The empty taxicab shot across the lanes, traffic diving every which way to avoid it, until finally it ran off the road and crashed.

That left just two taxicabs, running now on either side of us, still firing their guns and trying to herd us away from the badlands.

Puff the Magic Dragon had fallen silent. At two thousand rounds a second, it runs out of ammo pretty fast. The taxi guns fell silent, too, either because they'd realised their inventory was getting low as well, or perhaps because they'd finally realised the guns weren't doing any damage. The taxis pressed in close on either side, and a dozen long steel blades protruded from the sides of the cabs, aimed right at our windows. Long blades, with strangely blurred edges, and a chill ran through me as I realised what they were.

"Dead Boy," I said, doing my best to sound calm and concerned and not at all like I was filling my trousers, "do you see what I see?"

"Of course I see them," he said, entirely unconcerned. "The car's computers are already running analysis on the blades. Monofilament edges, one molecule thick. Cut through anything. Someone really doesn't want us going wherever it is we're going. Which means . . . they must be protecting something really interesting, and I want to know what it is more than ever. We're going to have to do something about those blades, John. The car says her exterior is no match for them, and while she does have a force shield, maintaining it for any length of time will put a serious strain on the engines. I think we're going to have to do this old-school. In their face, up close and personal. Just the way I like it. Sweetie, lower the window, please."

His window immediately disappeared, and Dead Boy calmly climbed out the opening. It took a certain amount of effort to force his gangling body through the gap, and then he braced himself in the window frame before throwing himself at the taxicab. It jerked away at the last moment, as the cyborged driver realised what Dead Boy was planning, but the unnatural strength in Dead Boy's dead muscles propelled him through the air, across the growing gap, until he slammed into the side of the cab, and his dead hands closed inexorably onto the steel frame. He clung to the side of the cab as it lurched back and forth, trying desperately to shake him off. His purple greatcoat streamed out behind him, flapping this way and that in the slipstream. I couldn't hear Dead Boy above the roar of the traffic, but I could see he was laughing.

He drew back a grey fist, and drove it right through the cab's window. The cyborged driver cried out as the reinforced glass shattered, showering him with fragments. The cab was all over the place now, trying to throw Dead Boy off, but he held his balance easily, the fingers of one hand thrust deep into the steel roof, his feet planted firmly on the wheel arch. He leaned in through the empty window, and punched the cabdriver repeatedly in the head with his free hand. Bone shattered and blood flew, and the driver screamed as the force of the blows slammed him all around the cab's interior. Dead Boy grabbed a handful of tubes and cables and pulled them free. Sparks flew and hot fluids spurted, and the driver's face went slack and empty. He collapsed forward across the jerking steering wheel, and Dead Boy threw the cables aside. He checked to make sure he'd done all the damage he could, and then backed out of the cab window. He turned and braced himself, his back pressed against the empty window frame. The cab was a good ten feet away now, but he jumped the increasing gap like he did it every day, and landed easily on the futuristic car's roof. I heard the thud above me, followed by whoops and cheers as Dead Boy applauded himself and challenged all comers to come and have a go, if they thought they were hard enough.

The futuristic car was still driving itself. It didn't need Dead Boy, and it certainly didn't need me, so I gave my full attention to the one remaining taxicab, closing in really fast from the right. Its vicious steel blades were now only a few inches away. One good sideswipe and those blades would punch right through the car's side and gut Liza and me. We'd already retreated as far back as we could, pressed up against the far door; but those blades looked really long . . . Dead Boy came suddenly swinging in through the driver's window, and dropped back into his seat. He grinned widely, and started to beat a victorious tattoo on the steering wheel before he realised one hand still had bits of glass sticking out of it. So he leaned back in his seat, and set about removing them one at a time from his unfeeling flesh.

"Hi!" he said cheerfully. "I'm back! Did you miss me?"

"You're a lunatic!" said Liza.

"Excuse me," Dead Boy said coldly. "But I wasn't talking to you." And he spoke loving baby talk to his car until I felt like puking.

I did point out the nearness and threat of the remaining taxi, but Dead Boy just shrugged sulkily, suggesting through very clear body language that he felt he'd done his bit, and it was now very definitely my turn. So I very politely asked the car to lower the window facing the taxi, and it did. I peered out into the rushing wind, concentrating on the distance between us as the wind blew tears from my eyes. We were still both moving at one hell of a speed, but the taxi was having no trouble keeping up. The blurry-edged blades were almost touching the car. The cyborged driver glared at me, his lips pulled back in a mirthless grin. His tubes and cables bobbed around him as he stuck close to the futuristic car, despite all it could do to lose him. I leaned out through the car's window and smashed the driver's window with the knuckle-duster I'd slipped on my fist while he wasn't looking.

I always make it a point to carry a number of useful objects in my coat pocket. Because you never know . . .

The taxi window shattered, glass flying everywhere, and the cyborged driver ducked, yelling obscenities at me as I leaned farther through the empty window and grabbed on to his door frame. I hung in midair between the two vehicles, very much aware that if they pulled apart, I'd very probably be torn in two. And I would have overbalanced and fallen, if Liza hadn't been clinging desperately to my legs in the back of the car. I hauled myself inside the cab, and the taxi driver pointed his arm at me. A dull grey metal nozzle protruded from his wrist, pointing right at my face. I really hadn't expected the driver to have an energy gun implant, but I still knew one when I saw one, and my mind raced for something to do. Time seemed to slow right down, to give me plenty of time to consider the possibilities; but since they all seemed to end with my face being shot off, that didn't help much. I was just about to try a really desperate lunge, when Liza let go of my legs.

I could feel myself sliding out of the car, only a few moments from falling and almost certainly dying, when Liza appeared suddenly beside me, forcing herself into the remaining gap in the car window. The cyborged driver hesitated, as surprised as I was, and while he tried to decide which of us to shoot first, Liza surged forward and grabbed his arm, forcing it to one side. She was more than half out of the car now, and only our two bodies wedged in the car window stopped her from falling.

The cabdriver struggled to bring his gun hand to bear on either of us, while Liza fought to control his flailing arm. I tried to reach him with my knuckle-duster, but I was too far away, and I couldn't risk trying to wriggle farther out the window. And all the time the taxicab and the futuristic car were hurtling through the Nightside at terrible speed, the ground rushing by only a few feet below us.

"Whatever you're planning on doing," Liza yelled to me, "now would be a really good time to do it!"

So I gave up trying to reach the driver, and wriggled back through the car window. Liza clung fiercely to the driver's arm, as she started to fall. He brought his energy gun to bear on her. And I pulled a small blue sachet from my coat pocket, ripped it open, and threw the contents into the driver's face.

Vicious black pepper filled his eyes, blinding him in a moment, shocked tears streaming down his face. He was just starting to sneeze explosively as I pulled Liza away from him, and both of us wriggled back through the window into the back seat of the futuristic car. We sprawled together on the bloodred leather seat, breathing harshly as we struggled to get our breath back.

The taxicab swayed away from us, the driver utterly blind and unable to control his cab for the force of his sneezing. The cab fell away behind us, and a fifty-foot articulated rig ran right over it from behind.

And that was very definitely that.

Liza looked at me speechlessly for a long moment, and then . . .

"*Pepper?* That was your great idea? Pepper?"

"It worked, didn't it?" I said reasonably. "Condiments are our friends. Never leave home without them."

Liza shook her head slowly, and then sat up straight, pushing herself away from me, and adjusting her clothes as women do. "Was that . . . All that just happened, was that normal for the Nightside?"

"Not really, no," I had to admit. "Most people have the sense to leave Dead Boy's car strictly alone. And they certainly should have known better than to take on Dead Boy and myself. We have . . . reputations. Which can only mean it has to do with your Frank. Someone knows we're coming. Someone who really doesn't want us to know what's happened to Frank. And to justify this kind of open attack . . . whatever's going on, it must be something really out of the ordinary."

"Which means," Dead Boy said cheerfully, "it must be something new! And I'm always up for something new! On, my lovely car, on to Rotten Row!"

"You're weird," said Liza.

THREE

And so we headed into the badlands. Where the neon gets shoddier and the sins grow shabbier, though no less dangerous or disturbing. If the Nightside is where you go when noone else will have you, the badlands is where you go when even the Nightside is sick of the sight of you. The badlands, where all the furtive people end up, pursuing things even the Nightside is ashamed of . . . because some things are just too tacky.

The traffic thinned out more and more as we left the major thoroughfares behind, dying away to just the occasional tattooed unicorn with assorted piercings and a Prince Albert, a stretch hearse with the corpse half out of its coffin and beating helplessly against the reinforced windows, and a headless bounty hunter on horseback. The flotsam and jetsam of the Nightside, all hot in pursuit of their own private destinies and damnations. The streets grew narrower and darker, and not only because maybe half the streetlights were working. The shadows were darker and deeper, and things moved in them. More and more buildings had boarded-up windows and broken-in doors, and where lights did sometimes glow in high-up windows, strange shadows moved behind closed blinds. The neon signs remained as gaudy as ever, like poisonous flowers in a polluted swamp. A few people still walked the rain-slick streets, heads down, looking neither left nor right, drawn on by siren calls only they could hear.

Homeless people lurked in the shadows, broken men in tattered clothes. Mostly they moved in packs, because it was safer that way. There are all kinds of predators, in the badlands. And a few good people, fighting a losing battle and knowing it, but fighting on anyway, because they knew a battle is not a war. I saw Tamsin MacReady, the rogue vicar, out in her rounds, determined to do good in a bad place. She recognised Dead Boy's car, and waved cheerfully.

The night grew quieter and more thoughtful, the deeper into the badlands we went, a shining silver presence in a dark place. Working streetlights grew few and far between, and the car cruised quietly from one pool of light to another. Dead Boy tried the high beams, but even they couldn't penetrate far into the gloom, as though there was something in this new darkness that swallowed up light. The roar and clamour of the Nightside proper seemed far away now, left behind as we moved from one country to another. The few people we passed ignored us, intent on their own business. This wasn't a place to draw attention to yourself; unless, of course, you had something to sell.

A tall and willowy succubus, with dead white skin,

crimson lingerie, and bloodred eyes, loped along beside the futuristic car for a while, easily matching its speed. She tapped on our polarised windows with her clawed finger-tips, whispering all the awful things she would let us do. Liza shrank back from the succubus, her face sick with hor-ror and revulsion. When the succubus realised we weren't going to stop, she increased her speed to get ahead of us and then stepped out into the middle of the road, blocking our way. Dead Boy told the car to put its foot down, and the car surged forward.

The succubus ghosted out, becoming immaterial, and the futuristic car passed right through her. A spectre, tinted rose red and lily white, the succubus drifted at her own pace through the car, ignoring Dead Boy, her inhuman gaze fixed on Liza. A succubus always has a taste for fresh meat. She reached out a ghostly hand to Liza, but I grabbed her wrist and stopped her. It was like holding the memory of an arm, cold as ice, soft as smoke. The succubus looked at me, and then gently pulled her arm free, the ghostly trace passing through my mortal flesh in an eerily intimate moment. She trailed the fingertips of one hand along my face, winked one bloodred eye, and then passed on through the car and was gone.

The badlands grew grimly silent, abandoned and forsaken, as we closed in on Rotten Row. We had left civilisation behind, for something else. Here buildings and businesses pressed tight together in long ugly tenements, as though believing there was strength, and protection, in numbers. Windows were shuttered, doors securely locked, and none of these estab-lishments even bothered to look inviting. Either you knew what you were looking for, or you had no business being here. Enter at your own risk, leave your conscience at the door, and absolutely no refunds.

Welcome, sir. What's your pleasure?

Few people walked the gloomy, desolate streets, and they

all walked alone, despite the many dangers, because no-one else would walk with them. Or perhaps because the very nature of their needs and temptations had made them solitary. And though most of the figures we passed looked like people, not all of them walked or moved in a human way. One figure in a filthy suit turned suddenly to look at the car as it drifted past, and under the pulled-down hat I briefly glimpsed a face that seemed to be nothing but mouth, full of shark's teeth stained with fresh blood and gristle.

It's all about hunger, in the badlands.

Glowing eyes followed the progress of the futuristic car from shadowy alley mouths, rising and falling like bright burning fireflies. They didn't normally expect to see such a high-class, high-tech car in their neighbourhood. They could get a lot of money, and other things, for a car like ours. And its contents. In the quiet of the street, a baby began to cry; a lost, hopeless, despairing sound. Liza leaned forward.

"Stop. Do you hear that? Stop the car. We have to do something!"

"No, we don't," said Dead Boy.

"We keep going," I said, and turned to Liza as she opened her mouth to protest. "That isn't a baby. It's just something that's learned to sound like a baby, to lure in the unsuspecting. There's nothing out there that you'd want to meet."

Liza looked like she wanted to argue, but something in my voice and in my face must have convinced her. She slumped back in her seat, arms folded tightly across her chest, staring straight ahead. I felt sorry for her, even as I admired her courage and her stubbornness. She was having to take an awful lot on board, most of which would have broken a weaker mind, but she kept going. All for her dearest love, Frank. Husband Frank. What kind of man was he, to inspire such love and devotion . . . and still end up here, in Rotten Row? I would see this through to the end,

because I had said I would; but there was no way this was
going to end well.

Interesting, that Dead Boy hadn't even slowed the car.
Perhaps his dead ears heard something in the baby's cry
that was hidden from the living.

"This is it, people," he said abruptly, as the car turned a
tight corner into a narrow, garbage-cluttered cul-de-sac.
"We have now arrived at Rotten Row. Just breathe in that
ambience."

"Are you sure?" Liza said doubtfully, peering through
the car window with her face almost pressed to the glass. "I
can't see . . . anything. No shops, no businesses, no people.
I don't even see a street sign."

"Someone probably stole it," Dead Boy said wisely. "Around
here, anything not actually nailed down and guarded by hell-
hounds is automatically considered up for grabs. But my car
says this is the place, and my sweetie is never wrong."

Someone in the tattered remains of what had once been
a very expensive suit lurched out of a side alley to throw
something at the futuristic car. It bounced back from the
car's windscreen, and exploded. The car didn't even rock.
There was a brief scream from the thrower as the blast
threw him backwards, his clothes on fire. He'd barely hit
the ground before a dozen dark shapes came swarming out
of all the other alleys to roll his still-twitching body back
and forth as they robbed him of what little he had that was
worth the taking. They were already stripping the smouldering clothes from his dead body as they dragged it off
into the merciful darkness of the alley shadows. Liza looked
at me angrily, more disgusted than disturbed.

"What kind of a place have you brought me to, John?
My Frank wouldn't be seen dead in an area like this!"

"The photo says he's here," I said. "Look."

I held up the two jaggedly torn pieces, pressed carefully

together, and concentrated my gift on them. The image of
Frank jumped right out of the wedding photo, to become a
flickering ghost in the street outside. He was walking hur-
riedly down Rotten Row, a memory of a man repeating his
last journey, imprinted on Time Past. His palely translucent form stalked past the car, his face expectant and troubled at the same time. As though he was forcing himself
on, towards some long-desired, long-denied consummation
that both excited and terrified him. His pace quickened
until he was almost running, his arms flailing at his sides,
until at last he came to one particular door, and stopped
there, breathing hard. The badly hand-painted sign above
the door said simply SILICON HEAVEN.

Frank smiled for the first time at the sight of it, and it was
not a very nice smile. It was the smile of a man who wanted
something men are not supposed to want, not supposed to be
able to want. This was more than need, or lust, or desire.
This was obsession. He raised a trembling hand to knock,
and the door silently opened itself before him.

The doors of Hell are never bolted or barred, to those
who belong there.

Frank hurried inside, the door closed behind him, and
our glimpse into Time Past came to an end. I busied myself
putting the torn pieces of photo away, so I wouldn't have to
see the disappointment and betrayal of trust in Liza's face.
Dead Boy turned around in his seat to look at us, calmly
munching on a chocolate digestive. He didn't care about
where we were, or what we were doing here. He was just
along for the ride. Apparently when you're dead you only
have so much emotion in you, and he doesn't like to waste
it. He would go along with whatever I decided. But this
wasn't my decision; it was Liza's.

"We don't have to do this," I said, as gently as I could.
"We can still turn the car around, and go back."

"After coming all this way to find Frank?" said Liza.

"Why would I want to leave, when all the answers are in there waiting for me? I need to know about Frank, and I need to know what happened to my memories."

"We should leave," I said, "because Frank has come to a really bad place. Trust me; there are no good answers to be found in Silicon Heaven."

Liza looked from me to Dead Boy and back again. She could see something in our faces, something we knew and didn't want to say. Typically, she became angry rather than concerned. She wasn't scared and she wasn't put off; she wanted to know.

"What is this place, this Silicon Heaven? What goes on behind that door? You know, don't you?"

"Liza," I said. "This isn't easy . . ."

"It doesn't matter," she said firmly, resolutely. "If Frank's in there, I'm going in after him."

She wrestled with the door handle, but it wouldn't turn, no matter how much strength she used.

"No-one's going anywhere, just yet," Dead Boy said calmly. "We are all staying right here, until John has worked out a plan of action. This is not your world, Liza Barclay; you don't know the rules, how things work, in situations like this."

"He's right, Liza," I said. "This is a nasty business, even for the Nightside, with its own special dangers for the body and the soul."

"But . . . look at it!" said Liza, gesturing at Silicon Heaven, with its boarded-up window and its stained, paint-peeling door. "It's a mess! This whole street would need an extreme makeover before it could be upgraded enough to be condemned! And this . . . shop, or whatever it is, looks like it's been deserted and left empty for months. Probably nobody home but the rats."

"Protective camouflage," I said, when she finally ran out of breath. "Remember the baby that wasn't a baby? Silicon

Heaven set up business here, because only a location like this would tolerate a trade like theirs; but even so, it doesn't want to draw unwelcome attention to itself. There are a lot of people who object to the very existence of a place like Silicon Heaven, for all kinds of ethical, religious, and scientific reasons. We like to say anything goes in the Nightside, but even we draw the line at some things. If only on aesthetic grounds. Silicon Heaven has serious enemies, and would probably be under attack right now by a mob with flaming torches, if they weren't afraid to come here."

"Are you afraid?" said Liza, fixing me with her cold, determined eyes.

"I try very hard not to be," I said evenly. "It's bad for the reputation. But I have learned to be . . . cautious."

Liza looked at Dead Boy. "I suppose you're going to say you're never afraid, being dead."

"There's nothing here that bothers me," said Dead Boy, "but there are things I fear. Being dead isn't the worst thing that can happen to you."

"You really do get off on being enigmatic, don't you?" said Liza.

Dead Boy laughed. "You must allow the dead their little pleasures."

"Talking of fates worse than death," I said, and Liza immediately turned back to look at me, "you have to brace yourself, if we're going in there. Just by coming to an establishment like this, Frank is telling us things about himself, and they're things you're not going to want to hear. But you have to know, if we're going in there after him."

"Tell me," said Liza. "I can take it. Tell me everything."

"Silicon Heaven," I said carefully, "exists to cater to people with extreme desires. For men, and women, for whom the ordinary pleasures of the flesh aren't enough. And I'm not talking about the usual fetishes or obsessions. You can find all of that in the Nightside, and more. In Silicon Heaven, science and the unnatural go hand in hand like lovers, producing new forms of sexuality, new objects of desire. They're here to provide extreme and unforgivable outlets for love and lust and everything in between. This is the place where people go to have sex with computers."

Liza looked at me for a long moment. She wanted to laugh, but she could see the seriousness in my face, hear it in my voice, telling her that there was nothing laughable about Silicon Heaven.

"Sex . . . with computers?" she said numbly. "I don't believe it. How is that even possible?"

"This is the Nightside," said Dead Boy. "We do ten impossible things before breakfast, just for a cheap thrill. Abandon all taboos, ye who enter here."

"I won't believe it until I see it," said Liza, and there was enough in her voice beyond mere stubbornness that I gave the nod to Dead Boy. We were going to have to go all the way with this, and hope there were still some pieces left to pick up afterwards. Dead Boy spoke nicely to his car, and the doors swung open.

We stepped out onto Rotten Row, and the ambience hit us like a closed fist. The night air was hot and sweaty, almost feverish, and it smelled of spilled blood and sparking static. Blue-white moonlight gave the street a cold, alien look, defiantly hostile and unsafe. I could feel the pressure of unseen watching eyes, cold and calculating, and casually cruel. And over all, a constant feeling that we didn't belong here, that we had no business being here, that we were getting into things we could never hope to understand or appreciate. But I have made a business, and a very good living, out of going places where I wasn't wanted, and finding out things no-one wanted me to know. I turned slowly around, letting the whole street get a good look at me. My hard-earned reputation was normally enough to keep the flies off, but you never knew what desperate acts a man might be driven to, in a street like Rotten Row.

The futuristic car's doors all closed by themselves, and there was the quiet but definite sound of many locks closing. Liza looked back at the car, frowning uncertainly.

"Is it safe to just leave it here, on its own?"

"Don't worry," said Dead Boy, patting the bonnet fondly. "My sweetie can look after herself."

Even as they were speaking, a slim gun barrel emerged abruptly from the side of the car, and fired a brief but devastating bolt of energy at something moving not quite furtively enough in the shadows. There was an explosion, flames, and a very brief scream. Various shadowy people who'd started to emerge into the street, and display a certain covetous interest in the futuristic car, had a sudden attack of good sense and disappeared back into the shadows. Dead Boy sniggered loudly.

"My car has extensive self-defence systems, a total lack of scruples about using them, and a really quite appalling sense of humour. She kept one would-be thief locked in the boot for three weeks. He'd probably still be there, if I hadn't noticed the flies."

In his own way, he was trying to distract Liza and make her laugh, but she only had eyes for Silicon Heaven. So I took the lead, and strolled over to the door as though I had every right to be there. Liza and Dead Boy immediately fell in beside me, not wanting to be left out of anything. Up close, the door didn't look like much; just an everyday old-fashioned wooden door with the paint peeling off it in long strips . . . but this was Rotten Row, where ordinary and everyday were just lies to hide behind. I sneered at the tacky brass doorknob, sniffed loudly at the entirely tasteless brass door knocker, and didn't even try to touch the door itself. I didn't want the people inside thinking I could be taken out of the game that easily.

I thrust both hands deep into my coat pockets, and surreptitiously ran my fingertips over certain useful items that might come in handy for a little light breaking and entering. A private investigator needs to know many useful skills. In the end, I decided to err on the side of caution, and gave Dead Boy the nod to start things off, on the grounds that since he was dead, whatever happened next wouldn't affect him as much as the rest of us. He grinned widely, and drew back a grey fist. And the door swung slowly open, all by itself. I gestured quickly for Dead Boy to hold back. A door opening by itself is rarely a good sign. At the very least, it means you're being watched . . . and that the people inside don't think they have anything to fear from you entering. Or it could just be one big bluff. The Nightside runs on the gentle art of putting one over on the rubes.

"Are we expecting trouble?" said Liza, as I stood still, considering the open door.

"Always," Dead Boy said cheerfully. "It's only the threat of danger and sudden destruction that makes me feel alive."

"Then by all means, you go in first and soak up the punishment," I said generously.

"Right!" said Dead Boy, brightening immediately. He kicked the door wide open and stalked forward into the impenetrable darkness beyond. His voice drifted back to us: "Come on! Give me your best shot, you bastards! I can take it!"

Liza looked at me. "Is he always like this?"

"Pretty much," I said. "This is why most people won't work with him. Personally, I've always found him very useful for hiding behind when the bullets start flying. Shall we go?"

Liza looked at the open doorway, and the darkness beyond,

her face completely free of any expression. "I don't want to do this, John. I just know something really bad will happen in there; but I need to know the truth. I need to remember what I've forgotten, whether I want to or not."

She stepped determinedly forward, her small hands clenched into fists at her sides, and I moved quickly to follow her through the doorway. My shoulder brushed against hers, and I could feel the tension in her rock-hard muscles. I thought it was something simple: fear or anticipation. I should have known better.

The darkness disappeared the moment the door closed behind us, and a bright, almost painful glare illuminated the room we'd walked into. Solid steel walls surrounded us, a good forty feet a side, and even the floor and the ceiling were made from the same brightly gleaming metal. Our own distorted images stared back at us from the shining walls. Dead Boy stood in the middle of the room, glaring pugnaciously around him, ready to hit anything that moved or even looked at him funny, but we were the only ones there. There was no obvious way out, and when I looked back, even the door we'd come through had disappeared.

"I don't understand," said Liza. "This room is a hell of a lot bigger than the shop front suggested."

"In the Nightside, the interior of a building is often much bigger than its exterior," I said. "It's the only way we can fit everything in."

There was no obvious source for the sharp, stark light that filled the steel room. The air was dry and lifeless, and the only sounds were the ones we made ourselves. I moved over to the nearest wall, and studied it carefully without touching it. Up close, the metal was covered with faint tracings, endless lines in endless intricate patterns, like . . . painted-on circuitry. The patterns moved slowly, changing subtly under the pressure of my gaze, twisting and turning as they transformed themselves into whole new permutations. As though the wall was thinking, or dreaming. I gestured for Dead Boy and Liza to join me, and pointed out the patterns. Dead Boy just shrugged. Liza looked at me.

"Does this mean something to you?"

"Not . . . as such," I said. "Could be some future form of hieroglyphics. Could be some form of adaptive circuitry. But it's definitely not from around here. This is future tech, machine code from a future time line . . . There are rumours that Silicon Heaven is really just one big machine, holding everything within."

"And we've just walked right into it," said Dead Boy. "Great. Anyone got a can opener?"

He leaned in close to study the wall tracings, and prodded them with a long pale finger. Blue-grey lines leapt from the wall onto his finger and swarmed all over it. Dead Boy automatically pulled his finger back, and the circuitry lines stretched away from the wall, clinging to his dead flesh with stubborn strength. They crawled all over his hand and shot up his arm, growing and multiplying all the time, twisting and curling and leaping into the air. Dead Boy grabbed a big handful of the stuff, wrenched it away, and then popped it into his mouth. Dead Boy has always been one for the direct approach. He chewed thoughtfully, evaluating the flavour. The blue-grey lines slipped back down his arm and leapt back onto the wall, becoming still and inert again.

"Interesting," said Dead Boy, chewing and swallowing. "Could use a little salt, though."

I offered him some, but he laughed, and declined.

Liza made a sudden pained noise, and her knees started to buckle. I grabbed her by one arm to steady her, but I don't think she even knew I was there. Her face was pale and sweaty, and her mouth was trembling. Her eyes weren't tracking; her gaze was fixed on something only she could see. She looked like she'd just seen her own death, up close and bloody. I held her up, gripping both her arms firmly, and said her name loudly, right into her face. Her eyes snapped back into focus, and she got her feet back under her again. I let go of her arms, but she just stood where she was, looking at me miserably.

"Something bad is going to happen," she said, in a small, hopeless voice. "Something really bad . . ."

A dozen robots rose silently up out of the metal floor, almost seeming to form themselves out of the gleaming steel. More robots stepped out of the four walls, and dropped down from the ceiling. It seemed Silicon Heaven had a security force after all. The robots surrounded us on every side, silent and implacable, blocky mechanical constructs with only the most basic humanoid form. Liza shrank back against me. Dead Boy and I moved quickly to put her between us.

For a long moment the robots stood utterly still, as though taking the measure of us, or perhaps checking our appearance against their records. They were roughly human in shape, but there was nothing of human aesthetics about them. They were purely functional, created to serve a purpose and nothing more. Bits and pieces put together with no covering, their every working open to the eye. There were crystals and ceramics and other things moving around inside them, while strange lights came and went. Sharp-edged components stuck out all over them, along with all kinds of weapons, everything from sharp blades and circular saws to energy weapons and blunt grasping hands. They had no faces, no eyes, but all of them were orientated on the three of us. They knew where we were.

Many things about them made no sense at all, to human eyes and human perspectives. Because human science had no part in their making.

They all moved forward at the same moment, suddenly and without warning, metal feet hammering on the metal floor. They did not move in a human way, their arms and legs bending and stretching in unnatural ways, their centres of gravity seeming to slip back and forth as needed. They reached for us with their blocky hands, all kinds of sharp things sticking out of their fingers. Buzz saws rose out of bulking chests, spinning at impossible speeds. Energy weapons sparked and glowed, humming loudly as they powered up. The robots came for us. They would kill us if they could, without rage or passion or even satisfaction, blunt instruments of Silicon Heaven's will.

I've always prided myself on my ability to talk my way out of most unpleasant situations, but they weren't going to listen.

Dead Boy stepped forward, grabbed the nearest robot with brisk directness, picked it up and threw it at the next nearest robot. They both had to have weighed hundreds of pounds, but that was nothing to the strength in Dead Boy's unliving muscles. The sheer impact slammed both robots to the steel floor, denting it perceptibly, the sound almost unbearably loud. But though both robots fell in a heap, they untangled themselves almost immediately and rose to their feet again, undamaged.

Dead Boy punched a robot in what should have been its head, and the whole assembly broke off and flew away. The robot kept coming anyway. Another robot grabbed Dead Boy's shoulder from behind with its crude steel hand, the fingers closing like a mantrap. The purple greatcoat stretched and tore, but Dead Boy felt no pain. He tried to pull free, and snarled when he found he couldn't. He had to wrench himself free with brute strength, ruining his coat, and while he was distracted by that, another robot punched him in the back of the head.

I'm sure I heard bone crack and break. It was a blow that would have killed any ordinary man, but Dead Boy had left ordinary behind long ago. The blow still sent him staggering

forward, off balance, and straight into the arms of another
robot. The uneven arms slammed closed around him immediately, forcing the breath out of his lungs with brutal
strength. But Dead Boy only breathes when he needs to talk.
He broke the hold easily, and yanked one of the robot's arms
right out of its socket. He used the arm as a club, happily
hammering the robot about the head and shoulders, smashing pieces off and damaging others. But even as bits of the
robot flew through the air, it kept coming, and Dead Boy
had to back away before it. And while he was concentrating
on one robot, the others closed in around him.

They swarmed all over him, clinging to his arms, beating at his head and shoulders, trying to drag him down. He
struggled valiantly, throwing away one robot after another
with dreadful force, but they always came back. He was
inhumanly strong, but there were just so many of them. He
disappeared inside a crowd of robots, steel fists rising and
falling like jackhammers, over and over again, driving Dead
Boy to his knees. And then they cut at him, with their steel
blades and whirring buzz saws and vicious hands.

While the majority of robots were dealing with Dead
Boy, the remainder closed in on me, and Liza. She'd frozen,
her face utterly empty, her body twitching and shaking. I
gently but firmly pushed her behind me, out of the way.
Our backs were to the nearest wall, but not too close.

I was thinking furiously, trying to find a way out of this.
Most of my useful items were magical in nature, rather
than scientific. And while I knew quite a few nasty little
tricks to use against the living and the dead and those
unfortunate few stuck in between . . . I didn't have a
damned thing of any use against robots. Certainly throwing pepper into their faces wasn't going to work. I don't
carry a gun. I don't usually need them.

I backed up as far as I dared, herding Liza behind me,

and fired up my gift. My inner eye snapped open, and immediately my Sight found just the right places for me to stand, and where and when to dodge, so that the robots couldn't touch me. Their blocky hands reached for me again and again, but I was never there, already somewhere else, one step ahead of them. Except the more they closed in, the less room there was for me to move in. I managed to be in the right place to trip a few and send them crashing into one another, but all I was doing was buying time.

I knew what was happening to Dead Boy, but there wasn't a damned thing I could do.

One robot aimed an energy weapon at me. I waited till the very last moment, and then sidestepped, and the energy beam seared past me to take out the robot on my other side. It exploded messily, bits and pieces flying across the room. They ricocheted off the other robots harmlessly, but one piece of shrapnel passed close enough to clip off a lock of my hair. Liza didn't react at all.

The robots had discovered they couldn't hurt Dead Boy, so they decided to pull him apart. They grabbed him by the arms and legs, stretched him helpless in midair between them, and did their best to tear him limb from limb. He struggled and cursed them vilely, but in the end, they were powerful machines and he was just a dead man.

Liza darted suddenly forward from behind me, grabbed up the robot arm that Dead Boy had torn off, and used it like a club against the nearest robot. She swung the arm with both hands, using all her strength, her eyes wide and staring, lips drawn back in an animal snarl. She wasn't strong enough to damage the robot, but I admired her spirit. We weren't in her world any more, but she was still doing her best to fight back. But she still couldn't hope to win, and neither could Dead Boy, so as usual it was down to me.

I concentrated, forcing my inner eye all the way open, till I could See the world so clearly it hurt. I scanned the robots with my augmented vision, struggling to understand through the pain, and it didn't take me long to find the robots' basic weakness. They had no actual intelligence of their own; they were all receiving their orders from the same source, through the same mechanism. I moved swiftly among the robots, dancing in their blind spots, yanking the mechanisms out, one after another. And one by one the robots froze in place, cut off from their central command, helpless without orders. They stood around the metal room like so many modern art sculptures . . . and I sat down suddenly and struggled to get my breathing back under control, while my third eye, my inner eye, slowly and thankfully eased shut.

I have a gift for finding things, but it's never easy.

Dead Boy pulled and wriggled his way free from the robots holding him, looked in outrage at what they'd done to his purple greatcoat, and kicked some of the robots about for a bit, just to ease his feelings. Liza looked about her wildly, still clutching her robot arm like a club. I got up from the floor and said her name a few times, and she finally looked at me, personality and sanity easing slowly back into her face. She looked at what she was holding, and dropped it to the floor with a moue of distaste. I went over to her, but she didn't want to be comforted.

A voice spoke to us, out of midair. A calm, cultured voice, with a certain amount of resignation in it.

"All right, enough is enough. We didn't think the security bots would be enough to stop the famous John Taylor and the infamous Dead Boy . . . or should that be the other way round . . . but we owed it to our patrons to try. You might have been having an off day. It happens. And the bots were nearing the end of their warranty . . . Anyway, you'd better come on through, and we'll talk about this. I said Liza Barclay would come back to haunt us if we just let her go, but of course no-one ever listens to me."

"I've been here . . . before?" said Liza.

"You don't remember?" I said quietly.

"No," said Liza. "I've never seen this place before." But she didn't sound as certain as she once had. I remembered her earlier premonition, just before the robots appeared, when she'd known something bad was about to happen. Perhaps she'd known because something like it had happened the last time she was here. Unless she was remembering something else, even worse, still to come . . .

A door appeared in the far wall, where I would have sworn there was no trace of a door just a moment before. A section of the metal just slid suddenly sideways, disappearing into the rest of the wall, leaving a brightly lit opening. I started towards it, and once again Dead Boy and Liza fell in beside me. You'd almost have thought I knew what I was doing. We threaded our way through the motionless robots, and I held myself ready in case they came alive again; but they just stood there, in their stiff awkward poses, utterly inhuman even in defeat. Dead Boy pulled faces at them. Liza wouldn't even look at the robots, all her attention focused on the open door, and the answers it promised her.

We passed through the narrow opening into a long steel corridor, comfortably wide and tall, the steel so brightly polished it was like walking through an endless hall of mirrors. It occurred to me that none of our reflections looked particularly impressive, or dangerous. Dead Boy had lost his great floppy hat in his struggle with the robots, and his marvellous purple greatcoat was torn and tattered. Some of the stitches on his bare chest had broken open, revealing pink-grey meat under the torn grey skin. I keep telling him to use staples. Liza looked scared but determined, her face so pale and taut there was hardly any colour in it. She was close to getting her answers now; but I think, even then, she knew this wasn't going to end well. And I . . . I looked like someone who should have known better than to come to a place like Rotten Row, and expect any good to come of it.

The corridor finally took a sharp turn to the left, and ushered us into a large antechamber. More steel walls, still no furnishings or comforts, but finally a human face. A tall, slender man in the traditional white lab coat was waiting for us. He had a bland forgettable face, and a wide welcoming smile that meant nothing at all. Slick, I thought immediately. That's the word for this man. Nothing would ever touch him, and nothing would ever stick to him. He'd make sure of that. He strode briskly towards us, one hand stretched out to shake, still smiling, as though he could do it all day. The smile didn't reach his eyes. They were cold, certain, the look of a man utterly convinced he knew important things that you didn't.

Fanatic's eyes. Believer's eyes. Such men are always dangerous.

He dropped his hand when he realised none of us had any intention of shaking it, but he didn't seem especially upset. He was still smiling.

"Hi!" he said brightly. "I'm Barry Kopek. I speak for Silicon Heaven. I'd say it's good to see you, but I wouldn't want to start our relationship with such an obvious lie. So let's get right down to business, shall we, and then we can all get back to our own lives again. Won't that be nice?"

He tried offering us his hand again, and then pulled it back with a resigned shrug, as though he was used to it. And if he was the official greeter for Silicon Heaven, he probably was. Even a ghoul in a graveyard would look down on a computer pimp like him.

"Come with me," he said, "and many things will be made clear. All your questions will be answered; or at least, all the ones you're capable of understanding. No offence, no offence. But things are rather . . . advanced, around here. Tomorrow has come early for the Nightside, and soon there'll be a wake-up call for everyone. Slogans are such an important part for any new business, don't you agree? Sorry about the robots, but we have so many enemies among the ignorant, and our work here is far too important to allow outside agitators to interfere with it."

"Your work?" I said. "Arranging dates for computers, for people with a fetish for really heavy metal, is important work?"

He looked like he wanted to wince at my crudity, but was far too professional. The smile never wavered for a moment. "We are not a part of the sex industry, Mr. Taylor. Perish the thought. Everyone who finds their way here becomes part of the great work. We are always happy to greet new people, given the extreme turnover in . . . participants. But they all understand! They do, really they do! This is the greatest work of our time, and we are all honoured to be a part of it. Come with me, and you'll see. Only . . . do keep Mrs. Barclay under control, please. She did enough damage the last time she was here."

Dead Boy and I both looked at Liza, but she had nothing to say. Her gaze was fixed on the official greeter, staring at him like she could burn holes through him. She wanted answers, and he was just slowing her down.

"All right," I said. "Lead the way. Show us this great work."

"Delighted!" said Barry Kopek. I was really starting to get tired of that smile.

He led us through more metal corridors, turning this way and that with complete confidence, even though there were never any signs or directions on the blank steel walls. He kept up an amiable chatter, talking smoothly and happily about nothing in particular. The light from nowhere became increasingly stark, almost unbearably bright. There was a sound in the distance, like the slow beating of a giant heart, so slow you could count the moments between each great beat, but they all had something of time and eternity in them. And there was a smell, faint at first, but gradually growing stronger . . . of static and machine oil, ozone and lubricants, burning meat and rank, fresh sweat.

"You said Liza's been here before," I said finally, after it became clear that Kopek wasn't going to raise the subject again himself.

"Oh, yes," he said, carefully looking at me rather than at Liza. "Mrs. Barclay was here yesterday, and we let her in, because of course we have nothing to hide. We're all very proud of the work we do here."

"What work?" said Dead Boy, and something in his voice made Kopek miss a step.

"Yes, well, to put it very simply, in layman's terms . . . We are breaking down the barriers between natural and artificial life."

"If you're so proud, and this work so very great, why did you send those cyborged taxis to attack us?" I said, in what I thought was really a quite reasonable tone of voice. Kopek's smile wavered for the first time. He knew me. And my reputation.

"Ah, yes," he said. "That. I said that was a mistake. You must understand, they were some of our first crude attempts, at melding man with machine. Those men paid a lot of money for it to be done to them, so they could operate more efficiently and more profitably in Nightside traffic. We were very short of funds at the beginning . . . When they found out you were coming here, Mr. Taylor, well, frankly, they panicked. You see, they relied on us to keep them functioning."

"Who told them I was coming?" I said. "Though I'm pretty sure I already know the answer."

"I said it was a mistake," said Barry Kopek. "Are they all . . . ?"

"Yes," I said.

He nodded glumly. Still smiling, but you could tell his heart wasn't in it. "I'm not surprised. Your reputation precedes you, Mr. Taylor, like an attack dog on a really long leash. It's a shame, though. They only wanted to better themselves."

"By having their humanity cut away?" said Dead Boy, just a bit dangerously.

"They gave up so little, to gain so much," said Kopek, just a bit haughtily. "I would have thought you of all people would appreciate . . ."

"You don't know me," said Dead Boy. "You don't know anything about me. And no-one gets away with attacking my car."

"Being dead hasn't mellowed you at all, has it?" said Kopek.

"Is Frank here?" I said. "Frank Barclay?"

"Well, of course he's here," said Kopek. "It's not like we're holding him prisoner, against his will. He came to us, pursuing his dreams, and we were only too happy to accommodate him. He is here where he wanted to be, doing what he's always wanted to do, happy at last."

"He was happy with me!" said Liza. "He loves me! He married me!"

"A man wants what he wants, and needs what he needs," said Kopek, looking at her directly for the first time. "And Mr. Barclay's needs brought him to us."

"Can we see him? Talk to him?" I said.

"Of course! That's where I'm taking you now. But you must promise me you'll keep Mrs. Barclay under control. She reacted very badly to seeing her husband last time."

"She's seen him here before?" I said.

"Well, yes," said Kopek, looking from me to Liza and back again, clearly puzzled. "I escorted her to him myself. Didn't she tell you?"

"No," Liza said quietly, though exactly what she was

saying no to, I wasn't entirely sure. She was all drawn up in herself now, looking straight ahead, her gaze fixed, almost disassociated.

The corridor finally ended in a flat featureless wall, in which another door appeared. Kopek led us through, and we all stopped dead to look around, impressed and overwhelmed despite ourselves by the sheer size of the glass-and-crystal auditorium spread out before us. It takes a lot to impress a native of the Nightside, but the sheer scope and scale of the place we'd been brought to took even my breath away. Bigger than any enclosed space had a right to be, with walls like frozen waterfalls of gleaming crystal, set so far apart the details were just distant blurs, under tinted glass ceilings so high above us clouds drifted between us and them. Like some vast cathedral dedicated to Science, the auditorium was so enormous it had generated its own weather systems. Kopek's smile was openly triumphant now, as he gestured grandly with outstretched arms.

"Lady and gentlemen, welcome to Silicon Heaven!"

He led the way forward, between massive machines that had shape and form, but no clear meaning or significance. So complex, so advanced, as to be incomprehensible to merely human eyes. There were components that moved, and revolved, and became other things even as I watched; strange lights that burned in unfamiliar colours; and noises that were almost, or beyond, voices. Things the size of buildings walked in circles, and intricate mechanisms came together in complex interactions, like a living thing assembling itself. Gleaming metal spheres the size of sheepdogs rolled back and forth across the crystal floor, sprouting tools and equipment as needed to service the needs of larger machines. Dead Boy kicked at one of the spheres, in an experimental way, but it dodged him easily.

Kopek led the way, and we all followed close behind. This wasn't a place you wanted to get lost in. It felt . . . like

walking through the belly of Leviathan, or like flies crawling across the stained-glass window of some unnatural
cathedral . . . So of course I strolled along with my hands in
my coat pockets, like I'd seen it all before and hadn't been
impressed then. Never let them think they've got the
advantage, or they'll walk all over you. Dead Boy seemed
genuinely uninterested in any of it, but then he'd died and
brought himself back to life, and that's a hard act to follow.
Liza didn't seem to see any of it. She had a hole in her mind,
a gap in her memories, and all she cared about was finding
out what had happened the last time she was here. Did she
care at all about husband Frank, any more? Or was she
remembering just enough to sense that her quest wasn't for
him, and never had been, but only to find the truth about
him and her, and this place . . .

There was a definite sense of purpose to everything happening around us, even if I couldn't quite grasp it, but I was
pretty sure there was nothing human in that purpose. Nothing here gave a damn about anything so small as Humanity.

"I was here before," Liza said slowly. "There's something
bad up ahead. Something awful."

I looked sharply at Kopek. "Is that right, Barry? Is there
something dangerous up ahead, that you haven't been
meaning to tell us about?"

"There's nothing awful here," he said huffily. "You're
here to see something wonderful."

And finally, we came face-to-face with what we'd come
so far to see. A single beam of light stabbed down, shimmering and scintillating, like a spotlight from Heaven, as
though God himself was taking an interest. The illumination picked out one particular machine, surrounded by
ranks and ranks of robots. They were dancing around the
machine, in wide interlocking circles, their every movement impossibly smooth and graceful and utterly inhuman.

They moved to music only they could hear, perhaps to music only they could hope to understand, but there was nothing of human emotion or sensibility in their dance. It could have been a dance of reverence, or triumph, or elation, or something only a robot could know or feel. The robots danced, and the sound of their metal feet slamming on the crystal floor was almost unbearably ugly.

Kopek led us carefully through the ranks of robots, and at once they began to sing, in high chiming voices like a choir of metal birds, in perfect harmonies and cadences that bordered on melody without ever actually achieving it. Like machines pretending to be human, doing things that people do without ever understanding why people do them. We passed through the last of the robots and finally . . . there was Frank, beloved husband of Liza, having sex with a computer.

The computer was the size of a house, covered with all kinds of monitor screens and readouts but no obvious controls, with great pieces constantly turning and sliding across each other. It was made of metal and crystal and other things I didn't even recognise. At the foot of it was an extended hollow section, like a large upright coffin, and suspended within this hollow was Frank Barclay, hanging in a slowly pulsing web of tubes and wires and cables, naked, ecstatic, transported. Liza made a low, painful sound, as though she'd been hit.

Frank's groin was hidden behind a cluster of machine parts, always moving, sliding over and around him like a swarm of metallic bees, clambering over themselves in their eagerness to get to him. Like metal maggots, in a self-inflicted wound. Thick translucent tubes had been plugged into his abdomen, and strange liquids surged in and out of him. Up and down his naked body, parts of him had been dissected away, to show bones and organs being slowly replaced by new mechanical equivalents. There was no bleeding, no trauma. One thigh bone had been revealed from top to bottom, one end bone and the other metal, and already it was impossible to tell where the one began and the other ended. Metal rods plunged in and out of Frank's flesh, sliding back and forth, never stopping. Lights blinked on and off inside him, briefly rendering parts of his skin transparent; and in that skin I could see as many wires as blood vessels.

The computer was heaving and groaning, in rhythm to the things going in and out of Frank's naked body, and the machine's steel exterior was flushed and beaded with sweat. It made . . . orgasmic sounds. Frank's face was drawn, shrunken, the skin stretched taut across the bone, but his eyes were bright and happy, and his smile held a terrible pleasure. Cables penetrated his skin, and metal parts penetrated his body, and he loved it. One cable had buried itself in his left eye socket, replacing the eyeball, digging its way in a fraction of an inch at a time. Frank didn't care. He shuddered and convulsed as things slid in and out of him, changing him forever, and he loved every last bit of it.

Liza stood before him, tears rolling silently and unheeded down her devastated face.

I turned to Barry Kopek. "Is he dying?"

"Yes, and no," said Kopek. "He's becoming something else. Something wonderful. We are making him over, transforming him, into a living component capable of being host to machine consciousness. A living and an unliving body, for an Artificial Intelligence from a future time line. It came to the Nightside through a Timeslip, fleeing powerful enemies. It wants to experience sin, and in particular the hot and sweaty sensations of the flesh. It wants to know what we humans know, and take for granted; all the many joys of sex. Together, Frank and the computer are teaching each other whole new forms of pleasure. He is teaching the machine all the colours of emotion and sensuality, and the very subtle joys of degradation. In return, the machine is

teaching him whole new areas of perception and concep-
tion. Man becomes machine, becomes more than machine,
becomes immortal living computer. A metal messiah for a
new Age . . ."

Kopek's face was full of vision now, a zealot in his cause.
"Why should men be limited to being just men, and machines
just machines? Human and inhuman shall combine together,
to become something far superior to either. But like all new
life, it begins with sex."

"How many others have there been?" said Dead Boy.
"Before Frank?"

"One hundred and seventeen," said Kopek. "But Frank
is different. He doesn't just believe. He wants this."

"Oh, yeah," said Dead Boy. "Looks like he's coming his
brains out."

Liza collapsed, her knees slamming painfully onto the
crystal floor. Her face was twisted, ugly, filled with a horrid
knowledge, as all her repressed memories came flooding
back at once. She pounded on the floor with her fist, again
and again and again.

"*No! No, no, no!* I remember . . . I remember it all! I came
here, following Frank. Following my husband, into the
Nightside, and through its awful streets, all the way here . . .
Because I thought he was cheating on me. I thought he had
a lover here. He hadn't touched me in months. I thought he
was having an affair, but I never suspected this . . . Never
thought he wanted . . . *this.*"

"She talked her way in, yesterday," said Kopek. "Determined to see her husband. But when we brought her here,
and showed her, she went berserk. Attacked the computer.
Did some little damage, before the robots drove her off. We
wouldn't let her hurt Frank, or herself, and after a while she
left."

"And she blocked out the memories herself," I said.
"Because they were unbearable."

"How could you?" Liza screamed at Frank. "How could you want *this*? It doesn't love you! It can't love you!"

Frank stirred for the first time, his one remaining eye slowly turning to look down at her. His face showed no emotion, no compassion for the woman he'd loved and married, not so long ago. When he spoke, his voice already contained a faint machine buzz.

"This is what I want. What I've always wanted. What I need . . . And what you could never give me. I've dreamed of this for years . . . of flesh and metal coming together, moving together. Thought it was just a fetish, never told anyone . . . Knew they could never understand. Until someone told me about the Nightside, the one place in the world where anything is possible; and I knew I had to come here. This is the place where dreams come true."

"Including all the bad ones," murmured Dead Boy.

"What about us, Frank?" said Liza, tears streaming down her face.

"What about us?" said Frank.

"You selfish piece of shit!"

Suddenly she was back on her feet again, heading for Frank with her hands stretched out like claws, moving so fast even the robots couldn't react fast enough to stop her. She jumped up and into the coffin, punched her fist into a hole in Frank's side, and thrust her hand deep inside him. His whole body convulsed, the machines going crazy, and then Liza laughed triumphantly as she jerked her hand back out again. She dropped back down onto the crystal floor, brandishing her prize in all our faces. Blood dripped thickly from the dark red muscle in her hand. I grabbed her arms from behind as she shouted hysterically at her husband.

"You see, Frank? I have your heart! I have your cheating heart!"

"Keep it," said Frank, growing still and content again, in the metal arms of his lover. "I don't need it any more."

And already the machines were moving over him, mopping up the blood and sealing off his wound, working to replace the heart with something more efficient. While the computer heaved and groaned and sweated, Frank sighed and smiled.

It was too much for Liza. She sank to her knees again, sobbing violently. Her hand opened, and the crushed heart muscle fell to the crystal floor, smearing it with blood. She laughed as she cried, the horrid sound of a woman losing her mind, retreating deep inside herself because reality had become too awful to bear. I gave her something to breathe in, from my coat pocket, and in a moment she was asleep. I eased her down until she was lying full length on the floor. Her face was empty as a doll's.

"I don't get it," said Dead Boy, honestly puzzled. "It's just sex. I've seen worse."

"Not for her," I said. "She loved him, and he loved *this.* To be betrayed and abandoned by a husband for another woman or even a man is one thing, but for a machine? A thing? A computer that meant more to him than all her love, that could do things for him that she never could? Because for him, simple human flesh wasn't enough. He threw aside their love and their marriage and all their life together, to have sex with a computer."

"Can you do anything for her?" said Dead Boy. "We've got to do something, John. We can't leave her like this."

"You always were a sentimental sort," I said. "I know a few things. I'm pretty sure I can find a way to put her back the way she was, when she came to us, and this time make sure the memories stay repressed. No memory at all, of the Nightside or Silicon Heaven. I'll take her back into London proper, wake her up, and leave her there. She'll never find her way back in on her own. And in time, she'll get over the mysterious loss of her husband, and move on. It's the kindest thing to do."

"And the metal messiah?" said Dead Boy, curling his colourless lip at Frank in the computer. "We just turn our back on it?"

"Why not?" I said. "There's never been any shortage of gods and monsters in the Nightside; what's one more would-be messiah? I doubt this one will do any better than the others. In the end, he's just a tech fetishist, and it's just a mucky machine with ideas above its station. Everything to do with sex, and nothing at all to do with love."

You can find absolutely anything in the Nightside; and every sinner finds their own level of Hell, or Heaven.

SOME OF THESE
CONS GO WAY BACK

London's heart is old and cold and sometimes very cruel. The sick, secret, magical heart of London is called the Nightside, but you won't find its teeming streets on any official map. Hidden by ancient agreements and protected by terrible forces, the Nightside is where the really wild things live. But if you can find your way in, by hook or by crook, you can find everything you ever lusted after in your dreams. Especially the bad ones. In the Nightside, it's always dark, always three o'clock in the morning, and the dawn never comes. Heroes and villains, gods and monsters get together to make the kind of deals you can only make in the dark; and afterwards they go clubbing together. Hot neon blazes over crowded streets where the buzz never stops, and love is for sale on every street-corner. Love, or something like it.

London has a heart; but it's rotten to the core.

My name is Harry Fabulous. These days. Always glad to see you, with a face to break your heart and clothes to break your wallet. I'm everyone's friend, when they need a friend in a hurry. I'm the Go To man, for all your pharmaceutical needs. I can get you anything your little heart desires, or I can put you in touch with someone who can. For a percentage. Of course, a lot of what I supply isn't exactly what I say it is; but most of my clients are too dumb or too desperate to make a fuss. Because, you see, I'm not really a dealer man. I'm a con man, and my delight is the nature of the deal. I could talk you out of both your legs, and you'd never even notice until you tried to chase after me. I'm Harry Fabulous, and you'll never see it coming till it's far too late.

But every profession has its ups and downs, and on that particular night I was out on the streets, losing myself in the crowds, staying one step ahead of certain indignant individuals who were after my body, and not in a good way. So I headed into Uptown, home to all the very best bars and night-clubs, looking to make a few unobtrusive scores and raise some serious cash in a hurry. The rich always make the best marks. They always think it can't happen to them. People and other types hurried past on either side of me, intent on their own business, chasing the kinds of dreams you can't even discuss with your loved ones. Perhaps especially your loved ones.

The Nightside doesn't judge. The Nightside doesn't care.

Hot jazz and heavy bass lines drifted out of the temptingly-half-open doors of night-clubs, where the show never ends, and you can dance till your feet bleed. Parties that go on forever, and the piper is never paid in money. All the latest bands, all the latest sounds. Everything that's hot, everything that's cool, everything that's bad for you, starts out in the Nightside.

I had my sights set on the club of clubs, Heaven's Doorway. As always, there was a long line of young hopefuls waiting outside the entrance, clamouring to get in, dropping names and even hard cash to the disinterested doorman, in the hope of jumping the queue. As if. Heaven's Doorway is the place to go, to get the kind of highs you can't get anywhere else. When taduki and tanna leaves don't do it for you any more, and you've run out of Martian red weed to smoke, you can be sure someone at Heaven's Doorway will have the very latest thing, at an only mildly extortionate price.

I strolled right past the queue like I hadn't a care in the world and nodded familiarly to the doorman, but he took a step forward to block my way more completely. We knew each other of old, he and I. I kept smiling. I have a very nice smile, chummy and charming in equal measure, with a winning touch of roguishness. I've put in a lot of practice in front of the mirror, getting that smile just right. The doorman scowled fiercely, utterly unimpressed. Prince Albert was a big, butch steroid queen, entirely naked, and secured to his position at the club's entrance by a long silver chain connecting his genital piercings to the door-post. The club's owners say it's because they couldn't bear to lose him to anyone else, but I think it's to make sure he stays in a permanent bad mood. Albert loomed over me, sneering down from his full six feet seven of bulging muscles.

"Now, now, Mr. Fabulous, we don't want any trouble, do we?" he said, in a voice like a low rumble of thunder. "The nice ladies and gentlemen come here for a bit of fun, not to be cheated out of their hard-earned by a cheap little con man like you, Harry."

"You wound me, Albert," I said. "I am never cheap. And besides, I have an invitation to a private party here, from the owners."

And I produced the very impressive piece of embossed pasteboard to prove it. Albert accepted it gingerly, the small card lost in his huge paw, and studied it carefully. I kept my smile going, but inside I was holding my breath. The card was actually a very impressive forgery, produced by one of my more useful junkie clients. Does really nice work when his hands aren't shaking. Albert finally scowled, shook his head in a what's-the-world-coming-to sort of way, and lifted the golden rope to let me pass. I swept past him as though I'd never had a doubt in the world. It's all about attitude. Albert hung on to my invitation, no doubt intending to have it checked by someone further up the food-chain, but I'd expected that. By the time the owners had confirmed the bad news, I'd have done my business and would be long gone.

I love it when a con comes together.

Inside, the dance floor was full, and the joint was jumping. I eased my way through the excited crowd, looking for a good vantage point from which to view the scene. Along the way, I used my old pick-pocketing skills to acquire several attractive objects, just to keep my hand in. I discovered a pleasantly rococo little stairway at the side and ascended the plush-carpeted stairs just high enough to get a good look. The usual unusual suspects were out in force, everything from teeny-boppers to elves to vampires, and even the odd Grey alien, all of them dancing with more enthusiasm than style. And all the usual pretty young things, with their hard faces and harder hearts, partying like there's no tomorrow to the surging sound of the very latest hot band, Night's Dark Agents. But I wasn't here for them. I was much more interested in the small groups forming and re-forming in the shadowy corners, drinking or smoking or popping the pills that the local faces were handing out as free samples. There's never any shortage of willing guinea-pigs at Heaven's Doorway. I descended the stairs like royalty, smiling and waving, and headed for one of the biggest groups, inwardly flexing my sincerity muscles.

I had some powdered black centipede meat I was hoping to pass off as demon's blood, along with a few other useful items that could look pretty damned tempting in a bad light. I needed to raise some decent money fast, pay off a few old debts, and get myself back into the high-stakes games. Because of a few rather misjudged business deals and a couple of cons that had gone spectacularly bad, I was temporarily embarrassed, financially speaking. I needed to make some new connections, get my feet under someone's table. When you've burned as many people over as many bad deals as I have, you always need to be moving on, moving up. And never ever look back.

I passed a small gathering of Bright Young Things in borrowed finery, crowded anxiously around one of their own, who was currently thrashing about on the floor in a somewhat theatrical way. I paused for a quick look. The girl didn't look too good. "Should that purple stuff be coming out of her ears?" said one of her friends, doubtfully. I didn't hang around to see the outcome. It was all I could do to keep from shaking my head in an adult, knowing way. I never touch any of the things I sell. I've got more sense. I get all my kicks from the thrill of the con.

There were a handful of celebrities in that night, and I had them in my sights. The Lord of the Dance stood as though posing for photographs, ostentatiously ignoring his ex only a few feet away, the Dancing Queen. Both had their own little coterie of fans and followers, glaring jealously at each other. The Lord was affecting a Celtic look, all black leather straps and splashes of blue woad, while the Queen had reverted to her most successful look, as a silver lamé diva. Any club would be glad to pay either of them to show up because no-one could inspire or madden a crowd like the Lord of the Dance or the Dancing Queen; but they only ever went where the mood or the fashion took them.

Also making the scene was that eternally reinventing phenomenon, the ultimate pop star, the Thin White Prince. Impossibly good-looking, infuriatingly tasteful, he dominated any scene he chose to favour with his presence. He wore a pure white suit, exquisitely cut, and all those gathered around him waited impatiently for their chance to tell him how wonderful he was. It would only have spoiled it for them to tell them he wasn't actually human; and I never do anything unless there's a profit in it for me.

And then there was the Painted Ghoul, resplendent in his tacky clown's outfit and sleazy clown's make-up. Never welcome, never turned away, because he could do things for you, get things for you, that no-one else could. Or would. The quintessential clown at midnight, who could make you laugh till you coughed blood. He was addressing a small, somewhat captive audience, who laughed in all the right places, until they could get a word in edgeways to plead very politely for what they needed. I've never found him amusing.

There's nothing funny about a clown with an erection.

But when I approached these stars of the scene, these celebrities of the night, all of whom had good reason to remember me fondly from the past, they froze me out. Turned their backs on me, pretended I wasn't there. Word of my current predicament had clearly preceded me. And after all the things I'd done for them, the bastards . . . But no-one ever wants to know you when you're down. Failure might rub off.

And that was the way it went, all through the club.

Refused and rebuffed, I retreated to the rococo stairway to lick my wounds and consider new strategies. I stood at the top of the stairs, pulling my pride back about me, and looked for some weaker members of the herd I could prey on. I couldn't afford to leave the club without doing somebody down, for the good of my reputation. And that was when I heard the singing. A woman's voice, trapped and plaintive, urgent and eerie, and the most beautiful thing I'd ever heard. It sure as hell wasn't coming from the band. I turned slowly, while the song built a fire in my heart and raised all the hackles on the back of my neck. There was a door at the top of the stairs, set so flush into the wall I hadn't even noticed it before. I headed towards it, drawn by the woman's voice. I tried the door-handle, but it was locked. I smiled.

I looked back, but no-one seemed to be paying me any attention. I reached into one of my many hidden pockets and brought out a very special skeleton key. Fashioned from the finger bones of the greatest locksmith who ever lived, I got it in return for a vial of what I swore was the pure Jekyll and Hyde formula. It was really an Adrenalin/amphetamine mix, but it had much the same effect, and by the time my client had come down, I was long gone with the greatest skeleton key ever made. I slipped it into the keyhole before me, and it worked the lock like a lover; and then all I had to do was open the door and slip inside.

I eased the door shut behind me, and the roar of the club cut off immediately. The singing stopped, too, and I turned to look. And in that bare and empty room, crouched on the bare floor-boards, within the glowing red lines of a pentagram, was an angel with broken wings. Even squatting on the floor, trapped and helpless, she was still heart-stoppingly beautiful. She was pure white, like an alabaster statue glowing from within, but her eyes were sea-green, and her long, flowing hair was a vivid red. She had a perfect figure and no navel, and her crushed wings slumped down her back like all the cruelty in the world. Seeing her there, broken and imprisoned, was like looking at the most beautiful butterfly in the world, pinned and mounted on a display card, but still alive, still suffering. I walked slowly towards her. I'd heard stories about an angel, trapped in some club's private room, kept for the amusement of its very special patrons; but I'd thought they were just stories.

She was so beautiful. She touched my heart in a way I'd have sworn was no longer possible.

Hello, she said, and her voice sounded in my mind like the chiming of silver bells, like a lover's voice as she lies cuddled in your arms after sex. *Are you here to hurt me, or enjoy me?*

"What?" I said. "I'm sorry, I don't . . ."

It's what men come to me for. Why I'm kept here, against my will. But you're not with them . . . are you?

"No," I said. "No, I'm not." My mouth was dry, and I was having trouble getting the words out. I crouched before her, at the very edge of the pentagram's glowing lines. They flared up briefly in warning, red as hell-fire. I felt drunk on her beauty, on the nearness of her. "Why . . . Why do they keep you here?"

There's a market for angel blood, and angel tears, and angel urine. She smiled sadly. *The price we messengers pay, for becoming material. I have been made into a commodity, nothing more. Sometimes they give me to really important people, for sex. Sex with an angel is better than any drug could ever be. But they never touch . . . me. I deny them that, at least.*

And just like that, I wanted her. Wanted her body, her unbelievable beauty, wanted her so badly I ached. My heart slammed painfully in my chest, and it was all I could do to breathe. She smiled, understanding.

"This . . . isn't right," I said. "You shouldn't be here. How can I free you?"

You mustn't. It's too dangerous. They would kill you if . . .

"I can't leave you here. Not like this. I can't. What do you need me to do?"

A good man has come at last. I had almost given up hope. The pentagram is the key. Its lines were drawn in the blood of a murdered unbaptised baby, mixed with salt and semen and sweat from the parents. Only the heart's blood from one of those parents can break these lines and set me free. She looked at me so sadly, my heart almost broke. *Do you understand what it is I'm saying? What I'm asking of you? To free me, you would have to commit one terrible, unforgivable act of your own free will. I can't ask you to do that for me.*

"I can't leave you here! It's . . . wrong. I can't walk away, not now I know . . ."

She smiled at me, and my heart leapt. *Most wonderful of men, and most beloved. I will worship you with my body and give you what I never gave anyone else—my heart. Sweet Harry. But you must move quickly. The mother of the murdered child is here, now. Her name is Aimee Driscoll.*

I knew Aimee. I could find her.

She deserves to die. She gave up her baby for the slaughter. Do it for me, my Harry. And we will be so happy together, afterwards . . .

I made my way back down into the club, looking for Aimee. Yes, I knew her. Professional good-time girl, living off Daddy's money, go with anyone, do anything, in the pursuit of the next big thing, the next big thrill. I'd supplied her with various items from time to time. Never stung her so badly she noticed. She had no reason to be frightened of me. I found her outside the ladies' toilet, chatting loudly with other bright, young, mindless things, who would laugh and chatter and enjoy her company right up to the point where her credit ran out. Aimee would always pick up the tab, as long as you could keep up with her. She smiled and waved at me as I moved in on her. She clearly hadn't got the word on me yet. She was drunk. Her eyes were bright but vague, and her lipstick was smeared.

"Harry, darling!" she squealed, throwing her arms around me and kissing the air somewhere near my cheek. "Have you brought me something new, something special? I've tried absolutely everything here, and I'm bored out of my mind. Harry always has the good stuff," she confided to her circle, who stared silently at me with cold, jealous eyes. "What have you brought me this time, you lovely man?"

"Not here," I said. "This isn't something I can give to anyone. It needs privacy. Come into the toilet, and I'll show you what I have for you."

She giggled and tripped unsteadily into the toilet on her high stilettos. I followed her in and checked out the room, all tiles and subdued lighting. A couple were having noisy sex in one of the cubicles, and a woman had passed out cold on the floor with her dress still hiked up around her hips, but otherwise we had the place to ourselves. Aimee pawed at my chest with her soft little hands, pouting and making kittenish noises. I drew the slim silver blade I keep for backup, and stuck it between her ribs. She squeaked once in surprise, and grabbed me by the shoulders. I twisted the blade, and all the strength went out of her legs. I helped lower her to the floor and held her in my arms till she died. There was a lot of blood. I emptied the black centipede dust out onto the floor and used the vial to hold some of her blood. I laid Aimee out on the floor and crossed her hands respectfully over her breasts. I stood up and looked down at her.

It helped that I'd never liked Aimee much.

There was blood on my clothes, but that was nothing new in Heaven's Doorway. No-one even glanced at me. I went back up the stairs to the secret room on the next floor. My hands were shaking. I'd never had to kill anyone before. But it wasn't as though I'd done it for myself. No. It was all for my angel. My lovely angel.

Back in the room, she looked at the blood on my clothes and smiled, like a child anticipating a present.

Did you kill her, Harry? Did you murder her for me?

"Yes," I said. My voice was dry and flat, even as my heart

leapt in my chest from seeing her again. "I'm here, to set you free."

I uncorked the vial and spilled Aimee's blood over the glowing red lines of the pentagram. Nothing happened. Nothing at all. I looked back at my lovely angel, confused, and she laughed at me. She dipped a finger into the blood, and sucked it off her finger like a child with a treat. And just like that, she wasn't beautiful any more. It slipped away from her like the illusion it had always been, and now what crouched inside the pentagram didn't even look human any more. It had a humanoid shape, with dark, membranous wings, but it reeked of otherness, like the huge spider you see scuttling across your bedroom floor. Flames leapt up in its eye-sockets, and its grinning mouth was full of needle teeth.

I should have remembered; there's more than one kind of angel.

That's right, Harry, it said, in a voice like spoiled meat, like the death of innocence or the torture of a loved one. *I'm a fallen angel, and you've made a very bad mistake. They summoned me up from Hell and bound me with these wards, but do you really think mere mortals could hold me here, against Hell's wishes? I'm here because I chose to be. Because it gives me so many opportunities to do what I do best, tempting fools like you and watching you fall. Aimee never had a baby or offered one up for sacrifice. You've mur-dered a relatively innocent young woman, Harry, and damned your soul to the Inferno, forever and ever and ever.* It laughed at me. *My work here is done. You can go now, Harry.*

I stood there, numb. Couldn't think where to go, what to do. "Trying to help you was the only half-way-decent thing I've done in years," I said finally. "I should have remembered; no good deed goes unpunished, in the Nightside."

Bye-bye, Harry. See you . . . eventually.

I stumbled out of the room, followed by the fallen angel's mocking laughter. I lurched through the packed club, blindly shoving people out of my way, ignoring their threats and curses. None of that mattered any more. *Damned, for all time.* I hadn't tried to set the angel free because it was the right thing to do. I did it because I wanted her. Conned, like any other mark. I was tempted, and I fell, brought low by my own desires. You might say that's the human condition—to be tempted by a pretty face. Or an apple.

Some of these cons go way back.

THE SPIRIT
OF THE THING

In the Nightside, that secret hidden heart of London, where it's always the darkest part of the night and the dawn never comes, you can find some of the best and worst bars in the world. There are places that will serve you liquid moonlight in a tall glass, or angel's tears, or a wine that was old when Rome was young. And then, there's the Jolly Cripple. You get to one of the worst bars in the world by walking down the kind of alley you'd normally have the sense to stay out of. Tucked away behind more respectable establishments, light from the street doesn't penetrate far. It's always half-full of junk and garbage, and the only reason there aren't any bodies to step over is because the rats have eaten them all. You have to watch out for rats in the Nightside; some people say they're evolving. In fact, some people claim to have seen the damn things using knives and forks.

I wouldn't normally be seen dead in a dive like the Jolly Cripple, but I was working. At the time, I was between clients and in need of some fast walking-around money, so when the bar's owner got word to me that there was quick and easy money to be made, I swallowed my pride. I'm John Taylor, private investigator. I have a gift for finding things and people. I always find the truth for my clients, even if it means having to walk into places where even angels would wince and turn their head aside.

The Jolly Cripple was a drinker's bar. Not a place for conversation or companionship. More the kind of place you go when the world has kicked you out, your credit's no good, and your stomach can't handle the good stuff any more, even if you could afford it. In the Jolly Cripple, the floor was sticky, the air was thick with half a dozen kinds of smoke, and the only thing you could be sure of was vomit in the corners and piss and blood in the toilets. The owner kept the lights down low, partly so you couldn't see how bad the place really was but mostly because the patrons preferred it that way.

The owner and bartender was one Maxie Eliopoulos. A sleazy soul in an unwashed body, dark and hairy, always smiling. Maxie wore a grimy T-shirt with the legend IT'S ALL GREEK TO ME, and showed off its various blood-stains like badges of honour. No-one ever gave Maxie any trouble in his bar. Or at least, not twice. He was short and squat, with broad shoulders and a square, brutal face under a shock of black hair. More dark hair covered his bare arms, hands, and knuckles. He never stopped smiling, but it never once reached his eyes. Maxie was always ready to sell you anything you could afford. Especially if it was bad for you.

Some people said he only served people drink so he could watch them die by inches.

Maxie hired me to find out who'd been diluting his drinks and driving his customers away. (The only thing that could.) Didn't take me long to find out who. I sat down at the bar, raised my gift, and concentrated on the sample bottle of what should have been gin but was now so watered down you could have kept goldfish in it. My mind leapt up and out, following the connection between the water and its source, right back to where it came from. My Sight shot down through the barroom floor, down and down, into the sewers below.

Long, stone tunnels with curving walls, illuminated by phosphorescent moss and fungi, channelling thick, dark water with things floating in it. All kinds of things. In the Nightside's sewers, even trained workers tread carefully, and often carry flame-throwers, just in case. I looked around me, my Sight searching for the presence I'd felt; and something looked back. Something knew I was there, even if only in spirit. The murky waters churned and heaved, then a great head rose out of the dark water, followed by a body. It only took me a moment to realise both head and body were made up of water, and nothing else.

The face was broad and unlovely, the body obscenely female, like one of those ancient fertility-goddess statues. Thick rivulets of water ran down her face like slow tears, and ripples bulged constantly around her body. A water elemental. I'd heard the Nightside had been using them to clean up the sewers, taking in all the bad stuff and purifying it inside themselves. The Nightside always finds cheap and practical ways to solve its problems, even if they aren't always very nice solutions.

"Who disturbs me?" said the sewer elemental, in a thick, glutinous voice.

"John Taylor," I said. Back in the bar, my lips were moving, but my words could only be heard down in the sewer. "You've been interfering with one of the bars above. Using your power to infuse the bottles with your water. You know you're not supposed to get involved with the world above."

"I am old," said the elemental of the sewers. "So old, even I don't remember how old I am. I was worshipped, once. But the world changed, and I could not, so even the once worshipped and adored must work for a living. I have fallen very far from what I was; but then, that's the Nightside for you.

Now I deal in shit and piss and other things and make them pure again. Because someone has to. It's a living. But, fallen as I am . . . No-one insults me, defies me, cheats me! I serve all the bars in this area, and the owners and I have come to an understanding . . . all but Maxie Eliopoulos! He refuses my reasonable demands!"

"Oh hell," I said. "It's a labour dispute. What are you asking for? Better working conditions?"

"I want him to clean up his act," said the elemental of the sewers. "And if he won't, I'll do it for him. I can do a lot worse to him than dilute his filthy drinks . . ."

"That is between you and him," I said firmly. "I don't do arbitration." And then I got the hell out of there.

Back in the bar and in my body, I confronted Maxie. "You didn't tell me this was a dispute between contractors, Maxie."

He laughed and slapped one great palm hard against his grimy bar top. "I knew it! I knew it was that water bitch, down in her sewers! I needed you to confirm it, Taylor."

"So why's she mad at you? Apart from the fact that you're a loathsome, disgusting individual."

He laughed again and poured me a drink of what passed for the good stuff in his bar. "She wants me to serve better booze, says the impurities in the stuff I sell is polluting her system and leaving a nasty taste in her mouth. I could leave a nasty taste in her mouth, heh heh heh . . . She pressured all the other bars, and they gave in, but not me. Not me! No-one tells Maxie Eliopoulos what to do in his own bar! Silly cow . . . Cheap and nasty is what my customers want, so cheap and nasty is what they get."

"So . . . for a while there, your patrons were drinking booze mixed with sewer water," I said. "I'm surprised so many stayed."

"I'm surprised so many of them noticed," said Maxie. "Good thing I never drink the tap-water . . . All right,

Taylor, you've confirmed what I needed to know. I'll take it from here. I can handle her. Thinks I can't get to her, down in the sewers, but I'll show that bitch. No-one messes with me and gets away with it. Now, here's what we agreed on."

He pushed a thin stack of grubby bank-notes across the bar, and I counted them quickly before making them disappear about my person. You don't want to attract attention in a bar like the Jolly Cripple. Maxie grinned at me in what he thought was an ingratiating way.

"No need to rush away, Taylor. Have another drink. Drinks are on the house for you; make yourself at home."

I should have left. I should have known better . . . but it was one of the few places my creditors wouldn't look for me, and besides . . . the drinks were on the house.

I sat at a table in the corner, working my way through a bottle of the kind of tequila that doesn't have a worm in it because the tequila's strong enough to dissolve the worm. A woman in a long white dress walked up to my table. I didn't pay her much attention at first, except to wonder what someone so normal-looking was doing in a dive like this . . . and then she walked right through the table next to me, and the people sitting around it. She drifted through them as though they weren't even there, and each of them in turn shuddered briefly and paid closer attention to their drinks. Their attitude said it all; they'd seen the woman in white before, and they didn't want to know. She stopped before me, looking at me with cool, quiet, desperate eyes.

"You have to help me. I've been murdered. I need you to find out who killed me."

That's what comes from hanging around in strange bars. I gestured for her to sit down opposite me, and she did so perfectly easily. She still remembered what it felt like to have a body, which meant she hadn't been dead long. I looked her over carefully. I couldn't see any obvious death wounds, not even a ligature round her neck. Most murdered ghosts appear the way they were when they died. The trauma overrides everything else.

"What makes you think you were murdered?" I said bluntly.

"Because there's a hole in my memory," she said. "I don't remember coming here, don't remember dying here; but now I'm a ghost, and I can't leave this bar. Something prevents me. Something must be put right; I can feel it. Help me, please. Don't leave me like this."

I always was a sucker for a sob story. Comes with the job, and the territory. She had no way of paying me, and I normally avoid charity work . . . But I'd just been paid, and I had nothing else to do, so I nodded briefly and considered the problem. It's a wonder there aren't more ghosts in the Nightside, when you think about it. We've got every other kind of supernatural phenomenon you can think of, and there's never any shortage of the suddenly deceased. Anyone with the Sight can see ghosts, from stone tape recordings, where moments from the Past imprint themselves on their surroundings, endlessly repeating, like insects trapped in amber . . . to lost souls, damned to wander the world through tragic misdeeds or unfinished business.

There are very few hauntings in the Nightside, as such. The atmosphere here is so saturated with magic and super-science and general weird business that they swamp and drown out all the lesser signals. Though there are always a few stubborn souls, who won't be told. Like Long John Baldwin, who drank himself to death in my usual bar, Strangefellows. Dropped stone-dead while raising one last glass of Valhalla Venom to his lips, and hit the floor with the smile still on his face. The bar's owner, Alex Morrisey, had the body removed, but even before the funeral was over, Long John was back in his familiar place at the bar, calling for a fresh bottle. Half a dozen unsuccessful exorcisms later, Alex gave up and hired Long John as his replacement bartender and security guard.

Long John drinks the memories of old booze from empty bottles and enjoys the company of his fellow drinkers, as he always did. (They're a hardened bunch, in Strangefellows.) And, as Alex says, a ghost is more intelligent than a watchdog or a security system, and a lot cheaper to run.

I could feel a subtle tension on the air, a wrongness, as though there was a reason why the ghost shouldn't be there. She was an unusually strong manifestation—no transparency, no fraying around the edges. That usually meant a strong character when she was alive. She didn't flinch as I looked her over thoughtfully. She was a tall, slender brunette, with neatly styled hair and under-stated make-up, in a long white dress of such ostentatious simplicity that it had to have cost a bundle.

"Do you know your name?" I said finally.

"Holly De Lint."

"And what's a nice girl like you doing in a dive like this?"

"I don't know. Normally, I wouldn't be seen dead in a place like this."

We both smiled slightly. "Could someone have brought you here, Holly? Could that person have . . ."

"Murdered me? Perhaps. But who would I know in a place like this?"

She had a point. A woman like her didn't belong here. So I left her sitting at my table and made my rounds of the bar, politely interrogating the regulars. Most of them didn't feel like talking, but I'm John Taylor. I have a reputation. Not a very nice one, but it means people will talk to me when they wouldn't talk to anyone else. They didn't know Holly. They didn't know anything. They hadn't seen anything because they didn't come to a bar like this to take an interest in other people's problems. And they genuinely might not have noticed a ghost. One of the side effects of too much booze is that it shuts down the Sight, though you can still end up seeing things that aren't there.

I went back to Holly, still sitting patiently at the table. I sat down opposite her, and used my gift to find out what had happened in her recent past. Faint pastel images of Holly appeared all around the bar, blinking on and off, from where she'd tried to talk to people, or begged for help, or tried to leave and been thrown back. I concentrated, sorting through the various images until I found the memory of the last thing she'd done while still alive. I got up from the table and followed the last trace of the living Holly all the way to the back of the bar, to the toilets. She went into the ladies', and I went in after her. Luckily, there was no-one else there, then or now, so I could watch uninterrupted as Holly De Lint opened a cubicle, sat down, then washed down a big handful of pills with most of a bottle of whiskey. She went about it quite methodically, with no tears or hysterics, her face cold and even indifferent though her eyes still seemed terribly sad. She killed herself, with pills and booze. The last image showed her slumping slowly sideways, the bottle slipping from her numbed fingers, as the last of the light went out of her eyes.

I went back into the bar and sat down again opposite Holly. She looked at me inquiringly, trustingly. So what could I do except tell her the truth?

"There was no murderer, Holly. You took your own life. Can you tell me why . . ."

But she was gone. Disappeared in a moment, blinking out of existence like a punctured soap-bubble. No sign to show that anyone had ever been sitting there.

So I went back to the bar and told Maxie what had happened, and he laughed in my face.

"You should have talked to me first, Taylor! I could have told you all about her. You aren't the first stranger she's approached. Look, you know the old urban legend, where the guy's driving along, minding his own business, and sees a woman in white signalling desperately from the side of the road? He's a good guy, so he stops and asks what's up. She says she needs a lift home, so he takes her where she wants to go. But the woman doesn't say a word, all through the drive, and when he finally gets there, she's disappeared. The guy at the address tells the driver the woman was killed out there on the road long ago, but she keeps stopping drivers, asking them to take her home. Old story, right? It's the same here, except our woman in white keeps telling people that she's been murdered but doesn't remember how. And when our good Samaritans find out the truth and tell her, she disappears. Until the next sucker comes along. You ready for another drink?"

"Can't you do something?" I said.

"I've tried all the usual shit," said Maxie. "But she's a hard one to shift. You think you could do something? That little bitch is seriously bad for business."

I went back to my table in the corner to do some hard thinking. Most people would walk away on discovering the ghost was nothing more than a repeating cycle . . . But I'm not most people. I couldn't bear to think of Holly trapped in this place, maybe forever.

Why would a woman, with apparently everything to live for, kill herself in a dive like this? I raised my gift, and once again pastel-tinted semi-transparent images of the living Holly darted back and forth through the dimly lit bar, lighting briefly at this table and that, like a flower fairy at midnight. It didn't take me long to realise there was one table she visited more than most. So I went over to the people sitting there and made them tell me everything they knew.

Professor Hartnell was a grey-haired old gentleman in a battered city suit. He used to be somebody, but he couldn't remember who. Igor was a shaven-headed kobold with more piercings than most who'd run away from the German mines of his people to see the world. He didn't think much of the world, but he couldn't go back, so he settled in the Nightside. Where no-one gave a damn he was gay. The third drinker was a battered old Russian, betrayed by the Revolution but appalled at what his country had become. No-one mentioned the ice-pick sticking out the back of his head.

They didn't know Holly, as such, but they knew who she'd come here after. She came to the Jolly Cripple to save someone. Someone who didn't want to be saved. Her brother, Craig De Lint. He drank himself to death, right here in the bar, right at their table. Sometimes in their company, more often not, because the only company he was interested in came in a bottle. I used my gift again and managed to pull up a few ghost images from the Past, of the living Craig. Stick thin, shabby clothes, the bones standing out in his grey face. Dead, dead eyes.

"You're wasting your time, sis," Craig De Lint said patiently. "You know I don't have any reason to drink. No great trauma, no terrible loss . . . I like to drink, and I don't care about anything else. Started out in all the best places and worked my way down to this. Where someone like me belongs. Go home, sis. You don't belong here. Go home. Before something bad happens to you."

"I can't leave you here! There must be something I can do!"

"And that's the difference between us, sis, right there. You always think there's something that can be done. But I know a lost cause when I am one."

The scene shifted abruptly, and there was Holly at the bar, arguing furiously with Maxie. He still smiled even as he said things that cut her like knives.

"Of course I encouraged your brother to drink, sweetie. That's my job. That's what he was here for. And no, I don't give a damn that he's dead. He was dying when he walked in here, by his own choice; I only helped him on his way. Now either buy a drink or get out of my face. I've got work to do."

"I'll have you shut down!" said Holly, her voice fierce now, her small hands clenched into fists.

He laughed in her face. "Like to see you try, sweetie. This is the Nightside, where everyone's free to go to Hell in their own way."

"I know people! Important people! Money talks, Maxie; and I've got far more of it than you have."

He smiled easily. "You've got balls, sweetie. Okay, let's talk. Over a drink."

"I don't drink."

"My bar, my rules. You want to talk with me, you drink with me."

Holly shrugged and turned away. Staring at the table where her brother died. Maxie poured two drinks from a bottle, then slipped a little something into Holly's glass. He watched, smiling, as Holly gulped the stuff down to get rid of it; and then he smiled even more widely as all the expression went out of her face.

"There, that's better," said Maxie. "Little miss rich bitch. Come into my bar, throwing your weight about, telling me what to do? I don't think so. Feeling a little more . . . suggestible, are you? Good, good . . . Such a shame about your brother. You must be sad, very sad. So sad, you want to end it all. So here's a big handful of helpful pills, and a bottle of booze. So you can put an end to yourself, out back, in the toilets. Bye-bye, sweetie. Don't make a mess."

The ghost images snapped off as the memory ended. I was so angry, I could hardly breathe. I got up from the table and stormed over to the bar. Maxie leaned forward to say something, and I grabbed two handfuls of his grubby T-shirt and hauled him right over his bar, so I could stick my face right into his. He had enough sense not to struggle.

"You knew," I said. "You knew all along! You made her kill herself!"

"I had no choice!" said Maxie, still smiling. "It was

self-defence! She was going to shut me down. And yeah, I knew all along. That's why I hired you! I knew you'd solve the elemental business right away, then stick around for the free drinks. I knew the ghost would approach you, and you'd get involved. I needed someone to get rid of her; and you always were a soft touch, Taylor."

I let him go. I didn't want to touch him any more. He backed away cautiously and sneered at me from a safe distance.

"You feel sorry for the bitch, help her on her way to the great Hereafter! You'll be doing her a favour, and me, too. I told you she was bad for business."

I turned my back on him and went back to the drinkers who'd known him best. And before any of them could even say anything, I focused my gift through them, through their memories of Craig, and reached out to him in a direction I knew but could not name. A door opened that hadn't been there before, and a great light spilled out into the bar. A fierce and unrelenting light, too bright for the living to look at directly. The drinkers in the bar should have winced away from it, used as they were to the permanent gloom; but something in the light touched them despite themselves, waking old memories, of what might have been.

And out of that light came Craig De Lint, walking free and easy. He reached out a hand, smiling kindly, and out of the gloom came the ghost of Holly De Lint, walking free and easy. She took his hand, and they smiled at each other, then Craig led her through the doorway and into the light; and the door shut behind them and was gone.

In the renewed gloom of the bar, Maxie hooted and howled with glee, slapping his heavy hand on the bar top in triumph. "Finally, free of the bitch! Free at last! Knew you had it in you, Taylor! Drinks on the house, people! On the house!"

And they all came stumbling up to the bar, already

forgetting what they might have seen in the light. Maxie busied himself serving them, and I considered him thoughtfully, from a distance. Maxie had murdered Holly, and got away with it, and used me to clean up after him, removing the only part of the business that still haunted him. So I raised my gift one last time and made contact with the elemental of the sewers, deep under the bar.

"Maxie will never agree to the deal you want," I said. "He likes things the way they are. But you might have better luck with a new owner. You put your sewer water into Maxie's bottles. There are other places you could put it."

"I take your meaning, John Taylor," said the elemental. "You're everything they say you are."

Maxie lurched suddenly behind his bar, flailing desperately about him as his lungs filled up with water. I turned my back on the drowning man and walked away. Though being me, I couldn't resist having the last word.

"Have one on me, Maxie."

HUNGRY HEART

The city of London has a hidden heart; a dark and secret place where gods and monsters go fist-fighting through alleyways, where wonders and marvels are two a penny, where everything and everyone is up for sale, and all your dreams can come true. Especially the ones where you wake up screaming. In London's Nightside it's always dark, always three o'clock in the morning, the hour that tries men's souls . . . and finds them wanting.

I was drinking wormwood brandy in the oldest bar in the world when the femme fatale walked in. The bar was quiet, or at least as quiet as it ever gets. A bunch of female ghouls out on a hen night were getting tipsy on Mother's Ruin and complaining about the quality of the finger buffet. Ghouls just want to have fun. A pair of Neanderthals had put away so many smart drinks they were practically evolving before my eyes. And four Emissaries from the Outer Dark were playing cutthroat bridge and cheating each other blind. Just another night at Strangefellows—until she walked in.

She came striding between the tables with her head held high, as though she owned the place, or at the very least was planning a hostile takeover. She slammed to a halt before my table, gave me a big smile, and let me look her over. A tall, slender platinum blonde, late teens, Little Black Dress . . . big eyes, big smile, industrial-strength makeup. Attractive enough, in an intimidating sort of way. An English rose with more than her fair share of thorns. She introduced herself in a light breathy voice and sat down opposite me without waiting to be asked. She tried her smile on me again. On anyone else, it would probably have worked.

"You're John Taylor, private investigator," she said briskly. "I'm Holly Wylde, and I'm a witch. My ex stole my heart. I want you to find it, and get it back for me."

Not the strangest thing I've ever been asked to find, but I felt obliged to raise an eyebrow.

"I'm being quite literal," she said. "All witches learn how to remove their hearts, and keep them safe and secure in some private place, so that no-one can ever fully kill us. As long as the heart stays safe, we always come back. Hardly sporting, I know, but if I believed in things like fair play I'd never have become a witch in the first place. My ex, bad cess to his diseased soul, used to be my mentor. Taught me all I know about magic, and rogered me breathless every evening at no extra cost. Gideon Brooks; perhaps you know the name?"

"No," I said. "Which is unusual. I know all the Major Players in the Nightside, all the real movers and shakers on the magical scene; but I don't know him."

She shrugged prettily. "When it comes to forbidden knowledge, Gideon is the reason why a lot of it is forbidden. A very powerful, very dangerous man, on the quiet. Anyway, I thought we were getting on splendidly. But when I decided I'd learned enough to leave Gideon and strike out on my own, he suddenly got all possessive on me. I thought we were just mentor and student, with benefits, but now he's all over me, declaring his undying love and how he can't live without me! Well. I was shocked, Mr. Taylor. I don't do emotional entanglements. Not at this stage in my career. I tried to be graceful about it, but there's only so many ways a girl can say 'No!' in a loud and carrying voice. So. After a while he calmed down, apologized, and said he was just worried about me. Which was fair enough. But then he persuaded me to hand over my heart, so he could place some heavy-duty protections on it, to keep me safe once I was out on my own. And like a fool, I believed him. He has my heart, Mr. Taylor, and he won't give it back! And whoever owns a witch's heart will always have power over her. I'll never be free of him."

She finally stopped for breath and gave me the big smile again, accompanied by the big, big eyes and a deep breath to show off her bosoms. I gave her a smile of my own, no more sincere than hers. For all her artless honesty and finishing-school accent, Holly was as phony as a banker's principles. All the time she'd been talking to me, her gaze had been darting all around the bar, hardly ever looking at me, and never making eye contact for more than a few seconds. Which is a pretty reliable sign that someone is lying to you. But that was okay; I'm used to clients lying to me, or at the very least being economical with the truth. My job is to find what the client asks for. The truth makes the job easier, but I can work around it if I have to.

"What kind of a witch are you, Holly?" I said. "Black, white, Wiccan, or gingerbread house?"

She bestowed a happy wink on me. "I never allow myself to be limited by other people's perceptions. I'm just a free spirit, Mr. Taylor; or at least I was, until I met Gideon Brooks. Nasty man. Say you'll help me. Pretty please."

"I'll help you," I said. "For one thousand pounds a day, plus expenses. And don't plead poverty. That dress you're wearing costs more than I make in a year. And don't get me started on the shoes."

She didn't even blink. Just slapped an envelope down on the table before me. When I opened it, a thousand pounds in cash stared back. I gave Holly my best professional smile and made the envelope disappear about my person. Never put temptation in other people's way, especially in a bar like Strangefellows, where they'll steal your gold fillings if you fall asleep with your mouth open. Holly leaned forward across the table to fix me with what she thought was a serious look.

"They say you have a special gift for finding things, Mr. Taylor; a magical inner eye that can See where everything is. But that won't help you find my heart. Gideon placed it inside a special protective rosewood box, called Heart's Ease. No-one can pierce the magics surrounding that box—and only Gideon can open it. And you won't be able to find him or his house, either. Gideon lives inside his own private pocket dimension that only connects with our world when he feels like it. I only saw him when he let his house appear, at various places throughout the Nightside. And I haven't seen him since he stole my heart." She looked me right in the eye while she told me this, so I accepted most of it as provisionally true.

She leaned back in her chair and gave me her big smile again. It really was quite impressive. She must have spent a lot of time practicing it in front of a mirror.

"I know: Find a missing heart, and a missing man, in a missing house. But if finding them were easy I wouldn't need you, would I, Mr. Taylor?"

She got up to leave. As entirely calm and composed as when she'd entered, despite her fascinating sob story.

"How will I find you?" I said.

"You won't, Mr. Taylor. I'll find you. Toodles."

She waggled her fingers at me in a genteel good-bye, and was off, striding away with a straight back, ignoring her surroundings as though they were unworthy of her. Which they probably were. Strangefellows isn't exactly elite, and you couldn't drive it upmarket with a whip and a chair. I sipped thoughtfully at my wormwood brandy for a while, and then strolled over to the long mahogany bar to have a quiet word with Strangefellows' owner, bartender, and long-time pain in the neck, Alex Morrisey. Alex only wears black because no-one has come up with a darker color, and he could gloom for the Olympics, with an honorable mention in existential angst. He started losing his hair while he was still in his early twenties, and I can't help feeling there's a connection. He was currently prodding the bar snacks with a stick, to see if they had any life left in them.

A bunch of spirits were hanging round the bar: shifting semitransparent shapes that blended in and out of each other as they drained the memories of old wines from long-empty bottles. Only Alex could sell the same bottle of wine several times over. I made the sign of the extremely cross at the spirits, and they drifted sulkily off down the bar so Alex and I could talk privately.

"Gideon Brooks," Alex said thoughtfully, after I'd filled him in on the necessary details. He cleaned a dirty glass with the same towel he used to mop up spills from the bartop, to give him time to think. "Not one of the big Names, but you know that as well as I do. Of course, the really powerful ones like to stay out of sight and under the radar. But the rosewood box, Heart's Ease . . . that name rings a bell. Some sort of priceless collectible; the kind that's worth so much it's rarely bought or sold, but more often prized from the dead fingers of its previous owner."

"Collectibles," I said. "Always more trouble than they're worth. And the Nightside is littered with those magic little shops that sell absolutely anything, no questions asked, and certainly no guarantees. Where the hell am I supposed to start?"

Alex smirked and slapped a cheap flyer down before me. ONCE AND FUTURE COLLECTIBLES, announced the ugly block lettering. I should have known. All kinds of rare and strange items turn up in the Nightside, from the past, the future, and any number of alternate earths. The jetsam and flotsam of the invisible world. And, this being the Nightside, there's always someone ready to make a profit out of it. The Once and Future Collectibles traveling show offered the largest selection of magical memorabilia and general weird shit to be found anywhere. Someone would know about the rosewood box. I made a note of the current address and looked up to find Alex grinning at me.

"You know who you need to talk to," he said. "The Queen of Hearts. She's bound to be there, and she knows everything there is to be known about heart-related collectibles. Big Bad Betty herself . . . I'm sure she'll be only too happy to renew your acquaintance . . ."

"Don't," I said. "The only good thing that woman ever taught me was to avoid mixing my drinks."

"I thought you made a lovely couple."

"You want a slap?"

I left Strangefellows and headed out into the narrow rain-slick streets of the Nightside. The night was bustling with people, and some things very definitely not people, all in hot-eyed pursuit of things that were bad for them. Hot neon burned to every side, and cool music wafted out of the open doors of the kind of clubs that never close; where you can put on the red shoes and dance till you bleed. Exotic smells from a hundred different cuisines, barkers at open doors shilling thrills so exotic they don't even have a name in polite company, and, of course, the twilight daughters, patrolling every street-corner; love for sale, or something very like it. You're never far from heaven or hell in the Nightside, though they're often the same place, under new management.

I was heading for the old Market Hall, where the Once and Future Collectibles were currently set up, when someone eased up alongside and made himself known to me. He was got up like a 1950s biker: all gleaming black leathers, polished steel chains, peaked leather cap, and an almost convincing Brando swagger. He couldn't have been more than sixteen, seventeen, with a corpse-pale face and thin colorless lips. His eyes were dark, his gaze hooded and malignant. He matched my pace exactly, his hands stuffed deep in the pockets of his leather jacket.

"The name's Gunboy," he said, in a calm, easy monotone, not even looking at me. "Mr. Sweetman wants to talk with you. Now."

"All lines busy," I said. "Call back later."

"When Mr. Sweetman wants to talk to someone, they talk to him."

"How nice for Mr. Sweetman. But when I don't want to talk to people, I have a tendency to push them off the pavement and let them go play with the traffic."

Gunboy took one hand out of his jacket pocket and pointed it at me, the fingers shaped like a child's imaginary gun. He let me have a good look at it, and then pointed the single extended finger at a row of blazing neon bulbs set above the door to a Long Pigge franchise. His hand barely moved, but one by one the bulbs exploded, sparks flying wildly on the night air. A large man in a blood-soaked white overall came hurrying out to complain, took one look at Gunboy, and went straight back in again. Gunboy blew imaginary smoke from his finger and then stuck it casually in my ribs. He wasn't smiling, and his dark gaze was hot and compelling.

"Conceptual guns," he said, his lips barely moving.

"Conceptual bullets. Real, because I believe they are. The power comes from me, and so do the dead bodies. Come with me, or I'll make real holes in you."

I considered him thoughtfully. Down the years, I've acquired several useful and really quite underhanded tricks for dealing with guns aimed in my direction, but they all depended on there being some kind of actual gun to deal with. So I gave Gunboy my best *I'm not in the least intimidated* smile, and allowed him to take me to his master. Gunboy was kind enough to put his hand back in his pocket as we walked along together. I'm not sure my pride would have survived otherwise.

Mr. Sweetman turned out to be staying at the Hotel des Heures: a very upmarket, very pricey establishment, where all the rooms were individually time-coded. Stay as long as you like in your room, and not one moment will have passed when you step outside again. The ultimate in assured privacy—as long as you keep your door locked. You could spend your whole life in one of those rooms—though don't ask me how they manage room service.

Gunboy guided me to the right room, performed a special knock on the door, waited for it to open, and then pushed me inside. The single finger prodding me in my back was enough to keep me moving. Mr. Sweetman was waiting for us. A very large Greek gentleman in a spotless white kaftan, he rose ponderously from an overstuffed chair and nodded easily to me. His head was shaved, he wore dark eye makeup, and he smiled only briefly as he gestured for me to take the chair opposite. We both sat down, looking each other over with open curiosity. Gunboy stayed by the door, his hands back in his jacket pockets, looking at nothing in particular.

"Mr. Taylor!" said Sweetman, in a rich, happy voice. "An honor, my dear sir, I do assure you! One bumps into so many living legends in the Nightside that it is a positive treat to encounter the real thing! I am Elias Sweetman, a man of large appetites, always hungry for more. You and I, sir, have business to discuss. To our mutual benefit, I hope. You may talk candidly here, Mr. Taylor; dear Gunboy will ensure that we are not interrupted."

Gunboy gave me a brief look, to indicate that I'd better behave myself, and then leaned back against the door. His eyes were immediately elsewhere, as he thought about whatever teenage thrill-killers think about. I was going to have to do something about Gunboy, for my pride's sake. I smiled easily at Sweetman while he arranged the folds of his kaftan for maximum comfort. He looked like a man who liked his comforts. He smiled on me like some favorite uncle who might bestow all manner of treats if he felt so inclined.

"Your reputation precedes you, Mr. Taylor, indeed it does, so let us not beat about the bush. You are currently in pursuit of a certain prize that I have a special interest in; the box, Mr. Taylor, the rosewood box. It has gone by many names, of course, inevitable for a treasure that has passed through so many hands down the centuries, but I believe you might know it as Heart's Ease."

"I know the name," I said, carefully noncommittal.

He let out a sharp bark of laughter. "I do admire a man who plays his cards close to his chest, indeed I do, Mr. Taylor! But there's no need to be bashful here. I have pursued the rosewood box for many years, through many lands in many worlds, disputing with equally serious collectors along the way, but now . . . the box has come to the Nightside. So here we all are. Yes . . . I must ask you, Mr. Taylor: what, precisely, is your interest in the box?"

I didn't see any good reason to conceal the truth, so I gave him the reader's-notes version of what Holly told me, concealing only her name. When I was finished, Sweetman gave his short bark of laughter again.

"Whatever the rosewood box may turn out to contain, Mr. Taylor, I can assure you it is most definitely not the heart of some unimportant little witch. No, no . . . the box contains a source of great power. A great man's heart, perhaps even a god's . . . Some say the box contains the preserved heart of the great old god Lud, the original foundation stone for London. Others say the box contains the missing heart of that terrible old sorcerer, Merlin Satanspawn. Or perhaps the heart of Nikola Tesla, the broken and bitter saint of twentieth-century science. No-one knows for sure; only that the box contains a power worth dying for. Or killing for . . . Certainly, the box has become so famous in its own right it has become a collectible in itself, whatever it might eventually prove to contain."

"So," I said, "a source of wealth, and possibly power. No wonder so many people want it."

"Passed from hand to hand down the years, acquiring blood and legends along the way, Mr. Taylor. Priceless because there isn't enough money in the world to buy it. You have to be man enough to take it, and hold on to it."

He was leaning forward now, licking his lips, his eyes gleaming. He was so close to what he'd chased for so long he could almost taste it, and only his need to be sure that he knew everything I knew kept him from harsher methods of interrogation. And since he had no way of knowing how little I did know, I made a point of leaning back in my chair and stretching easily.

"What do *you* think is in the rosewood box?" I said.

He leaned back in his chair and studied me thoughtfully, taking his time before answering. "I have been given good reason to believe that the box contains the heart of William Shakespeare, Mr. Taylor. The heart of England itself, some say."

"And what would you do with such a thing, once you got hold of it?"

Sweetman smiled widely. "I mean to eat it, Mr. Taylor! Only the rarest and most exquisite gastronomic experiences can arouse my jaded palate these days, and this particular delicacy should prove most satisfying . . . You have a gift for finding things, Mr. Taylor. Find the box for me. However much the little witch is paying you, I will double her offer."

"Sorry," I said. "But I have to be true to my clients."

"Even when they lie to you?"

"Perhaps especially then."

I got up to leave, and Sweetman immediately gestured to Gunboy at the door. He straightened up as I approached and brought one hand out of his leather jacket. I brought one hand out of my trench coat pocket, ripped open the sachet of coarse pepper I always keep with me, and threw the whole lot in his face. His head snapped back, startled, but it was already too late. He sneezed explosively, again and again, while shocked tears ran down his face from squeezed-shut eyes. He waved his finger back and forth, but it didn't worry me. With his nose and eyes full of pepper, there was no way Gunboy could concentrate enough to manifest his conceptual guns. Never leave home without condiments. Condiments are our friends. I easily sidestepped the weeping Gunboy and opened the door. I risked a quick look back, just in case Sweetman had his own hidden weapons, but he had lost all interest in me. He had his arm around Gunboy's shaking shoulders and was comforting him like a child. Or almost like a child.

I shut the door quietly behind me and left the Hotel des Heures. At least I hadn't wasted any time.

The old Market Hall is a great open barn of a place, and the Once and Future Collectibles traveling show filled it from wall to wall with hundreds of stalls, large and small, offering more rare and unusual memorabilia in one place than the human mind could comfortably accommodate. I strolled up and down the aisles, glancing casually at this stall and that, carefully not showing too much interest in anything. Not that there was anything particularly exceptional on offer . . . An old Betamax video of Elvis starring as Captain Marvel, in some other world's 1969 movie *Shazam!* One of Dracula's coffins, complete with original grave dirt and a certificate of authenticity. The mummified head of Alfredo Garcia, smelling strongly of Mexican spices. And the mirror of Dorian Gray.

I finally wandered over to the Queen of Hearts's stall, as though I just happened to be heading in her general direction. Big Bad Betty was running the whole thing on her own, as usual: large as life and twice as imposing. A good six feet tall and strongly built, she wore a stylized gypsy outfit, complete with an obviously fake wig of long dark curls and a hell of a lot of clanking bracelets up and down her meaty arms. The fingers of her large hands were covered in enough heavy metal rings to qualify as knuckle-dusters, and she looked like she'd have no hesitation in using them. She was attractive enough, in a large, dark, and even swarthy kind of way. I gave her my best ingratiating smile, and her baleful glare didn't alter one iota.

I pretended to look over the contents of her stall, to give her time to realize the scowl wasn't going to be enough to scare me off. Big Bad Betty liked to style herself the Queen of Hearts because she specialized in heart-related collectibles. She was currently offering the carefully preserved heart of Giacomo Casanova (bigger than you'd think), a phial of heart's blood from Varney the Vampyre, and a pack of playing cards that once belonged to Lewis Carroll, with all the hearts painted in dried blood. Nothing special . . .

"You've got some nerve showing your face here, John Taylor," Betty said finally.

"Just looking," I said easily. "I do like a good browse."

"I hired you to find my missing husband!"

"I did find him. Not my fault he'd had his memory wiped and didn't remember you any more. And not in any way my fault that he'd had his memory wiped to make sure he wouldn't be able to remember you. Maybe you should have tried counseling . . ."

She scowled at me. "You never called me afterward. Not once."

"That wasn't what you hired me for."

"What do you want here, Taylor? On the grounds that the sooner you're out of my sight, the better."

"What can you tell me about the rosewood box, called by some Heart's Ease?"

She couldn't resist telling me. She does so love to show off what she knows, and no-one knows more about hearts than the Queen of Hearts.

"The box is centuries old, supposedly first put together in pre-Revolutionary France, designed to contain the suffering of a brokenhearted lover. He put it all in the box, so he could be free of it. Hence the name, Heart's Ease. How very French. Though there are other stories . . . that what the box contains has become something else, down the centuries. Something . . . darker. Hungrier. Making the box the perfect container for all kinds of magical and significant hearts. Which is why the box has had so many other names. Heartbreaker, the Hungry Heart, the Dark Heart; you pays your money, and you believes what you chooses. Far as I know, no-one's dared open the box for years. Any collector with two working brain cells to bang together stays well clear of it.

"Now: Buy something, or get lost."

I nodded politely and moved away from her stall as quickly as possible without actually running. I'd got everything I needed from Betty, but I was still going to need a little specialized help if I was to find Gideon Brooks, his traveling house, and the rosewood box. So I concentrated and raised my special gift. My inner eye slowly opened, my third eye, my private eye; and I looked round the Market Hall with my raised Sight, searching for what I needed. A key that would unlock a traveling dimensional door. Something blazed up brightly, not too far away, glowing white-hot with mystical significance. I strode quickly down the aisles and finally stopped before a stall that offered nothing but keys, in all shapes and sizes. Skeleton keys to unlock any door, blessed silver keys to reveal hidden secrets, solid iron keys to undo chastity spells. Keys are very old symbols and can undo any number of symbolic magics.

One key stood out among all the ranks and rows of hanging keys, shining very brightly for my inner eye only. A simple brass key, marked with prehuman glyphs. I'd seen its kind before, in certain very restricted books. This was a summoning key, which could not only open any door, but actually bring the door to you. Just what I needed. Unfortunately, the key didn't have a price tag on it. And in a place like this, that could only mean that if you had to ask the price, you couldn't afford it. So, I used my gift to find the one moment when the stall-holder's attention was somewhere else, and I just reached out, took the key, and walked away.

I could always give it back later, when I was finished with it. When I found the time. The stall-holder really should have invested in some half-decent security spells.

I was heading casually for the nearest exit, the key tucked safely away in an inside pocket, when Holly Wylde appeared suddenly out of the crowd to block my way. She smiled at me winningly.

"I had a feeling you'd be here. And so you are! Aren't you glad to see me again?"

"I don't know," I said. "I do prefer my clients to tell me the truth, whenever possible."

"I didn't exactly lie," she said, pouting. "All right, yes, there's a lot about the rosewood box I didn't tell you, but I was pretty sure you'd find that out on your own, once you started looking. I didn't want to scare you off, after all; and I do so want my heart back! I just don't know what I'll do without it."

I sighed. It was hard to stay mad at her. Though probably worth the effort.

"Why would Gideon Brooks put your heart in such a precious and important box?"

"Because it was the only thing he had that he knew I couldn't get into," she said artlessly.

"And all you want is your heart back?" I said. "You don't care about the priceless and important box?"

"Well," she said, "if it should happen to fall into our hands, that would be a nice bonus. Wouldn't it?"

"You're batting your eyelashes at me again," I said. "Stop it."

"Sorry. Force of habit."

"Other people are looking for the box," I said, shifting onto what I hoped was safer ground. I told her about Sweetman and Gunboy, and she stamped her little foot and said a few baby swear words.

"The fat man and his toy boy; I knew they were sniffing around, but I didn't know they were this close. We have to get to Gideon before they do! All they care about is that box. They wouldn't care about my poor little heart."

"Sweetman seemed very sure the box holds some famous or important heart," I said.

"Might do. Who knows?" said Holly, shrugging easily. "Who knows how many hearts have ended up inside that box, down the years? I only care about mine. What are you doing here, anyway? Such a tacky place, all full of tat and kitsch. I can feel my street cred slipping away just for being here."

"I have acquired a useful little toy that will bring Gideon's door right to us," I said.

She squeaked excitedly and did a happy dance right in front of me. "Yes! Yes! I knew you wouldn't let me down!"

"I tell my clients everything," I said pointedly. "Are you sure there isn't something more you should be telling me?"

"I don't think so," said Holly Wylde, her wide eyes full of an entirely unconvincing innocence.

We left the Market Hall together, and I found a reasonably calm and quiet place to raise my gift again. I sent my Sight shooting up out of my head into the night sky, speckled with more stars than the outside world ever dreams of, and then looked down at the Nightside streets turning slowly beneath me. All around I could See the subtle flashes and occasional flare-ups of magical workings, and the more openly dramatic radiations and detonations of mad scientists at play. Giant wispy forms marched up and down the streets, passing through buildings as though they weren't even there; just the ancient Awful Folk, going about their unknowable business. All kinds of traffic thundered through the streets, carrying all kinds of goods and people, and never ever stopping. And some buildings just disappeared from view, coming and going, replaced by other buildings following their own inscrutable journeys.

Everyone knows a moving target is hardest to hit.

Down in my own person, I held the summoning key firmly in my hand and focused my gift through it; and immediately one particular building jumped out at me with extra significance, as the key locked on to the one special door I needed to find. The building hopped and skipped around the Nightside, appearing and disappearing apparently at random; but more like a fish on the end of a line now I had the summoning key. I chased Gideon Brooks up and down the Nightside, sticking close no matter how many times he tried to throw me off, my mind soaring impossibly fast from one location to another, invisible and undetectable, until finally Gideon Brooks just gave up, and his home settled down in one place and stayed put. It materialized right before me, presenting a quite unremarkable door, and squeezed into place between two perfectly respectable establishments, which rather grudgingly budged up to make room for it. I dropped back inside my head and released my hold on the summoning key. The door before me looked entirely unthreatening, but I checked it over with my Sight anyway, just in case. Heavy-duty protective magics crawled all over the door, and spat and sparkled on the air round the building.

I held up the key, muttered the proper activating Words, and unlocked all the protections, one by one. It took quite a while. Holly squeaked excitedly and clapped her little hands together.

And that was when Sweetman and Gunboy turned up. They were just suddenly there, strolling down the street toward us, Sweetman in his great white kaftan rolling along like a ship under full sail, Gunboy swaggering at his side like an attack dog on a short leash. Holly actually hissed at the sight of them, like an affronted cat, and moved quickly to stand behind me. I carefully shut down my Sight so I could concentrate on the matter at hand.

"My dear Mr. Taylor," said Sweetman, as he crashed to a halt before me. "Well done, sir, well done indeed! I knew I could rely on you to chase Gideon Brooks down, but I have to say, I never thought you'd be able to run his very special house to ground, too. You shouldn't look so surprised to see me, my good fellow, really you shouldn't. Dear Gunboy and I have been following you ever since you left the hotel."

"No you haven't," I said flatly. "I'd have noticed."

"Well, not personally following, as such," Sweetman agreed. "I took the liberty of slipping a small but very powerful tracking device into your coat pocket while you were preoccupied with poor Gunboy. The dear boy does make for such marvelous misdirection."

I looked at Gunboy. "And how do you feel, being used like that?"

He took one hand out of his pocket and pointed it at me. "I do what Mr. Sweetman says. And so will you."

"Are you going to let him talk to you like that?" said Holly, from behind me.

"As long as he's pointing that conceptual gun at me, yes," I said. "Mr. Sweetman, as I understand it, and I'm perfectly prepared to be told I don't, it's been that kind of a case . . . You want the rosewood box, and the very important heart you believe it contains. You are not, I take it, interested in this young lady's heart, also inside the box?"

Sweetman inclined his large head judiciously. "No offense, young lady, but I would have no interest in your heart under any conditions."

"For someone who didn't want to offend," said Holly, "I'd have to say you came pretty damned close."

"The point being," I said quickly, "that since we all want different things from Gideon Brooks, we don't have to be at each other's throat. We can work together to acquire the box, and then each take what we want from it."

"Are you crazy?" said Holly, hurrying out from behind me so she could glare at me properly. "Give up on the box?"

"You hired me to find your stolen heart," I said. "Or are you now saying the box is more important?"

"No," said Holly. "It's all about the heart." She looked at Gunboy. "We could use some serious firepower, if we're going up against Gideon Brooks."

Gunboy looked at Sweetman, and then put his hand back in his pocket.

"Don't sulk, boy," said Sweetman. "It's very unattractive."

I smiled around me. "I love it when a compromise comes together."

And then we all looked round sharply, as the door before us opened on its own. I felt a little disappointed that I wouldn't get to show off what I could do with my gift and the summoning key. We all stood looking at the open door for a long moment, but nothing menacing emerged, and there was only an impenetrable gloom beyond. We looked at each other, and then I led the way forward—if only because I didn't trust any of the others to react responsibly to anything unexpected. Sweetman and Gunboy fell in behind me, and Holly brought up the rear.

Beyond the door lay a simple, dimly lit hallway, with no obvious magical trappings. It could have been any house, anywhere. The door closed quietly behind us, once we'd all entered. The four of us pretty much filled the narrow hallway. A door to our left swung slowly open, and I led the way into the adjoining room. When in doubt, act confident. The room was open and warmly lit, with no furnishings or fittings; just bare wooden floorboards, and one very ordinary-looking, casually dressed middle-aged man, sitting on a chair surrounded by a great pentacle burned right into the floorboards. He was holding a simple wooden box in his hands; perhaps a foot long and half as wide.

The lines of the pentacle flared up abruptly as Sweetman approached them, and he stopped short. The lines shone with a fierce blue-white light, blazing with supernatural energies. Sweetman stepped carefully back and gestured to Gunboy, who smiled slowly as he took both hands out of his jacket pockets. And then he stopped, looked almost abjectly at Sweetman, and put his hands away again. Apparently conceptual guns were no match for older and more established magics.

I looked at Holly. She was staring unblinkingly at Gideon, but I couldn't read the expression on her face. She didn't look angry, or scared; just utterly focused on the box in his hands.

"You're a witch," I said to her quietly. "Can't you do anything?"

She scowled suddenly as she looked at Gideon. It might just have been the scowl, but she didn't look pretty any more. "If I could break his protections, I wouldn't have needed your help."

"You never did like having to depend on other people," the man on the chair said pleasantly. "And you really couldn't stand someone else having power over you, even when you came to them to learn the ways of magic. You were the best student I ever had, my dear—until you grew impatient, and tried to steal my secrets. And when that failed, you had to go looking for power in all sorts of unsuitable places." He looked at me. "Whatever she's told you, you can't trust it. She'll say anything, do anything, to get what she wants. She slept with demons so they'd teach her the magics I wouldn't, she stole grimoires and objects of power, and she would have stolen my heart . . . if I hadn't taken precautions."

"No-one tells me what to do," said Holly. "With your heart in my hands, you'd have taught me everything I wanted. And as for the demons, every single one of them was better in the sack than you."

Women always fight dirty.

"I kept my place moving so you couldn't find me," said Gideon. "I should have known you'd go to the infamous John Taylor, the man who can find anything. What did she tell you, Mr. Taylor? When she wasn't smiling her pretty smile at you?"

"She said you stole her heart," I said. "And put it in the rosewood box."

"Oh, Holly," said Gideon, and he actually laughed briefly. "It's *my* heart in the box, Mr. Taylor. I put it there after she tried to steal it. Because she couldn't stand the idea of anyone having a hold over her."

"So . . . you don't have any feelings for her?" I said, just to be sure.

"Ah," said Gideon. "I should have known that would be the heart of the matter, so to speak. Is that why you're here, Holly?"

"You never loved me!" said Holly. She stood directly before him, just outside the pentacle, both her small hands clenched into fists. "I did everything right, and you still never loved me!"

"You never loved anyone," Gideon said calmly. "You always loved power more. I was just your mentor."

Holly turned suddenly to me. "You believe me, don't you, John? You'll get the box for me. And then we can make him do anything we want!"

"Sorry," I said. "But I never believed you, Holly. You hired me to find the rosewood box. Well, there it is."

"She was the one who let word get out that I had the box," said Gideon. "So that avaricious men from all over would come looking for it, and she could set them against me. Just in case you didn't work out, Mr. Taylor. How does it feel, being used?"

I shrugged. "Comes with the job."

Gideon Brooks turned his attention to Sweetman and Gunboy. "It's really nothing more than a simple storage box, you know. Perhaps a little more famous than most. It may have contained any number of important or significant items, in its time, but the only heart it contains now is mine. Where Holly can't get at it."

Sweetman's brief bark of laughter held even less real humor than usual. "My dear sir, you don't really expect me to believe that? I have followed the box through unknown cities and blood-soaked streets, and I will have it. Gunboy, point those marvelous hands of yours at Mr. Taylor and the little witch. Now, Mr. Brooks. Give up the box, or everything my enthusiastic young associate does to these two young people will be your responsibility."

Holly looked at Gunboy, and then at Gideon. "You wouldn't really let him hurt me, would you, sweetie? You did say I was the best student you ever had . . ."

"I had students before you," said Gideon. "And there will be others after you. Though hopefully I'll choose a little more wisely next time. I am still quite fond of you, Holly, against all my better judgment. But not enough to put my heart at risk."

"What about me?" I said.

"What about you?" said Gideon.

"Fair enough," I said.

"Ah well," Holly said brightly. "Plan B." She turned her most charming smile on Gunboy and took a deep breath.

Sweetman chuckled. "Trust me, young lady; you have absolutely nothing that dear Gunboy desires."

"But he has something I want," said Holly. "I want his heart."

She made a sudden grasping gesture with one outstretched hand, and Gunboy screamed shrilly as his back arched and his chest exploded. His black leather jacket burst apart and the bare flesh beneath tore open, as his heart ripped itself from its bony setting and flew across the air to nestle into Holly's waiting hand. Blood ran thickly between her fingers as the heart continued to beat. Holly's pretty pink mouth moved in a brief moue of distaste, and then she closed her hand with sudden vicious strength, crushing the heart. Gunboy fell to the floor and lay still, eyes still staring in horror, his chest a bloody ruin. Sweetman let out a single cry of absolute pain and loss and knelt down beside Gunboy to cradle the dead body in his huge arms. Blood soaked his white kaftan as he rocked Gunboy back and forth, like a sleeping child. Silent tears ran down Sweetman's face.

"So," I said to Holly. "That's the kind of witch you are."

She dropped the crushed heart to the floor and flicked blood from her pale fingers. She smiled at me sweetly. "I'm the kind of witch you don't want to disappoint. I did tell you Gideon dealt in forbidden knowledge, and I was such a good listener. Now be a good boy, and go get the box for me. You can find a way past Gideon's defenses. It's what you do."

"Yes," I said. "But there's a limit to what I'll do."

She gave me a cold measuring look, and I met her gaze unflinchingly. Never let them see fear in your eyes.

"I bought your services, for a thousand pounds a day," Holly said finally. "And the day isn't over yet."

"I found the box for you," I said. "Not my fault your heart isn't in it. Still, after all my investigations, I probably know more about the box than you do. It was originally made to contain all the pain and horror of a man's broken heart; and it's still in there. Trapped inside the box for centuries, growing stronger and more frustrated. It's been alone so long, it must be very hungry for company by now. You may know the box as Heart's Ease, and perhaps it was, originally; but it has another name now. The Hungry Heart."

I raised my gift, found my way past Gideon's protections, and used my gift and the key to unlock the rosewood box. The lid snapped open, and the Hungry Heart within reached out and grabbed Holly and pulled her inside, all in a moment. It might have taken me, too, if Gideon hadn't immediately forced the lid closed again. We looked at each other, in the suddenly quiet room.

"She wanted my heart," said Gideon. "Now she can keep it company . . . forever."

Sweetman looked up, still cradling the dead Gunboy. "What is that . . . What's really inside the box?"

"The stuff that screams are made of," I said.

HOW DO YOU FEEL?

It's not easy having a sex life when you're dead.

I was sitting at the bar in Strangefellows, the oldest pub, night-club, and supernatural drinking hole in the world, smoking and drinking and popping my special pills . . . Trying to feel something, anything at all. I don't need to drink or eat, any more than I need to breathe, but I like to pretend. It makes being dead easier to bear. Without my special pills and potions, I don't feel much of anything. And even with the pills, only the most extreme sensations can affect me.

So I drank the most expensive Napoleonic brandy, and smoked a thick Turkish cigar threaded with opium, and still all I felt was the barest shadows of sensation, pinpoints of pleasure flaring briefly in my mouth, like stars going out. I was on the last of my pills, and my body was shutting down again.

I looked at myself in the long mirror behind the bar; and

Dead Boy looked back at me. Tall and adolescent thin, wrapped in a heavy, deep purple greatcoat with a black rose at the lapel, over black leather trousers and calf-skin boots; the coat hung open to show a pale grey torso, pock-marked with bullet-holes and other wounds, old scar tissue and accumulated damage. Including the Y-shaped autopsy scar. Stitches, staples, superglue, and the odd length of black duct tape, held everything together. A large, floppy hat, crushed down over thick, curly black hair. A pale face, dark, fever-bright eyes, and a colourless mouth set in a flat, grim line.

Dead Boy.

I toasted myself with the brandy bottle. I like brandy. It doesn't mess about, and it gets the job done. With the pills to push it along, I can almost get drunk; and, of course, I never have to worry about hangovers. I indulge my senses as much as I can, for fear of losing them. I sometimes wonder whether my human emotions might start to fade, too, if I didn't remember to exercise them frequently. I may be dead; but there's life in the old carcass yet.

I put my back to the unpolished wooden bar and looked around me. The place was packed, and the crowd was jumping. All the flotsam and jetsam of the Nightside, that dark and magical hidden heart of London, where the night people come out to play. Lost souls and abandoned dreamers, gods and monsters, golden boys and red-lipped girls, all of them hot in pursuit of pleasures that might not have a name but most certainly have a price.

It seemed like there were lovers everywhere that night, and I looked on them all with simple envy, jealous of the everyday joys I could never experience. A young man sat smiling happily while a female vampire chewed hungrily on the mess she'd made of his neck. If he could see past her glamour, and see her as I saw her, he wouldn't be smiling so easily. Any vampire is just a corpse that's dug its way up out of its grave to feast on the living.

Not far away, a couple of deeply butch ghouls in bondage gear snarled happily at each other over a finger buffet, playfully snapping at each other's faces with their sharp, sharp teeth. Two lesbian undines were drinking each other with straws and giggling tipsily as their water levels rose and fell. And a very ordinary young couple, with Tourist written all over them, were drinking a glass of something expensive through two heart-shaped straws, lost in each other's eyes.

Young love, in the Nightside. I wanted to shout at them, to tell all of them: do something, do everything, while you still can . . . Because at any time, any one of you can be snatched away. And then it's too late to do and say all the things you meant to say and do.

Off to one side, my gaze fell upon an off-duty rent-a-cop, still wearing his gaudy private uniform. Huge and stocky, he'd clearly been using knock-off Hyde extract to bulk up his muscles. He was having a good time yelling at his girl, a slender, blonde, upper-class, up-herself, business-woman type. She finally shook her head firmly, and the Hyde slapped her. A casual blow, but more than enough to wrench her head right round and send blood flying from her mouth and nose.

The Hyde looked around, daring anyone to say anything; and then his gaze fell upon me.

"What are you looking at, corpse face?"

I wasn't going to get involved. I really wasn't. But there are limits.

I got up and strolled over to his table. People and others hurried to get out of my way, and a kind of hush fell over the bar. Followed almost immediately by an expectant buzz, as everyone started placing bets. The Hyde looked uneasily around him. He was new here. But he still should have known better. I stood over the Hyde and smiled slowly at him.

"Say you're sorry," I said. "Doesn't matter what for. Say you're sorry, and you can still walk away."

The Hyde lurched to his feet. His size made him awkward. He snarled some pointless obscenity at me and punched me in the head. The blow had a lot of weight behind it, but not enough to move my head more than an inch. There was a sound like a fist hitting a brick wall, and the Hyde yelled in surprise as he hurt his hand. I sneered at him.

"You'll have to do better than that if you want me to feel anything."

The Hyde hurled himself at me, hitting me again and again with fists the size of mauls. I let him do it for a while, to see if he could hurt me. When you're dead, one sensation is as good as another. But the pills were wearing off, and the blows were as distant to me as the sounds they made, and soon enough, I got bored. So I hit him, with my dead hands and my dead strength, and he started screaming. His bones broke, and his flesh tore, and blood flew thickly on the smoke-filled air. We crashed back and forth among the nearby tables, and other fights sprang up along the way. With cries of *You spilled my drink!* and *You're breathing my air!* the bar regulars cheerfully went to war with each other. Chairs and bodies flew through the air, and all through Strangefellows, there was the happy sound of fisticuffs and people venting.

And behind me, I could hear the Hyde's girl screaming at me *Please! Don't hurt him!* Which was typical.

The Hyde hung limply from my blood-soaked hands. I shook him a few times to see if there was any life left in him, then lost interest. I dropped him carelessly to the floor and went back to my seat at the bar. The business woman crouched, crying, over the broken Hyde. You can't help some people. The bar fight carried on without me. I couldn't be bothered to join in. It's hard to work up the enthusiasm when you can't feel pain or take real damage.

I drank some more brandy, and it might as well have been tap-water. I drew cigar-smoke deep into my lungs, and they didn't even twitch. The pills' effects never last long. Which is why I always make a point of enjoying what I can, when I can. I was getting ready to leave when Walker came strolling casually through the bar towards me. Walker, in his smart city suit and his old-school tie, his bowler hat, and his furled umbrella. The Voice of the Authorities, those grey, background figures who run the Nightside, inasmuch as anyone does or cares to. Walker moved easily through the various fights, and not a single hand came close to touching him. Even in the heat of battle, everyone there had enough sense not to upset Walker. He strode right up to me and smiled briefly; and if my heart could have sunk, it would. Whenever Walker deigns to take an interest in you, it's always going to mean trouble.

"Dead Boy," he said, perfectly calmly. "You're looking . . . very yourself. But then, you haven't changed one little bit since you were murdered here in the Nightside, more than thirty years ago. Only seventeen years old, mugged in the street for your credit cards and the spare change in your pockets. Left to bleed out in the gutter, and no-one even stopped to look; but then, that's the Nightside for you. Very sad.

"Except, you made a deal, to come back from the dead to avenge your murder. You've never said exactly who you made this deal with . . . It wasn't the Devil. I'd know. But anyway, you should have read the small print. You rose from your autopsy slab and went out into the night, tracked down and killed your killers. Very messily, from what I hear. So far, so good; but there was nothing in the deal you made about getting to lie down again afterwards. You were trapped in your own dead body. And so it's gone, for more than thirty years. Have I missed anything important?"

Walker does so love to show off. He knows everything, or at least everything that matters. In fact, I think that's part of his job description.

"I killed the men who killed me," I said. "They didn't rise again. And after all the terrible things I did to them, before I let them die, Hell must have come as a relief."

"Well, quite," said Walker. "Except . . . they weren't your everyday muggers. Your death was no accident. Someone paid those three young thugs to kill you." He smiled again, briefly. "You really should have taken the time to question them before you killed them."

I just stared at him. It had never even occurred to me that there had been anything more to my death than . . . being in the wrong place at the wrong time.

"Who?" I said, and my voice sounded more than usually cold, even to me. "Who hired them to kill me?"

"A man called Krauss," said Walker. "Very big in hired muscle, back in the day. You'll find him at the Literary Auction House, right now. If you hurry."

"Why?" I said. "Why would anyone have wanted me dead? I wasn't anyone back then."

"If you're quick, you can ask him," said Walker.

"Why are you telling me this?" I asked him, honestly curious.

He gave me his brief, meaningless smile again. "You can owe me one."

He tipped his bowler hat to me, turned away, and looked at the mass of heaving, fighting bodies before him, blocking his way to the exit. They were all well into it now, too preoccupied with smiting the enemy to pay attention to Walker. So he raised his Voice and said, *Stop that. Right now.* And they did. The Authorities had given Walker a Voice that could not be denied. There are those who say he once made a corpse sit up on its slab to answer his questions. Everyone stood very still as Walker strolled unhurriedly through them and left.

And then everyone looked around and tried to remember what it was they'd been fighting about.

I sat at the bar, pondering the nature of my dead existence and my past. I'd been dead a lot longer than I'd been alive, and it was getting harder to remember what being alive had been like. To have a future, and a purpose, instead of going through the motions, filling in the time. Had it really been more than thirty years since anyone had said or even known my real name? Thirty years of being Dead Boy? I'd never made any attempt to contact my family or friends. It wouldn't have been fair on them. They all thought I was dead and departed; and they were only half-right.

I came to the Nightside looking for something different; and I found it, oh yes.

It's hard for me to feel anything much, being dead . . . But with the right mix of these amazing pills and potions I have made up for me specially, by this marvellous old Obeah woman, Mother Macabre, voodoo witch . . . my dead senses can be fooled into experiencing all the sweet moments of life. I can taste the spiciest foods and savour the finest wines, ride the lightning of the strongest and foulest drugs, and never have to pay the price.

I even have a girl-friend.

I do still feel emotions. Sometimes. They are what make me feel most alive, when I can be prodded into experiencing them. Good or bad, it makes no difference. I savour them all, when I can. And avenging old hurts is still at the top of the list of the things that make me feel most alive.

There was music playing in the bar, clear again now the sounds of battle had died away, but it was all noise to me. I can't appreciate music any more; and I do miss it. I have to wonder what else I've lost that I haven't even noticed. I don't shave, or cut my fingernails, or my hair. I had heard they go on growing after you're dead, but that turned out not to be the case. I wear brightly coloured clothes to compensate for my dead look, and I act large because I've lost my capacity for subtlety. I go on though I often wonder why.

I left the bar, walking unconcerned and untouched through the still-touchy crowd. Everyone gave me plenty of room, and many made the sign of the cross, and other signs, to ward off evil. I do try to be good company, but my people skills aren't what they were. I made my way out onto the street, and there waiting for me was my very own brightly gleaming, highly futuristic, car. A long, sleek, steel-and-silver bullet, hovering above the ground on powerful energy fields because it was far too grand to bother with old-fashioned things like wheels or gravity.

The door opened, and I got in. I announced our destination, and the car purred smoothly away from the curb. I settled back in my seat. I knew better than to touch the wheel. My car always knows where it's going. I opened the glove compartment and rooted around in it hopefully. And sure enough, there was one special pill left. An ugly, bottle-green thing that left a chalky residue on my pale grey fingertips. I washed it down with a few swallows of vodka from the bottle I always keep handy. I like vodka. It gets the job done. My dead taste-buds started to fire and flutter almost immediately, and I opened a packet of Hobnobs. I crammed a biscuit into my mouth and chewed heavily, the thick, chocolate taste sending a warm glow all through me.

"So, Sil," I said, spraying crumbs on the air. "How's it going?"

"Everything's going down smooth, sweetie," said Sil. My car's very own Artificial Intelligence has the rich and smoky voice of a very sexy woman. I never get tired of hearing it. She came to the Nightside through a Timeslip, falling all the way from the twenty-third century. She found me, and adopted me, and we've been together ever since. We're in love. My lover, the car. Only in the Nightside. Nobody else knows; she only ever speaks to me.

"You really shouldn't spend so much time in bars, sweetie," said Sil. "All that booze and brooding; it does you no good, physically or spiritually. Especially when I'm not with you."

"I like bars," I said, finishing the packet of biscuits and tossing the empty wrapper onto the back seat. "Bars . . . have food and drink, atmosphere and ambience, bad company and good connections. They help me feel alive, still part of the crowd. And it's not like I need to work. I only ever work to keep busy. To keep from brooding on the bitter unfairness of my condition."

"You mustn't give up," said Sil. "You have to keep looking. There has to be a way, somewhere, to break your deal and come alive again. This is the Nightside, after all. Where dreams can come true."

"Especially the bad ones," I said. "What if . . . all I find is how to become completely dead, at last?"

"Is that what you want?" said Sil.

"It's been so long since I could rest," I said. "I've forgotten what sleep's like, but I still miss it. Keeping going . . . can be such an effort. Sometimes, I think of how good it would feel . . . to be able to put down the burden of my continuing existence. If that was all I could find, could you let me go?"

"If that's what you want," said Sil. "If that's what you need. Then yes, I could do that. That's what love is."

I perked up as Sil bullied her way into the main flow of traffic. All kinds of cars and other vehicles, from the Past, the Present, and all kinds of Futures, thunder endlessly back and forth through the Nightside, never slowing, never stopping, intent on their own unknowable business. I'm one of the few people who actually enjoys navigating through the deadly and aggressive Nightside traffic because you can be sure that Sil and I are always the most deadly and aggressive things on the road.

A lipstick-red Plymouth Fury sped by, with a dead man grinning at the wheel. Followed by a stretch hearse, with two men in formal outfits and top hats in the rear, struggling to force something back into its coffin. Something with far too much chrome and truly massive tail fins, and a highly radioactive afterburner, slammed bad-temperedly through the slower-moving traffic, occasionally running right over smaller vehicles that didn't get out of its way fast enough. And something that blazed fiercely with an unnaturally incandescent light flashed in and out of the traffic at impossible speed, laughing and shrieking and throwing off multi-coloured sparks.

While I was busy watching that, an oversized truck pulled in behind Sil, sticking right on her tail. She drew my attention to it, and I looked in the rear-view mirror just in time to see the whole front of the truck open up like a great mouth, full of row upon row of rotating teeth, like a living meat-grinder. The truck surged forward, the mouth opening wider and wider, to draw Sil in and devour her. And me, of course.

Sil waited till the truck thing was right behind us, then opened up with her rear-mounted flame-throwers. A great wave of harsh yellow flames swept over the truck, filling its gaping mouth. The whole truck caught fire in a moment, massive flames leaping into the night sky. The truck screamed horribly, sweeping back and forth across the road as though trying to leave the consuming flames behind, while the rest of the traffic scattered to get out of its way. The truck thing exploded in a great ball of fire; and after a moment, chunks of burning meat fell out of the sky. I lowered the side window and inhaled deeply, so I could savour the smell. Take your fun where you can find it, that's what I say.

•　　•　　•

Sil finally drew up outside the Literary Auction House, in the better business area of the Nightside, and pulled right up onto the pavement to park, secure in the knowledge that absolutely no-one was going to dispute her right to be there. She opened the door for me, and I got out. I took a moment to adjust my purple greatcoat fussily and make sure my floppy hat was set at the right, jaunty angle. Making the right first impression is so important, when you're about to march in somewhere you know you're not welcome . . . probably make a whole lot of trouble, and almost certainly beat important information out of people.

The Literary Auction House is where you go when you're looking to get your hands on really rare books. Not just the *Necronomicon* or the unexpurgated *King in Yellow*. I'm talking about the kind of books that never turn up at regular auctions. Books like *The Gospel According to Mary Magdalene, The True and Terrible History of the Old Soul Market at Under Parliament,* and *101 Things You Can Get for Free If You Just Perform the Right Blood Sacrifices.* All the hidden truths and secret knowledges that They don't want you to know about. Usually with good reason.

I swaggered in through the open door, and the two guards on duty took one look at me, burst into tears, and ran away to hide in the toilets. Not an uncommon reaction where I'm concerned. Inside the main auction hall, the usual unusual suspects were standing around, enjoying the free champagne and studying the glossy catalogues while waiting for things to start. I grabbed a glass of champagne, drained it in one, and then spat it out. I never bother with domestic. Even my special pills can't make that stuff interesting. There were platters of the usual nibbles and delicacies and flashy, foody things, so I filled my coat pockets for later. And only then did I peer thoughtfully at the crowd, pick out some familiar faces, and head right for them. Smiling my most disturbing smile, to let them know I was here for a reason and wouldn't be leaving till I'd got what I wanted.

Deliverance Wilde was there, fashion consultant and style guru to the Fae of the Unseelie Court; tall and black and loudly Jamaican in a smartly tailored suit of eye-wateringly bright yellow. Jackie Schadenfreude, the emotion junkie, wearing a Gestapo uniform and a Star of David, so he could feed on the conflicting emotions they evoked. And the Painted Ghoul, the proverbial Clown at Midnight, in his baggy clothes and sleazy make-up. Chancers and con men, minor celebrities and characters for pay, the kinds of people who'd know things and people they weren't supposed to know. They all moved to stand a little closer together as I approached, for mutual support in the face of a common danger. It would probably have worked with anyone else. I stopped right before them, stuck my hands deep in my coat pockets, and rocked back and forth on my heels as I looked them over, taking my time.

"You know something I want to know," I announced loudly. "And the sooner you tell me, the sooner I'll go away and leave you alone. Won't that be nice?"

"What could we know that you'd want to know?" said Deliverance Wilde, doing her best to look down her long nose at me.

"You want a book?" said the Painted Ghoul, smiling widely to show his sharpened teeth. "I've got books that will make you laugh till you puke blood. All the fun of the unfair, with cyanide-sprinkle candy-floss thrown in . . ."

He stopped talking when I looked at him, the smile dying on his coloured mouth. Jackie Schadenfreude screwed a monocle into one eye.

"What do you want, Dead Boy? Please be good enough to tell us, so we can thrust it into your unworthy hands and be rid of you."

"Krauss," I said. "There's a man here called Krauss, and I want him."

"Oh him," said Deliverance Wilde, visibly relaxing. "Don't know why you'd want him, but I'm only too happy to throw him to the lions. Take him, and do us all a favour."

"Why?" I said. "What is he?"

"You don't know?" said Jackie Schadenfreude. "Krauss is the Bad Librarian. A booklegger. Specialises in really dangerous books, full of dangerous knowledge."

"The kind no-one in their right mind would want," said the Painted Ghoul, sniggering. "All the terrible things that people can do to people. Usually illustrated. Heh heh."

I nodded slowly. I knew the kind of book they meant. After I came back from the dead and found I was trapped in my body, I did a lot of research on my condition in many of the Nightside's strange and curious Libraries. I know more about all the various forms of death, and life in death, than most people realise. I'd acquired some of my more esoteric research materials from men like Krauss.

"Krauss is bad news," said Deliverance Wilde, mistaking my thoughtfulness for indecision. "He deals in books that show you how to open dimensional doorways, and let in Things from Outside. Books that can teach you to raise Hell. Literally. The book equivalent of a backpack nuke."

"Books full of the secrets of Heaven and Hell," said Jackie Schadenfreude. "And all the hidden places in between."

"Pleasures beyond human comprehension," said the Painted Ghoul, licking his coloured lips. "Practices to make demons and angels cry out in the night. Heh heh."

"Knowledge of the true nature of reality," said Deliverance Wilde. "That drives men mad because reality isn't what we think it is and never has been. Take him and be welcome, Dead Boy. It's bookleggers like Krauss that give people like us a bad name."

"Where is he?" I said.

All three of them pointed in the same direction. None of their hands were particularly steady.

I headed straight for Krauss, and everyone along the way fell back to give me plenty of room. Krauss was a nondescript, elderly man in a tweed suit with leather patches on the elbows, wearing an old-school tie he almost certainly wasn't entitled to. He was so immersed in his auction catalogue, circling things and making notes, that he didn't even see me coming until I was right on top of him. He looked up abruptly, alerted by the sudden silence around him, and peered at me over the top of a pair of golden pince-nez.

"Hello," he said, carefully. "Now what would the low-and-mighty Dead Boy want with a mere booklegger like myself? Can I perhaps be of service, help you locate something? Some suitable tome on the pleasures to be found in dead flesh, perhaps? Something explicit, on the delights of the damned? Satisfaction and complete discretion guaranteed, of course."

"You don't even recognise me, do you?" I said.

"But of course I do, my good sir! You're Dead Boy! Everyone in the Nightside knows Dead Boy."

"You only think you know me," I said. "But then, it has been thirty years and more since you paid three young thugs to mug and murder me, down on Damnation Row."

His jaw actually dropped, and all the colour fell out of his face. "That was *you*? Really? I can't believe it . . . I helped create the legendary Dead Boy? I'm honoured!"

"Don't be," I said.

Krauss chuckled a little, relaxing now he thought he knew what this was about. "Well, well . . . I can't believe my past has caught up with me, after so many years . . ." He tucked his catalogue neatly under one arm and looked me up and down, studying the results of his work. "I haven't been involved in the muscle trade for . . . well, must be decades! Yes! That was a whole other life . . . I was a different person, then."

"So was I," I said. "I was alive."

His smile disappeared. "But you can't blame me for what I did, all those years ago! I'm a changed man now!"

"So am I," I said. "I'm dead. And I'm not happy about it."

"What . . . what do you want from me?" said Krauss. "I didn't know . . . I had no idea . . ."

"Who paid you?" I said. "Who hired you, to have me killed? I want to know who, and why. I wasn't anybody back then. I wasn't anyone special. I was a teenager."

Krauss shrugged quickly. There was sweat on his face. "I never asked why. Wasn't any of my business. I only hired out muscle—that was what I did! I never asked her why, and she never said."

"She . . . She who, exactly?"

"Old voodoo woman," said Krauss. "Called herself Mother Macabre. Spooky old bat. Not the kind you ask questions of."

He had more to say, about how he shouldn't be blamed for someone else's bad intentions, that he only supplied a service, that if he hadn't done it, somebody else would have; but I wasn't really listening. Mother Macabre was the name of the old Obeah woman who'd been supplying me with all those special pills and potions for more than thirty years. Could it really be the same woman? Why would she pay to have me killed, then help me out? Guilt? Not likely; not in the Nightside. It didn't make sense; but it had to be her. She was why Walker had pointed me in this direction. I looked Krauss in the eye, and he stopped talking abruptly. He started to back away. I dropped one heavy dead hand on his shoulder, to hold him still. He winced at the strength in my hand and whimpered.

"I helped make you who you are!" he said desperately. "I helped make you Dead Boy!"

"Let me see," I said. "How do I feel about that?"

I closed my hand abruptly, and all the bones in his shoulder shattered. He screamed. I hit him in the head. The whole left side of his face caved in, and his scream was choked by the blood filling his throat. I hit him again and again, breaking him, watching dispassionately as pain and horror and blood filled Krauss's face because the last pill had worn off, and I didn't feel anything. I thrust one hand deep into his chest, closed my cold, dead fingers around his living heart, and tore it out of his body. He fell to the floor, kicked a few times, and lay still. I looked at the bloody piece of meat in my hand, then let it drop to the floor.

I'd killed the man who arranged my death, and it didn't touch me at all. I sat down on the bloody floor, picked up Krauss's body, and held it in my arms, cradling it to my chest. I still didn't feel anything. I let him go and got up again. I looked around me. Even hardened denizens of the Nightside were shocked at what I'd done. Some were crying, some were vomiting. I smiled slowly.

"What are you looking at?"

I didn't really care; but I had a reputation to maintain.

Outside, Sil was waiting patiently. She opened the door for me, and I took a rag out of the inner compartment and scrubbed the blood off my hands. There was more blood soaked into the front of my greatcoat, but that could wait. My coat was used to hard times. I got into the driver's seat, the door closed, and Sil set off again.

"Where now?" she said.

"Just drive for a while," I said. "And, hush, please. I have a lot to think about."

She drove on, cruising through the hot, neon-lit streets, while I looked at nothing and tried to make sense of what I'd learned. Mother Macabre, my trusted old Obeah woman, who'd helped me hang on to what was left of the real me for more than thirty years. Why would she have wanted me dead? I wasn't anybody, then. Nobody special.

What . . . purpose, could my poor death have served? The thoughts went round and round in my head and got nowhere. I'm not a great one for thinking. No; much better to go to the source and ask some very pertinent questions, in person.

"Sil," I said. "Take me to Mother Macabre. Take me to the Garden of Forbidden Fruits."

You can find the Garden of Forbidden Fruits not far from the main business centre of the Nightside. It's where you go when you want something a bit alternative to all the usual sin and sleaze. It's the place to buy an inappropriate gift, like a killer plant that will sneak up on the recipient while they're asleep. Or seeds that will grow into something really disturbing. And very special drugs, to give you glimpses of Heaven and Hell or rip the soul right out of you. If it grows, if it fruits and flowers in unnatural ways, you'll find it somewhere in the Garden of Forbidden Fruits.

I told Sil to wait for me and entered the Garden through its ever-open doors. It was just a long hallway that seemed to stretch away forever, lined on both sides with the kind of shop or establishment you only ever enter at your own risk. I'd been here many times before, to pick up my special pills and potions from my old friend, Mother Macabre. The withered old black crone, in her pokey little shop, the traditional image of the voodoo witch, who smiled and cackled as she made up my packages with her clever, long-fingered hands, and only ever charged me what I could afford. That in itself should have been enough to tip me off that something was wrong. You just don't get that in the Nightside.

I strode past The Little Shop of Horticulture, with its window full of snapping plants, past The Borgia Connection (for that little something he'll never notice in his food) and Mistress Lovett's Posy Parlour, (sleep without dreams . . .). I ignored the hanging plants outside shop doorways, which hissed at me as I passed or sang songs in languages I didn't recognise. I ignored the familiar, hot, wet smells of damp earth and growing things, the powerful perfumes of unlikely flowers, and the underlying stench from the bloody earth their roots soaked in. I just looked straight ahead, and everyone and everything in that long hallway shrank back from me as I passed. Until, finally, I came to the only shop-front I cared about, the one I'd visited so many times before and never thought twice about. Mother Macabre's Midnight Mansion.

I stood outside the open door. It wasn't any kind of mansion, of course. Just a shop. Dark and dingy and more than a little pokey. There was never anything on display, and the only window was blank. Mother Macabre's patrons liked their privacy. I put my shoulders back and lifted my chin. Never let them know they've hurt you. I strolled into the shop with my hands buried deep in the pockets of my coat, so no-one could see that my hands were curled into fists.

It looked as it always did. It hadn't changed because I was seeing it with new eyes. The familiar four walls of shelves, tightly packed with tightly sealed jars and bottles, full of this and that. Some of the contents were still moving. There was St. John the Conqueror root; mandrake root in sound-proofed jars; vampire teeth, clattering against the inside of the glass; all kinds of raw talent for sale, with colour-coded caps so the assistant could tell them apart at a glance; and a whole row of shrunken heads, with their mouths stitched shut to stop them screaming. All the usual tatt the tourists can't get enough of. And behind the counter, as always, a tall, young, strong-featured black woman dressed in the best Haitian style, with an Afro and a headscarf, speaking in broad patois for the middle-aged tourist couple dithering over their purchases. Her name was Pretty Pretty, and woe betide anyone who ever raised an eyebrow at that. She had always been very kind to me before; but I wasn't sure if that would save her now.

I waited patiently until she was finished with the tourists. They left happily enough, with their jar full of something that glowed with a sour, spoiled light; and I shut the door behind them and turned the sign to read CLOSED. Pretty Pretty looked at me curiously and started to say something in the patois. I raised a hand, and she stopped.

"Please," I said. "I'm not a tourist."

"Never said you were, darling," said Pretty Pretty, in the polished voice of her very expensive finishing school. "Now what on earth are you doing here? You can't have run out already, surely? I mean, honestly darling, you do get through those things at a rate of knots . . . You're not supposed to just pop them back like sweeties . . ."

And then she stopped, her voice trailing away. There must have been something in my face, in my eyes, because she stood very still behind her counter. She must have had defences there, but she had enough sense not to go for them. I smiled at her, and she actually shuddered.

"Mother Macabre," I said. "I want her. Where is she?"

"She just left, darling," said Pretty Pretty. She swallowed hard. "Maybe half an hour ago? You just missed her . . . Is it important?"

"Yes," I said. "Stay out of the way, Pretty Pretty. I'm prepared to believe you're not involved. Keep it that way."

I strode past the counter and kicked in the door that led to Mother Macabre's private office. The lock exploded, and the heavy wood cracked and fell apart. I pulled the pieces out of the broken frame and threw them to one side. There must have been magical protections, too, because I felt them run briefly up and down my dead skin; but they couldn't touch me. Pretty Pretty made an unhappy noise but had enough sense to stay behind her counter.

The private office looked very ordinary, very business-like. I tried the computer on her desk, but it was all locked down. And even I can't intimidate passwords out of a computer. I tried all the desk drawers, and the In and Out trays, but it was all everyday paper-work. Nothing of interest. So I trashed the whole office, very thoroughly. To make a statement. Pretty Pretty watched timidly from the doorway. When I tore the heavy wooden desk apart with my bare hands, she made a few refined noises of distress. When I'd finished, because there was nothing left to break or destroy, I stood and considered what to do next, picking splinters out of my unfeeling hands. I looked sharply at Pretty Pretty, and she jumped, only a little.

"Where would Mother Macabre be? Right now?"

"I suppose she could be at her club," Pretty Pretty said immediately. Anyone else she would have told to go to Hell, and even added instructions on the quickest route; but I wasn't anyone else. "She owns this private club, Members Only, called the Voodoo Lounge. Do you know it?"

"I know of it," I said. "I can find it."

"Should I . . . phone ahead? Let her know you're coming?"

"If you like," I said. "It won't make any difference. I'll find her wherever she goes."

"Why?" said Pretty Pretty. "What's happened? What's changed?"

"Everything," I said.

I'd heard of the Voodoo Lounge. Not the kind of place I'd ever visit but very popular with the current Bright Young Things keen to throw away their inheritance on the newest thrill. Voodoo for the smart set, graveyard chill for those just old enough to know better. Very expensive, very exclusive, very hard to get into—for most people. I told Sil to take me there, and she didn't say a word. We drove in silence through the angry traffic, each of us lost in our own thoughts. I was getting close now. I could feel it. Close to all the answers I ever wanted, and one final act of vengeance . . . that even I was smart enough to realise I might not be able to walk away from.

Sil pulled up outside the Voodoo Lounge. I got out and told her to wait for me. She didn't answer. She wasn't sulking, or even disapproving; it was simply that she knew better than to speak to me when I was in this kind of mood. The risen dead don't have many positive qualities, but stubbornness is definitely one of them. There were two guards on duty, outside the black-lacquered doors that gave entrance to the Voodoo Lounge. Very large black gentlemen, with shaven heads and smart tuxedos. I put on my best worrying smile and strode right at them. They knew who I was, probably even knew why I was there; but neither of them did the sensible thing and ran. You have to admire such dedication to duty. They looked at me expressionlessly and moved to stand just a little closer together, blocking my way to the entrance.

"Members only, sir," said the one on the left.

"No exceptions, sir," said the one on the right.

"We have orders to keep you out."

"By whatever means necessary."

"On your way, Dead Boy."

"Not welcome here, zombie."

I let my smile widen into a grin and kept on coming. One of them pulled a packet of salt from his pocket, and threw the contents into my face. Salt is a good traditional defence against zombies, but I've always been a lot more than that. The other guard produced a string of garlic and thrust it in my face. I snatched one of the bulbs away from him, took a good bite, chewed on it, and spat it out. No taste. Nothing at all. And while I was doing that, the first guard produced a gun and stuck the barrel against my forehead.

"When in doubt," he said calmly, "go old-school. Shoot them in the head."

He pulled the trigger. The bullet smashed through my forehead, through my dead brain, and out the back of my head. I rocked slightly on my feet, but I didn't stop smiling. The guard with the gun actually whimpered as I snatched the gun out of his hand and tossed it to one side.

"That's been tried," I said. "I'll have to fill the hole in with plaster of Paris again."

I punched the guard in the face, smashing his nose and mouth and jaw, and then back-elbowed the other guard in the side of the head. They both went down and didn't get up again. Normally, I would have taken the time to do them both some serious damage, to make a point, but I had more important things in mind. I stepped over the broken guards, kicked in the black-lacquered doors, and strode into the Voodoo Lounge.

"Hello!" I said loudly, as I strode into the entrance hall. "I'm here! Come on, give it your best shot! Do your worst! I can take it!"

And the next level of defence came running silently down the hallway towards me. A short, stocky Chinaman, the tattoos down one side of his face marking him as a combat magician. A very powerful and frightening figure—to anyone else. He waited till he was almost upon me, then he gestured sharply and snatched a blazing ball of fire out of nowhere. Vivid green flames shot up around his hand, and he stopped dead in his tracks to thrust them at me. Emerald fires blasted me like a flame-thrower. But I was already turning, putting my back to him; and the searing flames slammed against my deep purple greatcoat. A terrible fire roared over and around me; but it couldn't touch me. In my dead state, I couldn't even feel the heat. And when the flames finally died out, I straightened up, turned around, and smiled at the combat magician.

"I had my coat fire-proofed long ago, on the quiet, for occasions just like this," I said.

And while I was saying that, holding his attention, I surged forward, snatched the jade fire amulet out of his hand, and beat him to the floor. I heard his skull crack and break under the blows, but I hit him a few more times anyway, to be sure. I stood over him, listening to the bloody froth bubble in his mouth and nose, and felt nothing, nothing at all. I studied the fire amulet, a simple jade piece with a golden cat's-eye pupil at its heart. You can buy them at any market in the Nightside, though learning the proper Words of Power to make them work costs rather more. I turned the amulet back and forth, admiring the quality of the workmanship, then I said the right Words and set fire to the combat magician. His screams, and the sound of the consuming flames, followed me down the hall as I walked away.

The interior of the club had been painted all the shades of red and purple. It was like walking through the interior of someone's body. The air was thick with the scents of burned meat and spilled blood, and all kinds of illegal smoke. Smells so heavy even I could detect them. The air was hot and damp, and heavy beads of condensation ran down my face. I couldn't feel the heat or the moisture; I only noticed them when they fell down to stain my coat. The pills and the potions had worn off, and it was hard for me to feel anything.

There were doors on either side of the hallway, leading to very private rooms, for very private passions. I considered them thoughtfully. It might make me feel better, to kick the doors in and see what was going on behind them. It might make me feel . . . something. But then a Voice came to me, through some hidden speaker, saying *This way. Walk straight ahead. Come into my parlour, Dead Boy, and we'll talk. I've been waiting for you.*

A calm, confident, female Voice. Didn't sound like my Mother Macabre. I walked on, into the belly of the beast, into the trap that had been prepared for me. And the cold in my dead heart was the cold of dark and righteous anger.

Didn't take me long to come to the door at the end of the hall. It was standing just a little open, invitingly. I slammed right through it, almost taking the door off its hinges, and there she was, in her parlour. Mother Macabre's sweet little home away from home was more than comfortable, full of every luxury and indulgence you could think of and some you never even dreamed of. Tables full of drinks, bowls full of pills and powders, toys and trinkets to suit the most jaded sexual palates—decadence on display. All for the Bright Young Things . . . as they sat in chairs, or sprawled on couches, or lay giggling happily on the deep pile carpet. Young ladies and gentlemen from rich and powerful and well-connected families, still young enough to believe money could buy you satisfaction, or at the very least enough pleasure to convince you that you were happy. Spending Daddy's money and influence on the very latest thing, the newest kick, on something dark and dangerous enough to make them feel they were important, after all. They stared at me with blank eyes and meaningless smiles, and limited curiosity. And the dozen or so naked men and women, standing around the parlour to serve the young people's every need or whim, were all quite obviously dead. Well preserved, even pleasant to the eye; but you only had to look into their faces to know there was no-one home. They weren't dead like me; they were only animated bodies, moved by some other's will.

I wasn't interested in them. I fixed my gaze on the parlour's mistress, proud and disdainful on her raised throne, like a spider at the heart of her web. Mother Macabre, sitting at her ease on a throne made of human skulls. Bone so old it had faded past yellow ivory into dirty brown, stained here and there with old, dried blood. There was a cushion on the seat, of course. Tradition and style and making the right kind of impression are all very well, but comfort is what matters.

Mother Macabre looked as she always had: a withered old black crone, in tattered ethnic clothes. Deep-sunk eyes and a wide smile to show off the missing teeth. Very authentic. But I didn't believe that any more. I concentrated, looking at her with the eyes of the dead because the dead can see many things that are hidden from the living. And just like that, the illusion snapped off. And underneath the glamour she was just an ordinary middle-aged black business woman, neat and tidy in a smart business suit, her well-manicured hands folded calmly in her lap.

"Took you long enough to work it out," she said. "Mistress Macabre is just a trade name. Handed down through the generations, along with the trade and the look because that's what people want when they do business with a voodoo witch. There were many Mother Macabres before me, and no doubt there will be many more after. It's a very profitable trade. Because there will always be a need for women like us. But . . . this is the real me. You should feel flattered, Dead Boy. Not many are privileged to see the real me."

"Flattered," I said. "Yes. That's how I feel, all right. Tell me. Who did I really make a deal with?"

"And you've worked that out, too! Well done, Dead Boy. Yes; I'm afraid your memories of what happened after you died are as much a fake as anything else. You thought you made a deal with one of the voodoo loa, Mistress Erzulie; but everything you saw and experienced came from me. A show I put on, to distract you while I did the many vile and nasty things necessary to raise you from the dead. It was all an illusion, another mask. Just me. It's always been me."

"Why?" I said.

And there must have been something in my voice because everyone in the parlour stopped smiling and looked at me. Even Mother Macabre on her throne of skulls took a moment before she answered me. I fixed her with my unblinking eyes, and she actually squirmed uncomfortably on her throne.

"Why?" said Mother Macabre. "Because I needed someone to experiment on! Didn't matter who. Could have been you, could have been anyone. I was starting out in the Mother Macabre trade. I inherited it from my mother— after I killed her. She was so old-fashioned, couldn't see the potential in the business I saw . . . Anyway, I had all these marvellous ideas for new pills and potions, but I needed someone to test them on before I introduced them to a wider audience. I needed someone young and strong and vital, new to the Nightside, without friends or protectors. I picked you out entirely at random and paid to have you killed. And then I brought you back again, to be my test subject. You took everything I gave you, every new drug and concoction I came up with, and never once questioned any of it. And because it was my lore that brought you back, your body had no secrets from me. I've studied you, from a safe distance, for all these years . . . And oh the things I've learned from you! You have no idea how much money you've made me, down the years!"

"All the things I've been, and done," I said. "And all along I was nothing but your lab rat."

"Actually, no," said Mother Macabre. "You're a lot more than I ever intended you to be. I was just interested to see what would happen when I trapped a living soul inside a dead body, but you have made yourself into the legendary, infamous Dead Boy! You should be proud of what you've achieved!"

"Proud," I said. "Yes. That's what I'm feeling, right now."

Mother Macabre looked at me uncertainly, unable to read my dead face or my dead voice. "You really shouldn't take it personally, Dead Boy. It was only ever . . . business."

"It was my life!" I said loudly.

She smiled. "It wasn't as though you were doing anything important with it."

"All the things I could have done," I said. "All the people I might have been; and you took them away from me."

"None of them would have been as important, or as interesting, as Dead Boy." Mother Macabre sank back on her throne as though she were getting tired, or bored, with the conversation. "What does your life, or your death, matter, where there were fortunes to be made? I had a business to run! It's all about the pleasures of the flesh, you see. Control them, and you have control over the living and the dead." She looked fondly at the young people scattered around her parlour. "My lovely ladies and gentlemen. I give them what they think they want and take everything they have. And when they die . . . I raise them again, to serve me. The dead always make the best servants. No back-talk, no days off. And the dead make the very best lovers because they can go forever . . ."

She gestured to a naked man and a naked woman, and they came forward to caress her face and neck with their cool, dead hands. She smiled happily.

"They feel nothing. The only pleasure is mine. But then, I never was big on sharing. I knew you were coming after me, Dead Boy. Knew it the moment you killed poor old Krauss. I could have had you destroyed anywhere along the way; but I wanted to have you here, so I could watch it happen right in front of me. I have the right to destroy you because I made you. You belong to me. You always have. And after you've gone, I'll make another Dead Boy."

She snapped her fingers, and every dead man and woman in the parlour turned their head to look at me. And then they started forward, cold and implacable as death itself. All of them just as strong as me, and as capable of taking punishment. They reached for me with their dead hands, and the young ladies and gentlemen laughed and pointed, enjoying the show. I looked around me. The way to the only door was blocked, and I was clearly outnumbered. So, when in doubt, cheat.

I reached into my pocket and took out the jade fire amulet I'd taken from its previous owner. I said the right Words and set fire to all the dead men and women. They burst into bright green flames, burning with a fierce heat that consumed their flesh in moments. They kept coming as long as they could, reaching out blindly through the flames, bumping into the furnishings and fittings and setting them alight, too. They even set fire to the clothes of the Bright Young Things. Most of them just sat where they were, watching as the flames ate them up, and laughing. Giggling happily as they died, as stupidly as they'd lived.

Mother Macabre ran for the door the moment her servants started burning, but I was there before her. I took her in my dead arms and held her to me, almost tenderly. She beat at me with her fists, but I couldn't feel them, and she wasn't strong enough to do me any damage. I held her with all my dead strength, and she couldn't get away. The whole parlour was on fire now, burning the living and the dead alike, and the air was full of thick black smoke.

"You have to let me go!" shrieked Mother Macabre. "If we stay here, we'll both die! This fire's enough to destroy even you!"

"You say that like it's a bad thing," I said. "I'm tired. I

want to rest. It will be worth it, to die here, as long as I can be sure I'm taking you with me. Thanks to you, I can't feel any of the things the living feel; but dead as I am, I can still feel some things, even without your special pills. I'm watching you die, Mother Macabre, and that feels . . . so fine."

"I can make you new pills, new potions!" Mother Macabre said desperately. "I can make you feel all the things you felt before!"

"Perhaps. But what have I got that's worth living for?"

And then we both looked round, as a series of explosions shook the front of the building. There was the sound of energy weapons firing, and repeated sounds of something large and heavy and very determined crashing through the walls between us, heading right for us. And I began to smile. I looked at the door, still holding firmly on to the fiercely struggling Mother Macabre; and my futuristic car came smashing through the door and into the parlour, bringing half the wall with her. She slammed to a halt before me, her gleaming steel-and-silver body entirely untouched by all the destruction she'd wrought. And as I watched, smiling . . . as Mother Macabre watched with wide-stretched eyes and mouth . . . my car rose and transmogrified, taking on a whole new shape, until my Sil stood before me. A tall, buxom woman, in a classic little black dress, cut just high enough at the hip to show off the barcode and copyright notice stamped on her magnificent left buttock. Her frizzy steel hair was full of sparking static, and her eyes were silver, but she was still every inch a woman. My woman.

"Nothing to live for, sweetie?" said Sil. "What about me?"

"You were listening in," I said, just a bit reproachfully.

"You were taking too long," said Sil. "I became . . . concerned. You always go over the top when you go too far into the dark. You forget there are other feelings, other pleasures, than revenge."

"Of course," I said. "You're quite right. You always were my better half. I never needed pills to feel the way I feel about you."

"What the hell is that?" said Mother Macabre, staring at Sil with horrified fascination.

"I am a sex droid from the twenty-third century," Sil said proudly. "With full trans-morph capabilities!" She shot me a smouldering look. "I have always loved my job. It took more than one man to change my name to Silicon Lily. But I never met anyone like you, my sweet Dead Boy. And I won't let you die with her. She isn't worth it."

"You're right," I said. "You're always right. You're worth living for, inasmuch as I can. But . . . I can't go on, I can't just walk out of here and let her get away with what she did to me."

"You don't have to," said Sil.

She raised one hand and morphed it into a glowing energy weapon. She shot Mother Macabre in the face and blew her head apart. I let go of the headless body, and it crumpled to the floor, still twitching. I swept blood and brains from my face and shoulder with one hand, then nodded briefly to Sil. She's always been able to do the things I can't do. She swept forward, discarding her human shape, melting into a wave of metallic silver that swept right over me. She wrapped herself around me like a suit of armour, covering me from head to foot. Embracing me, and protecting me, all at once. And, together, we walked out of the burning building.

Outside, Walker was waiting for us, watching the building burn. He barely twitched an eyebrow as Sil peeled herself off me and resumed her human shape. She stood beside me as Silicon Lily, while I nodded politely to Walker. He tipped his bowler hat to both of us.

"Mother Macabre was getting a little too big for her boots,"

Walker said easily. "But I couldn't go after her, because of her . . . connections. So I pointed you at her. Well done, Dead Boy. Excellent work."

"How long have you known?" I said. "How long have you known the truth about me, and Krauss, and Mother Macabre?"

"I know everything," said Walker. "Remember?"

He smiled again, very politely, and walked off. Sil and I turned away, to watch the Voodoo Lounge burn.

"What am I going to do now, for my special pills and potions?" I said.

"There's always someone," said Sil. "This is the Nightside."

"True," I said. "If you're going to be damned, this is a pretty good place for it." I looked at her for a long moment. "Even with my pills, it takes more than an everyday woman to light the fires in my dead flesh."

"Good thing I'm not an everyday woman, then," said Silicon Lily. "I am a pleasure droid; and I do love my work! And it's good to know I can even raise the dead . . ."

"How can I love you?" I said. "When I don't have a heart any more?"

"I don't have a heart either," said Sil. "Doesn't matter. Love comes from the soul."

"Do we have souls?" I said.

She put her arms around me. "What do you think?"

It's not easy, having a sex life when you're dead. But it is possible.

"How do you feel?" said Sil.

"I feel . . . good," I said.

THE BIG GAME

ONE

The Nightside.

The secret, sour, magical heart of London, hidden away from the sane and sensible everyday world. Where it's always night, always three o'clock in the morning; and while it sometimes feels like the sun must rise eventually, after so many terrible things have happened in the shadows . . . still, the dawn never comes. The Nightside, where hot neon burns on every side, bright and colourful as hell's candy, and the come-ons never end. Where saints and sinners go fist-fighting down alleyways; where souls aren't so much sold as bartered, or thrown away with joyous abandon; where gods and monsters step out together, and love can bloom in the oddest of places. In the Nightside, everything is for sale, everything is up for grabs, and you can find everything you ever dreamed of. If it doesn't find you first.

Why would good men come to such a place?

• • •

I'm John Taylor, private investigator. I have a gift for finding things. I've never thought of myself as a good man. I
always tell my clients in advance, in the end, all I can ever
really find for them is the truth. Living with it is up to
them. I can solve mysteries, point out murderers, and now
and again I get to save the world. But I don't do divorce
work, and I don't fix relationships. I know my limitations.

I was drinking wormwood brandy in Strangefellows, the
oldest bar in the world. Coming down, after a particularly
vexing case. My white trench coat stood to attention beside
my table, in a private booth at the back of the bar. If I'm
going to be a private investigator, I like to look the part.
And the image does help distract people from who and what
I really am. I am, after all, one of the Nightside's better-
known legends.

My father drank himself to death after finding out his
wife wasn't human. My mother turned out to be a Biblical
Myth; from that part of the Old Testament where God gets
really angry. I have fought angels and demons, wrestled with
Heaven and Hell; and while there is blood on my hands, it's
mostly blood I can be proud of. I help people because there
was no-one there to help me, when I needed it. I don't give
up, and I don't give in, and I don't do comforting lies.

Case in point; the case I'd just finished. My client hired
me to find his missing wife, gone for over a year. He'd tried
all the usual agencies, and all the official channels, before
finally finding his way to the Nightside. Because when
you've tried everything else, including prayer, and nothing's
worked, there's always me. It didn't take me long to find the
missing wife. She'd come to the Nightside looking for the
one thing she needed that she couldn't get anywhere else. A
one hundred per cent sex change. A mystical, not surgical,
transformation into a real man.

He left the Nightside and went back into London Proper; where he became my client's best friend. Because he still loved him, and wanted to be with him, but as a man not a woman. A friend, not a wife. They got on great, without sex there to distract them. However, the client wasn't too pleased to learn the truth, about his wife and his best friend.

The husband killed the closest friend he'd ever had; and then sat down beside the body and put a bullet in his own head.

The truth? Overrated, if you ask me.

So there I was, hanging out in Strangefellows, drinking wormwood brandy straight from the bottle and telling myself none of it was my fault. And congratulating myself on getting paid in advance. Wormwood brandy isn't the smoothest of drinks; but there's no denying it gets the job done. I do most of my solitary drinking in Strangefellows. Not because it's peaceful, because it isn't, but because people there leave me alone. No matter how crowded or boisterous things get, no-one bothers me. Sometimes it's easier to be alone, in the middle of a crowd. And if you're into people watching, the weirdest and wildest people show up at the oldest bar in the world. That's what it's for.

The bar was packed full that night, and the joint was jumping. All the usual unusual suspects were in, desperate for distraction after a hard night's sinning. All the flotsam and jetsam thrown up by the night that never ends. Everyone comes to Strangefellows, usually on the run. From the comforting shadows of my private booth, I could see Lords and Ladies from a dozen Courts that didn't exist any more. Standing tall in their faded and shabby finery, wondering what to do now their old lives were gone, their worlds burned down. I could see a dozen different kinds of alien— beachcombers and remittance men—paid off by their own kind, on the condition they never tried to go home again. And here and there I could see hollow-eyed survivors of a hundred failed quests, the burned-out fall-out of a hundred psychic incursions. Ghosts and ghouls, madmen and murderers, hard-drinking men and hard-loving women. Old souls and memories of greatness. It's that kind of a bar. When no-one else wants you, and no-one else will take you in, Strangefellows is always waiting. As long as your cash and credit are good.

There was a lot of community activity going on: shouting and laughing, dancing and fighting . . . but I didn't feel like joining in. I've never been a joining-in sort of person. For much of my life, it was safer that way, for me and everyone I cared about, if I kept myself alone and apart. There were an awful lot of people, and a lot of awful things not anywhere near people, trying to find me and kill me. And even after I put an end to that, old habits die hard. I like to keep moving because a moving target is harder to hit. And I always sit with my back to the wall, so I can see who's coming for me.

Spiritual wounds never heal; and spiritual scar tissue is armour.

Rob Dougan's "Furious Angels" was blasting out of the bar's music system through carefully disguised speakers. The bar's owner keeps the speakers hidden so the patrons won't try to shoot them if they don't approve of his choices in music. A dozen members of the Tribe of Gay Barbarians were doing the lambada to the music, right in front of the bar, stamping and wheeling. Light flashed from their oiled, muscular bodies. They wore fur boots and loincloths, long swords hanging from their belts, and tall phoenix feathers thrusting up from their big eighties-style hair. Not far away, a young hex witch was putting on a hairdressing display by making the hair fall out of a werewolf's pelt in intricate patterns. The werewolf seemed to be enjoying it.

Those two disreputable legends, Dead Boy and Razor

Eddie, were holding a drinking competition, trying out some of the dustier bottles from the bar's back shelves. (The man who came back from the dead to avenge his own murder, and ended up trapped in his own corpse; and the homeless Punk God of the Straight Razor.) There was a lot of betting going on, as to which particular beverage would finally put a stop to the contest. Though given that Dead Boy was dead, and Razor Eddie was a living god, their inhuman systems could tolerate liquors that would have burned holes in most people. So far, the two of them had downed serious amounts of Tsothagua Tequila (eat the worm before the worm eats you), Vodyanoi Vodka (a killer surprise in every bottle), and Atlantean Ale (for that inevitable sinking feeling).

Dead Boy was swaying in his chair, singing an incredibly filthy song by the Sex Pistols and opening his long, deep purple greatcoat to show off his autopsy scar to passing young ladies. Razor Eddie was eating the shot-glasses, while attracting even more flies than usual. Though they still dropped dead out of the air before they got anywhere near him. I could have gone over and joined them. They were my friends, mostly. But I wasn't in the mood for company.

The music cut off briefly, and a raised voice hailed me from behind the bar. I looked up, to see Alex Morrisey scowling fiercely and gesturing for me to come over and join him. Alex is the owner and main bartender of Strangefellows, much to his continuing anger and distress, and the last in a long line of miserable bastards. He always wore black, right down to designer shades, and a snazzy black beret pushed well back on his head to hide his premature and rapidly spreading bald spot. (Proof, he always said, if proof were needed, that God hated him personally.) Alex is one of many reasons why there has never been a Happy Hour at Strangefellows. Permanently pissed off at the world and everyone in it, he mixes the most dangerous cocktails in the world, openly cheats you on your change, and wise men avoid his bar snacks.

I shrugged on my white trench coat and strolled through the packed crowd between me and the bar. People fell back to get out of my way, without quite seeming to, for their pride's sake. No-one spoke to me, but I could feel any number of eyes burning into my back. People are always curious about what I'm up to, if only to provide advance warning on the best way to jump once the inevitable trouble kicks off. I like having a bad reputation; it's better protection than Kevlar.

Alex glared at me as I eased up to the bar. "Someone wants to talk to you, Taylor. On the bar phone. How many times do I have to tell you; I am not your answering service!"

"You should pay me to come in here," I said. "I raise the tone."

"Would you like to hear some hollow laughter?" said Alex.

I took the phone from him, then stood there and looked at him until he took the hint and moved off down the long bar, out of earshot. Alex is a friend, sort of, but business is business. I looked at the phone for a moment, wondering why someone would call me at the bar rather than at my office or on my mobile phone. But then, discretion is a big part of being a private investigator. A lot of my clients don't want to admit that they'd have anything to do with the likes of me.

"Hello!" I said loudly into the phone. "John Taylor, at your service. Reasonable rates, an unreasonable attitude, and a dogged determination to find out things other people don't want me to know. Who am I talking to?"

"This is the Doorman at the Adventurers Club," said a deep, rich, and very cultured voice. "It would appear I am in need of your particular services, Mr. Taylor. There has been . . . trouble, at the Club. I require your assistance, immediately."

"Why can't the Adventurers deal with it?" I said. Not unreasonably, I thought. "I mean, you've got a club full of heroes and legends. What kind of trouble could there be at the Adventurers Club that they couldn't handle?"

"Everyone's disappeared," the Doorman said bluntly. "All the heroes and legends are gone, every last one of them. And not a trace left behind to suggest what might have happened. I am therefore forced to turn to you, Mr. Taylor. I need you to find out what has happened to the Club's missing Membership, and bring them back."

I couldn't help grinning. "That's why you phoned Strangefellows. Because you didn't want it showing up on the Club's official phone records, that you'd been forced to call me in your hour of need."

"Exactly," said the Doorman. "I have my standards. However, the missing Adventurers may be in dire need, and I am not allowed to leave my post to go in search of them. While you have a reputation for solving the most difficult of mysteries, rescuing those in trouble, and bringing them home safely. Will you help?"

"Of course!" I said. "Do you really think I'd turn down the opportunity to prove my superiority, once and for all, to the snobbish and snotty-nosed Members of your very exclusive club? Still, I have to ask. Can you afford me?"

There was a pause.

"You want paying?" said the Doorman. "Some of the greatest heroes of the world could be in mortal danger, and you want paying?"

"I never work for free," I said. "It's not the principle of the thing; it's the money."

"I'm sure we can cover it, out of the petty cash," said the Doorman. And he hung up.

• • •

Alex was there almost immediately, to take the phone from my hand. Which suggested he might not have been as far out of earshot as I'd supposed. I drummed my fingertips on the bar, thoughtfully. The Adventurers Club was home to some of the most powerful and experienced fighters and warriors of all time. So anyone who could make them all disappear all at once had to be pretty damned powerful in their own right. A more sensible and emotionally stable person would have turned the case down flat. But I really couldn't resist a chance to rub their poncy noses in it.

It was only then, as I peered absently down the bar, that I realised who and what I was looking at. I glared at Alex, almost shocked.

"Correct me if I'm wrong, but I'm sure I'm not . . . That elderly gentleman further down the bar; he is a Drood, isn't he? I mean, a member of that ancient established family who have made it their business to stand between Humanity and all the Evils that threaten us? Whether we like it or not? One of those high-and-mighty, very important people who lord it over the rest of us?"

"Oh sure," said Alex. "That's Jack Drood, the family Armourer. He often pops in here, for a quiet chat with someone he's not supposed to know."

"But he's a Drood!" I said, a bit excitedly. "They're banned from the Nightside, the whole damned family, by long compact and ancient charter!"

"He may be a Drood," said Alex. "But not here. Not officially. Everyone gives the Drood Armourer a lot of slack because . . . well, because you have to. He's that kind of person. Don't ask the questions if you can't cope with the answers, that's what I always say."

"But what's he doing here?"

"You never listen to a thing I say, do you? I pour him his

drinks and keep my distance and hope he doesn't decide to kill everyone here on a whim and burn down my bar. As Droods are sometimes prone to do. However, as to why he might be here right now . . . I'll say this. There has been an awful lot of gossip going around lately, as to where all the vampires have gone."

"Vampires?" I said.

"Yes! Blood-drinkers, undead walkers of the night, rip out your throat as soon as look at you . . ."

"All right, all right, I know what vampires are!"

"Then why did you ask?"

"Talk to me about the missing vampires, Alex," I said, hanging on to patience and self-control by my fingertips.

"No-one's seen any for some time," said Alex. "And there are usually one or two hanging around the place, stinking up the joint and drinking Really Bloody Marys."

"No great loss," I said. "Nasty things. Walking corpses, with pretty glamours and delusions of grandeur."

"Didn't you once go out with . . . ?"

"I was a lot younger then!" I said. "And it was a really good glamour. I sometimes wonder why there aren't more of them. Why they haven't tried to take over and colonise the Nightside. I mean, you would have thought a place where the sun is never going to rise would be perfect for them."

"The way I hear it, they have tried," said Alex. "Several times. But the various Authorities have always stamped down on them hard."

I nodded. The Authorities run things in the Nightside, inasmuch as anyone does, or can. We are protected; but it's often best not to ask how.

"I have to be on my way, Alex," I said. "And I'd prefer not to be noticed leaving. Is it okay if I use your backdoor?"

He sniffed loudly. "You use the bloody thing so often, I've started to think of it as my Other Front Door."

"Well," I said. "Strangefellows is that kind of bar."

TWO

The Adventurers Club is the long-established, very distinguished, home away from home for all the great heroes, gallants, and living legends who pass through the Nightside. I've never been sure why such people would want to come to such a morally dubious area as the Nightside; but I have my suspicions. Some are almost certainly just slumming, popping in for a quick visit so they can feel superior. And some are almost certainly here, on the quiet, for the same reasons as everyone else. To indulge the needs and pleasures that can't be satisfied anywhere else. But most of the Great Names who favour us with their presence are almost certainly above such things. Real heroes, who earned their legends the hard and morally inflexible way. So why do they feel the need for their own very private club, in the middle of the night that never ends?

I left Strangefellows by the backdoor, and ventured cautiously out into the dark-and-gloomy back alley. As always, it was filthy almost beyond belief and lit only by heavy blue-white moonlight. The moon is always full in the Nightside and far too large. I keep hoping someone will hire me to find out why. The shimmering light gave the back alley a sinister, uneasy air, like the streets we walk in dreams. I looked carefully about me. A lot of people use the backdoor at Strangefellows—for a little peace and quiet, a quick smoke of something unnatural, or to make the kind of deals that require privacy. But it seemed I had the alley all to myself, for once. Which was as well. I didn't want anyone to know where I was going, or why; and I definitely didn't want anyone to know how I was getting there.

The Adventurers Club is located in Uptown, the most civilised and snobbish part of the Nightside. Where even the Devil has to wear a tie if he wants to be allowed inside the very private and exclusive establishments of Clubland. Uptown is where the very best and very worst people go. To sample the sophisticated pleasures of all the very best bars and restaurants and night-clubs. Where Membership is always By Invitation Only, where dues are always paid, where it's hard to get in, and sometimes even harder to get out.

Uptown is right on the other side of the Nightside from Strangefellows; and it's never easy, getting across the Nightside. Because the roads are always packed with traffic that never stops; and driving through the never-ending rush hour is like swimming in shark-infested waters with a bloody steak tied to each ankle. There are no buses, and taxis have been known to eat the people who get inside them. I used to have to depend on the kindness of friends with transport; but they're never around when you need them. Luckily these days, I have my own personal short cut.

I reached into an inside pocket, and took out a gold pocket-watch. A small and apparently quite ordinary, functional object, it actually contains a Portable Timeslip. A dimensional doorway, powerful enough to bang two separate locations together and make them play nice. A way to get from here to there, while thumbing your nose at the distance in between. I carefully adjusted the rolled gold fob on the side of the watch, and the delicately engraved lid flew open, revealing an impenetrable darkness within. Looking into that dark was like standing on top of the world's tallest building and nerving yourself to jump. There are things, in that dark. Sometimes they speak to me. While I was still thinking that, and gathering my courage, the dark leapt up out of the watch and engulfed me; and when it let me go again, I was in Clubland.

•   •   •

After a moment to get my breath back, I carefully closed
the watch and put it away, and set off down the street.
No-one had noticed my arrival out of nowhere. No-one ever
did, that being one of the many useful properties built into
the watch. Who needs apps when you have magic on your
side? Or possibly advanced alien tech . . . Assuming there's
a difference. I strolled down the packed sidewalk, where
everyone made a point of never meeting anyone else's eyes.
None of them were interested in their surroundings; hot on
the trail of their own private satisfactions and damnations.
There was the occasional brief flicker of eyes in my direction, and no-one ever crushed or jostled me. Because they
knew who I was. No-one was surprised to see John Taylor in
Clubland, because no-one is ever surprised to see me anywhere. I turn up and do my job; and everyone with a burden
on their conscience runs like hell in the opposite direction.

The traffic roared past, never even slowing. Cars from
every period, from Model Ts to Edsels to slick things with
no wheels, all of them jostling for position or dominance
like rutting deer. Ambulances that run on distilled suffering, articulated vehicles carrying the kind of load best not
thought on, and hearses full of ghosts beating silently on
the closed windows. Something hideous swept past, on a
motorcycle made of bones, laughing shrilly, with its head
on fire. Long strings of melted fat fell away behind it.

The usual.

Clubland also looked much the same as always. A gaudy
collection of gathering-places and watering holes, dedicated
to everything from the outrageously erotic to the determinedly obscure. Quiet places of reflection, in which to
read and think. And very private back rooms, to serve the
kind of interests the rest of the world would not approve of.
It all started out as the ultimate extension of the Old Boys

Network, where all the real deals and decisions that mattered could be made in private, and behind the scenes, in a civilised and comfortable setting. The idea caught on; and these days there's a club for everyone and everything.

Familiar names caught my eye on every side. Club Dead, for the mortally challenged. Schrodinger's Club, for supernatural creatures so extreme they might or might not actually exist. You have to open the door and look in, to find out if there's anyone in there or not. Club Cannibal, where those who want to eat meet those who want to be eaten. (All done in the best possible taste, of course. Though it's never wise to hang around outside the front door.) And The End of the World Club, for those convinced the world really is coming to an end, anytime now, and are determined to do something practical about it. I subscribe to their monthly newsletter. Just in case.

The clubs in Clubland are rather like the churches and temples on the Street of the Gods. They come and they go, and they move around—the old being continuously replaced by the new, the weaker giving way and location to the stronger. It wasn't unusual for a Member to come looking for his club, and find it had been bounced half-way across Uptown by a bigger, more aggressive establishment. There are always traders standing on street-corners, selling street guides to the tourists; but since things move so fast in Clubland that the details in the guides can change before your very eyes . . . no-one ever buys them but the tourists. The longer-standing, established clubs never budge an inch. It's a matter of pride. The Adventurers Club hasn't moved in centuries.

I was probably the only person on that street strolling along. Everyone I passed was in a hell of a hurry, on their way to somewhere special, to do something the rest of us wouldn't want to know about. They were going to a place that would welcome them in and make them feel at home, among their own kind. I'd never been anywhere I felt like that, not even Strangefellows. Perhaps especially not at Strangefellows. I wasn't alone, any more. I had my Suzie Shooter, also known as Shotgun Suzie; the most respected and universally feared bounty hunter in the Nightside. We lived together, as closely as we could manage. But, still, it would have been nice to have somewhere else to go, a home away from home. Clubs might only be substitute families, but they're better than none.

I did wonder whether I should call Suzie on my mobile phone and ask if she'd like to be brought in on the case. Because I knew for a fact she had applied to join the Adventurers Club, sometime back; and they turned her down. Ostensibly because she didn't meet their high moral standards. And therefore wouldn't fit in. Suzie thought it was because they were all scared of her. She would love the chance to rub their noses in it by saving their heroic arses when they couldn't save themselves. But I couldn't justify asking for backup on what seemed like such a straightforward case. I have my pride.

I wondered, fairly casually, why I'd never applied to join the Adventurers Club. I'm not the joining kind, but . . . I did wonder what it would feel like, to be among my . . . well, peers. To talk about the kinds of things only we could understand and appreciate. But I am not an adventurer. I would never have fitted in. I've never thought of myself as a hero, only a man doing a job.

I finally reached the Adventurers Club—that huge, squat, and resolutely old-fashioned building, steeped in history and acclaim. The Doorman standing guard before the huge front door saw me coming, and a brief expression of relief flickered across his dark face before quickly disappearing behind a stoic, professional mask. I stopped right in front of him and nodded cheerfully. The Club's Doorman was a huge black gentleman, dressed in a long white Arabic gown, left hanging open at the top to show off the heavy necklace of sabre-tooth-tiger claws displayed on his massive black chest. Making it clear to everyone that he was a member of the were sabre-tooth-tiger clan, like all his predecessors. Every Doorman of the Adventurers Club is given the charm, and made a were sabre-tooth tiger, as they take office. To make it clear to all the world that they are tough enough to take on any and all uninvited visitors. Presumably the pay was good enough to make the curse worth it.

The Doorman was big and muscular enough in his own right to make me feel he could probably have taken care of business even without the claws. His face was broad and very dark, with raised ceremonial scars, dominated by fierce, dark eyes. He glared unblinkingly at me, as though daring me to justify my existence; so, of course, I smiled easily back at him.

"What do you want, tiny white man?" said the Doorman. In a deep, rich, cultured voice.

"Don't give me that crap," I said. "You know who I am."

"Of course," said the Doorman. "Who does not know the infamous John Taylor?"

"What happened to the old Doorman?" I said. "I liked him. He didn't give me any trouble."

"He got eaten," said the Doorman.

I decided not to press the matter. "You're not from around here, are you?" I said. "I can see Time hanging around you. Deep Time."

"I am from the Past," said the Doorman, a bit reluctantly. "I arrived here through a passing Timeslip. Abducted from ancient Africa, when it was a mighty place, full of great cities and marvellous civilisations. All gone now, and long forgotten. No-one now remembers the glories of the great city of Kor. I do not like it here. The people of this place and time are small and know not honour. I am merely keeping myself occupied, until I can find another Timeslip, to take me back to civilisation."

I didn't say anything; but I knew from experience how arbitrary most Timeslips are. I'd met a lot of people in the Nightside who were waiting for the right Timeslip to take them home again. Most of them were still waiting.

"You called me here," I said, to remind the Doorman which one of us was in charge. "I take it the Adventurers are still missing?"

"Of course."

"Have any of the Club's shields and protections been broached? From inside or outside?" I said, to show I was a professional.

"They are all still in place and still intact," said the Doorman.

"What first made you suspect something was wrong?"

"Just a feeling. A shiver in the bones, a chill in my soul."

"Do you think they might all be dead?" I said, carefully. "Do you want me to call in the Authorities?"

The Doorman shook his head firmly. "If I had wanted them involved, I would have contacted Walker, not you. I do not believe the Club Membership would want the Authorities' people sniffing around inside their very private rooms."

"You think I can be trusted?" I said.

"Of course," said the Doorman. "As long as you are being paid."

"Exactly!" I said. "You'd better take me in, show me around."

"I cannot help you," the Doorman said steadily. "It is my duty to stay at my post and guard this door against intruders. More than ever now, with the Club so vulnerable. I only left my position long enough to assure myself the Club Membership were all gone, then I returned to my post; and called you. It is not necessary for me to leave again, now you are here. I am sure you do not need my help, Mr. John Taylor."

"What if some of the Club Members die because you didn't help me?" I said, craftily.

"I am sure they would understand," said the Doorman. "There will be new Members, in the future, to make up the numbers. My duty is to the Club. To guard this door."

I gave him a hard look, but he seemed to mean it.

"All right," I said. "How long has it been since any Club Member passed through this door you're guarding so assiduously?"

"Not quite one hour," said the Doorman.

"Good," I said. "The trail is still fresh . . . Tell me, if you know. Why do so many honourable heroes and living legends come to the Nightside?"

"To go on safari, of course," said the Doorman. "To hunt the really Big Game. To test their skills and courage against the most dangerous prey of all."

"Suddenly, a great many things begin to make sense," I said. "In an alarming, and downright worrying, sort of way. Very well, Doorman. One last matter to be taken care of before I start work. My fee."

"You want paying in advance?" said the Doorman. "Before you've done anything?"

"Yes," I said. "It feels like that sort of case."

The Doorman reached inside his white gown, and brought out a credit card. It looked very small, in his huge black hand. He thrust the card at me, and I took it carefully. The card had the Club's name in it, and was attached to one of the biggest banks in the Nightside. Oh yes; we have banks. And none of them have ever needed bailing out. Sin has always been big business.

"You can access the card, and charge your fee, after you have found the missing Adventurers," said the Doorman. "I doubt they will quibble over details if you bring them back safely."

"And if I can't find them?" I said, tucking the card carefully away about my person.

"Then I will find you," said the Doorman.

I nodded, politely. Which is the best thing to do, when you've got a massive were sabre-tooth tiger towering over you.

He opened the door, and I strode through into the Adventurers Club with all the casualness I could muster. He didn't quite slam the door shut behind me. I stopped inside the entrance lobby and took a deep breath. I needed to do this right. I couldn't afford to screw this up. Bringing home the missing Adventurers would be a major feather in my cap, and it wouldn't hurt to have that many heroes and legends knowing they owed me. Never know when you might need to call in a favour, or protection.

I looked around the lobby, taking my time. It was open and roomy, quiet and utterly deserted. No sign of the Club Members, or any of their staff. It takes a lot of staff to run a club this size. Were the staff taken because the abductors had a need for them, too; or were they taken so no-one would be left to say what had happened? I shuddered, despite myself. I only had to be in the lobby to know something was wrong. Something really bad had happened here and left its mark. A subtle chill, an oppression of the senses, and the soul.

I moved slowly forward, across the patterned tiled floor. Everything felt wrong. Weird, and eerie. Tainted. When I'd been here before, the Club had always been full of larger-than-life individuals, all of them talking loudly, trying to top each other's tales of high adventure. Boasting of the amazing places they'd been, the appalling people they'd met, and the astounding things they'd done. The problem with heroes is that they can never do anything small, or everyday. I had been invited into the Club several times before this, to help them out with various problems, when the Members decided they needed an outsider, or at least an impartial view of things. That's why the Doorman had called me; I was probably the first name on his speed dial.

It did irk me, a bit, that I had never been asked to join the Club. I would almost certainly have said no; but it would have been nice to have been asked. But they never did. After all I'd done for them. I was good enough to clean up their messes, but not good enough to be one of them. I decided my fee had doubled.

I made myself concentrate on my immediate surroundings. The lobby was large, opulent, and entirely deserted. I moved over to the large mahogany reception desk and checked the phones and computers for any interesting messages. Nothing recent, nothing out of the ordinary. Nothing to warn anyone of what was coming. There was a large book, for Members to Sign In as they arrived. I checked through the most recent entries. Some names I recognised. Julien Advent, the Time-crossed Victorian Adventurer. Chandra Singh, the Sikh monster hunter. Augusta Moon, who looked like one of P. G. Wodehouse's more eccentric aunts but was actually one of the most dangerous women I've ever met. And I've been around. Sebastian Stargrave, the Fractured Protagonist, who'd battled so many forces, on so many sides, throughout Time and Space, in so many alternate time-lines . . . that even he wasn't sure who he was, any more. Monkton Farleigh, consulting detective. A great mind, and arrogant with it. A hard man to dislike but worth the effort. And a blotchy ink mark that was the sign of the Club's oldest Member; Tommy Squarefoot. The Neanderthal immortal.

Heroes and doughty fighters, all of them. I had to wonder why they hadn't fought off . . . whoever it was, when they came.

I left the lobby and moved on, deeper into the Adventurers Club. Passing from hall to hall and room to room, looking at everything, touching nothing. All the doors stood open; not one of them closed, anywhere. Which was odd. I peered quickly into every room, to make sure it was empty, then hurried on. Looking for one sign, one actual clue, as to what had happened here.

I saw flowers, wilted in a vase. And butterflies withered, inside a display case. But not a sign of violence anywhere. Not a drop of blood spilled, no overturned furniture, not even a section of rucked-up carpet. Nothing out of place. Just . . . empty deserted rooms, and a silence so absolute it was almost painful. I called out, again and again; but no-one answered. There wasn't even an echo.

I finally stopped in the bar. I felt in need of a good stiff drink. There was no-one present behind the bar to serve me, so I helped myself. The bar itself was almost overwhelmingly luxurious, a work of art, fashioned out of gleaming beech-wood and highly polished glass and crystal. I poured myself a large glass of single-malt whiskey because it was, after all, that kind of bar, and sipped thoughtfully. There were half-empty bottles and glasses set out the whole length of the bar top. Signs of drinking, interrupted. I could even convince myself I could detect faint traces of cigar-smoke on the air, from tobacco and opium and other less ordinary vices. But nothing to suggest what had happened here, or why.

Drinks left unfinished, cigar-butts in ash-trays . . . As though the Club Members had all got up and walked away. As though Someone, or Something, had called to them; and they had no choice but to obey. And yet none of the Adventurers had left through the front door; the Doorman would have spotted them. Which strongly suggested there had to be another entrance or exit, somewhere inside the Club. I emptied my glass and went forth in search of the hidden door.

The silence and the solitude were starting to get to me. The sense of life interrupted, suddenly, from outside. The Adventurers Club was starting to feel like the *Marie Celeste*. I went back through the Club, checking each room thoroughly. There had to be some clue, some evidence, something left behind.

In the Duelling Room, all the weapons were still in place on the walls. Swords and guns, and other equally nasty and destructive things. No-one had drawn a single weapon to defend themselves against the intruders. Could it all have happened so quickly, they had no chance to defend themselves?

There was a swimming pool. The waters should have been steaming hot; but when I knelt to check, they were freezing cold. What did that mean?

All the usual trophies and displays were still in place on the Club's walls. The distorted shadow of a Leopard Man, imprisoned in its great block of transparent Lucite. A hollowed-out alien skull, put to use as an ash-tray. Something from a Black Lagoon, stuffed and mounted, watched the proceedings from its usual corner, a melancholy look on its face. And a severed demon hand, forever burning but always unconsumed. I'd seen some Club Members light their cigars off the sulphurous flames. High up on one wall, proudly displayed on a memorial plaque, was the withered and mummified arm of the original Grendel monster; presented to the Club by Beowulf himself, back in the sixth century. The Adventurers Club goes way back.

And there had been one particular case that I worked

on, where one of the Club's most highly treasured exhibits turned out not to be what everyone thought it was. An ex–Ghost Finder had brought in a preserved mummified head, from the Egyptian Valley of the Kings, as his entrance fee. Except it turned out not to be just any old mummy, but that of a Djinn. And they can rebuild themselves from even the smallest fragment. The head grew itself a new body overnight and went rampaging through the Club. It took most of the Members acting together, along with my not-inconsiderable assistance, to bring it down. The Djinn was taken back to Egypt and ceremonially reburied deep underneath the Valley of the Kings, with all the proper Solomonic rituals. Along with the ex–Ghost Finder who'd caused all the trouble in the first place.

Which did make me wonder. Had someone else brought in a trophy that turned on them? There was no sign of violence anywhere . . . Perhaps the thing was some kind of Boojum, which could make people softly and silently vanish away. But even that would have left some traces behind, something I could pick up on.

The Doorman said . . . Adventurers came to the Night-side to go on safari. To hunt the really Big Game that couldn't be found anywhere else. Could one of the Adventurers have run into something too big for him to handle? Something that turned on him and pursued him back to the Club? Was something now hunting Adventurers?

It was the silence, and the unrelenting solitude. My head ached as wild ideas raced back and forth inside it.

I prowled from room to room, kicking the doors wide open and investigating every open space I could find; and still I couldn't turn up anything. Old rooms and new rooms, familiar rooms and refurbished rooms. Nothing moved anywhere, and even the shadows were creepily still. I was starting to feel the pressure of unseen watching eyes. My back crawled in anticipation of a blow I'd never see coming.

I ended up back at the bar. My breathing was coming uncomfortably fast, and I kept almost catching glimpses of something out of the corners of my eyes. So much time and effort, and nothing to show for it . . . So; time to draw the really big gun. I have a gift that enables me to find anyone, or anything. The gift has its limitations, but it rarely lets me down. I concentrated, reaching deep inside myself; and my gift unfolded like a flower with razor-edged petals, bursting forward to fill my mind. My inner eye, my third eye, my private eye, opened wide; and just like that I could See the bar before me with almost unbearable clarity. Every detail jumped out at me, full of meaning and significance. Ghosts of Adventurers surged back and forth before me, shimmering pastel shades that moved in absolute silence. Images from out of the recent Past.

I concentrated even harder, shutting out all unnecessary details. I asked my gift to show me where the missing Adventurers were; but all I got in return was a splitting headache. It was too vague a question. To get a specific answer, I needed a specific question. So I tried again, focusing on one Club Member I knew would have been here when it all went down; because he always was. Gareth De Lyon, the Resurrected Hero. He'd been at least a dozen different Members of the Club, at various times in its history; and probably a lot more, on the quiet. He spent a lot of time hanging out at the Club because it was one of the few constants in his lives. I fixed my gift on him; but all I got then was a horrible impression of utter darkness, like the dark inside a tomb, or right after they've nailed the coffin lid down . . . and the smell of spilled blood. Lots of it.

Except, I'd already established no blood had been spilled inside the Club.

I tried something else. I used my gift to find the last

place the Club Membership was, before it disappeared. My gift dug into my brain like a fish-hook, and dragged me out of the bar and through the Club, wincing and crying out all the way. My gift finally deposited me in the Club Reading Room, then released me. I swore at it a few times, on general principles, while my gift shut itself down, with the smug air of having done all that could reasonably be asked of it. I looked around the large, brightly lit room. I'd already been here once, but I checked it out again, taking my time, in case I'd missed something.

All four walls were covered in book-shelves, packed with oversized leather-bound volumes. No complete Dickens here, or modern literature of our times; it was all Histories of the Club, and its many Members, down all the years of its long existence. Everything they'd ever done, or seen, or been involved in. An invaluable treasury of facts and tactics and secret knowledge, wrestled from the hidden worlds. Including all the stories considered unsuitable for a general audience. All the best tricks of the heroing trade, and all the bitter secret truths. An accumulated body of hard-won knowledge, for new Members to learn from.

Along with all the usual secret histories and volumes of forbidden knowledge. I leaned forward to check out some of the titles and wasn't impressed. Nothing I hadn't seen before. The Nightside is lousy with back-street book-stores where you can buy over-priced volumes of forgotten lore, forbidden knowledge, and some of the more obscure cheat codes for the universe. Sucker bait, for the more gullible tourists.

So why had my gift brought me, so insistently, to the Club Reading Room? There was only the one door, the one I'd come in through; and that was barely large enough for two people to walk through, side by side. Even if all the Club's Membership had been here, how could they have all left, so suddenly? Answer—a hidden door. I raised my Sight again and studied the Reading Room carefully, and quickly found a Door, a dimensional doorway, tucked away in a shadowed corner, standing sideways to reality. So well shielded even my Sight had trouble focusing on it. A Door that could connect one place with any other, or any number of others. How very useful.

I used my gift to take a firm hold on the Door and ease it fully into existence. A perfectly ordinary-looking wooden door, except that it stood alone and unsupported, connected to nothing. Of course the Adventurers Club would have such a Door, so Members from all over the world, or worlds, could appear inside the Club without having to pass through the Nightside. If they were on safari, they wouldn't necessarily want their prey to know they were coming. I rattled the doorknob, in a hopeful sort of way, but the Door didn't open. I didn't really think it would, without the proper security-code words.

This was how the enemy got in, bypassing the Doorman. The front door was for show. This Door was the real entrance to the Adventurers Club, and perhaps its Trojan Horse, too.

I moved over to one of the book-shelves, looking for information on dimensional doors, and as I leaned in close to check a particular title, I heard a soft sound, a quiet whimpering. I pressed my ear up against the books, but the sound didn't get any louder. I grabbed at the books, pulling them off the shelves and throwing them to the floor. I ran my hands over the bare wooden shelf and quickly found a hidden catch. I tugged at it, and the whole section of shelving swung slowly out, revealing a hiding place beyond. A small bare room, with one Club Member lying on the floor. Eyes closed, knees pulled up to his chest, curled up tight in the foetal position.

I eased slowly and carefully into the concealed room, checking for defences or booby-traps; but there was nothing. What use would the Adventurers Club have for a hidden room? A panic room? I bent over the man on the floor. I knew him. Sebastian Stargrave, the Fractured Protagonist. He had his arms wrapped tightly around himself, tears running jerkily down his cheeks.

I knelt beside him, and said his name, but he didn't hear me. I tried my name; but that didn't help either. Something had driven him deep inside himself. Sebastian Stargrave was skinny and fragile at the best of times, with an air of exhausted nobility. He had a pale face, stringy jet-black hair, and eyes like cinders coughed up out of Hell. An air of quiet melancholy hung around him, all the time, like an old and familiar tattered cape. He'd fought in some serious battles, up and down the time-lines, and won quite a few of them. But along the way, he'd lost everything else that mattered. He wore shimmering futuristic golden armour; skin-tight, rising in a tall, stiff collar behind his head. The armour murmured to him constantly, in shifting alien tongues.

A fierce fighter and a fearless warrior, according to many of the accounts of his many lives. A good man to have at your side, or at your back. As long as you caught him on one of his good days. He'd been broken too many times to mend properly. He tended to drift . . . Most Members went out of their way to be polite to him, because he'd been down on his luck for so long. There but for the grace of God . . .

And now here he was, curled up in a ball on the floor, whimpering to himself. What could have done this to him? I took hold of his armoured arm and hauled him back up onto his feet, trying hard to sound comforting and supportive. I didn't like the feel of his armour. It seemed to suck all the warmth out of my hands. And no matter how close I got to the armour, I still couldn't understand what it was saying. The muttered words seemed to hover on the edge of meaning. Or maybe the armour was just as crazy as he was.

I held Sebastian Stargrave up and walked him round the room. He didn't seem to weigh much; like a starved child. His eyes were huge and shocked, barely taking in where he was or who was talking to him.

"Where are they, Sebastian?" I said. "Come on, you know me. John Taylor. You can talk to me. Where are all the other Adventurers?"

"They didn't want me," Sebastian said finally, his words distant but clear. "They came and took everyone else, but they didn't want me. So they left me behind. I would have gone with them! I would!"

"Who, Sebastian? Who didn't want you?"

"The angels!"

We looked at each other for a long moment.

"They were beautiful," he said. "And they shone so brightly. They said they loved us, and they were so glorious . . . how could we say no to them? I wanted to go with them, to go with the others, through the Door to the marvellous place they showed us. They showed us Heaven; but they wouldn't take me. They didn't want anything to do with me. My armour keeps saying it protected me; but who wants to be protected from Paradise?"

"Angels," I said. "Really?"

He couldn't answer me. Couldn't even tell me how he'd ended up in the hidden room. I patted him comfortingly on his armoured shoulder and let him lean on me, while I thought hard. It wasn't unknown for angels to appear in the Nightside, from Heaven and Hell. I was here the last time they appeared, in force, to fight a war over possession of the Unholy Grail; the cup Judas drank from at the Last Supper. An object of such great power, both sides were ready to destroy the whole Nightside to gain control of it. Or at the very least, keep it out of the opposition's hands. Luckily, I was able to defuse the Unholy Grail, and they all went home again, leaving us poor mortals to clean up the mess.

"All right," I said finally to Sebastian. "I'm sending you to Strangefellows. You'll be safe there, while I sort this mess out."

He nodded quickly, almost pathetically grateful. I got him to unlock the Door, using the Club's security words, and I ordered it to open onto Strangefellows. It swung back before us, and the raucous noise of a party still in full swing burst into the Reading Room. I yelled to Alex through the open Door.

"I'm sending you Sebastian Stargrave!" I said loudly. "Look after him! Keep him safe and protect him!"

"Who from?" said Alex.

"Everyone!" I said.

"Oh, it's like that, is it?" said Alex. "Like I haven't got enough to do . . . Do I look like a nanny?"

"There's money in it!"

"Okay. Fair enough. Send him through."

I bundled Sebastian through the Door, and Alex sent Dead Boy and Razor Eddie forward to collect him. I'd back them against pretty much anyone. Even angels would fear to enter Strangefellows without first sending in someone waving a white flag. I shut the Door firmly and looked thoughtfully about me.

If the Door had been the departure point for the missing Club Membership, it hadn't been a simple abduction. The Adventurers couldn't all have been taken at once, by force; they would have had to file through the Door, slowly and patiently, a few at a time. They would have had to go willingly. From what Sebastian said, it sounded like they'd been enchanted . . . Hypnotised and overwhelmed. And angels wouldn't have bothered with that. You did what they said, or you ended up as a pillar of salt. No. Whatever Sebastian had seen, it wasn't angels.

I called on my gift, and forced my inner eye open again. Even though the excessive use was burning up my resources. I peered through my third eye, to See the recent Past again. Immediately, the Reading Room was packed full of Adventurers, milling cheerfully before the open Door. I tried to look through it; but all I could see was an endless dark. The ghostly images of the Adventurers all looked the same; wide-eyed, with vague, happy smiles. Enchanted, mesmerised, by the vague forms that moved among them. Definitely not angels; I would have had no trouble Seeing them. In fact, the Sight would probably have burned the eyes right out of my head. No; these figures were hidden from me behind some kind of glamour. They ushered the Adventurers through the Door, hurrying them along, and not to any kind of Paradise.

What the hell could be powerful enough to overcome so many hardened and experienced Adventurers? Men and women who'd faced a thousand psychic attacks in a thousand undeclared wars? And could therefore be expected to have powerful mental shields in place as a matter of course? What kind of monsters was I dealing with here?

I thought hard, on what I knew for sure. Something, or more properly a number of Somethings, had found their way into the Adventurers Club through its hidden Door. They then enchanted and overpowered the Membership and led them away. Except for poor Sebastian Stargrave, who was either too broken to be of any use or protected by his armour. But who wanted the Adventurers? And for what?

I only had one trick left. One last permutation of my gift. I gathered up my thoughts and sent them flying up out of my head, through the ceilings of the Club and on up through the roof, into the night sky. I shot up and up, high above the many roofs of Clubland, where the stars whirled around me in the night like so many flaring Catherine wheels, and brightly coloured comets shot back and forth, zigzagging this way and that, shouting and laughing and crying out to each other in simple high spirits. The full moon roared with a great Voice, saying things I couldn't understand. Massive shapes flapped slowly by, big enough to block out whole sections of the night sky.

My mind moved slowly on the spiritual winds, looking in every direction at once. Down below, all kinds of traffic roared back and forth, and from this high, it was clear only some of them were vehicles. People swarmed along the streets, burning all kinds of guilty colours. But I wasn't looking for people. I set my gift searching for the presence of the vague monsters that had stolen away the Adventurers. And, surprisingly, they hadn't gone far.

A little way up the road, in fact, to another Club. I drifted slowly down, descending unseen towards this new Club. It wasn't one I knew. I didn't like the feel of it. It felt . . . like descending through bloody waters, towards hungry sharks. And then I slammed to a halt as something stopped me dead, hanging in the air above the new Club. *This far and no further,* said the Club. *You don't belong here.* I didn't try to push it. Something about the place made my head hurt and my skin crawl, sickening me to my stomach. Even though my body was far away, my mind was interpreting a spiritual threat in ways I could understand. This new Club was physically and spiritually dangerous. And the stolen Adventurers were somewhere inside it.

I fell back into my body, in the Reading Room, and cried out in shock and relief as I wrapped myself in warm flesh again. I lay spread-eagled on my back, breathing hard, getting my head back together again. All I had to do now was force my way into a well-guarded and protected Club, face down Something, or indeed any number of Somethings, all of them strong enough to overpower an army of experienced heroes, and bring the poor lost sheep home again. I sighed. I might as well make a start. It wasn't going to get any easier.

THREE

It's amazing how often it happens that even when you know where you want to go, it's really hard to get there. I knew where the missing Adventurers were now—up the street from the Adventurers Club. But getting there turned out to be a real pain in the behind.

I started with the dimensional Door, in the Reading Room. Since Sebastian Stargrave had given me the Door's activating words, I assumed that would give me access to its workings. In particular, to the spatial coordinates used by the Adventurers' abductors. That way, I could step directly from the interior of this Club to the next, in hot pursuit, and surprise everyone. But the Door wouldn't co-operate, remaining firmly and unhelpfully closed. Even when I tried kicking it. I hauled my gift forward again and tried to use it to find the correct command words that would force the Door to do what it was damn well told. But all that got me was a pounding headache, and a distinct feeling the Door was laughing at me. I should have known any door inside the Adventurers Club would have its own shields and protections. Which only made it all the more remarkable that Someone or Something had found a way past them. I put my gift back in its mental box, and my headache subsided. But I could smell blood again. Freshly spilled blood, and lots of it. Which did not bode well for the missing Adventurers.

•   •   •

In the end, I had no choice but to leave the Adventurers Club through the front door. With my back straight and my head held high, as though that was what I'd meant to do all along. When working a case, it's always best to at least look like you know what you're doing. I said something calm and comforting and basically misleading to the Door-man as I passed, so he wouldn't worry. And then I hurried off up the street before he could think of any questions to ask me. People on the street saw something in my face and gave me even more room than usual.

It was only a short walk, a few minutes. So short that I did wonder why the mysterious abductors hadn't just marched their enchanted victims out the front door and up the street to the new club. Rather than risk using a Door that had to be left behind; a major clue in itself, and some-thing that might point directly to the new club if anyone could get at its stored destinations. But then, the abductors would have had to get past the Doorman; and I very much doubted he would have seen them as angels. Enchantment might not have worked on a were sabre-tooth tiger; and you really wouldn't want to find that out the hard way . . . The abductors didn't want to be seen, or recognised, by anyone. And it was always possible they needed to get the Adven-turers away as quickly as possible, to buy them time to do something to their victims.

I stood outside the new club, both hands thrust deep into the pockets of my trench coat, rocking back and forth on my heels as I looked the place over. I didn't like the new building. It felt . . . wrong. This used to be the location for the Suicide Club. If the world had grown too much for you, and the Nightside no longer distracted you, then you could always depend on the happy smiling girls and boys of the Suicide Club to be there for you. Ready to see you on your way with a nice poisoned cup of tea, to somewhere hopefully better. No money required—the Suicide Club was a registered charity. Supposedly. I always suspected there was more to it than that; but no-one ever hired me to find out what.

The place wasn't as popular as you might have thought. The Nightside is, after all, one of the few locations in this world where you can be sure of coming face-to-face with representatives of Heaven and Hell on a regular basis. And there's nothing like an upfront and in-your-face encounter with the true nature of the Afterlife to make you very determined to avoid it for as long as possible. The Suicide Club was there for those who had seen it all, done it all, and were either very bored or completely burned-out.

But now the Suicide Club building was gone. Replaced entirely by the new arrival. Clubland embodies evolution in action, with the strong stamping out the weak. Sometimes literally. The old façade of dignified, gleaming marble had been replaced by a huge glowering display of purple-grey stone. Bulging out into the street, blunt and discoloured, like a bruised forehead. With a single, unmarked, and unremarkable door. The new club didn't even seem to have a name; just a single letter, carved in jagged deep cuts into the stone above the door.

V

I scowled, thinking hard. V for what? V could stand for any number of things in the Nightside, which has been known to stand for pretty much anything in its time. Or could it be the Roman numeral, for five? Five what? Thinking about that didn't get me anywhere, so I looked the place over some more. The rough stonework stared back at me, giving away nothing. No windows, no hot neon, no come-ons at all . . . not at all what you'd expect in Clubland. Nothing to suggest what kind of club this was or what kind of people it was intended for. Interestingly, none of the people passing by paid the new club any attention at all. They didn't even glance at it, just kept their heads down and hurried on past. As though they were scared of it, scared even of drawing its attention.

Odd behaviour for the Nightside, where people thrive on variety and anything new. Nothing draws a crowd faster than the promise of a new pleasure, or a new variation on an old sin. There's always someone desperate to be first to try something out and report back on how it felt. I'd assumed people were giving me plenty of room because of who I was, not where I was. But it wasn't me, it was the club. People actually flinched away from the rough stone façade as they passed. As though they knew something I didn't. Or, more likely, sensed something. No-one has more sensitive antennae than a Nightside regular. I glared at the front of the new club. I couldn't feel, or sense, a damned thing.

I looked at the new club, and the stone front looked back, like a blank, mad, unseeing eye.

So how was I going to get in? No handle on the door; no bell or knocker; not even an intercom. No Doorman. Nothing to suggest how anyone was supposed to get in. I did have a little plastique explosive about my person. And a few white phosphorous grenades. For emergencies. But they would make a lot of noise and draw rather more attention than I was comfortable with, for the moment. So I walked up to the door and knocked, politely.

The door swung slowly, invitingly open before me. There was nothing beyond it but an impenetrable darkness. Not the gloom of an unilluminated place but the cold, flat dark of an interior space without any kind of light. It could have been a few feet or a few miles deep. No way of telling.

It could have been a deep well, or a night sky that went on forever. There was nothing there for my mind to get a grip on. A cold shiver went through me. So I put on my most unimpressed face, folded my arms, and glared into the dark opening.

"How dumb do you think I am?" I said loudly. "Did you really think I was going to walk in there, like a cow into an abattoir?"

I waited, but there was no response. Just the dark; silent and still, not giving anything away. If I'd had any sense, I would have turned around and walked away. Come back later, better prepared. But then, if I'd had any sense, I would never have set up shop as a private investigator in the Nightside. I couldn't walk away. Not while the Adventurers were still missing and in need of help. Right now, I was all the hope they had. In the time it took me to go away and come back, that hope might disappear. Bad things can happen really quickly in the Nightside.

When in doubt, stare the bastards down. I took a deep breath and strode through the door into the darkness. The door slammed shut behind me, cutting off the light and sealing me in, like the lid slamming down on a coffin.

I stood very still, trying to get my bearings, waiting for my eyes to adjust to the dark. But there was nothing there for my eyes to adapt to, not even the smallest glimmer of light. No sound, and not even a breath of moving air. I reached out cautiously with both arms, extending them to their limits, but my fingertips didn't brush against anything. I lowered my arms and took two cautious steps backwards, but my back didn't slam up against the door.

"If this is supposed to intimidate me," I said, loudly, "you really don't know the Nightside. We're not scared of the dark; we embrace it. We eat it up with spoons. Now either someone turns the lights on, right now, or I am going to start throwing incendiaries around, in a highly irritating and destructive way. And we'll see what a few pounds of willie pete will do to brighten the place up."

I made it sound like I meant it. Even though I only had a few incendiaries, and I wasn't ready to use them up quite yet. I did have a small salamander ball tucked away about my person, somewhere, but I was reluctant to use it for illumination till I had to. Those things are expensive. Well, you only get two to a salamander. But bluffing can get you a long way in the Nightside, where you can never be sure who and what you're dealing with; and you never know what they might have tucked up a sleeve you can't even see. Somebody must have heard me because a light rose slowly around me.

Not a light I would have chosen. A flat, crimson glare, as though the air itself was stained with blood. It pulsed around me, as though generated by some massive, beating heart. Very dramatic. I made a point of curling my upper lip, to show how unimpressed I was. A long stone tunnel stretched off into the distance before me, for what seemed like forever. Great curving walls rose to close together above my head in a rounded ceiling. It was like standing in a great stone artery. The blood-red light gave everything a disturbingly organic look. As though I was . . . deep in the body of the Beast. And, of course, when I looked behind me, the door to the club that I'd come in through was no longer there. The stone corridor stretched far and far away, in front and behind me.

The walls weren't just stone. Set between the old stones were human skulls. Hundreds, thousands, of them. Dusty, dirty, uncared for, with empty, staring eye-sockets and grinning teeth. Many of the skulls were damaged, cracked apart and broken, the result of blows with appalling strength behind them. And they all looked old, very old, as though they'd been brought here and made a part of these walls long and long ago. Who could have killed so many people? And why? What kind of club was this . . .

All at once, the skulls were screaming. A horrid, unbearable, overpowering sound. Thousands of human voices, calling out in pain and loss and horror. It was so loud, I clapped my hands over my ears, instinctively; but it didn't help. These were psychic screams, not natural sounds. The dead, crying out, protesting their fate. I slammed down all my mental shields, blocking the screams out on level after level, until I couldn't hear them any more. You don't last long in the Nightside if you can't protect yourself on every level there is. There's always something trying to get in. And rarely in a good way. The terrible sound finally shut off, and the skulls were just bones again.

I slowly lowered my hands from my ears, breathing hard. Something was coming. I could feel it. The silence was broken again, this time by the sound of approaching footsteps, from far off down the tunnel ahead of me. I strained my eyes against the bloody glow, but I couldn't see anything. The footsteps were clear and distinct, drawing slowly nearer. As though they had all the time in the world. I ran through all the nasty little devices I keep about my person for emergencies like this. But it was hard to know what might be useful until I knew for sure what I was facing. And then suddenly a figure appeared, standing very still, right in front of me. I refused to let myself jump.

My first thought was how ordinary he looked. Though dressed in the height of fashion for the mid nineteenth century, he was a short and stocky figure, with an everyday face. And yet he had presence. A lot more than he should have had. As though merely by standing there, being there, he gave the moment significance and meaning. He was what I was here to see. Nothing else mattered.

I broke the mood with a loud and obnoxious sniff because

that's what I do. I looked him up and down, as though I were thinking of hiring him for some necessary but unpleasant task. And then all the hairs on my arms and the back of my neck stood up, as slowly and steadily, he changed, as though letting more and more of the real him come to the surface. Because he wanted me to see who and what he really was.

He stood unnaturally still. His face was deathly pale, without a touch of colour in it. He had a receding hair-line, a beak of a nose, sunken eyes, and a firmly closed mouth. His ears were pointed. He had his arms folded across his chest, the hands tucked away out of sight, in his armpits. And because I was beginning to think I knew what he was, what he had to be, I knew what to look for. His chest didn't rise or fall, and he didn't seem to be breathing. And for all the blood-red light, coming from every direction at once, he didn't cast a shadow. He smiled, slightly, his colourless lips twitching; and he inclined his head to me briefly, in something less than a bow.

"Welcome to my home, Mr. John Taylor."

His voice was dry and rasping, as though he didn't use it often. Just the sound of it made me want to cringe, every instinct I had yelling at me to run while I still had the chance. Some of these old monsters go way back.

"You know me," I said, carefully casual. "Can't say I know you. What is this place?"

His smile widened enough to show off the sharp points of his teeth. "Don't you know, Mr. Taylor?"

"V," I said. "V for vampire."

"Exactly, Mr. Taylor! Welcome to the Vampire Club. Where the blood really is the life. Just a small beginning in my colonisation of the Nightside."

"Oh bloody hell," I said. "Not another one. There's always someone who wants to take over the Nightside. I suppose it's the vampires' turn . . ."

"Ah, but I am not just any vampire, Mr. Taylor."

"It's been tried before!" I said loudly. "Those who will not learn from historical defeats are doomed to get their arses kicked really hard. The Nightside is a big place, and you're just a bunch of leeches with delusions of grandeur. What makes you think this attempt will be any different?"

"Because I am the King of the Vampires."

"You're a bit short for Dracula," I said. "I've met a dozen leeches, down the years, who claimed to be the old Count. None of them were in the least impressive, never mind convincing."

His smile widened a little further, showing sharp, pointed teeth, brown and blocky as a rat's. "No, no, Mr. Taylor. I'm not Dracula. I'm Varney."

And that actually did stop me, for a moment.

"Sir Francis Varney?" I said, my mind working swiftly. "The vampire who terrorised all of England, and most of Europe, more than fifty years before Dracula showed up. Who turned houses and homes into butcher-shops, and filled the gutters with blood . . . The very first vampire boogeyman. Just how many people did you slaughter, down the years?"

"I don't keep count," said Varney.

"I thought you committed suicide?" I said. "Threw yourself into Mount Vesuvius?"

He was grinning now, his teeth large and jagged. His eyes were dark and fierce and unblinking.

"What better way to get the hounds off my heels than to seem to be safely dead and gone? They should have known better. I was always the strongest and most powerful of vampires. I could walk in the brightest daylight, and it did me no harm. Garlic did not poison me, and the cross held no fears for me. So why would you think fire would hurt me? I swam down through rivers of liquid magma until I found a series of subterranean tunnels that led me eventually to the base of the mountain, and out into the world again."

"Then where have you been, all this time?" I said.

"Sitting in a cave," said Varney. "Far and far from the world of mortal men. Thinking, and dreaming . . . of a better way. Determined not to make the same mistakes, when at last I ventured out again. Human civilisation is such fun to play with; but it has grown too large, and too well educated, to be easily taken down. Even by the largest of vampire armies. No, I needed more than that. And then, finally, one of my disciples brought me news. Of a marvellous hidden kingdom, where the treacherous sun never shines, and it is always dark, always night. What better place for vampires to make a home, and a homeland?"

"It's been tried!" I said. "The Authorities always stop you and stamp you into the ground. They've probably got an instructional leaflet, tucked away somewhere, telling them exactly how to do it. I mean, come on. What do you have, oh King of the Vampires, that none of your predecessors had? To make your chances any better?"

"A new kind of army," said Varles. "I have taken the greatest heroes and adventurers and soldiers the world has ever known, right out of their very own Club, and I have made them mine. They shall be my vanguard, leading my forces, and all their strength and experience and tactics are mine to call on. I shall throw them at the throats of all those who dare oppose me. How do you think the Authorities' forces will feel when they see their most revered heroes running towards them, to tear out their throats and drink their blood? I think they will scream, before they die. Don't you?"

"Tell me how you did this," I said. "Come on; you know you want to tell me. Or you wouldn't have let me in."

"It has been such a long time since I have had anyone worth talking to," said Varney. "Yes . . . The heroes come to the Nightside to hunt the Big Game. And one of them had the temerity to think he could hunt me. Gareth de Lyon . . . He'd been around too long, you see. Getting old, and slow.

He thought he'd seen everything, done everything, fought everything. And then I let it be known, only to him, that I was back. He thought if he could track me down, and take me down, then he would be acknowledged among his peers as a hunter of the really Big Game. He liked the idea of bringing back the head of the King of the Vampires. That would prove he still had it. That he wasn't old and past it, after all."

"Gareth de Lyon?" I said. "The Resurrected Hero?"

Varney surprised me then, with a short bark of very human-sounding laughter.

"You believed that nonsense? Just a story, Mr. Taylor— propaganda to make him seem bigger and more important than he ever really was. So he could claim other men's victories as his own. I suppose you people encounter so many impossible things in the Nightside that you're prepared to believe anything . . . He's merely a man. Or at least, he was. He came after me, confident in what he thought he knew about vampires, armed with the cross, and garlic, and a stake. Like you, Mr. John Taylor. But you never met a vampire like me."

"You hypnotised him," I said. "And then used him to gain access to the Adventurers Club."

"Never waste an opportunity, Mr. Taylor. I've always understood the usefulness of the Judas goat. I looked him in the eye, and all his precious strength and experience went for nothing. He bared his throat to me; and I bit him. Not enough to change him, to turn him; but more than enough to make him mine. And then I gathered up my people, had Gareth open the Club Door from the other side, and in we went. Into the Adventurers Club. Charging through the rooms and passageways, overwhelming every living thing as we met them. You can't fight off an enemy if you don't want to. A few resisted; but their own friends and colleagues overpowered them and dragged them down.

Such fun, such sport . . . They all thought they were so important, and powerful; but a vampire's will has always been superior to any mortal man's. Because we are the predators; and you are the prey."

"Why did you take them away?" I said, steadily. To show I wasn't impressed or intimidated. "Why not feed on them, right there in their own Club?"

"Because it will be so much more fun to send them out to fight the Authorities while they're still human," said Varney. "Part of them will know what they're doing, and they'll scream and scream inside as they fight and kill old friends and colleagues. There will be time for feeding afterwards. And now, Mr. Taylor, that's enough polite conversation, I think. Now it's your turn."

He moved forward abruptly, without seeming to take a single step. He was suddenly right there in front of me, larger and taller and far more threatening. His eyes met mine, and I couldn't look away. Didn't want to look away. His eyes blazed like the fires of Hell, awful beyond bearing. His voice murmured in my ear, soft and seductive.

"You don't want to fight me, John. You want to fight the Authorities. You know you've always hated them. They've always hated you. Serve me; and I will see to it that those who survive will serve you. I will give you your heart's desire, John Taylor, in return for a little blood. The bite isn't so bad. You'll come to love it, in time. As you will learn to love and worship me. Bare your throat, John Taylor."

I laughed in his face; and suddenly he was back where he had been, standing some distance away. He looked suddenly smaller, less imposing. And he looked so shocked it was almost comical. I laughed again. So he wouldn't know how close it had been.

"Oh come on!" I said. "If Walker couldn't control me with his Voice, did you really think you stood any chance? I've been around. I've stepped on worse things than you!

I've faced angels, from Above and Below! I don't bow down to anyone! *I'm John Taylor!"*

It took Varney a long moment to regain his composure; and then he nodded, briefly.

"It seems the stories are true, Mr. Taylor. You are indeed your mother's son."

"Don't go there," I said. "Really."

"We could have done this the easy way," said Varney. "Your future suffering and degradation are therefore your own fault. It's time for you to meet my family. Come forth, my children!"

Holes and openings suddenly appeared everywhere, all the length of the great stone tunnel. Trap-doors swung down from the ceiling and burst up from the floor. Skulls and stones burst out of the curving walls. And the vampires came out. There was a sudden thick stench of blood and carrion, rot and corruption. Physically overpowering and spiritually sickening. A smell that said, *This is where Death is. Death, and so much worse than Death.* The vampires came crawling out of their holes, not moving in any human way. They burst out of the walls, like insects disturbed from their nest. They scuttled and scurried across the stonework, in sudden quick rushes. They hung down from the ceiling and crawled up and down the walls.

Some of them looked young, and some of them looked old; all were dressed in the styles and fashions of past periods. As though they couldn't bear to give up the last traces of what they were, the last time they were human. The last time they were still alive. They all had perfect faces, handsome and beautiful, which was how I knew I was only seeing what they wanted me to see. This was glamour, not reality. Pleasing illusions to hide the rotting corpses they really were. The undead don't wear their pleasing masks to hide what they are from the living but to hide what they really are from themselves.

Vampires are dead bodies animated by a spiritual infection. Blood will have blood because it must, because that's how the infection is spread. The infected wake up inside their coffins, break out, and dig their way up out of their own graves. Undead, unnatural things, driven by a need for blood and horror. Parasites that prey on the living. There's nothing romantic, or melancholy, about vampires. They're leeches on two legs.

They scurried back and forth, all around me, faster and faster. Running up and down the walls, clinging to the ceiling, scrabbling over one another, like insects. Hanging from the stones and skulls at impossible angles, their heads turning round impossibly far, like owl's. Fixing me with their dark, unblinking eyes. Showing me their pointed teeth in impossibly wide smiles.

I stood my ground, glaring back at them, showing them nothing but contempt. Because the moment I showed them the smallest sign of weakness, they'd be all over me. They were only holding off now because they were puzzled. What could I have, they were thinking, that made me so confident? What weapon could I possibly have that could hold them off? I had a few things about me that might prove useful. I had a few bags of powdered garlic, my incendiaries, and a handful of assorted religious items. No wooden stakes. Never thought I'd need any when I left the house.

I mean, vampires? That's so old-school.

I'd never seen so many of the nasty things in one place before. No wonder people in Strangefellows had been saying they hadn't seen any vampires recently. Varney had taken them all underground. And they'd never looked this dangerous before. He'd inspired them. No-one takes vampires seriously in the Nightside because they've been slapped down so many times. They'd learned to seem not so terrible, to keep their heads down, so they'd be tolerated.

Overlooked. Until the King of the Vampires came back, to tell them it was their time come round at last.

I was surrounded. The vampires ran in circles around me, scurrying up and down the curving walls, scuttling across the ceiling over my head, scrambling on the floor on all fours, circling me and circling me, darting in close, then back again, to see what I would do. Raking the air with their clawed hands, showing me their teeth, taunting me. But for the moment, they held back. Because they knew my reputation. And they didn't know what I might have hidden up my sleeve.

"Welcome to my home, and to my family, Mr. Taylor," said Varney. His voice was sounding less and less human all the time. "Do you understand at last why you are here? Why I let you in? Because the Adventurers aren't the only ones who appreciate the pleasure of the hunt. To us, you are the Big Game, Mr. Taylor!"

For once, I had nothing to say.

Varney giggled suddenly; but it was only a sound, with no real humour in it. "Time for you to see what will become of you, Mr. Taylor. My children will drag you down and hold you, and I will bite you. And then I shall send you forth, with the Adventurers. To lead my army out into the Nightside. We will run riot in your streets, tear out the throats and drain the blood of everyone we meet. Turn you into us. Until all that moves in this marvellous, endless night will be undead. Forever and ever and ever. And there's nothing you can do to stop it, Mr. Taylor. See . . . what you will be."

He gestured, and the vampires behind him fell back, hugging the stone walls, as Varney's possessed came forward. They moved slowly, stumbling, unsure of themselves. The abducted and bewitched Members of the Adventurers Club. Dulled in their minds, broken in their wills. I saw familiar faces: Julien Advent, Chandra Singh, Augusta Moon. Except there was no-one there, behind those uncertain eyes, those terribly fixed stares. They had been overwhelmed, made over into slaves to the Vampire King. I hoped . . . they didn't know what had been done to them. What they were doing, and what they would be made to do. If part of them was still alive, trapped inside and screaming helplessly, that would be so cruel.

So it was probably true. Vampires thrive on cruelty.

One small hope—they were, all of them, filthy dirty, and stained with fresh blood. Which suggested I was seeing them as they really were. Still human. If they'd been turned, made into actual vampires, they would have hidden behind their own glamours, like the things hanging from the ceiling and the walls. The Adventurers were still human, which meant . . . they were salvageable. They weren't a lost cause. I could still do something. If only I could work out what.

Varney must have seen the new strength and hope in my face; and he didn't like it.

"If you won't bend to my will, Mr. Taylor, you must be made to bend the knee and bare the throat. By force."

"Not going to happen," I said.

He laughed, breathlessly. "Surrender; and keep what is left of your dignity, Mr. Taylor. You won't enjoy the alternative."

"Stop using my name," I said. "You don't know me. You don't know me at all."

I produced my two incendiary devices, primed them, and threw them into the tunnel ahead of me. They exploded together, filling the tunnel with blazing flames and fierce light, blasting vampires right off the walls and ceiling. Many of them burst into flames and ran squealing and howling back and forth, leaving fiery trails behind them to set others alight. The fires ate them up even as they moved. Two pounds of white phosphorus doesn't mess around. And all of them cried out and flinched back from the unexpected light, covering their faces with their hands.

Apart from Varney. Who stood his ground, unmoved and unaffected.

He didn't say a word, didn't move a muscle; but suddenly all the other vampires were flying at me, throwing themselves through the fires and the flaring light. I pulled on a pair of studded silver knuckle-dusters, personally blessed by the Archbishop of Canterbury. A vampire reared up before me, all bared fangs and reaching, clawed fingers. I punched him in the face with my knuckle-dusters, so hard my fist slammed right through his features, smashing teeth and bones. I pulled my hand out of his head, and he fell back, screaming. But I could already hear his bones creaking and cracking as his face rebuilt itself.

I pulled a packet of garlic powder out of my pocket, broke it open, and scattered the contents around me, till I was surrounded by a protective circle. Another packet, to fill the air around me with a cloud of garlic dust. And the vampires that had been closing in on me fell back at once, hissing and spitting and crying out, as the garlic poisoned their unnatural systems. The protection would only last until the last of the garlic powder fell out of the air, but it should buy me some precious moments. To think and plan.

And still Varney stood right where he was, watching me with his dark, unblinking eyes, unmoved and unworried by anything I'd done.

I went to the last trick I still had up my sleeve. The one advantage Varney didn't know about, and couldn't anticipate. I used my gift, to find the door I'd come in by. The door Varney had made vanish. Except, of course, he hadn't. My gift found the door immediately, standing right behind me, where it had always been. Hidden behind a glamour. I turned to leave through the door, and all the vampires fell on me at once. Screaming in pain and horror as they forced their way through the garlic, and the terrible things it did to them, driven on, by their master's will.

I lashed about me with my knuckle-dusters, vampire faces and bodies cracking and collapsing under the impact. But I could only hit them one at a time. The vampires swarmed all over me, trying to drag me down through sheer force and weight of numbers. They grabbed me and clung to me even as I fought then off. Clawed hands ripped through my trench coat as though it were paper and scored bloody wounds in the flesh beneath. Jaws snapped shut, just short of my eyes and face and neck, as I surged desperately this way and that. I fought fiercely, fear lending me new strength. I threw vampires away from me, smashed in their skulls, stamped them hysterically under my feet. Forcing my way forward, inch by inch, towards the waiting door.

But there were so many of them.

Fires were still burning, further down the tunnel, casting strange, warped shadows on the walls, leaping and dancing. Too far off to do me any good. Vampires forced their way through the last of the garlic cloud to get to me even as their faces melted and ran away. And the controlled Adventurers lurched steadily forward, coming for me. To drag me down and hold me, so Varney could sink his filthy teeth in my neck and make me one of them.

Razor-sharp clawed fingers tore deep into my flesh, again and again, and I cried out despite myself. They were trying to madden me with pain, drive me back and forth like a bull in a bull-ring. My blood splashed on the tunnel floor, and the sight and smell of it excited and maddened the vampires. They hit me hard, from every direction at once. Until I couldn't tell one hurt from another, any more.

I pulled out the crucifix my old teacher Pew had given me, so many years ago. He always said it was special. I thrust it out, into the faces of my attackers; and the small wooden cross blazed with light, intolerably bright. The vampires let me go, falling back from the cross, crying out and turning their heads away. The whole length of the tunnel, vampires shouted and howled and backed away. The light was so fierce I couldn't bear to look at it myself. I held the crucifix out at arm's length, and looked for the door. It was right in front of me. A vampire clinging to the ceiling right above me struck down savagely, raking my forehead with a clawed finger, opening up a long, jagged wound. Blood coursed down, filling my eyes. I brushed it away with my ragged sleeve, and thrust the cross up into the vampire's gut. It exploded, splashing rot and corruption everywhere.

The tunnel was full of screams. Some of them might have been mine.

I hit the door with my empty hand, but it didn't open. There wasn't any handle. I looked back. Varney was still standing where he had been, looking at me. And if the light from the crucifix bothered him, he hid it well. I turned my back on him, giving all my attention to the door. I hit it with my shoulder, and it didn't budge. I hit it with the hand holding the crucifix, slamming it against the door like a battering ram, and it flew open. I burst through, stumbling out into the night, and the door slammed shut behind me.

I turned around and stabbed Pew's cross into the wood of the door. It sank in half its length; and stuck there, quivering. Still glowing, though not as fiercely. I fell back a few steps, not taking my eyes off the door. It didn't open. I couldn't hear anything moving behind it. Pew's cross was holding them back. For now. I sat down suddenly on the sidewalk, as the last strength went out of my legs.

I sat there, shuddering. I hurt all over. My white trench

coat was soaked in blood. I found a handkerchief and pressed it against the deep gouge in my forehead to keep the blood from running down into my eyes. People passing by gave me plenty of room, not looking at me, or the door. And I sat there, breathing hard. Waiting for a second wind that seemed a long time coming. I smiled briefly. Must be getting old. I used to be able to take a beating.

My head was swimming, and I had to concentrate hard to bring my thoughts into focus. I couldn't simply sit there. Had to do something. The case wasn't over just because I'd found out what happened to the missing Adventurers. I still had a lot to do. There were still good men and women waiting to be saved. It hurt like hell, getting my mobile phone out of my inside pocket. And it took a while before I could make my numbed and bloody fingers punch out the right number. I sat there, and waited, while the phone rang and rang; until finally someone picked up at the other end.

"Suzie?" I said. "John. I'm in trouble. Can you come and get me?"

FOUR

I sat slumped on the sidewalk, in the ragged remains of my trench coat, in a spreading pool of my own blood. My back almost but not quite touching the closed door to the Vampire Club. I couldn't hear, but I could feel, the army of vampires trapped behind the door; pressing against the wood, tearing into it with their clawed hands, trying to force it open. So they could get out and get me. But all their unnatural strength was nothing against the influence of old Pew's cross. He had put a lot of work into that down the years. To make it into a conduit and a focus for all the forces of Good, from outside this world. It was supposed to be his graduation present to me; but then he found out who my mother was and called me an Abomination. So I walked out, taking the cross with me. I thought I was owed, and he always said it would come in handy someday. Pew—old teacher, old friend, old enemy. Gone now, all these years. It disturbed me that I hadn't even thought of him in so long.

I felt tired. Bone-deep, soul-deep tired. It seemed to me that I wasn't hurting as badly as I had been. Not a good sign. It meant I was going into shock, growing numb as I bled out. I used to have a little werewolf in me, from an old case; enough to help me heal quickly . . . but that wore off long ago. I never get to hang on to anything that matters. It was a constant effort to keep from nodding off, because I knew that if I did, all these people who just happened to be casually passing by would notice. I could see them, edging closer. Trying to figure out how injured and damaged I was and whether it was safe yet for them to move in and rob me blind. Or kill me. There were a lot of people in the Nightside who'd been waiting for years for a chance to take me out while I was helpless.

I checked myself over, as best I could. I was honestly shocked, at the sheer number of wounds and injuries I'd taken. The vampires had hit me from every side, and they'd hit me hard and hurt me deep. The trench coat that usually protected me had been torn to rags and ribbons, by the supernatural strength behind those filthy, ragged claws. Under Varney, the vampires had rediscovered their old strength and viciousness. I was torn apart everywhere, my flesh laid open, blood pouring out of me.

I was in bad shape. Claws had sunk deep, muscles were ripped open, and tendons torn. I couldn't feel or move my left hand, not even when I looked right at it. And my left leg was twitching convulsively, white bone showing clearly in the ragged red meat. Blood was still pulsing down my face from the gouge in my forehead, slowly sealing my right eye shut.

I was so very tired; and my eyes kept closing, despite everything I could do to stay awake. I was actually starting to nod off when I felt a presence; and my eyes snapped open. I found myself face-to-face with a man leaning over me, caught in the act of reaching for my inside pockets. I met his gaze; and he froze where he was. He was wearing dentist's whites, and a white leather gimp mask. His eyes widened, and he slowly pulled his hand back. He straightened up, then hesitated and looked at me hopefully, in case my eyes might shut again. I started to sit up a little straighter, and he turned and hurried away. I smiled, slightly. Blood welled out of my mouth, and ran down my chin. Beaten half to death, and I still had it. Good to know.

My chin was just starting to descend onto my chest again when I heard a familiar sound approaching. A very individual car motor. I made myself look up; and there was Dead Boy's futuristic car slamming its way through the Nightside traffic towards me. A gleaming silver bullet that radiated advanced technology and a complete contempt for all scientific laws. It looked like it would quite happily run over or straight through any other vehicle dumb enough to get in its way. Dead Boy's always been a bit vague about how he acquired his car; I always supposed it fell off the back of a Timeslip.

The car eased smoothly to a halt right in front of me, a door flew open, and Suzie Shooter stepped out. A tall blonde in black motorcycle leathers, adorned with rattling steel chains and gleaming steel studs, with twin bandoliers of bullets crossing her impressive chest. Finished off with knee-high boots, with steel toe-caps. Shotgun Suzie, the best bounty hunter in the Nightside, because she never bothered with all that *bring them in alive* nonsense. She had a striking face with a strong bone structure, a grim smile, and fierce, dark blue eyes. She looked at what had been done to me, and there was murder and mayhem in her face for whoever was responsible.

My Suzie. My Valkyrie from Hell.

The moment she stepped out of the car, everyone else took one look at her and stopped dead on the sidewalk. The sensible ones turned around and hurried off in the opposite direction. Suzie glared about her, just in case there was anyone in need of immediate punishment, and the remaining people just ran for it. Suzie didn't say anything as she knelt beside me and checked me out with professional thoroughness. Her hands were as kind as they could be, but I still had to grit my teeth together to keep from crying out. She noticed. When she finally spoke, her voice was cold, and horribly determined.

"Someone is going to pay for this. My love."

I found that comforting. It's good to know there are some people you can always rely on, to stay the same.

"Never mind that," I growled. "Am I going to die?"

"Not necessarily right now," said Suzie. "As long as we get you professional help, and quickly. Who did you piss off this time? And why did you need me to come and pick you up? Why didn't you use the Teleport in your pocket watch to get you out of here?"

"Ah," I said. "Sorry. I'm not . . . thinking as clearly as I should. I just knew, I needed you."

"Of course you did," said Suzie.

Dead Boy came strutting round from the other side of the car, his deep purple greatcoat flapping in the wind. He looked at me and raised an eyebrow.

"Damn, John, you look like shit! I've taken less damage than that, and I'm dead!"

It wasn't that he didn't care. Dead Boy was casual about my wounds because he'd been dead so long he didn't remember what pain was like any more. But the sheer size of the pool of blood around me was enough to give even him pause. He looked quickly at Suzie, and she shook her head slightly.

"Good of you to come," I said to Dead Boy.

"Oh, I'm only here because Suzie decided she needed a lift in a hurry, and I was the one who didn't run away fast enough. You don't argue with Suzie when she says she needs you to do something for her; not if you like having your major organs on the inside. They might not work any more, but I'm still sentimentally attached to them." He stopped to look past me. "I don't know if it matters, but the crucifix stuck in the door behind you appears to be on fire."

"Get me on my feet," I said. "And then get me the hell out of here. It's not safe here."

Suzie and Dead Boy took an arm each, and between them hauled me up onto my feet. And then they held me up till I got my balance. My legs shook, I still hurt every time I moved, and every time I breathed; but I was holding it together. For the moment. I turned, slowly and carefully, to look at Pew's cross, where I'd stabbed it into the door. The wooden crucifix was charred and blackened, burning with an unnatural blood-red light.

"All right, I'll bite," said Dead Boy. "What's on the other side of that door?"

"An army," I said.

"Let them come," said Suzie. "I brought extra ammunition."

"No," I said. "Not here; and not now. We have to leave, before they get out."

"Who?" said Dead Boy. "Before who gets out?"

"Nightmares," I said. "With teeth and claws."

Suzie and Dead Boy shared another look.

"Nearest hospital is about half a mile from here," said Suzie. "The Hospice of Saint Baphomet. We might have to fight our way out afterwards, but they do a really good line in miracle cures."

"No!" I said, a bit more loudly than I intended. My head was swimming again. "No hospitals. Not safe enough. Take me to Strangefellows."

Suzie and Dead Boy exchanged another look they didn't think I saw. Dead Boy raised an eyebrow, and Suzie nodded; and Dead Boy gestured to the backdoor of his car. It swung open on its own, and he and Suzie man-handled me into the back seat as carefully as they could. Every movement hurt me, and I cried out several times, despite myself. But when I was finally settled on the back seat, propped up against the smooth leather, I felt decidedly safer. I let out a long, relieved sigh as Suzie settled in beside me. Her face was worryingly grim. She didn't like seeing me reduced to this. Dead Boy paused and looked back at the door to the Vampire Club.

"You want me to take the burning cross out of the door? I'm pretty sure it couldn't hurt me."

"No!" I said loudly. "Don't touch it! The power left in that cross is the only thing holding the door shut, keeping them back. We're going to need the time that cross is buying us."

Dead Boy shrugged, slammed the car door shut, then hurried round to slip into the driver's seat. The futuristic car moved smoothly out into the Nightside traffic, persuading all the other vehicles to get out of its way through brute force and vicious intimidation. Suzie sat as close as she could without hurting me further even as my blood stained her leathers.

"Dead Boy!" she said loudly. "Does this car have a med kit?"

"No," he said. "Why would I need one? Does he need one?"

"Drive faster," said Suzie.

She didn't look at my blood on her jacket, didn't give a damn. She kept her gaze on my face, her expression thoughtful and considering, her gaze icy-cold. I knew she was thinking of killing a whole bunch of people for what had been done to me. Because killing a whole lot of people was Suzie's usual first response to problems and difficulties. Except this time, I wasn't sure that would work. Whether even Shotgun Suzie could kill things that were already dead.

Dead Boy drove his car as smoothly as he could, but every sudden movement and change in direction was enough to send new pain blazing through me. I felt horribly broken, splintered inside. I wanted to let go, and black out, and not have to wake up again until I was safely inside Strangefellows, but I didn't dare. Because if I was as badly damaged as I thought I was, there was no telling how long it might be before I woke up again. And the clock was still ticking. I didn't know how long the abducted Adventurers had before Varney decided to turn them. To make them like him.

I couldn't let them down. I'd promised I'd save them.

I let my head loll slowly sideways, to look out the car window at the passing Nightside streets. All the blazing, coloured neon was smeared into long rainbow streaks by the car's speed. I broke open the dried blood sealing my right eye shut, so I could see more clearly, but it didn't help. Everything looked dim and strange, familiar but disturbingly wrong. I did my best to look for signs of pursuit, but I couldn't see any. Didn't mean it wasn't there, though. Vampires are masters at the art of moving unseen and undetected. It's how they survive. Only one of the reasons why I wouldn't feel safe until I was back at Strangefellows, behind its many ancient layers of puissant shields and nasty protections.

It worried me that I felt that way. All my confidence was gone, torn away. I didn't like feeling so helpless, so broken, that all I could think of was the need to be protected by someone else. I'd always been able to look after myself. Protect myself, against all comers. I'd had to, ever since I was a child, when I first learned the hard way that I couldn't afford to depend on anyone but myself. But everyone has their limits. And it was a long time since I'd been hurt this badly. I hadn't realised how bad until I saw the shock in Suzie and Dead Boy's faces when they first saw what had been done to me.

I felt weak and vulnerable and no longer in control of my life; and I hated it.

A car with no windows, not even a windscreen, swept in really close, challenging our position on the road; and I actually cringed back from it. Suzie saw me do it and scowled.

"Who did this to you, John? Tell me; and I will slaughter every damned one of them."

"Wait," I said. "Get me to Strangefellows. I'll tell you everything there. No telling who's listening, out here."

Suzie looked at me doubtfully, then her head snapped round as the car with no windows rammed us from the side. The futuristic car shuddered under the impact, and Dead Boy swore dispassionately. Up close, the other car didn't look like a car any more. The bodywork was an organic red, pulsing and sweating. The whole side of the car facing us opened up into a horrible wide smile, jammed full of heavy, grinding teeth. The Nightside is full of predators; some are more specialised than others.

Dead Boy swung the steering wheel round hard, and the futuristic car slammed back into the predator car. It cried out, in a loud, inhuman wail, as its teeth smashed and broke under the impact. The car pulled away, and Dead Boy let it get ahead before opening up with the futuristic car's concealed weapons. Heavy gunfire slammed into the predator car, raking it from side to side. Great chunks of meat were blown away, and blood spurted heavily into the air. The predator car swept wildly back and forth across the road, until it was run over and thoroughly chewed up by a heavy articulated vehicle.

"Traffic's murder tonight," Dead Boy said cheerfully.

I went back to looking out the car window, watching the streets pass, with all their familiar sights and sounds. They'd never seemed so open, so vulnerable, before. The Nightside thought it was untouchable. As I had till Varney showed me otherwise. The Nightside didn't know who was out there in the dark, didn't know what was coming. I wanted to lower the window, lean out, and shout at them, warn them of the hungry things plotting against them. But no-one would have listened. There's always someone shouting a warning in the Nightside.

I looked at the bustling streets, and in my mind's eye, I saw them littered with bodies, while blood ran like rivers in the gutters. I saw corpses piled up on street-corners, as the undead took control of the streets. I saw vampires running wild, cutting through panicked packs of tourists like wolves in among the sheep. I saw mad-eyed things with bloody mouths swarming over vehicles in the road, fighting to get inside. I saw them scuttling over the fronts of buildings, hanging from street-lamps, jumping from roof to roof. Saw them running down the streets after the last few human prey, snapping their teeth behind the slowest to keep them moving and prolong the sport. Until there was nothing left living in the night—just a sated, blood-drunk army of the undead, strutting proudly along empty streets, undisputed masters of their new territory. Lords of the night that never ends.

No more hot neon, no more music spilling out of clubs and bars because the undead would have no use for such things. They would drive all life out of the Nightside and leave it cold and silent as the grave.

Dead Boy finally brought his car to a halt outside Strangefellows. Or at least, parked on a street you could use to get there. The oldest bar in the world isn't supposed to be easy to get to. Dead Boy turned around in his seat, and looked at me.

"Front or backdoor?"

"Front," I said.

"John," Suzie said carefully. "Do you really think it's wise, to let people see you like this?"

"Word is bound to get around," I said. "Better to let them see how bad it is, so it will seem that much more impressive when I bounce back from it. This will make my reputation; you'll see."

"What if you don't bounce back?" said Dead Boy. He caught Suzie glaring at him and raised his hands defensively. "Just asking . . . All right; front entrance it is."

In the end, it took both of them to prise me out of the back seat and onto the sidewalk. And then they had to hold me up until I could get my feet under me. I was too tired, and hurting too bad, to feel embarrassed. I looked carefully about me but couldn't see anyone taking too much of an interest. I managed a small smile for Dead Boy.

"Sorry about the blood on your upholstery."

"She's known worse," said Dead Boy.

They took their hands away from me, and, somehow, I managed to stay upright. I took a few deep breaths and set off down the side alley that led to Strangefellows' front door. Dead Boy and Suzie stuck close, in case they might be needed. I looked straight ahead and pretended I didn't see them. My back was killing me, the leg with the bloody big hole in it kept threatening to collapse, and my strength came and went in sudden rushes; but I was damned if I'd give in to any of it. I stamped my feet down hard because I couldn't feel them, and lurched forward, using the momentum to keep me going.

The side alley wasn't that much cleaner than the back alley. It ended abruptly in a flat slab of steel set flush in a grimy brick wall. Above the door, a small but dignified neon sign spelled out the name of the bar in ancient Sanskrit. Alex has never believed in advertising. If you're meant to find your way to the oldest bar in the world, you will. If you're not, all the signs and directions in the world won't help you.

It's a destiny thing.

The door opened before us, and Suzie and Dead Boy accompanied me into the foyer. It never changes. The same old Tudor-period furniture, mostly occupied by people sleeping one off before they have to head home. The same obscene murals on the wall and ceiling, the same appalling stains on the Persian carpeting. There's nothing so comforting as the familiar. I felt a little stronger, merely for being in Strangefellows, hidden and protected behind the best shields in the world. I didn't like feeling that way. Another sign of how broken down and vulnerable I was.

We clattered down the heavy metal stairway, into the wide, stone-walled pit that holds the bar proper. The place was still packed, and just as raucous. I felt strangely angry—that I had been through so much, and they'd just gone on as normal. The music pumping through the hidden speakers was hot retro swing from The Cherry Poppin Daddies; but it shut off abruptly as Alex caught sight of me from behind the bar. The rest of the bar noise fell quickly away, replaced by a startled silence as everyone stopped what they were doing to look at the blood-soaked spectre, come to interrupt their feast. Many of the faces looked genuinely shocked on seeing the state I was in. The state I'd been reduced to. It was clear my reputation was taking a beating.

Some of the expressions I was seeing made me wonder if I was actually in worse shape than I'd thought; and given that I was feeling half-dead, that was a worrying thought. A lot of the faces were studying me carefully, judging the extent of my wounds and my weakness. The Nightside is always ready to see the Great brought low. Always waiting for a chance to shout *The King is dead; long live the new King!* Because there are always jackals, hoping for a chance to tear down a lion. I smiled around me, showing my teeth.

"All right!" Alex said loudly. "Everybody out! The bar is now closed, and this is a lock-in! By invitation only. If you have to ask, the answer's no. Go on; get the hell out of here!"

Dead Boy and Suzie supported me unobtrusively as I moved to the side of the stairs, and together we watched the crowd hurry past us, giving us plenty of room. Most of them made a point of not looking directly at me, to show that whatever was going on, they didn't want to get involved. But, of course, there are always a few who don't realise the party's over and don't want to go. A bunch of young merchant bankers, wearing sackcloth and ashes in a mostly ironic way, huddled together at the bar and protested loudly at having their fun interrupted. Until Alex lost patience with them and set his body-building bouncers on them.

Lucy and Betty Coltrane are large, forceful girls who never wear anything more than a T-shirt and tight shorts, the better to show off their impressive muscles. One is blonde, and one is brunette; but apart from that, there's not much to choose between them. They're married, to each other. They fell upon the merchant bankers, slapped them briskly about the head, kneed them in the privates, then frog-marched them to the foot of the metal stairway. By then they were all more than ready to leave.

But, of course, there's always one, isn't there. He pulled away from the pack, drew a sharp, golden sickle from inside his sleeve, waved it in my direction, and started to say something abusive. Suzie drew her shotgun from its holster with terrifying speed, and stuck both barrels up his nose. And after that, he couldn't leave quickly enough.

I walked slowly, and very carefully, up to the bar. My legs were shaking, and my vision kept blurring in and out, but I got there. Through sheer strength of will. Suzie and Dead Boy strode watchfully on either side of me. Only one customer had stayed at the bar. Razor Eddie perched on a high bar-stool, watching me calmly. The Punk God of the Straight Razor, a painfully thin presence in an oversized grey coat apparently held together by accumulated filth and grease. He lived on the street, slept in doorways, and killed all the people who needed killing that the rest of us couldn't get to. He had a hollowed face and fever-bright eyes; and he lived a life of endless penance for an atonement he wasn't sure he believed in.

"You look a mess, John," he said, in his quiet, ghostly voice. "I always thought that when the time came, I would be the one to do that to you. It seems I must have a quiet word with someone. Can't have someone else taking away my rightful prerogative."

"Thank you, Eddie," I said. "It's good to have friends."

"I wouldn't know," said Razor Eddie.

I propped myself up against the bar and looked about me. The open space seemed so much bigger, now it was deserted. Calm, and quiet. The bar felt slightly uncomfortable, as though it wasn't used to being empty and didn't like it. Dead Boy brought me a chair, and Suzie helped me settle into it. I looked at Alex.

"Put your strongest shields and protections in place. And I mean everything. Don't let anything in."

"Already taken care of," said Alex, coming out from behind the bar. "I did all that the moment I caught sight of you. Damn, you look like someone put you through a blender. Typical John Taylor, always bringing trouble to my door. Here. Drink this. It's good for what ails you."

He thrust a glass of some thick yellow liquid at me. The nasty-looking stuff churned and seethed in the glass, as though trying to get out. I looked at it suspiciously.

"What the hell is that?"

"If I told you what was in it, you wouldn't drink it," said Alex. "It's called Rassillonn's Restorative, if that makes any difference. It'll put you right."

"Is it any good?" said Suzie.

"It's expensive," said Alex.

And it was a sign of how bad I was feeling that I didn't argue with him. I took the glass in a slightly shaky hand and knocked the stuff back as fast as I could, trying not to taste it. The Restorative was thick and foul, but I got it all down. And then my eyes squeezed shut, as something exploded deep inside me. I shook and shuddered as something picked me up, gave me a damned good shake, then set me down again. And just like that, I felt fine. I felt better than fine. All my pains were gone, my wounds were gone, my head felt fine; and I was so full of energy, I felt like I could kick the whole world's arse. I laughed out loud, grinned at Alex, and handed him back the empty glass. He accepted it with his thumb and forefinger and handed it quickly to one of the Coltranes.

"Take this out back, destroy it, and throw the remains in the incinerator. And for God's sake, don't let any of the dregs touch you."

I looked at Alex, as the bouncer disappeared out back. "Is there something you're not telling me . . . ?"

"More than you can possibly imagine. Don't worry about it. If that stuff was going to kill you, it would have by now."

"Time to cut to the chase," said Suzie, and something in her cold voice cut right through everything else. "Talk to me, John. Who did this to you?"

"Vampires," I said. "A whole army of them, hiding out in Clubland, in their very own club. Led by the King of the Vampires. And no, I don't mean Dracula; I mean Varney. He's gathered all the vampires in the Nightside to him, so they can make the long night into a sanctuary and a homeland for all the vampires. Everyone else here goes to the wall."

"Vampires," Alex said disgustedly, moving back behind the bar. "Nasty things. Hard to kill. Worse than cockroaches."

I brought them up to date on everything that had happened since I was summoned to the Adventurers Club. They all listened intently, not interrupting. Which wasn't like any of them, so they must have been really interested. When I finished, ending with my narrow escape from the Vampire Club, Suzie growled dangerously, and everyone moved back a little.

"No wonder all the vampires seemed to have gone missing," growled Alex. "They were hiding out in their precious new club! It's hard to think of them as such a threat . . . I've had vampires in here, on and off, for ages. Never made any trouble."

"Varney has kicked them awake," I said. "Made them angry and ambitious."

Alex cleared his throat uncomfortably. "I can't believe I'm saying this, but . . . A whole army of vampires might be a little more than even we can handle. Does anyone here think we should . . . contact the Authorities? Let them deal with it?"

"No," I said immediately. "I need to do this myself. I can't have word getting out that I know my limits."

"Of course you have to do it," said Suzie. "But you don't have to do it alone."

"Damn right!" Dead Boy said cheerfully. "Vampires are vermin. I mean, I'm dead, but I still have standards."

"Exactly," said Razor Eddie. "Can't have the vermin getting above themselves. King of the Vampires . . . He'll be wanting his own church on the Street of the Gods next."

"There's a whole army of the things," I said.

"A whole army?" said Dead Boy. "Fantastic! It's been a long time since I took on an army. Those were good days . . ."

"I spit on armies," said Razor Eddie.

"I know you do," said Dead Boy. "I've seen you do it, and it's a disgusting habit."

"No-one messes with my man and gets away with it," said Suzie. "Not while I still have breath in my body. And ammunition. You're going back to the Vampire Club, John. And we are going with you."

"Why would you do that?" I said. "You saw what they did to me."

"Because we're family," said Dead Boy.

"Your family," said Razor Eddie. "In a highly dysfunctional sort of way."

"And, of course, none of us wants to miss out on the kind of fight this promises to be," said Suzie.

I nodded. I couldn't say anything.

"You all go right ahead," said Alex. "Kick the hell out of the ungodly bastards. I'll stay here and guard the bar. In case the vampires come here, looking for you. And then we can all have a nice party, if you get back. When you get back."

Suzie ignored him, looking at me thoughtfully. "The vampires were only able to abduct those Adventurers who happened to be at the Club when they forced their way in. What about all the other Adventurers, scattered across the world? Should we contact them, tell them what's happened, and inquire whether they want to join us? No shame in bringing in reinforcements."

"No," I said. "They'd be vulnerable to the vampires, too. More meat for the grinder. I'm protected, Dead Boy's dead, and Razor Eddie is a living god. And you're . . . you. Besides, this is the Nightside. We clean up our own messes. Can't have the heroes and do-gooders thinking we need them to do something we can't. We'd never hear the end of it."

"You want to save the day and hold it over the rescued Adventurers' heads for the rest of their lives," said Dead Boy.

"Got it in one," I said.

"After everything the vampires did to you, you're still ready to walk back into the meat-grinder yourself," said Suzie. "Not because you want to be able to look down your nose at the Adventurers. You do that already. Because you believe the men and women the vampires abducted are people worth saving."

"I never could hide anything from you," I said.

"My hero," said Suzie.

"I've never thought of myself as a hero," I said. "Just . . . your last chance for a little private justice, in the Nightside."

"I can live with that," said Dead Boy.

"You sure you want to come with me?" I said. "The odds are not good."

"We're family," said Suzie.

I had to smile. "I haven't been all that lucky when it comes to family."

"We're the family you chose," said Dead Boy. "The family that matters."

I stood up. I felt strong and sharp and ready to kick vampire arse. The horrors I'd been through were still with me; but you can't let things like that slow you down if you're going to work in the Nightside. Where blood and pain and horror are always going to come as standard. I brushed the dried blood off my coat and it fell away in clouds of blood-red confetti. And underneath, my long white trench coat was completely undamaged. Not a rip or a tear anywhere.

"A coat that repairs itself?" said Dead Boy. "Oh, I have got to get me one of those!"

"Sorry," I said. "It's a one-of-a-kind item. I had to go through a lot to get it; and you really wouldn't want to pay the price I had to."

"I still say he overcharged you," said Suzie. She was busy loading shells into her shotgun. "Special ammunition," she said, without looking up. "These particular blessed and cursed cartridges are greased with garlic. Should make the vampires' eyes water. You know . . . we could stop off along the way, pick up some more specialised weapons. The Weapon Shoppes of Usher are always open."

Razor Eddie's hand was suddenly full of a large, pearl-handled straight razor. The long blade gleamed supernaturally bright.

"Damn right!" said Dead Boy, striking a martial pose. "We don't need no stinking weapons!"

He punched a hole in the wooden bar front, with one dead-white fist. And then had to struggle to pull it out again. Alex glared at him.

"Did you have to do that?"

"Yes!" said Dead Boy. "I was on a roll!"

"That's going on your tab," said Alex.

"I don't have a tab!"

"You do now." Alex turned his glare on me. "And before anybody thinks to ask. No, I don't have any wooden stakes here!"

"Not even any firewood that we could sharpen into stakes?" I said.

"No, I don't have any firewood because I happen to live in the twenty-first century! Mostly."

"There must be somewhere in the Nightside that could

sell us some wooden stakes," said Dead Boy. "I mean, you can get everything else here. I know a place where . . ."

"I'm sure you do," I said. "But we don't need stakes. There are any number of ways you can take down a vampire, and I think we've got most of them covered, between us."

"Even the King of the Vampires?" said Alex.

"He . . . is going to be difficult," I said. "But in the end, it's all about faith. Do you have any crosses behind the bar?"

"Of course," said Alex, ducking and rummaging around. "You'd be surprised what people leave behind . . . Here, help yourselves."

He stood up and slammed a large wooden box down on the bar top, packed full of all kinds of religious items, from all kinds of religions. We all crowded round and sorted through the crucifixes. I took a small silver cross, in an old Celtic design. Dead Boy and Eddie squabbled over the more intricate designs. Suzie didn't bother. She met my gaze steadily.

"I'm not really a believer."

"How can you live in a place like the Nightside and not be a believer?" I said. "You've fought angels!"

"Just stubborn, I guess," said Suzie.

"You still carve a cross into the head of your bullets," I said.

"That's just being practical," said Suzie.

"Don't you believe in anything?" said Dead Boy, stuffing his pockets with assorted crosses.

"I believe in John," said Suzie. "And really big guns."

She caressed her shotgun in a disturbingly affectionate way; and we all found reasons to look somewhere else until she stopped doing it.

I stopped suddenly and looked at Alex. "Hold it. Where's Sebastian Stargrave?"

"Out back," said Alex. "Having a nice lie-down. Don't worry, I'll look after him."

"I feel I have to ask," said Dead Boy. "If it should all go wrong, suddenly and horribly, and the only way to stop a vampire invasion is to kill absolutely everything . . . What about the hypnotised Adventurers?"

"The whole point of this mission," I said, "is to rescue the kidnapped heroes. They are the victims here."

"But what if they attack us, under Varney's control?" Razor Eddie said softly.

"Then we take them down without killing them," I said firmly. "We save them from themselves."

"Not going to be easy," said Dead Boy.

"If this were going to be easy, it wouldn't take all of us," I said. "All right, let's go."

"Are we going by pocket-watch, this time?" said Suzie, just a bit pointedly.

"No," I said. "We'll take your car, Dead Boy. We need to pick someone up along the way."

FIVE

Dead Boy drove us back through the Nightside with all his usual casual disregard for traffic laws, natural laws, and any other laws he could thumb his nose at. Razor Eddie took the shotgun seat beside him because only a dead man could stand to be that close to Eddie for any length of time. Dead Boy could stand the smell because his sensory input was only ever a sometime thing. Suzie and I sat together in the back seat. All the blood I'd spilled all over the leather upholstery was gone. Not a trace left anywhere. I didn't say anything. Dead Boy's car has always been able to look after herself.

"Don't know if you've noticed," said Dead Boy, without looking round, "but it does seem to me that there's a lot more traffic coming out of Clubland, than there is heading in. Perhaps they've heard something . . . ?"

"Wouldn't surprise me," I said. "Nothing travels faster in the Nightside than bad news."

"Are you sure you're up to this?" Suzie said quietly. "You took a hell of a beating. Have you at least got a plan?"

"Of course he's got a plan!" said Dead Boy. "John Taylor always has a plan!"

"Except for when he doesn't," said Razor Eddie. "And then he improvises. Suddenly and violently and all over the place."

"How well you know me," I said.

Dead Boy stopped his car outside the Adventurers Club. He turned around in the driver's seat to give me a hard look.

"Why are we stopping here? The vampires have already taken all the Adventurers in the Club. So there's no-one here who needs rescuing. They're all gone!"

"Not everyone," I said.

I got out of the car, gestured immediately for Suzie to stay put, and walked over to nod respectfully at the Doorman. He was still at his post, the huge black man in the long white robe, with the were sabre-tooth-tiger charm hanging round his throat. He nodded to me, warily.

"I sent you out to find the missing Club Members, Mr. Taylor," he said, in his rich, deep, cultured voice. "Not to return here with some of your more disreputable associates."

"It's time for you to come with me," I said. "I have discovered where the missing Adventurers are being held."

"I told you before, Mr. Taylor; I cannot abandon my

post. I have to guard the door. It is not just a job; it is a sacred duty."

"But where does your true loyalty lie?" I said. "To the Club, or to its Members? You can come with us, and help save them; or you can stand here and guard a whole bunch of empty rooms. Which of those sounds more like a sacred duty to you?"

The Doorman looked at me steadily. "Who has them?"

"The King of the Vampires," I said. "And his vampire army. They want to make the Club Members into leeches like them, then make them part of an invading and conquering army, to take control of the Nightside. Well, I'm not having that. Not on my watch. So I and my very impressive friends are going to pay a visit to the Vampire Club, get the missing Adventurers back, while they're still human, and generally kick vampire arse till they cry like babies. We could use your help."

The Doorman smiled suddenly. "Well. If you put it like that . . . The door is locked, and the Club is secured. It can manage without me, for a while. So let us go."

"You've just been waiting for me to come and get you," I said. "Haven't you?"

"Of course, Mr. Taylor."

I hate being predictable. I led him over to the car and the backdoor swung open before us.

"You've been listening in again," I said to the car, accusingly. "Suzie, Eddie, Dead Boy, this is the Doorman of the Adventurers Club. He's coming with us."

"Why?" said Dead Boy immediately. "What's so special about him?"

"He's a were sabre-tooth tiger," I said. "Try not to upset him."

"All right," said Dead Boy. "That is a bit special, even for the Nightside."

Suzie sniffed loudly. "I could use a new rug for the den."

"Play nice," I said. "Or there will be spankings."

"Wouldn't be the first time," said Suzie.

"Oh God," said Dead Boy. "There's a mental image I wasn't expecting to take home with me."

Suzie budged up to the far side of the back seat, to let me and the Doorman climb into the back of the car. He had to bend right over, to squeeze his bulk into the limited space. Suzie and I were crushed together on the far side. It was all rather crowded, but we managed.

"Do you know everyone here?" I said to the Doorman.

"Let me say, I have at least heard of everyone present," said the Doorman. "Not always in a good way, perhaps, but this is the Nightside, after all. I know warriors when I see them. I pity the vampire . . ."

"All right," Dead Boy said to me, deliberately ignoring the Doorman. "Where to next?"

"The Vampire Club," I said. "A few streets along, and round the corner."

Dead Boy turned all the way round in the driver's seat again. "If it's that close, why are we driving? We don't we walk?"

"Because I want your marvellous car with us," I said. "In case we need the superior firepower built into her."

"Good reason," said Dead Boy. He turned round again, and set the car in motion. The Doorman looked at me steadily.

"This car . . . It is not just a car, is it?"

"Nothing is ever just anything, in the Nightside," I said.

The car eased to a halt right in front of the Vampire Club, and we all got out. And then we stood together before the single closed door and looked the place over carefully. There was still a great pool of blood drying on the sidewalk before the door. And all the people passing by were giving the door and the club a great deal of room; as though they could sense really bad things happening beyond the small wooden door in the bruised stone front. The door seemed exactly the same as before; except now there wasn't a trace of the blessed old cross I'd hammered into the wood. It was gone, with nothing left to show it had ever been there. Not even a scorch mark from its unnatural flames.

I was surprised at how angry and upset I felt. The cross had been the only thing I had left from my old teacher. Pew had been a good friend, and a better enemy. I still miss him.

"This is it?" said Dead Boy. He marched right up to the closed door and kicked it a few times. "Doesn't look like much."

"Don't show your ignorance, boy," said the Doorman. "This is a place of death and eternal suffering. Can't you feel it?"

"No," said Dead Boy. "I'm dead."

The Doorman looked him over carefully. "Of course you are. My apologies."

"If Pew's cross was the only thing preventing the vampires from coming out after you," Suzie said slowly, "what's holding them back now?"

"They're waiting for us," I said. "Waiting for us to go in. It's a wise predator that chooses to fight on its own ground."

"How did you get in last time?" said Suzie.

"I knocked," I said.

"He's so polite," Dead Boy said to Razor Eddie.

"He really is," said Razor Eddie. "Except for when he isn't."

"Is there a backdoor?" said Suzie. "Some way of sneaking in and catching the bastards by surprise?"

"I doubt it," I said. "As King of the Vampires, Varney has made his own world in there. He isn't just a vampire. He has power. The only entrances to this club are the ones he allows."

Dead Boy looked dubiously at the closed door before him. "Do you think he knows we're out here?"

"Of course he knows," I said. "He's watching us right now. Waiting to see what we'll do."

"Then why isn't he opening the door to us?" Dead Boy said loudly. He kicked the door again, with enough force to make the wood shake and shudder in its frame. "Come on! Let us in! I am Dead Boy, and I can take all you rotten leeches with both legs tied behind my back!"

The Doorman looked at me. "Is he always like this?"

"Pretty much," I said. "Nothing like having no self-preservation instincts left to make you always first into the fray. The rest of us mostly use him to soak up the opening fire, while we hide behind him. Dead Boy, please get away from the door."

"Why?" said Dead Boy, a bit plaintively.

"Because I think Varney is planning a surprise for us," I said. "I don't think he was expecting me to come back with reinforcements. He thought I'd be like him—arrogant enough to want to go head to head. He's probably taking a good look at who I've brought with me and asking his followers who you all are."

"That should scare him," said Suzie.

"No," I said. "Varney doesn't scare. He's the King of the Vampires. He doesn't believe anything can harm him, or stop him, or get in the way of anything he plans. He's being cautious. Planning something special for him and his army to enjoy. Remember, he doesn't want only to kill us. He wants to break us, enslave us to his will, make us leeches like him. Make us serve him and lead his invasion of the Nightside."

"That'll be the day," said Suzie. "You want to try knocking again?"

"No," I said. "Time for a display of power, I think. A little spiritual shock and awe. Eddie?"

"Love to," said Razor Eddie.

The Punk God of the Straight Razor showed his dirty brown teeth in a shifty smile, and suddenly his pearl-handled straight razor flashed supernaturally bright in his grey hand, a sharp, clean light in the neon-lit dark. People passing by cried out and turned their heads away, unable to look at the light. Even Suzie and I could only look at it out of the corners of our eyes. Dead Boy stared right at it because he was dead. And, surprisingly, the Doorman didn't seem at all bothered by the light. Which made me wonder what kind of things he had been used to, in his long-lost city of ancient Africa.

"You really believe he can cut through that door, with a single small blade?" said the Doorman. "It is an impressive weapon, I will agree; but I can see powerful shields and protections laid down upon this door and this structure. I would not bet on breaking it down with a battering ram blessed by all the dark gods. Even the most powerful weapons are only as strong as the man who wields them."

"Eddie isn't a man," I said. "And hasn't been for some time. He's the living god of the straight razor. I have seen him cut through Time and Space with that edge. Go for it, Eddie."

"Love to," said Razor Eddie.

He stepped forward, and his blade swept out impossibly quickly, faster than the human eye could follow. He cut deeply into the heavy stone front with no discernable effort, drawing a deep line from above the door to below it. Then another deep cut, on the other side. The flashing razor cut through the stone like a knife through fog. And then he cut again, above and below the door, his skinny figure moving with a terrible sense of unstoppable purpose. Because nothing can stand against Razor Eddie once he's taken his aspect upon him. He finished the last deep cut with a flourish, to complete the oblong he'd made; and then he stepped smartly away to one side as the wooden door fell forward, out of the wall. No longer supported by or connected to the surrounding stone, it measured its length on the sidewalk before the club, rattled a few times, and lay still.

We all moved quickly forward, to peer through the opening Razor Eddie had made, and see what lay beyond.

I got there first, of course. The narrow stone tunnel I remembered from before was gone. In its place was a white beach, with a red sea beyond. I moved cautiously forward, and leaned in through the opening. The stench hit me hard. That old, familiar smell of spilled blood, and so much death. I looked carefully around. The beach stretched away for miles and miles on either side, a beach made up entirely of bones. Human bones. Skulls and rib cages, leg-bones and arm-bones, packed tightly together. As though they'd been left there for so long that they'd settled down and compacted into place.

The ocean was red because it was blood. Nothing but blood. It moved slowly, sluggishly, an entire sea of spilled human blood. I could tell. I could feel it, in the depths of my soul. A beach of bones and a sea of blood, under a night sky empty of everything but a piss-yellow moon. An atrocity of a world.

I stepped back and let the others take a good look. Dead Boy and Razor Eddie squeezed in together, shoulder to shoulder. Then Suzie, and finally the Doorman. We all looked at each other.

"Nasty," said Suzie, apparently unmoved. "Not the worst thing I've seen in the Nightside, but pretty damned nasty, all the same."

"Varney's work?" said the Doorman, looking at me.

"Of course," I said.

"Is it real?" said the Doorman.

"Real enough," I said. "Real enough to kill us if we let our guard down. Let's go."

Dead Boy looked back at his car. "If we're not back in half an hour, come and get us. Or avenge us."

The car seemed to nod at him.

I led the way in, stepping carefully over the stone lip and out onto the bone beach. The others hurried in after me, then spread out, so as not to present a single target to whatever might be waiting. The bones creaked and cracked under our weight. The stench from the blood ocean was sickening. The deep, dark night sky had no stars at all, just that full yellow moon. Yellow as sickness. There was more than enough light to see by, but none of it came from the moon. Varney wanted us to see clearly the world he'd made for us.

It was cold—the harsh, unwavering cold of the grave, or the graveyard. And not a breath of air moving anywhere.

"Oh, I do like to be beside the seaside," murmured Razor Eddie. He stood very still, both hands thrust deep in the pockets of his filthy coat.

"Where the hell are we?" said Dead Boy. He looked around interestedly, apparently unmoved and unconcerned by his surroundings. "I thought we were going clubbing."

"So much blood," said Suzie. She held her shotgun at the ready, prepared for the first hint of a threat.

"It smells of death and horror," said the Doorman.

"I can't smell anything," said Dead Boy, just a bit sadly. "Look at all these bones! How many people died here? Thousands? Millions? I don't get it. Why kill so many people? I thought Varney wanted to make everyone like him."

"Only up to a point," I said. "Too many predators in one place, and they'd run out of victims. Turn on each other."

"So what, or where, is this?" said Suzie.

"This is the vampires' world," I said. "Or, at least, the world as they would like it to be. Their fantasy, perhaps, of where they originally came from. Who knows how vampires came into our world, originally?"

I looked around me, and the bleached white beach of bones stretched away for as far as I could see. The blood ocean reached away into the distance, all the way to the far horizon, heavy blood, moving sluggishly in slow waves. And when I finally turned and looked behind me, the opening we'd come in through was gone. No door, no doorway. Just more bones and more beach, stretching away forever. The others followed my gaze. They didn't seem particularly surprised, or upset, and not in the least intimidated. We'd all known what we were doing when we entered the world Varney made for us.

"Nobody panic," I said. "I can find the door again."

"Who's panicking?" Dead Boy said immediately. "I do not panic! What have I got to panic about? The worst thing that could possibly happen to me has already happened. I got over it."

Suzie turned her shotgun this way and that, frowning thoughtfully. "I don't see any vampires, John."

"I'm sure they're around, somewhere," I said. "Watching us. Checking out who I brought with me. Seeing how we're affected by . . . all this."

"Should we do something, to make sure they know we're here?" said the Doorman. "I grow impatient to see my missing Adventurers, Mr. Taylor."

"They know," I said. "That's why Varney redecorated. He's trying to impress us."

Suzie made a rude noise.

"This is the world as vampires see it," said Razor Eddie. "A fantasy, nothing more. It's not real."

"Yeah, well," said Dead Boy. "That word can cover a lot of ground in the Nightside."

The Doorman stamped a heavy sandaled foot on the bones beneath him; and they cracked and shattered loudly. "Feels real enough."

"Some kind of mass-broadcast illusion, perhaps?" murmured Razor Eddie. "Vampires do love to play mind-games. They hide their true appearance behind glamours, so they can move among us, and we won't see them as the walking corpses they really are. They mesmerise their victims, so they won't fight back. Maybe this is their idea of a good fighting ground. A killing ground. I can't believe there ever was a place like this . . ."

"Who knows?" I said. "We've all seen stranger places. It's probably as real as it needs to be, for us and them. We can die here."

"Speak for yourself," said Dead Boy.

"Would you prefer, destroyed?" said Suzie.

"A killing ground, for us and them," said the Doorman. "What more do you need?"

"Something to shoot at," said Suzie.

A shaft of heavy yellow moonlight fell across the bloody waters, a phosphorescent path shining out across the crimson ocean, all the way to the bone beach. And walking along that sick yellow path, walking on the bloody surface without disturbing it at all, came a single figure. A man wearing the stark black uniform of the Nazi SS, complete in every detail, down to the lightning flashes on his epaulettes and the silver deathface on his peaked cap. He strode forward with an easy swagger until he finally stepped off the moonlit path onto the bones of the beach. His boots made no sound at all as he strode across skulls and leg-bones. He cast no shadow. He finally stopped before us and smiled easily, the colourless lips in his dead-white face peeling back to show jagged teeth. His eyes were blood-red, no pupils. There were several bullet-holes in the front of his uniform, but no blood-stains.

I just smiled back at him because I didn't believe any of it. His appearance was another illusion, another glamour.

"Welcome back, John Taylor," said the vampire, in a deep guttural voice. "We knew you couldn't stay away. And you've brought some friends for us to play with. How nice."

"Who the hell are you?" said Suzie, her shotgun trained unwaveringly on him.

The vampire ignored her, his dead gaze fixed on me. "Back for more pain, Mr. Taylor? What a glutton for punishment you are. You must know, you won't get away this time."

Suzie stepped forward, putting herself bodily between the vampire and me, so he had no choice but to look at her. And then she stood very still as he caught her gaze with his, and held her in place with it. Her shotgun lowered slightly as the vampire smiled at her.

"Hello, Shotgun Suzie. We've heard of you. Little bounty hunter, who thinks she knows all there is to know about death. You know nothing. We know because we are death, and worse than death. We were hoping you would follow John back here. Like the obedient little puppy-dog you are. We're so pleased all of you are here, to share John Taylor's awful fate. To share in his punishment for daring to defy our will. This is our world, and nothing happens in it but what pleases us. So please me, Suzie Shooter. Turn your gun on your precious John Taylor and see how many times you can shoot him without killing him. You mustn't kill him because that is ours to do. But make him hurt, and make him bleed; for me."

"Look down," said Suzie.

"What?" said the vampire.

He looked down, and suddenly stood very still as he

realised Suzie had stuck both barrels of her shotgun right up against his crotch.

"Before I came out," said Suzie, "I greased all my shells with oil of garlic. Which everyone tells me is just like rat poison to vampires."

The vampire started to say something strident, and Suzie let him have it with both barrels. The vampire's words became a sudden, horrified shriek, as the shotgun blast all but tore him in two. His whole crotch area just disappeared, blown out in long, bloody streamers behind him. He was thrown back a dozen steps across the bone beach before he finally collapsed, screaming horribly, trying to hold himself together with his hands. He crawled away, scrabbling painfully across the bones, until he could throw himself into the blood sea and disappear beneath the slow, heavy waves. Suzie looked at me.

"Start as you mean to go on, that's what I always say."

"You can always rely on a woman to fight dirty," I said, and all the other men nodded solemnly in unison—until Suzie glared at them, and they stopped.

"We should have finished him off," said the Doorman.

"No," I said. "We want him to go back to Varney and the others. Tell them we're coming."

And then we all looked round sharply, at sudden disturbances in the bones all around us. Skulls overturned, and arm- and leg-bones rose and fell, as the abducted Adventurers rose through them to form a great circle all around us. The Doorman called out to them eagerly, but none of them answered him. The Adventurers stood unnaturally still, with slow, crafty faces and someone else staring out from behind their eyes. Dozens of famous heroes and adventurers, men and women of great renown, staring at us with deadly, unblinking eyes. The Doorman looked to me.

"What is happening here, Mr. Taylor?"

"The vampires have sent their slaves to do their fighting for them," I said. "Because they know that being forced to fight those we came here to save would prove most distressing for us. I hadn't realised the vampires had taken so many . . ."

Forty, maybe fifty of the doughtiest heroes and fighters of all times surrounded us. The most familiar faces at the front, where they would have the most effect. Julien Advent, the Great Victorian Adventurer. Chandra Singh, the monster hunter. Gareth de Lyon and Augusta Moon. And more, so many more. All at once, as though in response to some unheard signal or order, they began to shuffle forward, across the bones of the dead. Heading right for us with bad intent. I turned to the Doorman.

"This is why I brought you; because I thought Varney would try something like this. I need your other self—the sabre-tooth tiger. You can use your bulk and strength and speed to keep most of these poor bastards occupied, without killing them. I can rely on the others to win this battle, but only you can keep the majority back until I can figure out a way to get to the King of the Vampires and put a stop to this."

"Don't take too long," said the Doorman.

He changed suddenly, abruptly, without any sense of strain or pain. He didn't stretch or change or transform. One moment, there was a man standing before me, then a huge, black-striped tiger crouched in his place. He had to be at least eight feet long, with massive muscles rippling under his streaked hide and a great leonine head with two terribly large teeth stabbing down from his upper jaw. The Doorman was a sabre-tooth tiger, and the air was heavy with the rank smell of cat. He growled, once, like a roll of thunder, and launched himself at the approaching Adventurers.

He hit the first handful like a living battering ram, bowling them over and throwing them off their feet. He twisted and turned, slamming his great body into the mesmerised heroes, sending them flying this way and that. He moved incredibly quickly for a beast of his size, in and among the possessed heroes and out again, before they had time to react. Some struck out at the great beast, but he was always gone before they could touch him. He charged back and forth among the Adventurers, knocking them down with his heavy shoulders or the occasional slap from a massive paw.

Augusta Moon lurched forward, her fierce gaze fixed on Dead Boy. Augusta Moon, the professional trouble-shooter, who always looked like someone's favourite middle-aged auntie, complete with country tweeds and a monocle screwed into one eye. She raised her famous walking-stick, that long staff of blessed oak with a silver top, that had beaten many a monster to death in its time, and brought it hammering down with both hands on Dead Boy's head. And he stood there and took it. The staff rebounded without hurting him. Augusta blinked at him uneasily, then rained a series of vicious blows upon Dead Boy, belabouring him again and again about the head and shoulders. Dust flew up from his long coat where the blows landed, but Dead Boy didn't react. He didn't feel anything, and he wasn't in any danger; so he just stood there politely and let her get on with it. Until her strength began to wane, and she slowed down, and he stepped quickly forward and took her in his arms, crushing the breath out of her.

Chandra Singh came forward, resplendent in his height of the Raj finery. All splendid silks and satins, with a jet-black turban fronted by a magnificent diamond. He carried a long, curved sword, glowing fiercely with ancient enchantments from another world. Razor Eddie stepped forward to block his way, and Chandra Singh's sword came sweeping around in a tight arc, to cut off his head. The Punk God of the Straight Razor met the enchanted sword with his own glow-ing blade. The straight razor blocked and stopped the sword in midswing, absorbing the impact easily, and great sparks flew on the air from the vicious impact. Chandra cut at Eddie again and again, but couldn't get past Eddie's defence. Because Chandra wasn't himself, and so wasn't fighting at the height of his powers; and because Eddie was Razor Eddie.

Chandra pressed forward, swinging his sword wildly, but he couldn't force Eddie back a single step. The grey little man just stood his ground, putting his razor blade where it needed to be, every time, his fever-bright eyes entirely unmoved. Until Chandra, too, began to tire and slow, and Eddie stepped neatly forward inside Chandra's reach and kicked him hard in the knee-cap. Chandra went down on one knee as his leg betrayed him, and Eddie back-elbowed him in the side of the head. Chandra's head swung round under the impact; and while he was stunned, Razor Eddie slashed him neatly across the back of his right hand. Chandra's fingers flew open in spite of themselves, and he dropped his glowing sword. Eddie kicked it away, and it came to rest right in front of me. I didn't touch it.

Gareth de Lyon headed straight for Suzie, and she raised her shotgun to cover him. For a moment I really thought she might forget she was there to save the heroes or decide she didn't care. But I should have known better. Suzie always knows what she's doing. She waited till Gareth was almost upon her, then reversed her shotgun and slammed the butt into his gut. All the breath exploded out of him, and he fell onto his knees before her. Suzie took another swing, and clubbed him down with the butt of her shotgun. The sound from the impact was enough to make even me wince. Gareth de Lyon fell forward onto the bones and lay still. Suzie kicked him in the ribs a few times, to be sure, and looked around for someone else to take down.

And then it was my turn, as I found myself facing Julien Advent. Another old friend and old enemy, we'd fought side by side on a dozen cases and gone up against each other on as many more. A very moral man—when he wasn't being possessed by a vampire. I met his gaze steadily as he stumbled towards me.

"Come on, Julien," I said. "It's me, John. You know me. You don't want to do this. Whatever hold Varney has over you, fight it. You can do it. You're Julien Advent, the Great Victorian Adventurer! You're better than this!"

And he stopped. He stood there before me, and I could see his own personality rising in his face. His eyes cleared, and he looked at me and knew me. I could see him fighting the vampire's control with all his iron will. He started to say something . . . and then a look of slow horror passed across his face as the vampire's will took hold again. Because in the end he was a man, a natural creature, under the control of a supernatural creature. I saw the last of his consciousness drown in his eyes, replaced by the cold, deadly gaze of the King of the Vampires. Varney glared at me through Julien's eyes, and he came at me again. And I could see in his face and in his eyes that Varney meant to make Julien kill me. Or make me kill Julien.

So I reached into an inside pocket, and brought out a sealed packet of coarse black pepper. I ripped it open, and threw the whole contents in Julien's face. He stopped dead in his tracks and sneezed explosively. And then he did it again, and again, huge, overpowering sneezes that shook his whole body. Great helpless tears ran down his face, forcing their way past squeezed-shut eyes.

Condiments are our friends. Never leave home without them.

I looked across at Razor Eddie. "Time we were leaving, Eddie! I've had an idea."

"About time," said Eddie.

"I've had enough of this place," I said. "Let's take the

fight to the vampires. Use your razor and cut me a doorway, between this world and wherever the vampires are hiding!"

"You don't want much, do you?" said Razor Eddie.

He struck at the air before him with his shining blade; and it sank in deep, leaving a bloody trail behind as it descended. He cut at the world again and again, until it shuddered under his blows, and the false reality collapsed, unable to withstand the terrible godly power contained within that supernaturally bright razor blade. The bone beach and the blood sea and the piss-yellow moon all disappeared at once, as the illusion was replaced by the underlying reality of the Vampire Club.

We were all suddenly standing in a great stone amphitheatre. Illuminated by that old familiar blood-red glow. A huge stone circle, of curving stone steps rising up and up into a covering darkness. Old grey stone, soaked and caked with dark stains and fresh running blood from new victims. And vampires, vampires, everywhere. Hundreds of them, scattered across the raised steps of the amphitheatre. Many of them feeding on human prey. Men and women seduced or snatched in, from the street outside the club. Some might even have been volunteers; there's always someone ready to try a new kick. Some might even have been fooled by the modern romantic lies about vampirekind. But none of the victims looked like they were enjoying the experience. The victim's horror is part of the vampire's feeding.

They didn't feed daintily, like in the books and films. No small puncture marks in the side of the neck. The vampires tore at the flesh, biting deep, worrying at the wounds they made like dogs with a fresh kill. Gulping down the blood, lapping it up from the skin, making deep, grunting sounds of satisfaction like pigs at the trough. Some fastened onto the neck, others the wrist. Some went for the breast or the belly or the crotch.

Right in front of me, a vampire had his face sunk deep in the bloody mess he'd made of a young goth girl's neck. She was past the point of struggling, her whole front soaked in her own blood, but she looked at me pleadingly. I pointed her out to Suzie; and she stepped forward, put both barrels of her shotgun against the vampire's head, and blew it right off. The vampire's body convulsed and fell away, clawed hands still grasping convulsively for the goth girl. She didn't move. Even when Suzie shot her head off, too. I didn't say anything. The goth girl had already lost so much blood, all that was left for her was to die, or turn. I nodded to Suzie; and she nodded back.

The mesmerised Adventurers stood still and confused, in the great open circle at the centre of the amphitheatre. Unable to cope with the sudden change. The huge sabre-tooth tiger prowled among them, herding them together, ready to bring down anyone who tried to start anything.

The vampires slowly became aware of us, aware that we had invaded their private domain. They raised bloody mouths from their victims, to shout and scream from every side, demanding Varney do something. One vampire launched itself at Dead Boy, and sank its sharp teeth deep into the side of his neck. And then the vampire recoiled and fell back, spitting and shaking his head.

"Formaldehyde! There isn't a drop of blood in him!"

"What would I do with blood?" said Dead Boy. He grabbed the vampire's head with both hands and ripped it right off. He threw the head away, and the body went stumbling off after it.

I yelled to Dead Boy to get his attention, then to Suzie and Eddie.

"Take out as many as you can! Maximum damage; no mercy."

"And what will you be doing?" said Suzie.

I pointed at the one figure standing alone, at the top rank of the amphitheatre. Varney, King of the Vampires.

"He is going down," I said.

Suzie nodded, and opened fire with her shotgun, blowing away vampires left and right. Heads blew off, chests exploded, and stolen blood flew on the air. Some of the vampires pulled themselves back together almost immediately, but Razor Eddie was quickly there to carve them up with his brightly shining blade. Dead Boy walked right into the biggest collection of vampires and smashed their heads in with his dead fists.

"Come on!" he roared. "Give me your best shot! I can take it! Come and have a go if you think you're hard enough!"

The sabre-tooth tiger prowled among the Adventurers, keeping them from getting involved. Most stood where they were, dazed, abandoned for the moment by their vampire puppet masters, who had more immediate troubles of their own. And Varney . . . stood alone, on the top rank of the stone amphitheatre, looking down in disbelief on what I and my friends were doing to his vampire army. I walked steadily towards him, climbing the stone circles, one by one.

"You can't win," Varney said finally. He had to raise his voice, to be heard over the shouts and screams and the roar of the fighting. "You can hurt my people, but you can't stop them. Eventually, they will pull themselves together, overpower you and your friends, and drag you down."

"You forget," I said, closing in on him. "I find things. That's what I do. I can find sunlight from outside the Nightside and bring it here."

"I didn't forget," said Varney. "I heard you did that once, in the past. But it won't work here. I have never been troubled by sunlight, thanks to a certain deal I made, long ago.

And now I am King of the Vampires, I have shared that gift with all my followers."

"Ah," I said. "But did you think to share that gift with the Adventurers you hypnotised?"

Varney looked at me. "What?"

"I thought not," I said.

I reached out with my gift, found the brightest sunlight in all the outside world, and brought it slamming down into the stone amphitheatre. Blazing sharp sunlight, bright as the day and twice as powerful, blasted into the Vampire Club like a single vicious spotlight, piercing the heart of the Club like a stake driven into a vampire. Most of the vampires present screamed and howled and fell back, turning their heads away from the light. Varney might have told them they were protected from the light of day, but clearly most of them were having trouble believing it. They scrabbled backwards, across the stone circles, abandoning their victims. And in the meantime, the sunlight hit the mesmerised Adventurers like a slap in the face, waking them from their hypnosis and freeing their minds.

Just like that, they were themselves again, and back in command of their actions. It was clear from the looks on their faces that they knew what had been done to them, that they remembered what they had been forced to do by the vampires' will. And that they really weren't at all happy about it.

They burst out of the central space and threw themselves at the nearest vampires, striking them down with outraged fury.

I used my gift again, to find the door that led out of the Vampire Club and into the street in Clubland. The doorway appeared out of nowhere, standing alone in the centre of the amphitheatre, an opening cut out of Space and Time by Razor Eddie, showing the bright lights and hot neon of the

Nightside. I called out to the sabre-tooth tiger, and it spat out the vampire it was mauling to look at me with fierce cat eyes.

"Doorman!" I said. "I need you."

And like that, he was there, that tall black warrior in his sweeping white robe.

"Round up the Adventurers!" I said quickly. "Have them gather up the surviving victims and get them safely out of here!"

The Doorman nodded quickly and set about it. I turned and yelled to Suzie. I had to yell her name a couple of times, to get her attention, as she shot down vampire after vampire with a terrible cold smile on her face.

"Suzie! Work with Eddie and Dead Boy, and hold off the vampires while the Adventurers get the victims to safety! When they're out, you follow them!"

"What about you?" said Suzie.

"I'll deal with Varney and his army," I said. "And then I'll come out after you."

"Do you have a plan?" said Suzie.

"Of course I've got a plan! I always have a plan!"

"Except for when you don't, and you wing it," said Suzie. "That doesn't always work out so well."

"Trust me, I have a plan," I said. "And it's a really nasty one."

Suzie grinned briefly. "Best kind."

The Doorman and the Adventurers gathered up the victims, and half led and half carried them down the stone circles and out through the doorway, out of the club and into the street. Suzie and Dead Boy and Razor Eddie covered the rear, doing terrible things to any vampire who tried to interfere with the rescue. Not all the victims could be saved, but you learn to settle for what you can get in the Nightside.

• • •

Surprisingly quickly, it was all over. All of them were gone, through the doorway and out into Clubland. Leaving me standing alone at the top of the stone steps, facing Varney. Behind me, I could hear his followers stirring, gathering their strength to come up the steps after me. I let the daylight go, and it snapped off. There was just enough light left in the Vampire Club to let me see Varney, standing before me, studying me with a cold, implacable eye. He walked slowly forward to meet me. I could hear vampires hissing and scrambling behind me, rising up the stone circles, drawing closer. I didn't look back.

"You must know," said Varney, almost conversationally, "that I will never let you leave here, John Taylor. An army of my kind stands between you and the only exit; and all your little friends are gone. You shamed me to save a few debased heroes and some human cattle. It won't make any difference. We can always get more. You hurt some of my people; but they will get over it. You have stopped nothing, changed nothing. But for what you have done, and tried to do, I promise you, there will be an eternity of suffering."

"Save it," I said. "I really have heard it all before, and from far worse than you."

"There is no-one worse than I," said Varney.

I had to smile. "You never met my mother."

Varney shrugged impatiently. "I have to say, you're looking well, John. Considering how badly my children hurt you the last time. Trust me—that will be as nothing, compared to what I will do to you now. Why did you stay behind, John, when the others left? You have no friends to defend you now, no weapons, not even the sunlight."

"I don't need them any more," I said. "I have something better in mind."

Varney chuckled easily. "You do bluff well, John. It's actually a pleasure to have an enemy worthy of me. But there's just you, and so many of us. You really shouldn't have let your friends go."

"You didn't really think I'd go off and leave him, did you?" said Suzie Shooter. I looked around and there she was, standing beside me, shotgun at the ready.

"I told you to go," I said.

"Yeah, like that ever works," said Suzie. "I never leave a job unfinished when there's still killing to be done."

"Dear Suzie," said Varney. "You will make such a wonderful vampire. You have just the temperament for it."

"Over my dead body," said Suzie.

She raised her shotgun and gave him both barrels, at point-blank range. And he just stood there and took it. She shot him again and again, working her pump action with savage speed; but the garlic-smeared shells did him no harm at all. She slowly lowered her gun, and Varney smiled at her; completely unharmed and entirely unmoved.

"I made a deal, many years ago," he said. "To become more than just another vampire. And part of the deal I made was that I could never be harmed by any weapon of this world."

"I thought it might be something like that," I said. "A deal with whom, exactly?"

"Who do you think?" said Varney.

"Ah," I said. "You always have to be careful, with deals like that. There's always a loophole, or two. The Devil really is in the details."

I glanced behind me. The vampires were closing in, crawling up the stone steps on all fours, to get to me and Suzie. Hundreds of them, with hate and viciousness stamped on their dead faces. Suzie moved quickly to stand back-to-back with me, covering the approaching vampires with her shotgun. Many of them stopped when they saw her. They remembered what her special ammunition had done to them, if not to Varney. But they could afford to be patient. There were so very many of them, surrounding Suzie and me on all sides.

I looked back at Varney and smiled. Because I had one last trick up my sleeve. One last and very nasty rabbit to pull out of my hat.

"What are vampires, really?" I said to Varney. "When you get right down to it? You're all just walking corpses that have dug your way up out of your graves. And what eats corpses? Insects, maggots . . . worms. Since you're not ordinary dead bodies, you're not bothered by ordinary eaters of the dead. But here in the Nightside, we have our very own private cemetery—the Necropolis. We keep it locked up in a separate dimension because of the kind of people, and things not even a little bit people, that get buried there . . . We don't want them coming back. And of course, the worms that eat the bodies buried in the Necropolis can't just be ordinary everyday worms. After generations of feeding on the Nightside's dead, they have grown very strong and very hungry. Supernaturally strong and hungry."

I saw the look of understanding and dismay grow on Varney's face, and I savoured it as I reached out with my gift, found all the worms in the Nightside Necropolis, and brought every damned one of them to the Vampire Club.

They fell down from above, a never-ending waterfall of millions of fat, wriggling worms. They fell upon the vampires and ate their dead flesh, burrowing deep into their dead bodies with supernatural strength and speed. The vampires screamed and howled, and tried to beat the worms away with their hands. But more and more worms fell out of nowhere, an endless tumbling rain of them. They ate their way into the vampires' bodies and burrowed through them, chewing rapidly through organs that didn't work any more. Stolen blood burst out of widening holes in crimson gushes. It seemed the supernatural worms had a special taste for undead flesh. Vampires ran and scrabbled on all fours, in all directions, beating at themselves, tearing away chunks of their own flesh with clawed hands as they tried to rip out the worms. But already they were falling, and flailing helplessly, as the worms ate up their muscles. More worms burst out of vampire eye-sockets and wriggled in their screaming mouths.

They fell upon Suzie, and on me, too; but they didn't trouble us. They had no taste for the living.

And Varney, King of the Vampires, screamed loudest of all. The worms burrowed into him, all over his body. The deal he'd made only covered things of this world; and the worms came from a separate dimension. He beat at his body with his hands, unable to believe this was happening to him. And I bent down and picked up the sword I'd seen gleaming on the top steps of the amphitheatre. I saw it fall from Chandra Singh's hand when he went up against Razor Eddie on the bone beach. It had come through with us, to the Vampire Club; because it was an enchanted sword, bound to Chandra Singh. He never said where he had acquired the magical blade, only that it was a thing not of this world. Which meant Varney's deal didn't cover it.

I picked it up and advanced on Varney. He was too busy with the worms to see me coming. I swung the enchanted sword with both hands, and the glowing blade took his head right off.

The severed head fell away, still trying to scream, and I grabbed hold of it quickly, before it could roll away. Varney's body stumbled forward, reaching out with clawed hands. The glamour was gone, and now Varney looked like what he was: an old rotting cadaver in disintegrating clothes. I turned around and gave Suzie the nod, and we ran back down the stone circles, heading for the open doorway. I had the sword in one hand, and Varney's worm-ridden head in the other. Suzie blasted away any vampire that got in our way. The amphitheatre was full of screams.

We left the Vampire Club through the open doorway and stepped out into the Nightside street. The Doorman, Dead Boy, and Razor Eddie were waiting for us, leaning against the futuristic car. I looked behind me. The doorway had disappeared, along with the rest of the Vampire Club. The whole building was gone, no longer a part of Clubland without Varney's will to support it.

I placed Varney's head carefully on the sidewalk. There wasn't much of it left. Most of the flesh was gone, and worms crawled all over the skull, spilling from the empty eye-sockets, and rioting in the still-weakly-snapping mouth. I raised Chandra Singh's sword and brought it swinging down one last time. The skull exploded into a hundred pieces. They melted away into mists and were gone; and all that was left were the worms.

"Is that it?" said Suzie. "Is it over now?"

"I think so," I said. "Without the King of the Vampires to hold them together, the few vampires who do survive will just scatter and go to ground, and hope not to be noticed." I looked at the Doorman. "Thanks for your help. Take your Adventurers home and give them a few stiff drinks. And let this be a salutary lesson to them of what can happen, when they go after game so much bigger than they are."

The Doorman looked down at the worms wriggling on the sidewalk. "It would seem to me that it's not the Big Game you have to worry about."

"That's the Nightside for you," I said. "There's always something nastier than you."

"He always has to have the last word," said Suzie.

"Yes," I said.

SIX

Later, at the Adventurers Club:

Many famous faces insisted on buying me many drinks, at the Club bar. And I let them. All the heroes and adventurers, and the Club staff, were back where they belonged, and mass celebration was the order of the day. Gareth de Lyon was the only absent face because he was off in the Library, overseeing the reprogramming of the Club Door, to make sure it could never be misused again. Nobody was really mad at him (*Could have happened to any one of us,* being the general feeling), but Gareth wouldn't allow himself to relax until he was sure the Club was secure again.

Augusta Moon and Dead Boy were re-enacting their encounter at the Vampire Club, to the amusement of all. He just stood there calmly, while she belaboured him mightily with her walking stick; until he got bored, snatched the stick away from her, and kissed her heartily on the mouth. Hardened Adventurers leaned on each other, helpless with laughter, as Augusta pursued a fleeing Dead Boy round the bar, demanding he make good on his promise.

Suzie Shooter and Razor Eddie were firmly ensconced at the bar, already well into a drinking game that seemed to involve drinking double measures from every bottle stacked behind the bar. Lots of bets were being made; not so much on which one of them would pass out first—more on which direction they would fall.

I had a number of drinks lined up on the bar top before me and was happily considering which order to try them in, when the Doorman came up to me. I nodded amiably to him and raised an eyebrow.

"I thought you weren't allowed to abandon your post at the door when there were Members present in the Club?"

"I have been upgraded," the Doorman said solemnly. "I have been declared an official hero, and a Club Member in good standing. But I am still the Doorman."

"Why?" I said.

"Because being a Member is an honorary position, while being Doorman comes with a wage."

"Ah," I said.

"At least now I can stop off in the bar for a quick drink, now and again," said the Doorman. "The front entrance can look after itself. It has its own security system. The Doorman is only there to impress people."

"You do it very well," I said generously.

"Thank you, Mr. Taylor. You will now oblige me by returning the Club credit card I gave you."

I retrieved the card from an inside pocket and handed it back to him.

"I was rather hoping you'd forgotten about that . . ."

"Not a chance in Hell, Mr. Taylor."

"I have already deducted a substantial sum," I said. "I'll submit my expenses later."

"You're certainly welcome to try, Mr. Taylor."

"What's happened to the victims we rescued from the Vampire Club?" I said.

"Mr. Advent has escorted them to the nearest hospital, or church sanctuary, as required," said the Doorman. "He has assured me they will all be cared for. Might I enquire, what has happened to all the appalling worms you summoned from the Necropolis?"

"I sent them back," I said. "Don't want to upset the ecology of our one and only cemetery. Besides, I didn't want them hanging around the Nightside streets long enough to acquire a taste for living flesh. No-one would be safe."

"What an odd place the Nightside is," said the Doorman.

I looked around the packed Club bar. Everyone seemed to be enjoying themselves, in a relaxed and unconcerned and very noisy way.

"They all came close to dying," I said. "And worse than dying. And the whole Nightside came very close to being overrun and conquered by the undead. All because one of these people bit off more than he could chew. Heroes don't belong in the Nightside. They think it's all a game."

"It is," said the Doorman. "The Big Game. At least I understand why they do what they do. Why do you do what you do, Mr. Taylor?"

"It's a dirty job, cleaning up after heroes," I said, reaching for my first drink. "But someone's got to do it."